# The Spy on Putney Bridge

# The Spy on Putney Bridge

## A Mystery Novel of Espionage, Murder, and Betrayal in London

Col. David Fitz-Enz

*To: Bob,*
*My friend. I hope you*
*enjoy the story,*
*Col. David Fitz-Enz*
*Happy Holiday*
*2021*

HAMILTON BOOKS
*Lanham • Boulder • New York • London*

Published by Hamilton Books
An imprint of The Rowman & Littlefield Publishing Group, Inc.
4501 Forbes Boulevard, Suite 200, Lanham, Maryland 20706
www.rowman.com

6 Tinworth Street, London SE11 5AL, United Kingdom

Copyright © 2021 David Fitz-Enz

Maps by Rhys Davies.

Translations of Goethe by Hyde Flippo.

British Library Cataloguing in Publication Information Available

Library of Congress Control Number: 2020952351

Dedication

Lynn Weber, Editor.

Five years from conception to publication a novel is a very
tricky thing. Over the six books I have authored, Lynn added
the touch that made characters come alive and relate to the
readers. *The Spy on Putney Bridge* is my favorite.

## OTHER BOOKS BY DAVID FITZ-ENZ

*Why a Soldier?*
*Memoir of an Army Combat Photographer*

*The Final Invasion*:
*Plattsburgh, the War of 1812's Most Decisive Battle*

*Old Ironsides*:
*Eagle of the Sea*

*Redcoats' Revenge: A Novel*
*An Alternative History of the War of 1812*

*Hacks, Sychophants, Adventurers, and Heroes*:
*Madison's Commanders in the War of 1812*

# Contents

# Preface and Acknowledgments

Having lived for four years near Cambridge, England, while a member of the American armed forces and later serving with British troops in both Germany and Belgium, I became absorbed with the British Army's rich history. That led me to read, in particular, about their influence in Europe and the world during the beginning of the twentieth century. In my previous books, I attended to the truth and nothing but the truth of non-fiction but found it didn't tell the stories of people who lived through harrowing events. In my novel *Redcoats' Revenge,* an alternate history of the American War of 1812, I found the release I was looking for.

One spring day, on the way to the grocery store in the High Street of Putney, London, I stopped to read a bronze plaque on the outer wall of a commercial building tucked away on the tiny side street of Brewers Lane. It read, "At this, the site of the Castle Pub, 43 customers, attending a party, died when German bombs rained down obliterating the structure." Later, while sitting on the balcony of my flat on the shoreline of the Thames River a mere block away, I imagined a massive German zeppelin as it loomed into the shaft of a spotlight from an anti-aircraft gun as it passed over the rail bridge to Fulham and the sheer terror that must have consumed the former resident of my chair during the blackout of 1915. What did he do, where did he go, and did he survive?

I had been reading about German spies during World War I and how a writer bragged that "the British Secret Service caught all the German spies and either shot or turned them to British service to send false reports home to Germany." When I read the history of the same period written by Germans, they disagreed. *The Spy on Putney Bridge* is the story of spies who maintained their true identities though two wars in spite of their close proximity to the center of activity.

I soon found that it was a necessity that I walk the ground in England, France, Germany, Rome, Alexandria, and Turkey. The first and most unusual in-depth investigation that I did, however, was the medical ramifications of the suffragettes' imprisonment and their treatment just before the outbreak of the First World War. The force-feeding of the suffragettes during the hunger strikes resulted in severe medical complications. What I found, when consulting with Dr. Eugene Cassone, a very prominent gastroenterologist, was disturbing. Those who survived often died later of pneumonia. BBC television presenter and author Andrew Robertshaw, a renowned expert on WWI battlefields, accompanied me as I trudged through the trenches of France, painting a clear and horrifying picture of the carnage. Colonel Timothy Weeks, Her Majesty's military attaché to the United States, reconstructed the internal workings of the British Army during the period. I was also aided by the staff of the Kew Bridge Steam Museum who operated the water pumping station one winter Sunday morning at my request. An afternoon spent with the staff of the Thames Water Authority was well worth the visit. The thirty-foot tides twice a day made a lasting impression. When I lectured at the National Army Museum, I met Mr. Julian Farrance, whose dedicated work on the lore of regiments and tireless research on the fascinating history of the British Army ensured my narrative would be accurate throughout the book. The RAF museum near Collingdale Tube station, north of London, provided both a complete inventory of World War I aircraft and a chance to research the archives of first-hand accounts. Wherever I went for assistance during the composition of this book, the British were always there for me. Over the length of the creation and composition, one contribution must be especially recognized. My childhood sweetheart and wife of fifty-eight years, Carol, was not only there but kept me on topic and always added the right words to poorly constructed sentences.

Historical fiction allowed me to blend real people with past events to create an image in the mind for the reader not found in non-fiction. Spies and intrigues have been a part of every era of conflict and elevate the reader's interest and imagination beyond the mere historical facts and timelines of warfare. To write a tale of spies and espionage that is convincing to the reader, the author must have the appropriate background and real-world experience. I have tried to bring both my background and experience to the task of writing this novel. It has taken me years to explore on foot—and also in my mind—all the places associated with this story. Connecting the dots to complete the story has been truly rewarding.

As a genre, the spy novel is a constant taskmaster demanding that a thread be maintained throughout, woven within the text and sometimes seemingly hidden. I hope you enjoy searching for the threads in this one.

# Note to the Reader

In Britain the word "lieutenant" is pronounced "leftenant." This is the pronunciation I had in mind as I wrote *The Spy on Putney Bridge* and hope that it rings in the readers' minds as they progress through the novel as well.

# Cast of Characters

## THE STETCHWORTH AND UNTERHART FAMILIES

Charlotte Howard Stetchworth, née Grayling: Matriarch of the Stetchworth family. Daughter of Martin Grayling and Lattice Howard. Mother of Roland.

Marcus Stetchworth: Charlotte's deceased husband.

Roland Augustus Grayling Stetchworth: Charlotte's son, known as Rolly to Charlotte and Rags to everyone else.

Grace Moss-Jones: Nurse and friend of Rags.

Nathan Frederick Stetchworth (Freddy), first lieutenant: First-born son of Rolly.

Martin Stetchworth: Second-born son of Rolly.

Christian August Manfred von Thurn und Taxis Unterhart: Charlotte's youthful love interest, an Austrian aristocrat.

## CHARLOTTE'S HOUSEHOLD

Mrs. Jayson, Charlotte's cook.

Mrs. Alberry, former housekeeper at Charlotte's.

Mrs. Brooks, current housekeeper at Charlotte's.

Teddy and Valerie: West Highland White terriers.

## AT HORSE GUARDS AND THE MILITARY FIELD

Major General Sir Avery Hilliard Hopewell, known as Uncle Hilly to family and Hilly to friends: Staff director on the Chief of the Imperial General Staff's office at London's Horse Guards Headquarters and deputy inspector general.

Mildred Box: Hilly's secretary.

Beryl White: Member of Hilly's staff at Horse Guards.

British Army Inspector General Badington-Smyth: Hilly's boss at Horse Guards.

Lieutenant Colonel David Moss-Jones: Welsh Guards regimental commander and Grace's father.

Private Stack: Lt. Col. Moss-Jones's batman.

Captain Rory Edgerton-Gray: Captain in Rags' regiment and a friend of Grace.

## OTHER CHARACTERS

Pieter Luskey: Charlotte's friend from Regensburg, later known as Monsignor Peter Merchanti.

Mr. and Mrs. Booker: husband Harold, wife Reeny, son Horatio, owners of Booker's World of Stamps, number 11 The High Street.

Bunny Rodney: Charlotte's friend at the Registry Office.

Helene: Swedish employee at the Registry Office.

Chief Petty Officer Marks: Employee at the Registry Office.

Mr. Cable: Employee at the Registry Office.

Rupert Mannering: Employee at the Registry Office.

Major J. R. M. Chard: King's Messenger.

## HISTORICAL FIGURES

Field Marshal Lord Herbert Kitchener: Secretary of State for War.

Henry Segar: Kitchener's personal aide and confidant.

Winston Churchill: First Lord of the Admiralty.

Field Marshal Sir John French: Commander in chief of the British Expeditionary Force, 1914–1915.

General Sir Ian Hamilton: Commander of the Mediterranean Expeditionary Force in Gallipoli.

Lieutenant General Aylmer Hunter-Weston: Commander of the British 29th Division in Gallipoli.

Lieutenant General William Birdwood: Commander of Anzac in Gallipoli.

Lieutenant General Sir Frederick Stopford: Commanding officer of the IX Corp on Gallipoli.

Royal Naval Captain Mansfield George Smith-Cumming: First director of the British Secret Intelligence Service.

Edith Cavell: British nurse captured by the Germans.

General Ferdinand Foch: French Allied commander.

Marshal Joseph Joffre: Commander of the French Army.

General Philippe Petain: Commander of the Second French Army.

# Timeline

| | |
|---|---|
| 1939, August | Construction finished of Churchill's War Rooms |
| 1939, September | Chamberlain declares war on Germany |
| 1940, May–June | Battle of Dunkirk |
| 1940, July | Beginning of the Battle of Britain, the German Luftwaffe's bombing of Britain |
| 1941, December | Japanese attack on Pearl Harbor; the US enters World War II |
| 1945, May | End of World War II in Europe |

# Maps

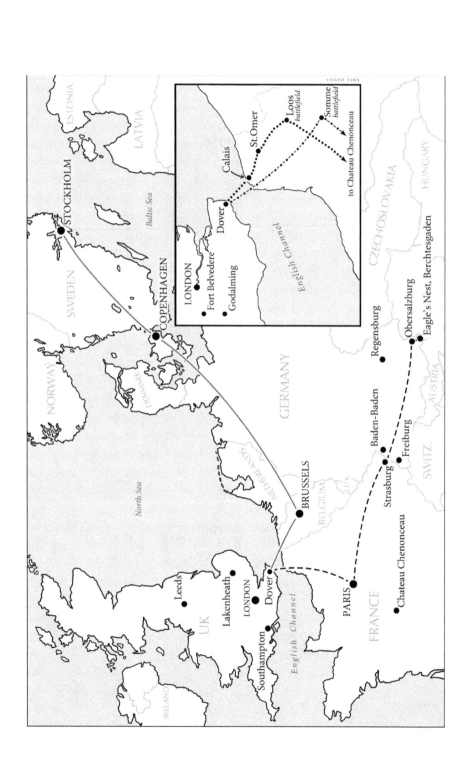

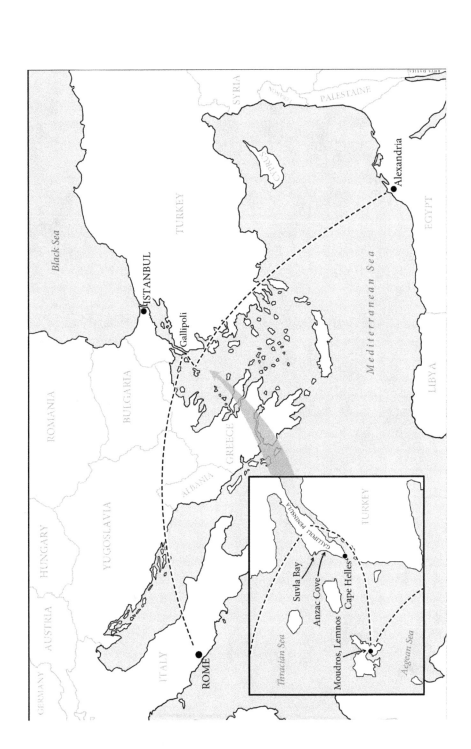

*Part I*

# CODE (1945)

# Chapter One

# London, Just Prior to Christmas, 1945

PROBING THE THRESHOLD WITH HIS cane, the British soldier carefully shuffled to the edge of one of the open doors on the underground train carriage. Though the war was over, for many the sacrifice continued.

"Let me be of assistance; there's a bit of a gap, Lieutenant." A fellow passenger debarked and offered his gloved hand. "Been to Normandy and beyond, I'll wager."

"Kind of you, sir," the young officer muttered, head down as he took two poorly coordinated steps onto the wet platform at the elevated Putney Bridge Tube station, on the north bank of the River Thames. There was a snap in the air now that the snow had let up, leaving a white sheen on the rooftops. The doors slammed shut in unison. A whistle screamed, and the lumbering train shook the concrete platform as it crept off across the ice-covered bridge toward Wimbledon.

Standing as steady as his wounded leg would allow, the officer shifted and paused to get his balance. "You'd be a winner at the betting shop with that pick. It's been months of one thing and another, but I'm back on my pins, by Harry," he said with confidence, in spite of lingering pain that twisted his lip. "The first few steps are the tough ones—thanks, I'm on my way."

His Samaritan, more than likely a veteran in his demob suit, reluctantly released the young man's elbow and saw him steady before leaving. "Merry Christmas, take care. Hope all goes well, Lieutenant."

"And you as well." First Lieutenant Nathan Frederick Stetchworth—Freddy to those who knew him well—trundled along the nearly empty platform high above the neighborhood shops and peered at the curtained windows of the upper floors that backed on to the elevated tracks, looking for signs of life. It was the first holiday season in years that families would be gathering for tea unafraid of German bombs and rockets. Nearly dark, a hint

3

of dim amber light sneaked out past sheer curtains. There was considerable damage to half of the block of pale brick row houses, no doubt the legacy of a dreadful "V"—vengeance—flying bomb.

"More blasted stairs," he muttered as he neared the end of the platform. They had never been a consideration before in his young life. Once, he had danced down them, missing the odd one or two, chasing his younger brother Martin in a gleeful race to the tiny ticket hall two flights below. But that was a dozen years ago in a happy past when fun was the only priority. "Now then, Lieutenant, one step at a time, hand on rail, stick first." It was all he had heard for weeks while fighting his way back from despair and depression. So real was the refrain that he wouldn't have been surprised, when he turned the corner at the bottom of the steps, to see Private Marks, his batman, taking his ticket rather than the uniformed guard. Safely on the ground level, the awkward descent brought a throbbing to his mangled leg—but a whiff of sausage rolls from the shop across the narrow street distracted him from the pain. He recalled stopping there on the way home from school as a boy, the hot grease burning his tongue, then trickling from the corner of his mouth on to his stripped school tie. His mother was not pleased by that.

The guard stepped forward to assist him as he presented a military token in lieu of a ticket. The attendant's dark jacket sported a single row of colored ribbons from a previous campaign, and he touched the bill of his blue cap in respect. Catching the sole of his shoe on the exposed edge of the damp black-and-white mosaic floor tiles, Freddy skimmed a few inches across the slippery floor on his heel before regaining his balance.

The guard put out his hand and apologized. "Careful now, sir. Folk keep draggin' in slush from the street all day—can't keep up with it."

FREDDY EMERGED FROM THE UNDERGROUND station and splashed his way under the long canopy next to the adjoining bus stop. A left turn and then a few more steps to the brick arch of the railway bridge. Framed by the opening on the far side, his grandmother's aged mansion, which rested on the north bank of the Thames half a block along Ranelagh Gardens, loomed in all its Victorian trappings. His boyhood home, for he had known no other, was a four-story tribute to the great queen. Broad porches and fake towers surrounded a great box of a structure pierced with large, high windows darkened by thick blackout drapes. When a train rumbled overhead he looked up and noticed the addition of a cement bunker with telltale machine-gun slits near the upper edge. These civilian precautions amused him; they had no idea what a German soldier was like. He'd toss a potato masher through that slit and kill them all before they got a shot off.

The family home had been built by his great-grandfather to house the little Stetchworth clan. A single daughter, Charlotte Howard Stetchworth—Grandmamma—took her middle name from her mother Lattice Howard, known as Letty to the family, a member of the powerful Howard family of York. Now Charlotte, long a widow, tucked inside the stately structure suffering from a pulpy heart, waited anxiously for her eldest grandson to take on the responsibility of the family debt, which she was about to lay upon his young shoulders.

It was not a debt of money, for the family held inherited wealth in firmly clenched hands. Frugal northerners with Christian ways, they had money in unprobed pockets and purses. Money was never spoken of, no matter the expense. The social standing of the family demanded certain luxuries that, while necessary, were not to be enjoyed but rather used to maintain appearances. Things simply materialized on schedule—according to social expectations. The boys were enrolled in Eton at birth. The family country estate, Stetchworth House, near New Market's racing community, indulged Freddy's mother's passion for horses while providing fresh air, seldom found in stuffy London. A townhouse in Sussex Gardens spared his father a tedious commute on the Underground to army headquarters at Horse Guards. Along with the family's seasonal jaunts to the Continent to take the waters, all things were possible; that is, as long as they were *proper* and *in season.*

At this time of year in London, darkness fell hard just after four o'clock. Emerging from the solid brick arch, Freddy recognized the pavement along the slippery, uneven, cobbled embankment. Early in this war, the entire metropolitan population had clung to the safety of that gloom and huddled together below the throbbing multiengine German bombers. When the Luftwaffe was smashed by the pursuit planes of the Royal Air Force, calm would return to the night, but the blackout in lonely places continued. Crouching, in an attitude somehow both helpless and defiant, became an integral part of British survival. Captive Londoners remained on edge, sleepless in damp underground shelters or cramped together beneath dusty stairways, while a few slept night after night in a Morrison shelter smack dab in the center of their homes. As the war droned on, the manned bombers were replaced with the dreaded "doodlebugs," followed soon by the silent V2 rockets that arrived without knocking, taking out whole blocks of row houses in a single maddening stroke.

Freddy made his way to the smooth stone walkway that led to his home. At the door, a servant he didn't recognize withdrew the noisy metal bolt and asked Freddy to give his name. "Lieutenant Stetchworth, here to see my grandmother." The servant's embarrassed apology accompanied him into the entryway. Much had changed during his absence. In the once bright and airy foyer, the Dresden chandelier hung darkly, covered by a muslin cloth.

Only a pair of wall sconces threw a dim light up the divided marble staircase, and the scent of carbolic dominated the center hall where he left his service trench coat.

The house held a chill, and Freddy ascended the staircase to a wide carpeted hallway, hoping his grandmamma's chamber would be more inviting. A faded rose silk wallpaper was hung with Howard family portraits that alternated with dark wood doorways. He came to her door and took a deep breath. He hoped she was in good spirits. There had been enough gloom in their recent lives. She had summoned him a month before, but only now had his injury healed enough to allow the journey. His childhood in this great house had been a happy one, but it had been five years since he had seen the great lady. Five long years since he left for the service as a mere teenager.

He found her drawn up to the glowing fireplace on a shelter chair that wrapped around her like a shroud. Very frail, he thought, she who had ruled the hearth with good cheer and high spirits, always prepared to buoy up childhood dreams and drop a few coins into an empty pocket when parents withheld a shilling for miscreant behavior. Though untitled, the family had become wealthy through the innovative dyeing process developed by her clever father, Martin Grayling. She dismissed titles "as prefixes and suffixes for fools and wasters not fit to hold the hat of a real man like your great-grandfather." She was proud that her father had begun as a laborer in the cloth mills. Freddy's parents had lived in the house as well, with only occasional retreats to the country home that his mother insisted on keeping for her own sanity. But it was his grandmamma who was the lion of the family, always there to scold, reprove, protect, and dote.

FREDDY CLOSED THE DOOR GENTLY behind him. "Grandmamma, you look in the pink," he said, taking her direction to sit in the wingback chair facing her. Secretly he saw his mother was correct, that while still strong in mind his grandmother had shrunk to a waif. "Dreadful," he thought, "she's taken on the skeletal image of death." Her slippered feet were propped on a damask-covered stool drawn tight against the matching chair. Her maid had stuffed cushions on either side, propping her in place.

Charlotte Stetchworth didn't greet him or comment on his uniform, medals, or injury. This was unlike her. She was always proud of her grandson, eager to bolster his fortunes and hear of his accomplishments. Today she seemed totally absorbed by her own plight. At first Freddy thought she was merely in pain or grieving the approaching end of life. But he knew there was more to it when she lifted her head and said, "It's my fault entirely, Freddy."

His grandmamma lifted a white marble hand in his direction, straining to reach out to him, but quickly sank back deep into her chair. She looked down.

"I was so sure I was right: I wouldn't let it go no matter what. And now . . ." Her words began to tumble out: "Now I can't make it right or change so much as the turning out of a lamp." Extending thin fingers that were still strong, like the claw of a bird of prey, she confessed, "It's gone from my grasp. But you, my dear"—she reached once more—"you must know before my story is whisked away to the graveyard."

The cold right hand was joined by the other in a grip Freddy could only describe as desperate. It was an anxious grasp, and he took care when he helped her settle back in place among the cushions. "It's all right, Grandmamma, I'm here. We're old friends—you can tell me anything."

"I'm afraid my story's one that will shock and haunt you, Freddy. I mustn't keep it secret any longer. It's my only way to heaven. For you see, *mein liebchen*, I've been selfish and I'm afraid the saints will not testify for me until I rid myself of this burden and place it upon your young shoulders. The war's over—I know the Germans are dashed to the ground for the second time in my life. I had a role to play, and now you must be made aware of my treachery."

Freddy smiled at the use of *liebchen*. She had always called him that, despite the times they lived in. He smiled too at her use of "treachery." She was ridden with guilt, that was clear. But what could an old woman who had lived within the bosom of her family for nearly seventy years possibly do that was treasonous? Perhaps she had made an enemy at a tea party or said boo to a goose? Charlotte had never been prone to exaggeration or hysteria. She chose her words carefully, never wasting her breath or a farthing. But Freddy was sure this was a tempest in a long-forgotten teacup.

"Poke up the fire, Freddy. I find the cold has descended deep into my core, where it persists no matter what I do to warm myself." Her subject was family history—one that would shock if it were not carefully contained between pages interspersed with tales of love and heartbreak designed to evoke sympathy rather than blame. Charlotte knew she would have to paint a portrait of herself as a girl since her cherished grandson was not yet thirty and would not understand all she had been through. She must erase the image before him—that which perched on the forward edge of the overstuffed chair—and replaced it with the image of an eighteen-year-old, rushing into life with no bounds to hold her back. It was going to be a long saga and she sat back to gather both wits and strength, preparing to confess to indiscretion and misjudgment on a scale that would not be easy for her grandson to accept.

A servant knocked and entered. "Supper, Madam? How many will it be—is the young gentleman staying the night?"

"It will be two, Nicole, here by the fire. Tell Cook to make it heavy for the officer: he's in need of bucking up. My grandson will be staying the night.

Put him in his father's room, warmer there than his own. He'll want a bath as well. There's no hurry. I'll ring later—tell Cook to keep it warm." She gave orders like a sergeant-major, Freddy thought.

The maid sounded French to Freddy, and he was surprised to find a French maid in the house. The servants had always been Austrian peasant girls brought over between the wars, a gesture, or so his father said, at reconciliation after 1918. The French—*frogs*, according to Grandmamma—were beaten at Agincourt, venerated that ogre Napoleon and his silly nephew, were obstructive in the Crimea, ran at Sedan, wept like children in 1914, and wet themselves at the very thought of Hitler. Like most English, she had no truck with the French.

"Grandmamma, the French are in the house? Is that what you wanted to see me about?" He was pulling her leg.

"No, no, don't be absurd. She is not French; Luxembourger, from Echternach, she's—German really. We won't be disturbed for at least an hour. I suggest you pour yourself a drink." She gestured toward a crystal container of Scotch. "Freddy, a sweet sherry for me, perhaps it will take the chill from the river—and my soul. That solemn river has not been able to wash away my sins in all these years."

He took a swallow of the Glenfiddich that he had poured from a decanter warming on the stand next to the coal fire and sat down to listen.

"YOU DIDN'T KNOW MY FATHER—your great-grandfather. Martin Grayling was a great and generous man. He created our family fortune, which we still enjoy these many years later. My mother was ascending up the social ladder, and when she reached the top in Leeds she ventured here to Fulham to build this country house—and soon found herself back in the city." She was clearly amused at her mother's self-inflicted wound. "That was prior to the construction of that dreadful Putney rail bridge that obscures our riparian view and cut the value of the property in half. The town grew to embrace that monstrosity and those rumbling trains into the City. In time the property took on a new luxury, and Mother regaled herself with smart friends from the large houses that sprang up all round."

She raised her right forearm just above her lace cap and let the wrist go limp in a simple wave: "The lovely and charming Miss Charlotte Howard Grayling was about to come out in 1895. I was as light as a thistledown, seventeen years old. And Mother whisked me off to Europe for my first trip abroad." As she gushed, her voice softened and her green eyes took on a light that shone from behind as she recalled the excitement of a first-class excursion to the Continent. In all the years before, she had been left behind each spring in the company of a governess to stagnate in the great house. Now she was stretched out on the window seat, watching steamboats negotiate the heavy bridge pillars and the swirling tide eddies they created, waiting to join in the promised swirl of society in Europe.

Her attention was drawn back to Freddy's face. "My world was very different from yours, my dear. The times were nearly feudal. Men of substance ran everything. The City of London was the hub of the world's moneylending. Men were encouraged to amass great fortunes and, like Silas Marner, keep it all for themselves while the workers and their unfortunate families decayed. This bothered me not at all. In that wonderful spring I was caught in the center of a whirlwind. We arrived in Paris with our steamer trunks filled with bright, gay clothes and our striped hat boxes filled with fluff and feathers. I was the center of attention at every party. I must admit I was very pretty—everyone agreed."

The tiny figure straightened up and came alive. "Paris hotels were crowded with a crop of yearlings ready for the marriage market. Oh, Freddy, the shops and frocks and the food, what luxury, what fun! Within a week we traveled first class in a heavy train carriage, stuffed with dowagers and debutantes, right across France to Baden-Baden on the Rhine. There my father gambled while I preened on the terrace and was mobbed by young officers intent on making a good impression upon the heiress." She turned toward the red coals to absorb the warmth on her transfixed face. "That's right, the heiress. I was a catch, you see. Mothers shepherded their handsome sons to court me with the most perfect attentions. We strolled the gardens and watched old men play outdoor chess on the terrace, lugging pieces about half the size of the competitors." She laced her fingers together out in front of her tiny frame and puffed out her cheeks as if lifting a fat rook to the next giant square.

Freddy rose to straighten his throbbing leg and warm it close to the fire. With one elbow on the mantel and a cut crystal tumbler half full of Scotch in his hand, the lieutenant smiled. "Grandmamma, you must have been a vision from heaven for those poor fellows, all hoping for just a smile or wink."

"I was—I flirted my way through the lot of those hopeful boys, withholding my favors, a coquette in a foreign land. Mother was tiring of watching my father lose money when she was introduced to the Countess de Billatch, who suggested they abandon their tiresome husbands at the card tables and take a house at Spa Bad Abbach near Regensburg during the August heat. You remember, don't you? Your father took you there during your school holidays."

Freddy did remember warm summer holidays paddling in frigid lakes and hiking through the pristine forests dotted with little restaurants where he discovered *pommes frites* smothered in mayonnaise. Listening to his grandmamma's tale brought back the scent of wet ground moss that he had kicked along Bavarian forest trails. The memory helped soften that of the dry stench of rotting German corpses squashed under tank treads on the roads that led away from the beach at Normandy.

Charlotte pressed on. "During a visit to the unfinished St. Peter's Cathedral in Regensburg, my world changed. Our guide, the bishop, introduced us to an intent, young, handsome student who was poring over an illuminated manuscript in the library. Freddy, he was a vision—a light from a high window streaming from behind setting him in a shimming halo." Now her voice became reverent as she remembered. "The mixed choir was practicing a Tallis piece of soaring voices that reverberated off the painted ceiling and showered down on my spinning head. When I came close to shake his hand, his light blue eyes pierced right through me. He was tall and slim and spoke with a hushed church voice. My mother found him charming as well. She stuttered and stammered through a history of our family. As long as she was talking, she was in control—she dared not allow this young man to speak, for she was afraid she could not come up with a coherent answer and thus look small and addled. When she took a moment to breathe, I boldly thrust myself in the conversation and inquired about his work and complimented him on his choice of text. I was never shy and had been waiting for a moment like this all my life. I knew this heavenly creature was meant for me." She paused. "His name was—and still is—Christian August Manfred von Thurn und Taxis Unterhart."

She stopped once again, took a sip of sherry, and looked up at me. "You should be interested in this man, Freddy, for he is your real grandfather. I couldn't talk my mother into Manfred, so I settled for Marcus."

Freddy went stock still. Until that moment he had believed that he was descended from Marcus Stetchworth. This was another bombshell dropped on his young life by the Germans. "Grandmamma, I'm not a Stetchworth—but a Hun, a member of the von Thurn und Taxis Unterhart clan? My father was not a real Englishman and those trips to the castle in Linz—"

"They were to visit your father's homeland, of course. Only you, your dear brother, and your mother were unaware of the connection." It was a relief to let the kitty out of the old black bag she had kept sewn shut for her entire adult life. She smiled. "But that is only the start of the story, my *liebchen*."

Freddy leaned forward. "There's more?"

"I haven't even begun."

## Chapter Two

# Regensburg, Germany, and Yorkshire, 1898

FREDDY'S HEAD BUZZED—REELING, HE lifted his glass to find it empty. He glanced at the drinks tray, his only hope. The top of the decanter clinked on the rim of his heavy glass tumbler as his unsteady hand poured a large Scotch. He thought, "My life, it's a lie, who am I—for that matter, who is she—how could we all exist in this maze, this deception?" He wanted to form a response, but where to start?

His grandmother was not ready to brook interruptions; that much was clear. She watched Freddy pour his drink but marched on with her tale. "I soon learned that Christian had come to Regensburg to study the classics. He rented a room in a great rambling *schloss* on the edge of town, a great manor house owned by Count von Thurn und Taxis Unterhart and rented to students to supplement the house's upkeep. An impressive structure, it was in marked contrast to the college itself, which had been part of a monastery at one time, very bleak and severe. Christian's room at the *schloss* was small but functional, and the baroque, sand-colored palace had a large inner court-yard that was an ideal cloister for serious study. Rather than a crenelated top like one of our castles, the roof was darkly shingled with a cupola on each corner, which softened the exterior, making it rather inviting. The student rooms were overrun with young privileged offspring from the southeastern edge of Europe. Those turbulent early years were filled with hijinks that might have provoked Regensburg's authorities. But as long as the students were dependent on the Count's hospitality, it was unlikely they could spiral out of control, in spite of raging hormones and the freedom found away from strictly structured homes."

Freddy fortified himself with a quick snort of Scotch. "So this boy *Christian* was my grandfather? And you met in a church with a bishop acting as matchmaker?" he scoffed.

Charlotte cut in. "Now, now, *liebchen*. I know it sounds fanciful, but that is nearly how it happened. I was tired of my parents' company and endless days at the spa, listening to that dreadful crowd of old biddies spouting free advice. Their lives were driven by gossip, character assassination, and pride of place. There was no interest outside the social season. Frills and feathers, my father called their cackling. Fashion was at the top of list. Not to snare men, but to vie with each other in a contest that was as brutal as any sport. For my part, I wanted to converse with those involved with the meaning of life, the political state of the game. I had always hated the stifling convention of Mother's luncheons and teas—the endless talk of marrying well and setting the *proper tone*.

"At least I thought of a way out. I scouted the university syllabus for a course of study that would be acceptable to English culture. The only one that presented possibly was 'Fine Art, the Study of.' More than an actual course of study, it was the pretext for the *grand tour*, a must for all enlightened Englishmen, and more particularly their women. The English upper classes cluttered their homes with silly *objets d'art*. After Mother consulted with her clutch of bigots, the curriculum was assessed as suitable as long as it didn't dwell on inappropriate images of the human body. It was a brilliant choice. I learned wonderful things and made many German friends. The course would last the whole summer, that wonderful summer."

Freddy saw Charlotte lift herself up out of the soft cushions. She became bright eyed. He thought her countenance lost the pallor he had been so concerned about earlier that evening. It was a story she must have told herself a thousand times to comfort herself during hard times, but tonight was a special occasion. She needed to impress upon her grandson its importance before she pressed on with conflicting decisions and events.

"It was my art studies that took me to the cathedral where I met Christian. And of course we had many mutual friends from Regensburg. We would meet at the student haunts where his friends were so free and gay. It was so much fun to talk to people of my own age who had broken away from convention and debated ideas one could not even dare to refer to in the circle of my mother's acquaintance. But the benefit lay not in the pursuit of art but in that beautiful boy, Christian. He was best described in terms of the day. I would tell my girlfriends at the spa that he was 'athletic.' Freddy, in those days 'athletic' was the modest way to indicate a man was virile, dangerously handsome. Blonde, of course, with a square jaw and wide mouth with a phalanx of white teeth. He was a sharp contrast to those English lads raised in glass houses, no more than overly nurtured plants slightly wilted from the cold and rain. Christian had a purposeful voice I can still hear. Strong, positive, not laced with convention. His mind was focused on important questions that could only be answered in the future. I was not his only admirer. He cast a wide net among the felines who clustered about him in the guesthouse. We made a show of praising his keen mind but were in reality overcome by his magnetic personality. And he knew it.

"I knew I had to strategize carefully if I were to hold the field of battle and vanquish my rivals. I had set my hat; he was going to be mine and mine alone. I worked hard at improving my German and coached him with English, which gave us time alone. I learned about his interests, prepared myself on topics he found interesting in life, in study, in me. I scoffed at the memory of those stiff English boys in the company of their strait-laced mothers, bent on capturing me and marching me down the same dismal marital path as my mother, a prisoner of convention.

"Poetry was my most powerful weapon. Christian loved Goethe and Schiller, poetry that rang in my ears like the singing of the church bells in Regensburg's cathedral. Christian and his friends taught me to speak and read German, which my mother dismissed as useless nonsense. When I quoted in English, Mother called it *a guttural attempt to disguise obscenity in poems that were not fit for cultured folk.* But my mother's counsel and the nodding agreement of her cronies meant nothing to me. I had my eye on the target; I besieged Christian on every front—language, poetry, laughter, attraction— and soon he fell."

"He was besotted with you, then?" said Freddy.

"More than besotted." His grandmother's earlier nerves had given way before the advance force of her memories, and she seemed the conquering hero once again as she settled into her story. "We spent every day together. Regensburg was a charming town at that time, built around several large squares and pastel-painted five-story dwellings on the edge of the raging Danube rapids. It held its medieval past with pride. Washed stucco homes, neat as a pin, lined every lane. Devout Catholic families honored street corner shrines with cut flowers. Minor churches clustered along lanes that led to the cathedral. Christian took me there once to light a candle asking God to bless us. All those old ladies with black shawls over bowed heads shuffling about the worn stone block floors like mice looking for the cheese gave me a fright. I was not eager to linger. Christian could see how ill at ease I was and countered with a walk down through the picturesque old town to the storied banks of the Danube, strolling across the long Roman Bridge, hand in hand, entranced by the rush of water shredded by the ancient arches, feeling that its chaotic power matched our own attraction.

"Regensburg was similar in design to the northern city-states of Tuscany. Rough blocks of sand-colored stone were piled high near windowless towers topped with peaked red tile roofs. These towers were more of a family status symbol than of practical use. In truth, their stark interiors were merely ware-houses and places for the family youths to get out of the villa where the adults conducted their business. We often ended our walks at Rathaus Platz, the upper floors of the tower owned by the Luskey family, whose son was a great friend of ours. That tower had become a meeting place for the restless student generation. The higher floors were the safest since mothers were reluctant to climb rickety wooden stairs to satisfy their curiosity about the goings-on. Jutting above the red tile roofs of the surrounding low buildings, the complex took on the look of children carelessly playing with blocks. While our friends played games that would have shocked their parents, Christian and I climbed to the topmost chamber filled with soft, sweet-smelling sacks of grain. He had cleared out a corner for us. Placed over the rough plank floor was an ornate oriental rug strewn with fat Turkish cushions. It smelled of wood and grain, things of the earth and animals. In the solitude Christian and I would bed down, alone at the top of a tower in the darkened chamber lit only by a pair of candles."

Charlotte looked up at her grandson then. "I must confide, Freddy, that I swooned to Christian's body as much as his readings of Goethe in that tower." There in the London chamber Charlotte looked up at the ornate white plastered ceiling that danced to the tune of the open fire across from her chair and quoted Christian from memory:

"Found"

I was walking in the woods
Just on a whim of mine,
And seeing nothing,
That was my intention.

In the shade I saw
A little flower standing
Like stars glittering
Like beautiful little eyes.

I wanted to pick it
When it said delicately:
Should I be picked
Only to wilt?

I dug it out with all
Its little roots.
To the garden I carried it
By the lovely house.

And replanted it
In this quiet spot;
Now it keeps branching out, And blossoms ever forth.

Charlotte continued to look upward, lost in her reverie. "The cool stone chamber became heavily scented from the hot charcoal turning to ash at the top of the samovar. I brewed tea. The atmosphere turned to passion as my young hero began once more—"

"Nearness of the Beloved One"

I think of you,
When I see the sun's shimmer
Gleaming from the sea.
I think of you,
When the moon's glimmer
Is reflected in the springs.

I see you,
When on the distant road
The dust rises.
When on the narrow bridge
The traveler trembles.

I hear you,
When with a dull roar
The wave surges,
In the quiet grove I often go to listen
When all is silent.

I am with you,
However far away you may be,
You are next to me!
The sun is setting,
Soon the stars will shine upon me.
If only you were here!

Silence for a moment. Then she looked back at Freddy. "Now tell me, Freddy, what chance did I have against that?" she said, smiling coyly. "I became a woman in the arms of my Teutonic knight. He made me who I am. That tower became our second home. No longer a whale-boned Victorian debutante, I saw Christian as often as I could, his friends keeping guard in the chamber below. When servants appeared with refreshments, a tap on the floor from a broom handle below tore us apart and we'd go back to our books, the very picture of studious innocence.

"The long summer days alone with Christian turned into weeks. The summer passed too quickly. The classes I had assured my mother were critical to my position in society as a sophisticated debutante? I ignored them. I stopped going to classes, never intending to write my papers or take exams. Life at the top of the tower made me resolute. I would defy my upbringing and break from convention. I would stay in Regensburg with Christian and become a true 'Bohemian.'

"I looked forward to shocking my mother with these plans and my abandonment of my debutante obligations. I would tell her of my passion for a young man of aristocratic family and my intention to remain in his company until his studies were completed and our intention to marry. I was going to be brave. My mother would have something to shock her friends.

"On that momentous morning when I intended to proclaim my desertion to Christian, I dressed not as a young Englishwoman abroad but like my continental girlfriends from the college. Swathed in colorful eastern printed silk, wearing suede slippers with gold tassels, I waited until breakfast was well under way and I was sure they were criticizing my slovenly ways. I slipped down the stairs and swirled into the bright sunlight morning room. Three sets of open French doors allowed a scented breeze to fill the room with a whisper of fall. To add to the scene, several family guests had joined us, expecting to go out on the last river excursion of the holiday. I thought it a good omen. My mother couldn't make a great deal of my assignation with a local boy in their company. Sitting at the long, dressed table, I cheerfully greeted the company and proceeded without hesitation. I knew if I allowed time to pass and wait for just the correct moment, it would never come and all would be dismissed and out the door before I could declare myself.

"'Mother, Father, I must tell you about this remarkable boy,' I swallowed, 'I mean, young man I have become interested in. He is one of the von Thurn und Taxis Unterharts—from the university.' I hoped the connection to the aristocratic family would relieve and impress both my mother and their guests. 'We are very close, studying together that is. You must meet him.'

"Inside I was getting nervous. And I realized I was still being the proper English girl, prissy and subdued. This would never do. If I wanted to be a Bohemian, a brave rebel, I needed to begin right then. I erupted with my adoration for Christian and told all! The tower, the poems, the long afternoons in his arms came tumbling out in a stream. I couldn't stop talking. I was a little hysterical, to be honest, Freddy.

"All the while my mother had been turning bright red as I spoke. At last I paused and she exploded. She forbade me to spout such nonsense, calling Christian *Continental trash*, not fit for a young girl with high prospects! My mother condemned Goethe as wicked, and the boys who read him as well.

She felt the malevolent influence of German culture on my soul: 'Europeans may indulge themselves in an obsession with Germanic poets, but we English know it to be nothing but an appeal to the lower instincts, which the Church of England has spent generations expunging from our souls. We're no longer children imprisoned by the sins of Adam and Eve. And I will not have you acting as one.'

"I realized then that I was wrong to have proclaimed my love and devotion there in front of outsiders. It left my mother with no other choice than to dismiss the affair out of hand, as a silly but dangerous misadventure. I could see it in the visitors' eyes: Throughout London that season, my self-confessed melodrama would be repeated over and over by proper mothers as evidence of the hazards of youth abroad. I knew from the looks in the attending ladies' eyes that it would be the hit of the season. A one-act play, starring Charlotte, a silly girl infatuated with a wily Austrian aristocrat, who fed on the romantic notions that consumed young ladies while studying inappropriate paintings of 'European Ways.' It would become a cautionary tale repeated to young impressionable debutantes that season at numerous parties.

"Finally my mother barked, 'Go to your room and stay there until you are told to come out. Martin, I believe we should make plans to return home immediately; see to it.' The party broke up. I went to my room. And somehow, in the space of two days, instead of making a heroic escape from my parents' domination and being firmly ensconced in Christian's arms, I was on a train back to England. Back to my parents' home. Back to the marriage mill of the season."

Pain crossed Charlotte's face. "I only had time to send Christian word of our departure, not to see him myself, as my parents were vigilant about my confinement in our rooms as they prepared to leave. Once back in England, my mother, ignoring my outburst, as she called it, launched into preparations for the coming social season in London. I dreaded the coming-out ritual now that I had fallen in love with Christian. I drove my mother to distraction with my apathy and constant questioning of *do's and don'ts*, which simply washed over me. My brain buzzed with memories of days in his strong arms atop our heavenly tower, memories that only increased my present misery.

"Then it happened: I realized that I was carrying Christian's child. I wrote to him before my mother suspected anything was amiss, and he responded immediately, asking me to marry him. His family approved: They needed the money I would bring. Their only condition was that I become a Catholic. To me it was a perfect solution. I didn't care about religion, so it made no difference to me whether I was Catholic or a Mohammedan. I just wanted relief from my situation and to be united with my Christian. And the baby would be the solution that turned the tale on its head.

"The time had come for my announcement. I knew that I couldn't remain in London once the news was out. Convention demanded that a young lady who slipped the bonds of convention and became *in a family way* wasn't to be accommodated, condoned, or supported in her situation. Social prospects were out of the question and her family was to be both pitied and spurned. Her mother would be whispered about if she dared appear at a social occasion. I rehearsed my proclamation for an hour before confronting my unsuspecting parents with the whole story in a tour de force performance. Standing up proudly at the supper table, I formally announced to my mother, father, and grandmother, 'I'm going to have Christian's child and he has asked me to marry him in the Catholic Church and live in Austria at the family *schloss*.'

"My father and grandmother stared in shocked silence, but my mother ignited. She could see it all: the scandal, the shame, the society muckrakers who would reproach her family on the one hand and gleefully rake them through the mud with the other. My indiscretion would send her directly to the bottom of the social heap.

"'Charlotte, your behavior is unforgivable! How dare you?' Mother was seething, burning with anger. She declared that I had betrayed her. In a way I had; it made me feel for just a moment that I was a very bad girl. My grandmother Howard was speechless at first, as she calculated the repercussions. But she had lived long and seen these things before. She took a practical approach: 'Charlotte is ill. She must be sent to convalesce somewhere quiet, remote, and not on the Continent where wagging tongues will surely find her. Of course there's the shooting lodge at Catterick between the moor and the army training preserve. It isn't used much these days since my brother's riding accident.' My father was quiet, weighing the longer-term consequences, but none of them gave the slightest consideration to my own desire to marry Christian."

Lowering her voice to a whisper, Charlotte looked down at the fire beside them. "I should've anticipated my family's response, but I was lost in a haze of my own dreams. Their world, built on layers of tidy social convention, placed demands on us that could not be altered or resisted. 'Austria is out of the question,' my mother proclaimed. My father nodded: 'You will go to the country.' And so it was decided, with no concession to my feelings or the offer of the von Thurn und Taxis Unterhart family. Mother insisted that Christian had played his part and was not to be rewarded for it. As for me, it was as if I did not exist. If only an overture had been made to Christian's family, it all could have come out differently."

Freddy felt the pain in her voice, but he doubted that there was ever the climate in England when such a soiled match would have found approval. While the Continent drew high interest, Europeans did not. The English embraced the art, cuisine, and general ambiance, but that never included the natives, whom they fervently believed to be flawed and filthy. They and their cultures could all be summed up with one word: *foreign.*

Charlotte's voice grew angry. "I was given a train ticket north to the wilds of Yorkshire, where a cousin would see to my confinement while a marriage of convenience was arranged to my father's junior partner, a Mr. Stetchworth. Stetchworth was not well respected at the factory. He could be slapdash in his approach to the chemistry, and he did not have a warm manner. But he was ambitious and, most of all, he was *agreeable.* It would not be just any young man who could be bribed into marrying a pregnant woman he barely knew. There must be a sweetener.

"So with little ceremony, in the fall of 1897 I was shackled to the mostly bald Marcus Stetchworth." Her mouth curled as if she were about to spit. "I'd known him for years, since I was a little girl. A sycophant to my father's every word, but with not even half my father's stature in science or business—a clerk who had wheedled his way into the business and now into our family. I assure you, Stetchworth was no match for me. He traveled north and stood in what should have been Christian's place that afternoon while the words were spoken in a private chapel on the grounds of the estate. It was a dreary fall day. My mother insisted that the obliging groom not be offered the marriage bed in consideration of my condition and Marcus was confined in a carriage driven away by my father, who put him on the late train south along with his thanks."

Charlotte looked up at Freddy briefly: "You can't imagine what that winter was like for me. Foisted on minor northern relatives, stuck in the corner on all communal occasions, as my body changed, exiled from the man I loved. I fantasized about abandoning my baby and running off to meet Christian. I wrote letters to him, but I knew they would never get past the entry hall table from where the servants carried off the post each morning to the gatehouse for pickup by the passing Royal Mail carriage. Rather than grow attached to the child filling my inside, I began to despise what it was doing to my young body that Christian had venerated. In those days many infants did not survive, so perhaps it would be a stillbirth. Then I would be sent on a tour of Italy for an extended time while society was told of my miraculous cure in some Swiss spa and all would be forgotten. Such things were known to happen, according to my minders. I imagined disappearing while on a boat to Capri, presumed to have taken my life, but secretly returning to Austria to change my name, become Christian's wife, and live happily ever after." Her glistening dark eyes caught the yellow light of the fire. "I admit that I had many such daydreams that filled the lonely months as I gazed out the upper floor window at the cold rains that swept like sheer curtains across the rolling desolation of the lifeless moors.

"Finally the delivery time came, and after a few hours of frantic labor my son arrived. Resting in my arms, he peeked out at me through dark slits on a chubby face. That was your father, Freddy. I can't explain it, but the past seven months of hate and conflict must have exhausted me and there was nothing left but love for the child that was mine and Christian's. I decided then that I would raise him to be the son of his real father and see to it that Stetchworth would not interfere with his upbringing."

"WE TOOK UP RESIDENCE IN the townhome that was my birthplace in the center of the Midlands village of Pudsey, near the city of Leeds, just streets away from my father's dye factory. From the start I must admit that I neglected the unfortunate Mr. Stetchworth. He had little charm. Short, stocky, rough, and barely mannered, he was just that much shorter than me." She held up her frail white fingertips spread about two inches between her thumb and first finger. Looking at her hands, Freddy remembered the sewing gloves with the tips cut away—allowing exact movement while the remainder of her hand was kept warm—in that drafty old mausoleum of a house. As a child sitting on the window seat watching the riverboats negotiate the bridge spans, she would bring him a treat and then touch his cheek with an icy finger. Freddy could hardly believe that woman, his beloved grandmother, was the same person telling this story of betrayal.

"Stetchworth, in revenge for my disdain, treated me worse and worse every month that went by. I confronted him daily with my discontent and we wrangled over what he called the value of tradition. He called me the most vile names and raised his hand to me one evening and struck me down before locking me in the pantry. Only the cries of the startled baby made him release me from the darkness. The house became a prison and Marcus my warden. Unlike my mother, I didn't read the *London Times* society pages but devoured the news of women's agitation for the vote, which was at the top of a list of oppression brought by men like Marcus down upon the women of England. I could see that my life was only going to suffer daily at his brutal hands, and I vowed to be rid of him."

Freddy's face registered his surprise. "Surely you called upon your father to remedy the situation and bring you to safety."

"No, indeed. I was a woman with a child, not a girl, and I wasn't going to take that from any man. Nor did I need my father to protect me. But he did inspire me indirectly. My father had developed an incessant low cough that followed him wherever he went. He told me that the chemicals in his factory and workroom had weakened his lungs and thickened the walls of his heart.

In the basement of our London home he had constructed a laboratory where he continued to fiddle with dyes. I would help him by cleaning beakers, and he amused me with silly tricks that changed the color of liquid in a jar as if by magic, made acid bubble on a plate, or set off small explosions. He also warned me about the corrosive and toxic effects that he had noticed among the workers. They developed hand and head tremors and the inability to follow directions.

"Father began examining the chemicals more closely and found that mercury cyanide, used in the synthetic dye for the color mauve, was toxic. Several men's kidneys were affected and he sent them away on extended absence to cleanse their systems." Freddy didn't like where the yarn was taking him, but he nodded and girded himself for what was to come.

"Dyes are very important to England and the Midlands mills. Great-Grandfather Grayling learned his trade in the Arkwright Factory at Chorley in the West Riding where they developed the beginnings of what would become the synthetic dyes and provided them to textile centers at Leeds. Not only was the range of color expanded well above the old vegetable dye, the accelerated chemical process increased output and quality. New colors were coming out of the crude laboratories weekly after 1862. My father, though only a teenager when he started, was in the vanguard of this group who produced stunning colors over the next twenty years. Grayling's indigo caused the family fortune to skyrocket.

"I began to reacquaint myself with my father's laboratory. Your father, whom I named Roland, after his father's family, had begun to grow, and it was easy to find reasons to travel to London to visit my family. While my mother rested or went to the shops, I would go to the basement and begin to read and test. I settled on mercury chloride. The salts dissolve in water and are tasteless in tea. I took a canister from my father's lab and hid it in my valise. Stetchworth, in his greed, had already been working long hours to gain a firmer foothold in my father's company. He spent every hour that God gave in the laboratory, and his health had begun to suffer. Returning to Pudsey, I saw a golden opportunity to accelerate his condition. I began to prepare Stetchworth's evening meal laced with the granules. I added just a little at first, watching to see if there was an effect. Within days he developed stomach pain, much to my relief, for, you see, I was unsure of the process and feared it would take too long.

"Within a month Marcus Stetchworth developed a tremor which I chided him about for my own amusement, happy to watch the progress of my revenge on this haughty, self-assured, really very stupid man. I sympathized and cooed to him when he was in great distress as if he were a child: 'Sit right there while I get you a sachet of Doctor Falkirk's pain infusion: it might be just the thing to relieve the trembling.' Of course it worsened the condition. I increased the dosage, a little more each evening.

"I exchanged mercury chloride salts for his medicine, and that, in addition to the poisonous atmosphere of the factory laboratory, soon produced the desired result. On Christmas Eve I got the only present I wanted. An out-of-breath messenger bade me to go to the factory office where Marcus had suffered convulsions and lay unconscious. The doctor arrived soon after and pronounced my husband quite dead. The cause of death was recorded as mercury poisoning, a surprise to no one at the factory. Rolly and I, the grieving widow, were free to close up the house in Pudsey and move to London, where I could pursue a life free from all but Mr. Stetchworth's name."

Freddy looked at his grandmother's contented face. He could hardly reconcile it with what he just heard and thought he must have misunderstood. So he put it to her with a simple yet extraordinary question: "Did you murder your husband, Grandmamma?"

With little concern, and a bit of triumph in her cracking voice, she corrected him: "Eliminated, *liebchen*. 'Murder' . . . such a horrid word."

# Chapter Three

# London, 1898–1910

A TAP ON THE DOOR broke their reverie. Dinner was served on tiny mahogany stands that wobbled precariously in front of the overstuffed chairs. The chambermaid came in and revived the coal fire. Served an hour after intended, the lamb was dry, the gravy congealed, and the vegetables shriveled, but it was still better than the army rations and hospital food Freddy had been enduring for the last three years.

Freddy took the opportunity to change the subject, however briefly. "It went from bad to worst. Military training school meals, cold field rations, and unit mess dinings-in were an assault on the lining of my stomach, which was at the point of combustion. Home-cooked food was my nightly dream. You can't imagine the things they had me put in my mouth these last few years." His faced screwed up. "Disgusting meat pies, bully-beef left over from the Great War, tins of mush that were labeled veg, and coffee that was practically all chicory. The sausage was halved with sawdust and the chocolate mixed with wax that coated the tongue. Many of the German prisoners refused to eat our rations."

Charlotte sympathized, "My, but the army has a lot of to answer for. Feeding our boys like rats in a sewer. Well, you'll be pleased to hear that I've arranged a special pudding put up just for you—jam tarts, like the ones before the war. I expect you to eat them all, no rationing in my house, you can be certain of that!"

The war was won and yet rationing continued. It was one of Charlotte's favorite topics: "I'll wager the Continentals are served up nicely, and they lost the war." It was a common complaint, which swept through every shopping queue. The British were aware that food was being diverted to feed the French. It was true that the Germans were the enemy, but in every British heart there was a special place, down low, for the "frogs." Some say it went back as far as 1066.

Rationing had begun during the early battle of the Atlantic in 1939, when the British Isles were in a submarine stranglehold; it was endemic even at this late date. Freddy knew that the goodies that went into supper's sweet treat must have come by way of the black market. In a household as affluent as the Stetchworths', the ration rules were bent, if not broken, and extravagant delicacies would magically appear when the occasion warranted. Cook was expected to establish liaisons, no questions asked, with suppliers beyond the High Street shops. Visitors from the northern Howard clan, young things as a rule seeking the high life away from the moors, needing a place to kip, were expected to arrive with a considerable quantity of ham, salmon, or game. Cook had her hand out for a brown paper package containing lard, flour, cheese, and eggs donated by His Lordship's kitchen staff. It was an accepted custom for manor houses once the U-boats scrambled the convoys in the North Atlantic. Some large homes in London claimed rations for servants who had left for military service. Freddy's father's connections at Horse Guards and Whitehall would yield alcohol in endless variety, and the odd tin of smoked salmon was never out of reach.

The crockery was cleared away, with the exception of a three-tiered pastry stand holding clusters of jam tarts. The meal had revived Charlotte, and she continued her tale. "As you know, your father was christened Roland Augustus Grayling Stetchworth. If anyone bothered to check, Augustus is in honor of Rolly's real father, Christian August. It was my little joke. Our son copied his father's good looks. My little boy was blonde, fair, and hardy. My mother found it difficult to resist his cheerful disposition but succeeded in keeping him under wraps until school days loomed. Harrow and Eaton were never in the cards, but with the help of my mother and the Howard family, who had experience concealing indiscretions, my darling boy was enrolled at Charterhouse. There his schoolmates dubbed him 'Rags' for his initials, a name I've never allowed to be repeated in this house—too common. Rags, indeed: it never fit him in the slightest. He was a neat boy, not a vagabond or traveler—the perfect young gentleman," she snorted.

Freddy was well aware that his father was known far and wide as Rags, which, contrary to his grandmother's supposition, gave him an aristocratic air. Many titled boys—the little Honorables, Lords, Marquesses, and Earls—had a nonsense moniker hung on them by their schoolmates that lasted a lifetime. It was a defensive mechanism established to deal with particularly privileged youths in an egalitarian academic situation. The House of Lords was crammed with Bunnys, Birdys, and Tubbys.

Charlotte continued: "When the old queen passed on, so did her era. To the great displeasure of my mother, I embraced the spirit of the new century. I chose to become a rebel, a new woman. I hated my mother's elitism and was inspired by social reformers and the early Bloomsbury Group." She hesitated, thinking she had gone a little too far. But Freddy showed no reaction, so she surmised that his education had not touched on such risqué topics. "I grew," she said, sweeping her right hand across her seated body in a gesture of indignation, symbolizing her departure from oppression. "Since I had no part in London society, I owed them not so much as a pin. I was as free as a bird to support any and all causes that flew in the face of those whose rigid values had driven a wedge between Christian and me. I blamed my misfortune on blind compliance with arbitrary and capricious rules. When I told my mother I was intent on joining my sisters in the fight for the vote, she sought to cast me out of her house, but my father, in an unaccustomed show of initiative, put an end to it one night during a heated argument barked over a lamb casserole: 'Let it be, my dear. Half the young things in London have picked up the banner. It'll run its course for in the end there is nothing that can stop it. It's nonsense to allow these goings-on to break up our family.'

"Fuming, my mother relented and the topic was dropped. When a grand Victorian lady, such as my mother, wished to extract herself from an unpleasant situation, she simply turned her back on it and *it* no longer existed."

Freddy shifted in his seat, impatient with the details of turn-of-the-century social upheaval. "It's hard to believe the vote was ever in question," he proffered.

Undeterred, Charlotte continued. "You have no idea what it took to break the stranglehold men had on the lives of women. It was a long struggle that began with the right to own property, sign contracts, and possess a bank account. It took generations to tear our rights from the oppressive grasp of men. Courageous women banded together in the face of ignorance and the façade of slavish obedience to seek the assistance of Parliament to accept women as equals. I was in the early fray along with Mrs. Pankhurst and others who risked home, reputation, and social ruin. We banded together as sisters in *the cause*, as it became known."

Freddy's impatience for his family story was mollified by the passion and pride in his grandmother's voice. "We were composed of middle- and upper-class heroines dressed for war and ornamented with accessories of spring green, white opal, and rich purple. Those were *our* battle colors. Like soldiers we suffered; like criminals we were incarcerated. Can you picture your grandmamma in a coarse brown dress covered in broad black arrow points? The same mark painted on crates of government property. They pinned a wooden disk to my shoulder. You didn't know I was number '41,' did you?" She smiled proudly and Freddy couldn't help laughing a bit at the image.

She pointed toward the fire. "There on the mantel is my suffragette brooch: we proudly wore it as a badge like the regimental one on your cap." Freddy rose, his leg now stiff from sitting, and shuffled to the fireplace. She described it in detail as he turned it over in his hand. "It has a crystal dome covering a purple flower with a green leaf background on a gold flat disk with a thin white ribbon that reads 'Vote for Women.' Most striking, don't you agree?" Freddy brought it over and laid it in Charlotte's birdlike hand. She held it to her shoulder and gave a coquettish twist of her head. Reprimanding him, "Of course, they didn't teach you about suffrage in your posh schools, did they?"

Freddy thought back to the freezing classrooms and the tedious hours spent translating Greek and Latin. There was the whirl of mathematics and endless hours memorizing English poetry and French verbs as well as a smattering of scientific facts dominated by Newton's laws. In his time, history stopped with Trafalgar and Waterloo. During his nine months as a cadet at the Royal Military Academy, drill, polish, and shouted commands did little to expand his academic horizons. "Grandmamma, according to my school masters, politics was an unsavory subject better left alone."

"Pah! Of course they said that. Stupid men. Mr. Charles Dickens endlessly wrote about the ills of our class system. He opened the eyes of those who had chosen to be blind to the living conditions wrought by the migration from farm to factory. Low wages, crowded conditions, loss of family identity, illiteracy, cheap liquor, and disease spawned a squalor you can't imagine. The vaunted industrial revolution. Parliament didn't care what happened to the workers as long as England was the supplier to the world. One-third of all manufactured goods in the world were traded in England. Disraeli called the industrial boom a convulsion of prosperity. The streets of London were paved with gold, but those who polished it with their unending labor lived in a sewer. The upper classes listened to the miracle of the wireless, enjoyed bank holidays abroad on Cooks' tours, took holiday snaps with Kodak detective cameras and gossiped on the telephone. The poor masses paid the price while the upper class frolicked. The church pandered to the middle class, ignoring the debasement and rot in the slums. A prime Dickensian character, the aloof Mr. Pecksniff, uttered the words, 'I don't want to know about it, I don't want to discuss it, I don't want to admit it.'

"The spirit of the new century affected everything. The jumble of Victoriana seemed out of place and the simpler 'Queen Anne' elegance reduced the clutter of the home furnishings. The fuss of fashion feathers became more restrained and frocks more subdued in straight lines. In the salons King Edward's female companions openly set the fashion while Gaiety Girls were openly courted by peers of the realm. In the streets the 'new women' like me and my suffragette friends rejected fashion articles on the social pages. We were there to challenge the old hobble skirt and set women on the path to freedom and meaningful work outside the suffocation of the home and children.

"We formed groups in parlors across the city to assault the status quo and protest the lack of progress promised but not delivered by Liberal politicians. They continued to campaign on vague reforms, hoping it would hold us off or turn us back. Prime Minister Campbell-Bannerman told us he could do nothing and suggested that we strive for change in a manner more fitting for ladies. We had been fobbed off by government, and we fought back. In 1903 we formed the Women's Social and Political Union—the WSPU. The term 'union' was a deliberate threat to the government, as were the labor unions, which had become so troublesome at that time. Our manifesto mounted an attack on the social position of women. We demanded redress over issues ranging from the inability of women to own property, make contracts, own businesses, and vote. We were an affront the government didn't want to deal with.

"Such a provocation was in direct contrast with our mothers and the majority of the middle- and upper-class women and—naturally—all the men. Mature Victorian women at the close of the old queen's reign maintained a composed façade, delicate health, demure manner and a revulsion of all things violent or vulgar." She paused to catch her breath. "We didn't care. We swept them along with their conventions aside in our vigor to right the wrong and pressed on in the most virulent manner. I formed a cell in this very room." Her frail right hand reached for an unseen goal, and he knew she saw those suffragettes standing and applauding her appeal.

"We were great warriors, Freddy. The Pankhursts, mother and daughters, Bohemians from Bloomsbury, broke from the mainstream to reject the methods of the other well-meaning women who had spent their energy petitioning Parliament. She sent us into the street for the sole purpose of creating negative publicity. The newspapers could not resist and censured us for our militancy. The most radical was dear little Emily Davidson. She took her protest to the Derby racetrack. Alone, she positioned herself at inner trackside rail and thrust herself at the king's charging racehorse. Trampled to death, her statement galvanized the two sides into immovable camps for years to come. As a widow and mother with an unencumbered means, I was untouchable and, I must admit, a leader in the militant wing of the suffragettes."

"Militant, that is quite a title, Grandmamma. Isn't that rather over the top?"

"Over the top?" There was just a hint of a snarl in the back of her dry throat. "Nonsense, I wasn't an aged matron all my life, Freddy. I too was young once, and like you I had a war to fight and fight it I did."

Freddy looked around the large chamber, with its tall windows overlooking the water which reflected the golden house lights of Putney three hundred yards across the black, ebbing river. He tried to imagine the clucking women milling about in big hats, drinking tea and devouring sweet cakes and tiny sandwiches. He knew his grandmother had a will of steel but never dreamed she was a leader of a militant movement in her youth, that she had so eagerly defied convention. He felt a pang of sympathy for her opponents, not knowing what they were up against.

"We picked out targets within central London that were bound to attract crowds and hopefully newspaper reporters. We made placards and banners. Others cut and sewed sashes or movement rosettes so there would be no mistake. Suffragettes wore three colors—white for purity in private and public life; purple, the royal color which flows in everyone's veins; green for hope and new life in spring: amethyst, chalcedony, peridot," she purred. Freddy glanced at the brooch that she clutched in her hand, making an impression in the thin flesh. "We gathered stones from our gardens and concealed them in our purses. Naturally I insisted that our first engagement be at the Houses of Parliament.

"Our indomitable leader, Mrs. Pankhurst, who claimed her birth on the date of the storming of the Bastille in Paris, activated my plan. We gathered at midstream on Westminster Bridge, where I took the lead, banners flying, three hundred strong, determined women all. We marched four abreast, snarling traffic and scaring horses. We had put together a sort of musical band, a few brass instruments and a number of drums; the noise brought the reporters and photographers to heel. I was up in front." Freddy noticed the twinkle was back. He was enjoying the tale now that she re-enacted it with little bounces in the soft chair.

"When my dear mama saw me in the van on the front page of the tabloids, she nearly spit. The article praised our zeal but denounced our method. Once across the bridge we wheeled left along the iron fence to a point near the entrance where we could launch the stones secreted away in large purses. My, Freddy, it was a sight. Mrs. Pankhurst, in a high-pitched voice that sounded quite comical, hollered like a screech owl, 'Now, ladies!'" Charlotte did a delightful imitation that took Freddy by surprise. He couldn't help but laugh.

"We unleashed a fusillade of missiles. A few cracked windows, and the newspapers, as expected, exaggerated the effect. When the police intervened we stood our ground, chanting and waving signs demanding the vote for women. Our voices grew stronger while crowds gathered round the edge and omnibuses stood still honking horns, which only added to the effect. Sir Somebody, in a cheap suit and bowler hat, stood on the deck of a police wagon and directed us to disperse and then threatened to read the 'Riot

Act.' We jeered him off his perch and waved placards for the cameras. Mrs. Pankhurst made an impassioned speech and, when heckled, shot back in a most unladylike manner. It was a great deal of fun, but a policeman crashed into the front line and jostled me rather severely. I proceeded to knock his helmet off with my umbrella. I, along with those who attempted to rescue me, was arrested and taken off in a police van.

"I tell you, Freddy, it was a great day, but the arrest was the beginning of the most harrowing experience in my life. I mentioned earlier that I had been a guest of His Majesty's prison. Prison in those days was medieval. Once through the grim iron-clad horse gate we were met by women of a sort I had never encountered. Worse than men, they seized me by the cloth on my shoulders and dragged me, feet pawing the ground for balance. There were five of us, each with her own personal warder. Reception was at the bottom of stone stairs in a cold chamber where we were told to undress and place our clothes in a barrel marked with a broad black arrowhead. Thrust together as a wad of humanity, we were pressed into a shower room, there to huddle in the center as streams of cold water beat down on our bodies. Screaming, we attempted to flee but were thrown back showered with expletives and threats we were convinced were real. Frightened, we clung together shivering as our long hair, which had been unpicked, matted over our faces and made it hard to breathe.

"Cleansed and rubbed dry by our warder's angry hands, we were tossed threadbare towels to finish our private parts. Rough undergarments were stacked on benches along with the brown shapeless dresses that made no attempt to fit. Slippers, obviously made for men, were thrust at us. We donned them quickly, anything to get free of the wet, freezing stone floor. Up metal ladders and down balconies we trudged, pushed along by our keepers. Each was shoved into an eight-by-six-foot rock wall cell with a tiny window too high up to see through. With a bench for a bed, I sat and wrapped myself with a rough blanket marked by the king's broad arrow. I will never forget the feeling—like being a possession rather than a person."

Freddy got up from his chair and knelt at her feet. Taking her cold hands in his, "Grandmamma, I am sorry. How could they do that to free women? To be treated like criminals just for voicing your right to protest . . . I had no idea." Charlotte looked at him with clear eyes, thankful. He had made the breakthrough she had been seeking. Her grandson was on her side at last. She knew this would be important when she came to tell him those terrible things she still had to reveal.

"Freddy, that was only the beginning. But it was worth it. Many applauded our arrest, but I knew that we were turning a corner. I may have been mishandled, humiliated, and incarcerated, but I was not cowed, not Charlotte

Stetchworth. I refused my dinner when it was passed through the slot in that dreadful iron door. Taking only water, I held out." Charlotte's chin went out and up along with her upper lip, as she continued her saga. "One level of official after another interviewed me, but I was not for turning. My sister inmates were released after three days and put on probation. They carried my defiant comportment to the newspapers. My pastor visited me and told me of the commotion I was raising, the damage suffered by my family and most importantly the tarnish to my reputation. He begged me to take food, tempting me with the promise of release forthwith. I refused. On the outside the ladies rallied round and committed similar offenses in order to join in my protest. They too were brought under the same condition and, like me, refused to take food.

"It was decided by the Home Secretary, the Honorable Winston Churchill, that we were to be force-fed. Two doctors and several warders were waiting for me when I refused the next meal. Taken like a naughty child to another chamber in the infirmary, they strapped me to a sturdy wooden chair. One doctor, standing behind me, grabbed me under the chin and forced my head back while the other inserted a wedge between my back teeth. He pinched my nose closed and brandished a long red rubber tube where I could see it. 'It doesn't have to be this way, madam; if you would accept a meal of good food we can dispense with this procedure. Which will it be, the tube into your stomach or a nice hot dinner?'"

IN RETELLING THE ENCOUNTER, CHARLOTTE'S eyes rolled up to the ceiling as if reliving the atrocity. Freddy squeezed her hands, hoping she had reneged. Force-feeding was a procedure fraught with danger, especially in 1910. The critical moment came when the descending tube was forced through the open mouth down the throat into the esophagus. There, a flap that allowed food to go down the esophagus into the stomach rather than the lungs was opened a little while still allowing air to pass into the lungs. In order to accomplish this delicate maneuver, the patient had to swallow at the moment the end of the feeding tube was presented at the conjunction. If done properly, the tube continued down to the sphincter muscle at the top of the stomach, which was penetrated. A slurry of milk and cereal was then forced down the tube with a hand pump. It was a very painful procedure, and often the patient vomited during the attempt. In addition to injuring the esophagus with the tube, other, more catastrophic results could occur. Many times the tube would be misplaced and would descend into the lungs rather than the stomach. The doctors at the time had no way of knowing exactly where the end of the tube rested. Later doctors learned to listen to the stomach with a stethoscope for the production of air bubbles, indicating that air was filling the stomach, before beginning to pump in the food. Back in 1910, however, a misplaced tube could not be diagnosed. Many British suffragettes died of pneumonia when food had accumulated in the bottom of the lungs. The symptoms appeared similar to pleurisy as well and could haunt the victims for many years if it did not kill them.

"Freddy, I underwent force-feeding twice a day for two weeks. Finally the doctor declared that if I wasn't released, I would probably die. I went home to my family, disgraced but not bowed. My *liebchen*, the pain was like no other. I could not talk for weeks. I felt buoyed by my sisters who cared for me in private while my family bore the stigma in public. Like you, I was wounded in my fight but not killed."

Freddy felt like leading a cheer for the firebrand that was his grandmother. "And did that do it, Grandmamma? Did the government give in? Were you the hero of this story?"

"No, indeed. Those years brought the motor car, juggernauts, and a new king, but our efforts only solidified the nation into two distinct opposing camps. We had great hopes for George V, but the world was beginning to come apart, and he had bigger fish to fry."

## Chapter Four

# Charterhouse and Putney, 1910–1914

"BIGGER FISH." FREDDY CHUCKLED. "That's an understatement. This was 1910, you say?"

"1910, yes. Your father was twelve years old and was at school by then. Your grandmother Letty insisted he go to Charterhouse, a public school built around what she called sensible discipline and 'sound Christian values.' It was founded in 1611 near Smithfield Market, you know, and had been a Carthusian monastery. It was a beautiful place and was considered a stepping-stone to prominence. Your father loved it. When he was on school breaks, he proudly wore the black, red, and pink-stripped cravat that marked an Old Carthusian when picking through Putney Market. So proud.

"You know, there is a quote in gold letters on a mahogany plaque in Charterhouse's reception area, from John Hancock's *God's Dealings with the British Empire*: 'We are God's chosen people, His inheritance, the salt of the earth, His loved ones, His glory, the people He delights in, His sons and His daughters.'" Her boney index finger pointed up to the unseen inscription in front of her ashen face. "That's just how those boys felt. And how I felt about my son.

"Remember I told you at the start of this evening of my treason?" Freddy's face fell at the reminder. "Yes, my treason. That's where it started. I was full of myself in those days: a leader of suffragettes, a lady of means, mother of an extraordinary boy fathered by an extraordinary man. But I was disgusted by those around me. My husband had been a brute. My family had thwarted my happiness with their petty biases. And my country had imprisoned me. My father died in 1913, and my mother followed the next year. If you think I mourned them, you are wrong. They had kept me exiled in my own country, and good riddance to them both. My parents had left their entire estate to Rolly, with me as the sole guardian. Rolly was sixteen and would not come

33

of age until he was twenty-five—plenty of time for me to maneuver the estate into a safe harbor." Suddenly she threw her head back and looked up as if in thanks to a great unseen power: "I was free, and I had only one goal: to get back to Christian."

"He had not married?" Freddy asked.

"He had not. Christian had preferred to live within the confines of the military establishment. He'd become a soldier like his father before him. Educated first at Regensburg and later at Freiburg, he had become a field grade officer on the Austrian General Staff. That same year, the Emperor Franz Joseph bestowed upon him the noble prefix of Graf—that means Count, you know. With my parents gone, my plan was to marry and take up my place in my adopted country—with my son."

Freddy was shocked. "Did my father want this? To leave England and become an Austrian?" He could not believe that an Englishman could so easily slip the bonds of his heritage to go off and become a "Kraut."

"Of course he did! I'd been preparing Rolly for this day from his formative years. He *knew* his father. He and I spent every summer and fall holiday with my parents on the Continent visiting the same old haunts with friends they'd dragged along. While my father gambled at Baden-Baden, I would slip away with Rolly to Freiburg to be with Christian. We three spent many a summer day strolling the worn paths of the deep dark Black Forest. We would rest at the edge of a stony cliffs while Rolly, to his great delight, threw stones into the raging forest stream below, which fed into the Rhine.

"Christian would tell Rolly stories from his homeland. One favorite was the story of the great stag pursued by hunters who were determined to take his life. He would begin by standing and waving his arms." Charlotte lowered her voice in imitation: "'Crashing through the tangled undergrowth, the imposing animal stopped on this very rock,' Christian would say, pointing to where Rolly rested. 'He turned his magnificent head'—his father raised his hands to his ears and spread his fingers stiff like antlers—'and snorted in derision at the pursuing hunters scrambling up behind. The stag sprang high up over the chasm.' Christian pointed to the other side. 'Mightily leaping into the air, easily clearing the stream below he lightly touched down and settled soft as a feather, stopped, turned his head to look back at his amazed pursuers. Flicking his short furry tail in disdain, he walked away into the thicket before they could get off a shot.' Rolly would look in admiration of the great feat and jump like the stag into his father's arms. They were so happy together.

"In later years I would press my unwitting parents to return to Regensburg. I told them that Rolly and I would visit friends, which was no lie. Linz, Christian's home, was only a short boat ride down the Danube. My parents, immersed in their puerile lives, never dreamed I would defy them and return to Christian, the cause of their shame. But defy them I did, and the von Thurn und Taxis Unterharts became our surrogate family. Rolly learned to speak German like a native, playing at the Albach Baths and buying candy with his local chums in the sweet shops of Regensburg's market. He loved the old castle owned by Christian's family and was treated like a little prince. At first he was accepted—then acknowledged. That was very important to me. Contrary to British opinion, the Germanic peoples are most loving and welcoming."

Freddy bristled in his uneasy chair at the accolade given to a people who had done their very best to kill him in the recent past. His generation had seen British soldiers, now invalids, begging in the streets. They had marched from the schoolyard directly into battle with the hated Huns. They did not seem to Freddy to be of a loving and welcoming nature.

Charlotte saw Freddy's face but didn't back down. "It's true, Freddy; they were wonderful. And your father and I looked forward, every spring, to spending extended languid days surrounded by mountains, lakes, and streams of that heavenly corner of Europe. By the end of his sixteenth year, Rolly felt as much an Austrian as an Englishman."

Freddy took a long drink but kept quiet. Sitting quietly in his ancestral home on the Thames in 1945—after two devastating wars—such a feeling was nearly unthinkable. But he realized as his grandmother spoke that the woman who felt these things was simply a young mother in love, with no idea of what was to come. There had been no war, no bombing of London, no millions of deaths. Charlotte Grayling Stetchworth had a dream of life with her great love—and no idea that war would soon take her by the throat and smother those dreams.

"We intended to travel to Austria in July of 1914, but dark clouds were already gathering. The German army began to mobilize, and Christian's movements became clouded. His letters were short. Yet he also believed the war would be over by Christmas and, whatever the outcome, our plans would be honored and we would unite at Linz on that happy day. Far too soon mail from the other side was read by some faceless bureaucrat before delivery. By July communication stopped entirely. But if July was difficult, the month of August was hell. If the shot fired at Concord Bridge had turned the world upside down, the pistol shot from that postman's son that killed the Austrian heir to the throne in Sarajevo sent the world into a spin that could not be stopped with anything short of catastrophe. The declaration of war rang like giant bells from the cathedrals of Europe. The British Expeditionary Force, later dubbed the 'Old Contemptibles,' crossed the Channel to France on the 9th of August, unaware they were bound for destruction." With eyes fixed on her grandson, Charlotte soldiered on. "Every nation thought they had something to gain from a few short months of glorious war. But I had lost it all as soon as those shots were fired. The borders closed. Friends became enemies. And Christian left for war."

CHARLOTTE EXPRESSED HER PANIC AT that hour. "The wheels were coming off, Freddy. Suddenly Englishmen were dying on a foreign field and the population cried that spies and collaborators were everywhere. Three major newspapers ran a story that there were 66,000 Germans in London in disguise and an arms cache in a depot near Charing Cross railway station in central London. German spies, according to Sir Mansfield Cumming, leader of the national intelligence services, had infiltrated the army, navy, and the Foreign Office. Turf disputes between government departments filled the newspapers.

"Worst of all, I was afraid for Rolly. Soon he would be of service age. All his schoolmates were consumed with the war, and he was bound to envy the upperclassmen who were volunteering en masse. I knew he'd be swept up like the others. Popular opinion drove youngsters into the arms of the recruiter." Freddy began to see a wave of deep emotion once again consuming the frail old lady. She was looking directly at him, but he was sure her inward gaze was focused on the iconic poster of Field Marshal Lord Kitchener pointing to the young men of England with the words "Your Country Needs YOU!" She continued. "Lines of young men surged forward to join up, overwhelming the services, who were unable to cope with demand. Rather than uniforms, they were issued dark armbands with white royal crowns embroidered in the center. To me, it was as if Kitchener were pointing right at my heart and saying 'I want Rolly for the army.'"

Charlotte continued, recalling her frenzy. "It wasn't helped when the stories of German atrocities came pouring in from the helpless people of little Belgium. And that old fool Kitchener spouted rubbish to the troops leaving for France: 'Be invariably courteous, considerate and kind. Never do anything likely to injure or destroy property, and always look upon looting as a disgraceful act.' As if the British had never dirtied their hands. Early reports from the battlefield were appalling. British newspapers printed the names of the dead and wounded daily, drowning the nation in shock and sorrow. Rolly heard from his British schoolmates that in the first four months 300,000 British lads had been killed and 600,000 wounded out of a male population of ten million of military age. Rolly was troubled: 'They say that the cadet program will lead directly to commissioning. Can you imagine, Mother, seventeen-year-old lieutenants in command of a platoon of farm lads and factory laborers fighting the Germans?'"

Charlotte stopped and looked at her grandson. She could see that Freddy's attention was in and out, and she suspected that his leg was beginning to hurt.

He was a dear boy and had been through a great deal. Normandy had been his first experience in combat and it had taken a toll. He was no longer the little boy filled with happy energy. It was more than his gait that had slowed; his mind had suffered as much as his leg. Charlotte picked up the pace of her story.

"Rolly, in his last year at Charterhouse, had participated along with his fellows in a modified military program one afternoon a week. Geared to interest the young in furthering an army career, the cadet program was more fun than practical in the eyes of the boys. They were taught drills and became acquainted with the Enfield rifle. Not allowed to fire it, they were content to look like soldiers under arms, just short of becoming one. One day he came to me in this very room, sorely troubled. I was worried that he was about to sign up with his schoolmates, but he surprised me. He looked out the window at the running river, not making eye contact, and said, 'Ma, I want to be a soldier, but not an English one. I want to be with Father and fight for the Austrians and Germans.'

"Freddy, you can't imagine how I felt. I think he was afraid I would chastise him for deserting his friends—his country. He was sure that I, like everyone else, had been caught up in the wave of patriotism that had swept the country. But I realized then that my nurturing had placed a bond between us that would never be broken. I seized him, almost violently, and felt him startle and stiffen in surprise and then relax in my arms—we were one. I told him I would find a way to make that dream come true for us both.

"I began to search for an escape route. We had to get to the Continent. They might be able to cut me off from Christian's letters, but I could pack up and go to France, a boy and his mother on holiday. By spring of 1915 the war had established strict lines that stretched from the shoreline of the North Sea to the Swiss Alps. England had become a fortress and the Channel a moat. Civilian travel to the Continent became a suspicious activity. In past wars, wealthy family members appeared on battlefields from India to South Africa and stood aside to witness the conflict as spectators who were out of bounds and therefore safe. The range of artillery and overflight of aircraft increased lethality and ended the time of safe havens. The high casualty rate and need for critical supplies of war material along with extended troop movements had complicated the process and eliminated civil travel.

"Restrictions were nearly iron-clad. Many reasons were given—fear of spies, contraband, black market, aid to the enemy, deserters. But I had a plan. Rolly and I would cross the Channel on a packet boat to Brittany, then go by train to Switzerland and Liechtenstein, where we could slip across the mountain pass on a hiking holiday into the Tyrol and then travel by coach to Linz. This plan, while highly practical, was destroyed when I was unable to secure

a passage without a government pass from the inspector general of communications at British Army headquarters. I enlisted the aid of the Howard family,
but I think they suspected an ulterior motive and ignored my plea."

Freddy's heavy meal and promised jam tarts—combined with most of
the Scotch in the decanter—was taking its toll. The heat of the fire and
the darkness of the chamber didn't help, and he felt his eyelids fighting to
stay open. But his interest was piqued when his grandmother's story took
its next turn.

"I had begun to despair, Freddy. But then God smiled on us. A stranger
appeared at my door one day in April. A priest—well, a monsignor from the
Vatican—he showed me his credentials, which was certainly a surprise. His
name was Monsignor Merchanti. I offered him tea, and we sat in the salon at
that little marquetry table, the one by the painting of your great-grandfather.
The monsignor was a most impressive man—in his thirties, quite trim, a man
of quiet demeanor whose whispered tone made it difficult to detect his country of origin. Not accustomed to entertaining unannounced Catholic clergy in
the middle of the afternoon, I was about to tell him that the family didn't support the church, no matter the cause or appeal. But once tea was served and
pleasantries concluded, he reached into his inside pocket of his black coat and
produced a small envelope. Handing it to me, he turned it over, to reveal the
wax seal of the von Thurn und Taxis Unterharts. I must have jumped because
he nearly pulled it back. Trusting it into my outstretched trembling hand, he
apologized—'My dear lady, I would like to leave this message with you to
read in seclusion. I can see that I am intruding.' My smile came like a reward
he was not expecting.

"The monsignor rose, bowed slightly, and turned toward the heavy closed
door to the hallway. He paused as if he had forgotten something. I thought
that perhaps he was expecting someone to open it from the other side. It was
an awkward moment. Half turned back, looking reluctantly over his shoulder.
'You don't recognize me, do you, Charlotte?'

"The use of my Christian name startled me and I thought of reproaching
him. But there was something familiar about him, and I paused. I had no
connection with the Catholic establishment; on the contrary, I was C of E.
Neither had I been to Rome. But then I thought—Christian is Catholic, the
family as well. Could I have known this young man from Linz? Facing me,
a hint of a smile curled the corners of the priest's mouth. I could see he was
enjoying the little game, but I was not. I asked, holding up the envelope, 'Did
Christian give you this?'

"The priest shook his head. 'No, not directly; I've not seen him in some
time. He sent it to me through the diplomatic pouch from Rome.'"

"'Christian is in Rome?'

"The monsignor tried to explain. 'According to the note I received, he was in Rome in order to set up this channel of communications with you. I think it must be explained in his message; as you can see, I've not read it.'

"'Oh.' I dropped my gaze to the letter.

"'I guess, Charlotte, that you never knew my last name back in those heady days in Regensburg when you and Christian used to visit my family's tower and my friends and I stood guard for you on the floor below.'

"'Pieter, my God, it's Pieter—that teenager who kept our secret on those long lovely days.' I nearly burst as those happy days came flooding back. Those wonderful hours that seemed so far away now. All I had thought of for weeks was danger, disappointment, death. But now, a letter from Christian. Oh my, it was good. The channel for communications my clever man had chosen—I could breathe once again.

"Freddy, can you fathom? There was a priest, a monsignor, right in that chair you're sitting in now. An envoy from the Papal See in my salon with a message from behind enemy lines just for me from the one person I most longed to hear from. Freddy, it saved me, that day meeting an old friend from a time when I was truly happy, ready for the world and whatever it could throw at me. I had renewed strength; the sky had opened and I would be all right, war or no war.

"Pieter had been apprehensive of meeting me. He knew that I was now a proper English lady, no longer the effervescent girl that in spite of the age difference he had admired, loved a little, in those growing-up times. I admit to being a coquette, playing the younger boys. But when he saw my reaction, his doubts fled.

"'May I come again, Charlotte? I mean, may I be your willing delivery boy? It would be suspicious for you to come to the Westminster Cathedral grounds; the church is watched, not fully trusted. The old schism remains unresolved. My diplomatic immunity has been only reluctantly granted.'

"'Oh, of course, come even if you don't have a message; it'll do me good to renew happy times with an old friend.' I grasped him tightly by his upper arm and pulled him forward for a kiss on the cheek. 'My dear Pieter, it is so very good to have you back in my life.'

"Pieter smiled. 'Before I leave, may I offer my compliments; I will be at your service in the very near future. You might know that the Holy Father is in delicate health and so my schedule is in doubt at the moment.' He produced his card that contained an unfamiliar name:

Monsignor Pieter Merchanti
Papal delegate of His Holiness,
Pope Pius X,
in residence at Westminster Cathedral,
Victoria, London.

Pieter placed his index finger in front of his pursed lips, then turned and left."

Charlotte sighed contentedly. "I'm sure you can imagine, Freddy, how I felt. A gateway had opened to my beloved Christian, one I could walk through, a hidden doorway in the midst of the Great War. The content of the letter I am sure you can guess: He asked for my help in the war. It lifted my heart and put me back on a firm footing. I wrote to him immediately and had the communiqué hand-delivered to the monsignor, as instructed. In it I told him of Rolly's desire to join his father and his adopted land to fight on the side of right and my hope that somehow I could join and make the family whole. Surprisingly I was soon given an answer by courier, whom I presumed was in the pay of the priest. I worried that it could have been intercepted and read or altered. But before leaving the courier slipped the monsignor's calling card into my hand. Handwritten on the back was the name Luskey. I knew then that this was Pieter's way of assuring me that the correspondence was legitimate and had not been tampered with by authorities, for no one would fathom the deep meaning of the Luskey tower in Regensburg.

"When the courier left, I sat down to read the miraculous letter in my hand. Christian wrote: 'My darling *liebchen*, if you are both sincere about joining the cause of the Kaiser, and I am sure you are, I believe that Rolly would be of greater service to the cause if he were to join the British Army. I am certain your family can make space for a young officer in a high department, out of harm's way, but close to the affairs of the Allied General Staff. We know this conflict will last for some time. I am building a spy network, but I believe it will be very hard for us to infiltrate the British Army without being compromised. We require a real Englishman in a vital spot who we can rely on, who cannot be turned against us. You and Rolly are the only ones we can trust. Arrangements can be made to transmit the vital information he learns concerning plans, strengths, equipment, and intentions through a special channel to me for our use in the imperial intelligence service of the German General Staff.'"

FREDDY HAD KNOWN WHAT WAS coming, but his mouth torqued in disgust all the same. "A spy, a German spy, in the service of the Kaiser." Charlotte nodded her head slightly but kept her bright blue eyes on her grandson's countenance. "How could you do it, Grandmamma?" His father's loyalty had never been questioned. All his life Freddy had known his father as a hero, and the pain of betrayal poured out of him. "My father, Lieutenant Colonel 'Rags' Stetchworth, who served through two wars . . . a German spy. He put the family, the nation at risk, for what—your pipe dream of Heidi skipping through a mountain meadow." Freddy felt sick. How could he be a traitor's son? How could his beloved grandmother be a turncoat? His stomach heaved as his mind cracked at what he had learned.

Charlotte looked on at his distress with quiet equanimity. Freddy held his head in his hands, his whole family identity breaking before him. He got up, stumbling over a wrinkle in the carpet as he crossed the bedroom chamber and sought the solace of the decanter. Freddy grasped the crystal tumble tightly and clinked the narrow mouth on the edge, chipping his glass. He tossed down one and refilled it again before resuming his seat across from the old woman he suddenly felt was a stranger.

Charlotte looked at Freddy with sympathy and suggested they retire. "Tomorrow is another day, *liebchen*." The moment it left her lips, she knew the German endearment would only inflame Freddy, but it was too late to stop. Freddy snapped his head up, realizing the term had lost its German context until tonight. "To bed, help me up, my dear." Freddy had no choice and took her arm and pulled her slightly forward. There was little sinew between her arm and shoulder, and it popped as they both strained to bring her upright. She extended her forearm: "My stick, Freddy, over there by the hearth." He retrieved it leaving her unsteady for just a moment. He rang for her maid, who must have been asleep in the hallway chair, for it took three calls to produce the young woman. They parted company and Charlotte thought the worst was over; it would go smoother now that he knew. But of course there was much more to come. Much more.

## Chapter Five

# Putney, 1914–1915

WHILE THE MORNING WAS CLEAR and crisp, Freddy was not. He was suffering from both a hangover and lack of sleep. He'd laid awake in the darkness listening to the boats tethered to the floating docks bang back and forth as the thirty-foot tide played with them. He must have slept, for the bells of Saint Mary's church across the river on Putney High Street didn't wake him at eight. Reluctantly he rose; his leg was calm, which he attributed to the quantity of Scotch whisky he had poured down his throat the long evening before. Groggy, he slipped on the robe the maid had left at the end of his bed and answered the light knock at the door.

"Morning, Lieutenant, sir. Breakfast is served in the dining room. Madam will not be joining you; she doesn't rise until eleven o'clock."

Freddy pushed his straight brown hair back, teetered on his injured leg, and asked, "Who are you? I didn't meet you last evening."

"I'm Anna, Madam's chambermaid. I'll be looking after you while you stay, Lieutenant."

Her Germanic accent was lilting, like a little bird. Well, he thought, I better get used to it. After all, I *am* part Austrian, I guess. The conversation from the previous night came flooding back like bad news. Anna left the room and he stepped to the bedchamber mirror. In the solitude of his room, he confronted his roughened face and asked himself, "Am I really Austrian? I've sliced a few in my time; I wonder if we were related." It actually made him chuckle, with a bitter smile.

All he had packed for the short stay were army uniform items. He refrained from wearing mufti, not wanting his relatives to think that he was demob-happy. Unlike his brother, Martin, who was young and wild, acting out his newfound joy in civilian life in every pub in London and then at the Cote

43

d'Azur, where he had decamped after presumably running through all the pretty girls in London.

If Freddy were lucky, he'd be retained on active service. The regular army was in transition. It was contracting from millions of soldiers to thousands. If he were to remain on active status, it would require intervention from someone with influence at Horse Guards, the headquarters of the British Army. His mother's father, Colonel David Moss-Jones, was a Welsh Guardsman who had used his position to transfer Freddy from the Honorable Artillery Company rolls to a Guards regiment. The fact that he had been in hospital recovering from wounds with a Military Cross pinned to his pillow gave him hope in this respect. The old regular army was a gentlemen's club fit for heroes. As a Guardsman serving the king, a chest full of meaningful decorations set the proper tone.

He was fortunate since the Welsh Guards were the latest addition to the Household Brigade; the Welsh Guards were created as a separate regiment at the start of the World War I as part of the largely ceremonial Foot Guards regiments. Less competition was to his advantage. Besides, he felt comfortable in uniform, which complemented his cane and tortured gait. The looks given him on the street were honorable ones, not pity. As an officer, even a lieutenant, it placed him in a class above, where he wanted to be. It was once said to him about service in the Guards, "you'll never be rich, but you'll walk with kings." His father had walked with kings—well, one king. Besides, he looked rather good in khaki.

Freddy had meant to follow his father's example. But as he gave a quick rub to his buttons and regimental badge, he was struck anew with what that actually meant. He was aghast that he had trained his whole being on emulating a man whom, he now realized, he didn't know at all. His grandmother's words echoed in his mind: *Your father and I were German spies.* Descending the heavy staircase to the center hall, he thought, "What's going to happen to all my plans? I'll never be free of this stain."

He negotiated the carpeted stairs one at a time, holding the rail, with his batman's voice chuntering in his ear: "Mind the steps, sir." Of course, his batman had been right. It had been a rather nasty fall at the hospital when he got cocky. It was a hell of a tumble and had set him back weeks.

Off the cavernous center hall, across from the library, his breakfast waited for him in covered silver dishes atop the long Georgian buffet. The Howard coat of arms was embossed in the center of each plate that he took from the warmer: a wedding set from the family to his great-grandmamma Howard. He grazed among the row of gleaming serving dishes, knowing they contained special delicacies for the war hero. Mrs. Jayson, the family cook, favored him over the other family members since Freddy had always been such a good eater. It had made him very popular in the kitchen. Freddy made a mental note to visit her as soon as he gorged himself. His hospital mates would have killed for Mrs. Jayson's plain English cooking. Kippers, kidneys, fried eggs, field mushrooms, Cumberland sausage, blood pudding, fried tomatoes, baked beans, and thin slices of gammon warmed above alcohol burners. A small silver framework with a half dozen triangles of cold toast waited at his place. Small pots of orange marmalade, berry jam, and butter surrounded the rack. A warm coddled egg in a Beatrix Potter porcelain holder rested on a small plate at his place. Embossed on the side, Peter Rabbit scurried away from Farmer McGregor, who brandished a rake. Nothing had been left out. There was only one place set in the cozy breakfast room, which made him a little lonely. Bygone days of family meals were precious memories. He always thought of himself as a gifted son in the heart of a grand family, and now he shuddered inside as his world-view took another blow.

After breakfast he strolled outside on to the low-walled terrace. Although it was an early December morning, it was bright and just above freezing. There was a thin layer of ice on the dark metal furniture soon to be melted by the winter sun. The stone dressing on the top of the wall had been the perfect surface for him and his brother to race their Dinky cars. He could still detect tracings of dark rubber from their wheels in rows that crisscrossed on the white stone. Freddy loved the river, its power and indifference to the heavy railroad bridge. Its many pilings acted as a sieve, trapping debris until the next tide cleared it away. The tide was about to change as the clock crept toward noon. Even though the sky was a vivid blue, the rushing water paid no mind and reflected the same dark color that enveloped his heart.

How did they do it? How could they have fooled the spy hunters that roamed the country, ever watchful, ever vigilant? The British were famed for their counterintelligence, from the book adventures of Bulldog Drummond to Sherlock Holmes to the real-life feats of MI5. Relentless, that was the British way. Freddy's heart sank as the probability of discovery dawned on him. The day would almost certainly come when someone snooping around some dusty archive would find them out. What then?

Freddy looked down at the crushed cigarette butts surrounding his boots. He must have been there a long time. A soft voice came from the dining room's French doors: "Madam is up, Lieutenant." Freddy turned and saw a spritely middle-aged woman in a modest dark dress and sensible shoes. Her hair was pulled back in a bun, leaving her face exposed. She had a rather sharp nose that was protected by pronounced cheekbones, providing an air of authority. The woman's only makeup was a thin line of rose lipstick on a pleasant mouth. Thin hands were clasped before her at the belt. He glanced to see if she had a wedding ring, a soldier's habit.

"Ah, you must be Mrs. Brooks. I knew you must be somewhere in the background, since the house is in order, as always. My mother told me that you had taken charge when Mrs. Alberry passed away."

The housekeeper smiled at the compliment. "Welcome home, sir. I hope your confidence in me will be justified. This is your home once again—that is, as soon as you have completed your convalescence. Will you be staying for a while, recovering here perhaps?" It was an acceptable question for the housekeeper to ask. She would have to make some adjustments to schedules and assignments once a young man was in residence.

"No; I'll be off early on Monday, unless Grandmamma isn't done with me." He grimaced inwardly. Remembering his earlier resolve, Freddy asked, "I must visit Mrs. Jayson; is she in the kitchen?" The housekeeper nodded before she withdrew to her duties.

Freddy's army boots clattered on the hardwood floors and down the uncarpeted back stairs, announcing his presence long before he stepped through the open door to the kitchen below. The morning light came in through high windows sunken below the sidewalk level of the tradesman entrance. Mrs. Jayson was unmarried, the "Mrs." a customary honorific in such positions. She was short and round, like Mrs. Tiggeywinkle, a middle-aged woman with a red face and enormous smile to welcome him home. But upon settling her eyes on him, her smile fell. "Master Freddy! My, my—you're a stick of your old self! What have those Germans done to you?" Tears filled her green Welsh eyes, prompting Freddy to look away for a moment to avoid his own eyes misting up. Mrs. Jayson had always been the nourishing force in the home, ready to bolster a bad boy who was in hack for something she knew he didn't really mean, or sneak a sweet roll to one just because. He loved his mother, but it was of Mrs. Jayson and her warm kitchen that he dreamed on those terrible nights in France and later in hospital. She gave him a quick hug and Freddy sat down at the worn oak table.

"Now then. How was breakfast, Master Freddy? Was it a treat, or do you get your marmalade in Peter Rabbit's jar in the mess as well?" He smiled and then spied the biscuit tin resting on the corner of the table. "Any chocolate-topped survivors from the ration book?" he asked, pointing past her.

With a twinkle in her eye, "There might be a 'bicky' for a very good boy." Turning, she pried open the tight square lid from the Fortnum & Mason's decorative box painted with soldiers of the regiments.

Freddy dove in as if he had never left home. Seated, calmly crunching the treats, he asked, "Tell me: What can I expect from Mrs. Brooks? Is she the tyrant old Alby was?" It was no secret that the boys had been the bane of Mrs. Alberry's existence. The housekeeper didn't appreciate their high spirits so indulged by their mother. Unamused, she was an endless tattletale, providing Charlotte with plenty of ammunition during school holidays.

Mrs. Jayson was always ready to tell a story. "Mrs. Brooks came to us in most disturbing circumstances. Her husband was a waterman, caught in a zeppelin raid down by the docks. They never found his body. Their daughter, Alice, a ten-year-old, such a pretty girl, was sent up to the Howards when her mother took the job here—the poor lamb. The parting was difficult, but since her house, across the river on Deodar Road, was set on fire—" She took a quick breath. "When one of those monstrous bombers jettisoned at Putney Bridge, Mrs. Brooks agreed to let the girl go north to protect her. Now Alice stays up there because she likes the school. I'm afraid our housekeeper is a rather lost soul; the war has been very hard on her." Freddy had not realized how much destruction Putney had endured. Several miles inland from Westminster, with no industry in evidence, the railway bridge was the only target. The German attempts to hit a narrow bridge a couple hundred yards long in the dark from 8,000 feet ensured that everything around would be struck but the bridge would survive.

It was a treat to sit in the cozy kitchen, the warmest room in the house. As a boy he and Martin were always under Mrs. Jayson's feet. Like all cooks in grand houses, she had a special dispensation. Her liaison with the local merchants, who delivered foodstuffs to the house, allowed her to manage the accounts to her advantage. Her value was not just in the procuring of high-quality food for the table at the lowest price; within her network, she managed to supply anything that Charlotte fancied. She had a free hand, and it was acceptable for her to extract a small stipend for her own purse. She might barter as well, especially in the face of rationing restrictions. Such goings-on would build into a nice sum for the inevitable day when she could no longer work. Of course the family would provide her a small pension or grant, but she needed to squirrel away what she could.

Mrs. Brooks interrupted: "Lieutenant, Madam is asking for you in the library. She thought you might be more comfortable there; a fire has been laid."

Mrs. Jayson winked at Freddy: "Oh dear, you better get up there. It sounds serious, Master Freddy."

PREVIOUSLY THE DOMAIN OF HER father, the library had been transformed once Charlotte took over the mansion. The original floor-to-ceiling bookcases were intact, but that was all. The grand style of Napoleon III and Victoria—which favored an abundance of bric-a-brac, each home like a small V&A museum—had given way to the era of the *objet d'art*—single polished pieces that stood out in a clean and uncluttered space. The drapes and fringed swags were gone along with the feathers and china dogs that had sat imperiously on the corners of the mantelpiece.

Charlotte was seated close to the fire on a buttoned leather-backed shelter chair. She appeared withered in the harsh daylight, slumped, knees covered with a heavy, brightly colored afghan wrap. She seemed vulnerable as a stream of sunlight hit the vivid threads and washed her out. But as she saw Freddy walk toward her, she drew herself up straight and looked him steadily in the eyes. "Did you sleep well, *liebchen?*"

Freddy felt anger at her apparent ease. "Grandmamma, I didn't sleep well and may never again. I am amazed that you could."

Charlotte smiled wryly. "I sleep perfectly fine, Freddy. I made my peace with our choices long ago." Her grandson hoped there was more regret than she was willing to admit. If the Germans had won the war, she would have been proud to take some credit. But since they were soundly beaten, perhaps she repented of her efforts in the privacy of her own mind.

Freddy sat down across from her. "Are you going to tell me the rest? I'd rather hear it from you than from the MI5 boys. You know that the day may come, long after you're no longer with us . . ." He paused; it was a little strong but honest. "A knock will come at my door and I'll be expected to explain it."

"Certainly. You should know all that your father and I accomplished. I must say, we were very good at spying, very careful. There were times when I thought things were going to get out of hand. We had to take drastic action at times, but I don't think our missteps will ever come back to haunt you."

"You mean mistakes, blunders?" Freddy was surprised. Until that moment she had been positive. Oh, this was bad.

Charlotte changed gears. "I'm getting ahead of myself; we must take things in order, that's the best way." Freddy was dumbstruck. Mistakes would surely come to light on his watch. In his silence, his grandmamma continued as if she were relaying a bit of gossip, nothing more.

"CHRISTIAN'S SUGGESTION TO PLACE OUR son within the heart of the British Army was honored. I appealed to the Howard family for assistance and they arranged an interview for Rolly with the Honorable Artillery Company. Howards had joined the HAC for generations, practically since it was chartered in 1537, *For better defense of our realm.*"

Freddy knew this story. He too had been commissioned by the HAC. Graduates began as long bowmen, gentlemen of the artillery garden, and then were integrated into the Territorial Army as the London contingent. Members had served as officers in HAC light cavalry and horse artillery since before the Victorian age. Often seconded across the functional elements of the army, HAC graduates had made a name for themselves in nearly all walks of life. The HAC home barracks was Armory House, a Georgian-style, block-long complex with crenelated, white stone corner towers. The mock castle in the heart of the city announced its military intentions, as did the two-story stained-glass window of Saint George slaying the dragon that loomed over its entryway. Young men of good character from public schools were the first choice for acceptance into HAC. Recommendations from respectable quarters were reviewed and letters inviting applicants to appear for the pre-commissioning course of study were sent.

Charlotte got specific. "Since it was near Spitalfields and Charterhouse, Rolly was familiar with the area. He told me that on his first day it was crowded with candidates who lingered in long lines waiting for their personal interviews held at rickety, green field tables. Clerks took down basic infor-mation, putting it on large shoe tags affixed to candidates' buttonholes on their waistcoats before they met the medics. These formalities didn't apply to your father. Of course the sergeant-major attending at Rolly's interview had been informed of Rolly's application and eliminated the medical phase. He directed Rolly to the Queen's Room, where accepted applicants waited for the swearing-in.

"Rolly loved the HAC. He had three months of field training and then his class was commissioned in January of 1915." Freddy reminded her that he had undergone the same routine and that it sounded very familiar.

Charlotte glowed at the thought of Freddy following in his father's foot-steps. "I was as proud of him as I was of you. Once he had his commission in hand, he marched directly to the family tailor at Jermyn Street, across from Churches' Shoes near Piccadilly Arcade, for measurement. His body had been altered from the rigorous training. He was even a little taller, he thought, but I told him that he was just standing up straight for the first time. He was told before he left that his entire kit would be ready in a fortnight. He wore his undress uniform out of the shop complete with pips on his shoulders. He felt like a king. He took a taxi straight home, hang the expense. Once I gushed over his smart appearance, we composed a message to Christian announcing his suitability." She lowered her tone now: "I was most concerned that it not be intercepted. I phoned Monsignor Merchanti, who sent a messenger boy from the Chancery of Westminster Cathedral round on his bike. I was sure it was safe once it was in the priest's hands. I expect it was put in a diplomatic pouch for the Vatican. But still I worried. In the note I asked that a safer means to the cathedral be found if a stream of information was to be transmit-ted over a long period of time. Or perhaps we should leave the monsignor out of it entirely for his own sake?"

Freddy was distraught listening to the tale she was spinning. She seemed to have no compunction at her treason, seemed to take delight in recalling it all. His anger burst out: "How could you calmly plot the destruction of young

Englishmen? They could have been classmates of your son! How could you, Grandmother?"

Charlotte went rigid and cold. She spoke as to a child who had schemed against her wishes and must be brought to heel. The gloves came off. "The British are a mongrel merchant nation—soulless, decadent, corrupt. Full of money-grubbers like their American offspring, wanting only physical comfort, security, money, and reputation. Who could possibly prefer Britain to Germany who knew any better? German culture is authentic, spirited, and pure-blooded. And noble—their leaders expect Germans to sacrifice themselves for a greater cause, the survival of the fatherland. It was not Germany's fault that it was attacked by those Slav cavemen, that the other European nations conspired against them to deny their rightful place among nations. Russia and France seized a chance to humiliate the Austrians by squeezing the life out of them."

Freddy recognized Charlotte's justifications from the many antiwar pamphlets circulated by German agents in England and America, fifth-column propaganda that had been resurrected during the run-up to the recent war with Germany. Prominent political families, mortally wounded by the loss of kinsmen in the Great War, were desperate to appease Hitler and avoid more bloodshed. They backed publications, speakers, and broadcasts advocating concession to prevent another costly war. His grandmother may have been taken in, but Freddy suspected that she was motivated more by her love for Christian and her pathological hatred of her parents and all that they represented. Her bitterness at being sold off to the miserable "protection" of Marcus Stetchworth had twisted her irrevocably. Freddy fumed at this invective, but Charlotte stared him down: "May I continue?"

"ROLLY BEGAN WORK IN JANUARY 1915, straight after his commissioning. His initial orders billeted him as a forward artillery observer, but I wasn't about to let my son lead a platoon of doomed infantrymen or set out forward to scout for guns. I called upon an uncle of mine on the Howard side—Major General Sir Avery Hilliard Hopewell, a staff director on the Chief of the Imperial General Staff's office at Horse Guards, the British Army headquarters. Uncle Hilly was a distinguished, long-serving soldier. He had fought the Madhi of Sudan as a subaltern and battled the Boers in the Transvaal. A political ally of Churchill's, you know, with whom he shared a service record. His contribution led him to the Army Council, there to advise the War Secretary, Lord Kitchener. His war experience and wide-ranging inquisitiveness slotted him as an inspector general. Uncle Hilly met Rolly, found him impressive, as I knew he would, and offered him a position as his own aide-de-camp—a 'dog robber,' as they were known. I was delighted;

what could be safer? He'd be in England, not in some trench, and he'd be positioned at the heart of strategic planning for the war. An inspector general was not only invited to staff meetings but was expected to travel, observe, and report back to the directors both good and poor implementation of the war minister's intentions and directives. He held no command authority and was regarded as a nuisance—a tattletale—in the field. But he was a distraction to be treated with the upmost care, for he had the ear of the War Cabinet. Across his desk passed the keys to the kingdom.

"Rolly was so impressed to be at the heart of the war planning that he gave me the most minute review of his first day. For once I didn't have to prod and peel to get him to tell his mother the full story."

Freddy was intrigued as well and began to enjoy the tale, forgetting for the moment the purpose of his adventure.

"He reported to my uncle's office that same week, a warm April morning. As a junior officer attached to the Army Council staff, his tunic was modified to accommodate the plain red markings separating him from the officers of the line. It was an honor in the eyes of the general public. Tommies, ordinary soldiers, saw the tabs as a near noncombatant and sycophant of less distinction. Do you think this bothered me, Freddy?" she scoffed. "The simple red devices set him apart and allowed him into the best of places on government sites. They would keep him from becoming another honored dead among the nameless thousands. What did I care what the Tommies thought? They might die in countless numbers, but Rolly would make a name for himself in the halls of his Teutonic kin.

"The Chief of the General Staff could be found in the rooms of the Horse Guards headquarters building on Whitehall just down the way from the Cabinet offices where Lord Kitchener served as the war minister. Rolly said he rubbed shoulders with uniformed officers in the crowded corridors that afternoon asking directions to Uncle Hilly's chambers, which turned out to be on the top floor. Everyone he encountered had three things in common. They were in army khaki, carried paper folders marked 'most secret,' and were in a terrible hurry. He always seemed to be going against the grain.

"Little by little he progressed until he found an office door marked Deputy Inspector General, Imperial Army Staff. Safe inside, he found that no one paid any attention to his brand-new pip on the end of his shoulder strap. It was dazzling, he thought, in gold with a dark enameled Maltese cross designating him as an officer commissioned by the Honorable Artillery Company. Officers in all directions, heads down at desks, or deep in discussions in small groups, were oblivious to his entrance. The noise was disorienting. Telephones rang, pretty girls pounded massive clattering typewriters, and in each corner of the large, high-ceilinged room were booths with Morse code operators tapping away or listening on headphones. Messages, on soft yellow paper, were stacked in trays on the corner of every desk. What he concluded to be mass chaos would indeed turn out to be mass chaos.

"A pretty young lady took his arm and pulled him out of the way of the double office doors he was blocking. 'Lost, Lieutenant?' He admitted he was and said, 'I'm on Major General Hopewell's personal staff, the aide-de-camp, don't you know,' hoping it would impress.

"'General Hilly, oh yes, he's a darling old fellow, follow me—quick march.' Back out in the gloomy corridor, Rolly followed as quickly as traffic would allow. The young woman was obviously experienced and wove her way untouched along the wall past three doors and into a rather posh set of rooms the general shared with three other high-ranking gentlemen. The wide-open central area held half a dozen small wooden desks. The small windows rationed the light. The high ceiling was hung with a half dozen globe-covered lights that did little but cast shadows. One of the places was unoccupied, and that turned out to be Rolly's. It was just outside Hilly's connecting glass office door, which lead to his secretary chamber, the walls for which were chockablock with filing cabinets.

"'Here you are, just your size.' It was a bit of a jab—Rolly took it person-ally. 'The general's in a meeting with all the others down below, but he'll be back soon. They're never late for morning tea. I'm Beryl, by the way; if you need anything my number is 173—there on the phone.' She smiled again, and before he could thank her, she whirled around and disappeared into the bustling corridor.

"Rolly began to shift through the trays that littered the top of his desk. Some were loose papers, memos, letters, and the like. The trays were labeled Dispatch, Secret, and Most Secret. Dispatch was for outgoing messages, which turned out to be his responsibility. He shifted his eyes around the room to the other occupants shuffling frantically through messages and forms. No one was paying the least bit of attention to him. He felt reassured.

"He soon found even more reason for confidence: The army had no intel-ligence department of its own. The Esher Report on army structural reforms, issued shortly after Victoria's death, eschewed any intelligence department within the army proper. Spying was considered 'unsuitable' for the regular army. Can you imagine, Freddy? The English can be so very stupid. They left spy matters to the Home Office, which meant that Rolly could conduct his affairs in perfect peace and safety.

"While he waited, Rolly picked up an unmarked folder entitled the Bryce Report, which had been released that morning. The author was the Right Honorable Viscount James Bryce. He was a famous Lord, former ambas-sador to the United States and liberal political. It was a condemnation of the

German army's trek through Belgium, a neutral nation, the very action that had prompted England to enter into the war the year before. Rolly began to read it, the first government document he had ever seen.

"I still remember how upset he was that night. The report had condemned the German army for civilian casualties in its march through Belgium. Bryce chronicled atrocities committed by German soldiers. Of course, Germany had given Belgium every opportunity to allow them safe passage through unmolested! To my mind it was a simple choice; if they had just allowed them to pass, none of the incidents would have taken place. You can't expect soldiers in a peaceful column to ignore snipers as they pick off their officers, now can you? Were they expected to stand at ease as peasants attacked their formations and sabotaged their camps? Ridiculous. I saw it for what it was, a whitewash. The British government was champing at the bit for a chance to take down Germany."

Freddy struggled to maintain his calm. He wanted to know all he could of what had happened with his family during the wars, but he was seeing a side of his grandmother he never had before. Freddy knew, as did practically everyone, how vicious the Germans had been in Belgium, burning farms, firing on hospitals, killing civilians. The Belgium town of Battice had been burnt to the ground and all its citizens shot for allegedly sniping at the German soldiers as they entered the town limits. German General Moltke had been clear: "All who get in our way must be destroyed." The nausea that had been building in Freddy worsened, but he was determined to hear the story through. "Scotch," he thought, "and quick." He moved toward the decanter as his grandmother continued.

"I told Rolly all this and reminded him that such things were merely propaganda written to enflame hatred of the Germans. The British people didn't hate the German people; why would they? After all, our history is entwined with the Teutonic culture. The Saxon civilization is everywhere in these isles. Their kings became our kings; their language is woven into our daily speech. Even the Kaiser's mother is the first daughter of our great Queen. Thousands of Germans live and are intermarried within our communities. It seems every other shop front bears a Germanic name. Our people had to be *made* to hate them, or the British Army wouldn't be able to recruit. It was just so much twaddle.

"Rolly returned to Horse Guards the next day in a better state of mind. He met with Uncle Hilly in his posh inner office for his orientation. Ornamented bookcases and framed hanging maps lined the chamber. Rolly, as he often did, acted out the encounter with funny voices and gestures. Hilly, seated behind an oval mahogany desk—reported to have been one of Wellington's—was his usual self: 'Now then, my boy, your job is quite simple: take orders from no one but me and look after my interests. I take a great deal of looking after, as Mildred can attest to.' His secretary Mildred Box stood behind him and offered one of her infrequent smiles. Mildred was of indeterminate age. Rolly said she looked middle-aged, but she could simply have been worn down from being at Hilly's beck and call all those years, prematurely grey with a yellow pencil forever stuck in an elastic armband to record Hilly's every request. He could see that the two had a bond that, though platonic, was nevertheless intimate. He knew he had to somehow endear himself to them both if he was to succeed in his mission. Uncle Hilly was a pushover; family ties were important in his world, and Rolly could depend on them for protection. Mildred was not going to be so easy. She was a wary old cat who had meet many a sycophant who attempted friendship with the general while satisfying his own agenda over that of the boss. Rolly thought that little demonstrations of loyalty would be most important to start. He knew she would be watching. He must remain in the background, eager to serve. A clever boy, my Rolly.

"After that brief introduction, Hilly stood, said, 'I'm off,' and looked at his hat on the top of the coat rack and then at Mildred. Smiling with grim satisfaction, Mildred turned to Rolly. 'Your first task, Lieutenant,' she said. 'You are in charge of the general's hat.'"

## Chapter Six

# Putney, Lakenheath, and Horse Guards, February–March 1915

"I GOT MY WISH FOR a safer channel. The monsignor—that is, my old friend Pieter—sent a note on his gold-edged Vatican stationery with the pope's miter at the top, by bike messenger boy: *Madam, May my friends Mr. & Mrs. Booker and I call upon you and your son on the afternoon of the second of February. We are engaged in Belgium Relief and hope that you are also in favor of this humanitarian pursuit.*

"My reply, which I returned by the same messenger, offered afternoon tea at four o'clock in the afternoon. Belgium Relief was the charity of the day as refugees flooded into London by the trainloads. Of course I wasn't interested in sponsoring any filthy French-speaking peasants in my home, but it was a good cover for meeting with our collaborators. I instructed the cook to prepare a special tea with all the imagination and specialties she could muster. Late on the day of February second, hearing the party shuffle through the hall set my heart aflutter. Rolly, in uniform, stood behind me in this very chair. I thought to myself, 'What if the British authorities burst through the doors at that moment to arrest us—how thrilling!'

"Mrs. Alberry led the party into the library and introduced each member of the party while waiting for further instructions in the open door. When none came, she left, closing the twin oak doors behind her. Not the inquisitive type.

"The time had come, and I was so proud of Rolly: 'Monsignor, may I introduce Lieutenant Roland Augustus Grayling Stetchworth, my son with Christian von Thurn und Taxis Unterhart.' Rolly saluted in the most military fashion to Peter's slight bow. 'He is much like his father, isn't he, Charlotte?' I smiled my broadest smile: 'Isn't he, though?'

"'My dear Charlotte, may I present Mr. and Mrs. Booker, friends of mine involved in Belgium Relief.' He looked at me for a sign that the coast was clear to speak openly about the true purpose of the visit.

"I put him at ease. 'The staff will respond to the bell if they are needed. Have no fear that we will be disturbed. Be seated, everyone. Monsignor, speak freely. I assume this meeting is a result of a communiqué from Christian?'

"Pieter led the conversation. 'Yes, Madam Stetchworth, it is indeed.' He turned to Rolly. 'Lieutenant, you should know that your father is very happy that you have committed to aiding your fatherland. He is very proud of you. And he's thought carefully about how best to use your talents. Although passing messages to me through the Vatican has been useful in these initial consultations, Christian believes a close liaison with the Vatican would attract suspicion over time. The Home Office is watching the Church carefully, and they pride themselves on grubbing out spies. We must not assist them in their vital work,' he said ironically. 'Christian believes that a close-knit independent team known only to him within the intelligence service of the Kaiser will be sustainable. While the Bookers are British citizens in good standing, they are communications experts trained in Germany with the latest equipment. You may already know of them? They own a shop on Putney High Street. Yes—do you recall?'

"I looked at the couple seated across from me. 'Really, Pieter, I rarely go to Putney. If I go anywhere, it is into central London to Swan & Edgar's and lunch at Simpsons. But Rolly, you've spent many a shilling on the High Street, or at least the High Street pubs.' Rolly looked at them and then at the ornate ceiling. He sifted through the names of the pubs he liked—but drew a blank. Rolly inquired, 'Booker's . . . what do you trade in, Mr. Booker, may I inquire?' unable to recall the name from the storefronts. The High Street was only three blocks long and ended at the train station on the crest of a hill.

"Holding his gloomy wife's hand, he replied in a public-school voice. 'I am the proprietor of Booker's World of Stamps,' he said proudly, indicating that the firm was of some importance within its own domain. 'My wife Reeny and I are purveyors, surveyors, valuers, and philatelic auctioneers at number 11 The High Street, across from the bank. We have been there these ten years now, isn't it, Mother?' His use of 'Mother' was a sure indicator that the couple had a young child at home.

"'The bank, yes'—Rolly's favorite stop before the pub. 'But I don't recall your stamp shop. Well, a good lesson for an aspiring spy—I had better become more observant in the future.'

"I sat summing them up, allowing them to talk. After all, an Englishman betrays his station the moment he opens his mouth. I must say, they looked unpromising. His accent was provincial, schooled but not proper. His suit, brown pinstripe, was off some ghastly rack. He was thin and tall, rather Nordic but not German. I wouldn't be surprised if his surname once ended in 'wait'—Bookerwait, I should think. There was a hint of the salesman about his personality, which was a good thing for our purposes, I suppose. The wife's frumpy dress was hardly appropriate for tea at our fine table, and she appeared to be not as young as her husband, if the lines in her forehead and wrinkled neck were any indication. I wondered why a couple was enlisted for such a dangerous and sophisticated task. Surely a single man in a basement somewhere would be more appropriate. But the pair would not impress or stand out in a crowd, and perhaps that was their appeal. 'Have you always lived in England, Mr. Booker?'

"'Oh, yes. Born and bred in the fens. I attended cathedral school in Ely, a chorister. I did spend time abroad doing the tour of cathedral choirs, as does many a youth involved in music, I am sure you know. I settled down in Norwich, where I met my wife.' Mrs. Booker remained silent at her husband's recitation. The story had all the hallmarks of a cover story. The more he talked about his shop, life, their home across the river and their son Horatio, the more I realized I was not alone. There were others who had seen through England's hypocrisy and recognized the superiority of the German nation, even this unpromising pair. I began to warm to them. When I turned to the monsignor, he leaned over and whispered, 'Good, aren't they? They fooled me.'

"Rolly could not ascertain how a stamp dealer could mail his reports without being suspected and carefully watched. 'Are you expecting to send my messages by the Royal Mail, or do you have some other way of getting them to the Continent?'

"'I pride myself as a highly skilled Marconi technician. We occupy a house just across the river, number six, Deodar Road, down the block from Mrs. Booker's former home. You may have noticed our place, tucked up against the terminus of the railroad bridge? We're next to the maintenance catwalk attached to the east side of the bridge. You can see it from your window here.' He gestured to the tall library window.

"Rolly and I crossed the room to the window and noted the two-story red brick house with the high gable that indeed appeared to lean against the bridge abutment. I had seen Rolly many a time skirt along the rickety walkway when in a hurry to get to the pub. A hundred yards beyond the railway bridge, further upriver, was the conventional broad traffic bridge to the High Street and beyond to Wimbledon and Richmond. The railway bridge was rarely used by the general public since it was covered in soot from the trains that thundered past a mere yard away. Signs at both ends notified trespassers to stay off the pathway for their own safety, indicating that trespassers would be fined.

"The stamp dealer continued his explanation: 'I've concealed a transceiver at the top of the attic in a recess just under the ridge. I've been operating for the last week to see if we arouse any suspicion or stirred up the radio detecto van that passes through the area on a regular basis. The location of the house is critical to our operation. The electronic surveillance direction-finding efforts are stymied by our location,' he said with obvious pride. 'First of all,' he lowered his voice before giving away his cunning plan, 'the volume of moving tidal water is a reflective base which interferes with identifying our base station.' Touching his nose with his finger, 'Very tricky for the finders. And . . . I have no roof antenna,' he said triumphantly."

"Grandmother," Freddy objected, "they must have had an aerial antenna if they expected to reach Germany, that is a certainty."

"I will get to that, *liebchen*. The truth is, they were clever, despite their crude manners," she noted with an air of excitement. "If there was to be a message for Rolly that night, Mrs. Booker would leave her curtains open in the afternoon for me to make a note of; if Rolly had a message to leave, I would do the same. On message days, Rolly would walk the bridge to where the steps meet the abutment on the Putney side. There was a loose brick adjacent to the bolt that holds the top rail to the bridge masonry. He would remove it and place the message in the space behind it. Booker would put messages to Rolly on his way home from the pub near the Tube station. The code name would keep us from accidentally dropping his name in front of the staff. With this arrangement, any dispatch would be exposed for a half hour at the most.

"Freddy, it was so much fun. The code they used was unbreakable—a one-time pad for each message. The only two holders were Mrs. Booker and Christian himself. It was quite complicated and took considerable time and patience to encode it faultlessly. Apparently Mrs. Booker was more intelligent than her worn day dress would lead one to believe. Rolly knew the protocol: Each evening he would stop in the center of the bridge and smoke a cigarette before completing the span and dropping off or picking up a message. If he sensed danger or compromise, he was to toss the message into the water as you would a spent cigarette. Since the message would be in ink, the water would erase it. The catwalk provided a good deal of security. Few people ever used it, especially in the dark. It can be dangerous on a wet and slippery evening. It was the perfect rendezvous.

"But, Freddy, you will never guess what the crowning achievement of the Bookers' modest talent for spycraft was. It had nothing to do with bricks or code names: it was for Rolly to get a dog."

Freddy laughed. "A dog, good heavens why?"

"Because a dog, my dear *liebchen*, requires walking in the late evening. The darkness hides movement and the dog provides a reason for being out and about at that time of night. Whoever thought that our first action as spies would be a trip to the dog breeder? Pieter had recommended a terrier; the cook had one at the chancel, a real ratter, just the thing for the scullery. And a terrier would have no trouble negotiating that narrow walkway and would alert if anyone were to follow them.

"So the next weekend we boarded the train from St. Pancras rail terminal and rode northeast two hours to visit the Karendore Kennel at Lakenheath to buy a West Highland White terrier. We got off several stops beyond Cambridge. Shippia Hill station was a mere concrete platform positioned next to an unattended crossing gate where a single taxi waited. Lovely country—watery fens and low crops like lavender, beets, and rye hugged the ground, all neatly arranged between dark green hedgerows like a homemade quilt. We took an open car to the kennel—a model T, you know, Freddy, in those days.

"And it's a good thing we did. When the driver heard we were going to Lakenheath, he said he had gotten one free from the kennel himself. 'You'd best be quick, then. With the ration they're havin' to thin the stock, there's talk that all the pets are to be kilt, you know. Told we aren't s'pose' to waste food on dumb critters. Now I ask you, a dog's no dumber than those blokes in London writin' silly rules while sittin' on their backside. We're still feedin' them, ar't we?' We had heard about the decree, of course. More proof if we needed it that it was the English and not the Germans who were the barbarians. In the end we took both a puppy named Teddy and his mother Valerie. The breeder could see we were taken with Valerie—we needed a mature animal immediately. But he convinced us to take the puppy too. 'I know, Valerie is a lot of name for little terrier, but she's a grand one. She's awful fond of that puppy, hard to separate them, and, you know, he may not survive on his own, if you take my meaning.' Clearly a bit of blackmail there. The farmer convinced Rolly that the mother would train Teddy. Rolly loved those dogs, played with them like a little boy and even slept with them, for heaven's sake.

"Just a few weeks after starting work Rolly had barely gotten his coat off when Mildred handed him a file. 'Here. Read this and be prepared to back up the general in his mid-morning meeting with the Air Defense Board.' Rolly sat down at his desk with his heart pounding. On the front of the file was the word he had been excited to finally see but half-dreading as well: SECRET."

It was then that Freddy discovered the difference between a professionally trained spy and his grandmother. She went over to the long bookcase that lined the inner wall of the library. With her back to him and a little sleight of hand, she caused a panel to slide open between carved pillars. The opening was unlit, closet size, and shelved from top to bottom. Freddy, who had been facing the books, moved cautiously forward and looked over her shoulder. "You must become aware of this space, *liebchen*; it holds my secrets. Did you ever imagine there was a hidey-hole here, even as a child?"

Freddy raised his eyebrows and shook his head. He peered past Charlotte's shoulder to see reams of papers in folders slipped methodically into wooden recesses. Shelves were marked with dates, beginning at the topmost with January 1914. "Fetch me those library steps, would you, Freddy? The file is right up at the top." The polished dark wood ladder was on wheels connected to the top of the bookcase on a rail. Freddy slid it in place. "Take down February 1915 up at the far left. I'm not a mountain goat, you know." Freddy reached as she continued. "This is not the only secret in this old house. My mother never trusted banks, and her planning has served me well. Now, there it is. Sit down and read it, Freddy." He pulled the yellow pages from the folder. It seemed to be the original report. Had his father taken it as a trophy?

SECRET
Record of zeppelin engagements since the beginning of the German air campaign begun in January 1915:

*German Zeppelins as a war machine*
*Beginnings, Employment and Countermeasures*
*Militarized Airship 450 or 650 feet in length*

Commander Peter Strasser, German Imperial Navy, is responsible for the bombing campaign over England. Strasser has declared that it is total war and no one is exempt from the target lists. All citizens are combatants. This change in the rules of civilized status in warfare can be expected to persist when under attack from the Empire of Germany.

Launched from occupied Netherlands and Belgium, the airship, traveling at 85 mph, in calm air, gives us about two hours before it reaches the east coast on route to London.

Both the imperial German navy and army have in excess of fifty serviceable Zeppelins presently available in service in our area.

A Zeppelin is capable of dispensing 28 high explosive bombs and 91 firebombs. The incendiaries are a combination of Thermite & Benzod wrapped with tar-impregnated rope which will continue to burn for five minutes after ignition.

Capable of flying at 21,000 feet, the crews experienced illness from the lack of oxygen and cold, forcing them to operate at ten thousand feet. The ships are vulnerable to several effects.

Weather limits flight. In particular, high or cross winds in excess of fifty mph prevent safe handling. Additionally, precipitation in any form make the skin of the ship too heavy to maintain altitude.

Poor visibility over the target can be overcome with the employment of a cloud car. An unpowered aerodynamic pod is lowered one thousand feet below the airship and accommodates an observer with a telephone line to the mother ship. There below the clouds he can spot targets and assess damage.

The numerous airtight bags, made of collagen from cow's intestines, are filled with hydrogen, a volatile gas. The beef skin bags require 250,000 cow intestines to make one airship. The sausage industry in Germany has suffered as a result. Although the bags leak, it does not affect the viability of the airship.

### Counter Measures

Anti-Aircraft guns. French 75 mm artillery pieces are mounted vertically on motor vehicles but are unable to reach the altitude of the airships. However, it is a morale booster to civilians to have them deployed.

Fighter aircraft take thirty minutes to reach the altitude to attack by which time the airship has departed.

Special bullets (the Buckingham incendiary bullets) will not make a hole large enough to affect the flight characteristic of the airship and will not set it on fire. They merely pass through. The machine gun must be fired from the rear seat of the aircraft, which makes it difficult to land the aircraft.

An early warning service is being tested on the eastern coast at the point where airships enter our waters. Acquisitive acoustic reflectors are being tested to ascertain the direction of the flight path of an approaching attack and the information telegraphed to launch the fighters earlier.

At this stage there is no effective counter measure.

"That was an exciting day, Freddy. On just his first month on the job, your father diverted a copy of this report and concealed it in his dispatch case. No one questioned the bag's content when he left the office. Aides often carried sensitive documents. He told me that just in case he was stopped, he left by a service entrance on the loading dock. You see, he was a natural," she said with pride.

"That night we worked together to convert the material into precise form for transmission, taking out what was irrelevant and inserting explanatory phrases when needed. Instead of smaller, the document got larger, but we were very pleased with ourselves. I raced against time to render the document in block print, and Rolly scurried to dress for the dog walk. He dressed in dark civilian clothes and donned a trilby he pulled down over his brow. He had been watching other dog walkers, you know, and saw how they dressed to be braced against the weather. He must look natural, one of those trekkers who fought the elements, like it or not.

"Little did we know that harnessing the dog would be the hardest part of our evening! Valerie, initially sleeping in a basket with her puppy near the fire, was resolute. She saw no need to be tramping about on a lead at that time of night when a quick outside on the terrace would treat her fine. She led Rolly on a merry romp around the furniture with Teddy in close pursuit. He cajoled and chased, but when the grandfather clock in the hall struck the three-quarters hour with a deep bong, bong, bong, Rolly knew he could wait no longer. He called for servants to corral the unruly pair. The dogs loved it and sped through the rooms, which were closed off one by one until they were confined in the library. Finally they were grabbed up, harnessed, and all three dashed out the front door. Taking rapid giant steps, Rolly headed for the catwalk and the dead drop on the opposite end of the long railway bridge. The dogs assisted, pulling him up the steps.

"I tried to keep my eyes on him from the front window. He was out of breath by the time he climbed the thirty feet to the catwalk, and it was at least two hundred yards to the far end. Just then an electrified train thundered up behind him, blowing his expensive hat into the river. There was nothing for it; he quickened his pace to a trot. All the time he was thinking up alibis, reasons to justify his rapid pace. He could be a businessman coming home late and trying to placate the wife by hurrying through the dog walk. There wasn't time to stop for a cigarette, but he did look over his shoulder and noticed a figure behind him, still a considerable distance behind. He reached the end of the handrail at the wall, breathless. He fumbled for the brick with gloved hands. Sliding it out halfway, he thrust the folded papers in and squeezed the brick back in place.

"Relieved his first mission was complete, he ambled down the wet pavement. He was much wetter than Valerie and Teddy, who kept dry under their double coarse coats. They paid no attention to the man holding the leads as their noses explored every anomaly in the bushes that lined the front of the town houses. To Rolly it felt like an eternity to make it to the park and complete one go-round. To the dogs it was a never-ending delight. As he mounted the bridge, the half-hour had passed and he paused at the abutment at the top of the stairs once again. He knew he should pass by without taking a look, but he could not resist. He checked the bottom of the stone steps and listened for footsteps. There were none. He could see a light on in the attic of the Bookers and thought they must be hard at it. To be sure, he slid out the brick and found the space empty. Pushing it back in place, he could now say with confidence that we were spies."

"A SHORT TIME LATER, FREDDY, your father picked up a message at the drop-off that was addressed to me. The little hausfrau, Mrs. Booker, had requested a meeting. The operation had been going swimmingly, and I was puzzled by this breach of protocol. Nonetheless, I sent back an invitation, and a few days later Mrs. Booker was on my divan with the other ladies from the aid society, wrapping bandages from bolts of white cotton.

"It was no great difficulty to spirit Mrs. Flopbottom—her code name— away to the library for an hour, and there she revealed her purpose: Apparently our messages were proving overly difficult to encrypt. I was doubtful that she could tell me much about language, but I nonetheless bent my ear to her instructions, resolved to do what I needed in order for our little team to succeed. Flopbottom pulled out a page torn from the one-time pad encryption book and began to explain her method."

Freddy couldn't hold it in any longer; his chuckle turned into a laugh and then a guffaw. "Mrs. Flopbottom . . . really, Grandmamma, so descriptive."

Charlotte smiled at her own wit and continued. "Each letter of the alphabet had a string of random letters after it. The first bogus letter was substituted and crossed out on the pad so it would not be used again for the actual letter when it occurred again in a sentence. She explained that the message would be made up of groups of five letters each so the length of words would not tip off their meaning. The way the British could unravel the code was by repetition and substitution. If the same bogus letter is used again for 'A,' then a pattern is established and a good guess can break some of the message. Sometimes a single letter can represent an entire phrase. In addition to the alphabet for spelling out a word, there is a listing of common phrases that can represent entire ideas. They might be titles, locations, or phrases such as 'go to,' 'my location is,' 'headquarters' and so forth. It will also speed up decryption. The longer the message, the easier it is for the codebreakers. Once the message is encrypted, the page is destroyed. Each page in the one-time pad book is different."

"I learned a bit about one-time pads in the army, Grandmother. They're still used, you know. There is no safer means of encryption."

"Yes, Freddy, they're nearly unbreakable when used correctly. Flopbottom informed me that my job thereafter was to review the final communiqué and take out all unneeded words and phrases. Pare it down to the shortest number of words while ensuring the meaning was clear. We had been using proper English, of course, but transmission time, the time it takes to tap out a message, had to be as short as possible, giving the British detecto vans roaming the streets little chance of homing in on their attic. Each message was broadcast several times during the twenty-four-hour period until an acknowledgment code letter was received from the distant end to indicate that it had been received and decoded. Your father and I worked hard to streamline our missives and succeeded brilliantly, I must say. Rolly pilfered documents from Horse Guards, we quickly reduced the facts to their essentials, and we tossed our copies into the fireplace. As you know, I also kept a working copy in the cupboard within the library, just in case something went wrong and we had to reconstruct the text. I never told anyone, not even Rolly, about my cache."

Freddy look into the blackened grate and wondered how many young British lives could be counted against the ashes left behind in the flue. He shuddered at the thought of his grandmother and father on their knees raking through the hot ashes to ensure that all was consumed. How proud they must have been, how misguided.

Charlotte continued. "A few evenings later I watched the attic window across the river and excitedly grabbed Rolly as he came in. 'It's here, there's a message for us. You must corral Valerie earlier and get up on the bridge after the stamp man passes by.' I was excited to receive our first message directly from Christian, and Rolly's trek became the template for all his pick-ups.

"Teddy made a fuss when he discovered his mother in harness at the front door where Rolly was to join in that lonesome throng of nocturnal dog walkers. A little too early, eager to get feedback from his first gambit as a spy, he actually passed Booker on the wet brick stairs to the catwalk. Neither acknowledged the other, while the irrepressible Valerie gave out a low growl before being jerked to one side. As usual, Rolly smoked his cigarette, which was hard to light in the evening drizzle that was becoming more intense. 'I must get myself a windproof lighter at Dunhill's; these matches aren't the ticket,' he told me later. He proceeded calmly to the end of the catwalk and fumbled for the loose brick. Just as he did, a train burst past, which sent Valerie into a terrier tirade of spinning, barking, and snarling. Startled, Rolly dropped the brick on his foot, and the message attached floated down to the damp walkway. 'Damn and blast' was held tightly between his teeth. Valerie put a wet paw on the envelope and sniffed it. 'Good girl, hold it there.' Rolly picked it up before another train whizzed by, but he was shaken at how close it had come to floating out of his grasp.

"Dog and master proceeded to clamber down the steps to Deodar Road. Turning left, Valerie tugged her way down the dampened sidewalk, pausing at the red postal pillar-box while Rolly tried to secure the message in his inside pocket. She could smell the green grass of Wandsworth Park from a block away. They quickly paced once around the grounds, though she never found a smell she didn't like, and then back to the bridge. Fortunately, the blackout and gloom didn't faze the terrier as she led him home without a paw going wrong. The humidity rising off the tidal river combined with a cold front from the east reminded Rolly how spring stuck to his bones. It took nearly an hour to complete the circuit, and upon their return your father wanted to flop down with Valerie in her basket."

"The message from Christian, I must say, was less than pleasing. It was short and pointed directly at us both. Rather than a compliment, it began with a rebuke. 'ZEP STRIKES COMMON KNOWLEDGE. REPORT ON INTERNAL MILITARY MATTERS ONLY. TROOP STRENGTH, WAR MATERIALS, MOVEMENTS, RESTRICTED CONTENT, CONFLICTS OVER INTERNAL & ALLIED STRATEGY.' With Christian's dispatch Mrs. Flopbottom had felt free to add her two cents: 'That is how one writes a message, high on information and low on rhetoric.' The little hausfrau was quite full of herself," Charlotte snorted. "She obviously thought we were amateurs whose indiscretion would endanger her, her son Horatio, and Harold in that order. Naming their son for an English hero must have been Harold's idea."

"THAT SPRING WAS EXHILARATING, FREDDY. Rolly flourished in his dual roles, attending to Hilly in the hub of Horse Guards, smack in the middle of all the excitement, and honing his spycraft in the evenings at Putney. Every evening without fail he walked Valerie and Teddy along the catwalk of the bridge—after 9:30 in the evening but before ten o'clock."

"But Grandmother, you still haven't explained how the Bookers got along without an aerial antenna. It's simply impossible."

"Ah, that was their cleverest bit of all. Your father had spent a week training on radio equipment and had the same question you did. At Rolly's skepticism Booker puffed himself up.

"'Oh, I have an antenna, an excellent antenna—one supplied free of charge.' Booker loaded his words, preparing to amaze the young upstart. 'I have a probe on a pole that I can use to clamp onto it. In the evening, after dark, it can't be seen. Cut to the proper length for the frequency, you understand. I have run a heavy-gauge wire under it which is nearly invisible and even if found leads to nowhere, until I make the connection to the transmitter. Like all omni-antennas, it radiates equally poor in all directions and drives the detecto folks bonkers. But the sky wave skips perfectly into your father's headquarters.'

"Rolly and I looked at him with blank stares. What on earth was he talking about? But then he looked at me with great satisfaction. 'The cast iron railroad bridge is my antenna, madam. And they will never know it.'"

## Chapter Seven

# Putney Bridge, April–May 1915

FREDDY FELT HIS JAW DROP but didn't seem to have the wherewithal to close it again.

"You can't fault their ingenuity, I suppose." He couldn't help letting a tiny bit of admiration slip through his defenses for the small group of collaborators his grandmother had worked with. "The railroad bridge—the biggest, most powerful, and most deceptive antenna a group of traitors could have hoped for. That's brilliant."

"And it worked beautifully, Freddy. All that spring, Rolly continued to pick up important news from Horse Guards. He generally accompanied Uncle Hilly to meetings with members of the War Cabinet, and this provided an enormous amount of intelligence. One of his most important pieces of news was that the First Sea Lord, Winston Churchill, and Lord Kitchener had put forth a proposal to divert the attention of the Germans away from the stalemate in France, which was eating troops and supplies at an alarming rate. Neither England nor France could sustain the exertion in men and material that trench warfare in France was costing them. The Germans were unexpectedly winning in Russia ever since the huge victory of the Battle of Tannenberg in late August 1914. The victors of that great battle, Generals von Hindenburg and Ludendorff, were in the process of taking over the reins of both battlefronts. Churchill's navy was out of touch in this land war while taking terrible losses in the Atlantic submarine conflict. A great deal of money had been spent on dreadnought construction prior to the war and the newspapers were wondering why.

"Kitchener and Churchill were looking for some strategy to break the stalemate. They contemplated making a beachhead at Antwerp to draw the Germans' attention to their rear. But this was discarded in favor of a bold plan to kill two birds with one stone: They would delve into the Middle East, where the Ottoman Empire was twinned with Germany. This would accomplish two highly desirable goals: to break the stranglehold the Turks had on the eastern edge of the Mediterranean and divert German attention away from the Western Front. Germany had been entrenched in Turkey—that 'sick old man of Europe'—ever since the Kaiser visited the great mosque and declared himself to be a Muslim as well as a Christian." Charlotte smiled at Freddy's look of amazement. "Are you surprised at my grasp of affairs, Freddy? It was not for nothing that I spent all those months with my student friends in Austria. Rolly was present that day when the proposal was made for a spring offensive in the Dardanelles. My brilliant son had insinuated himself into the top echelons of the military.

"Nearly as important were his communiqués regarding Lord Kitchener. The field marshal had called a meeting at Whitehall's Cabinet Office, inviting Hilly along with major members of the staff. Kitchener was known to keep politicians at arm's length, but he trusted military confidants who had served alongside him in past campaigns. Rolly was anxious to see the legendary Secretary of State for War. Like the rest of Englishmen, he knew Kitchener from the stern image on the recruiting posters that were plastered all over the empire. In August 1914, the day war was declared, Kitchener relinquished command of forces in Egypt to join the government. The ministers assembled that day agreed that the war would be over by Christmas. Nearly all the military and political leadership in London believed that the French army, augmented by a small British volunteer force, could win the conflict quickly. Kitchener had shocked the chamber with his opening words: 'The war will last three years.' Kitchener told them that they would have to raise a grand army in which resources would have to be switched from the navy to the army. Colonial troops would play a major role. It would be the navy's mission to safeguard the soldiers' transport, equipment, munitions, raw material, and rations sent to and from England.

"Naturally the Admiralty objected. The Royal Navy had bottled up the Kaiser's imperial fleet in the Baltic and turned the North Sea into an English lake. The Royal Navy didn't take the threat of untried German submarines on the high seas as serious warfare. Kitchener could speak freely because he had spent years overseas and had no hard political connections or obligations. The secretary's assessment panicked the other cabinet ministers since no allied nation could afford a long war, especially Great Britain.

"In a short time Kitchener proceeded to raise, train, and equip a land army from scratch. He marshaled industry to convert to wartime production. Women were called upon to leave the home and domestic service to take men's positions in the labor market, allowing them to enlist. In the field, Field Marshal Sir John French insisted on deployment of the British

Expeditionary Force deep into western Belgium, per the pre-war agreement with the French command. Kitchener advised that they should take up a position at Amiens deep in France, near Paris and at the center of communications links. Kitchener insisted that if sent to Belgium, they would be run down with significant loss of men and equipment since the Belgium army would not hold. Unfortunately, he was proven correct. As the spring of 1915 warmed over a particularly cool winter, Kitchener displayed vision not shared by anyone in the Cabinet or armed forces, with the exception of Winston Churchill.

"On the day of the meeting, Rolly was seated on a hard-wooden chair against the chamber wall along with the other low-ranking aides, eager to see the great warrior in the flesh. He hoped the image on the recruiting poster would not disappoint. The elegant conference room was filled with noisy mumbles from uniformed figures conversing, chuckling, and shifting in their seats around the edges of the long, shiny, dark wood table. Anticipation filled the room. What secret solution would he trust them with? The Secretary of the General Staff had cleaned away any debris. No notes were to be taken. Kitchener insisted that the conversations were informal, 'not on the record.' He was gun shy since some inflammatory utterances had found their way into the tabloid press, who were not always complimentary. Always in a hurry, he entered, seated himself at the head of the table, and began to speak extemporaneously. Rolly was close enough to notice that the great general was cross-eyed. It made the lieutenant giggle into his hand. 'Not on the poster,' he thought. He quipped to the officer next to him, 'The real Kitchener poster would have cost us the war.' Henry Segar, Kitchener's personal servant and confidant, seated to Rolly's right, overheard and smiled. 'Yes, Lieutenant, we know,' he whispered.

"Uncle Hilly had indicated that the tenor of the meeting might be over Kitchener's inauguration of the 'Pals Battalions.' In an effort to bring fit young men to willingly enlist, they were encouraged to join as a social group. As you know, Freddy, English boys are devoted to their mates to see them through trial and tribulations of the teen years. The apprehension of leaving home and joining the army was somewhat diminished if done with buddies, especially during the early transition from civilian to soldier. So it was that hundreds of thousands appeared fresh from the rugby, football, cricket, and social clubs arm in arm. Small villages enlisted their sons as one, and schoolmates all together joined territorial companies. It eased the task of raising a fighting force in a hurry since there was no conscription.

"Unfortunately, as the war quickly progressed past Christmas, the reality of Kitchener's war took hold. Because of the introduction of multiple rapid, accurate weapons employed over flat ground, whole platoons could be decimated in minutes, stripping entire neighborhoods of all their young men. By the end of April Kitchener's reputation had turned sour in the mouths of his countrymen. He had also alienated the Welsh. He fought the creation of the Welsh Guards Regiment for the Household Brigade as a battlefield formation, saying, 'In an all-Welsh formation all commands would be given in Welsh, most unsuitable,' and he called the Welsh 'wild and insubordinate.' However, he didn't object to colonial troops using native language. A newspaper reporter suggested that on some previous campaign he 'had been bitten by a Welshman.' The minister was also fond of expanding on previous faux pas that hit the news like a bombshell: 'Men enlisted because of unemployment, crossed in love, financial trouble or patriotism and adventure, the romance of war, escape the boredom of work, please others, go with friends, and the immortality of youth.' He was probably correct, but deep offense was taken.

"It was in this state of unpopularity that the field marshal called the meeting at Whitehall. Kitchener wasted no words. He reported that during a recent push plans were left unfulfilled due to a lack of available artillery rounds for the supporting fires. Kitchener had not anticipated the unrelenting firing of the heavy guns that would be needed in order to keep the Germans in place— the amount of artillery needed overreached the capabilities of Kitchener's factories and transportation links. He believed that the infantry's ability to take and hold ground was lost in the bedlam of incessant artillery barrages fired 'to keep their heads down,' as he put it. Rather than blaming himself for unpreparedness, he simply assumed that the Royal Artillery had gone berserk with these new high-speed reloading guns. Later your father remarked on Kitchener's complaints: 'It's like a shooting gallery out there, the guns fire night and day and at what, I ask you. Shooting willy-nilly at everything and nothing. This level of action can't be sustained.'

"Rolly was bubbling with excitement at the import of this intelligence. He was restricted from taking notes, but Rolly did his best to mentally record the event. At last he had something no one else would report to Berlin and saw that his father had been correct when he told Rolly to stay in England. A well-placed mole deep in the establishment could do so much more for the Kaiser than an individual soldier in the front lines!

"As the conference wrapped up, he was approached by Henry Segar again, this time at a back corner table where caps were being retrieved. Rolly was half expecting a reproof for his comment about Kitchener's crossed eyes and was prepared to plead that his remark was spontaneous and not meant to offend. Segar leaned in close so as not to be overheard: 'Those eyes. When you get closer, you think he is looking right through you. Most distracting, one never gets used to it, I'm afraid. Be prepared to look away if you feel a giggle coming on; I do.' It was a mischievous warning, but Rolly was pleased, feeling accepted into the ranks of the aides, assistants, and secretaries who gossiped among themselves in order to keep their sanity. Rolly could expect to be present with Uncle Hilly on numerous occasions with Lord Kitchener, who kept his comrade from the South African campaign close at hand when trouble arose. It also meant that Segar and Rolly would be working together, which suited them both, though for different reasons.

"When the conference concluded, generals besieged Kitchener, all wanting to embrace his position and cement their loyalty in that political game they called government. The press was not so naïve as to accept his excuses. Your father recalled a piece he had read in Lord Beaverbrook's newspaper that morning: 'Since strength for the purposes of war was the total strength of each belligerent nation, public opinion was as significant as fleets and armies.' The shortage of artillery shells was not going to be blamed on a change of tactics but on one person: Kitchener. It could bring him down. And thanks to your father, Freddy," Charlotte noted with pride, "Christian would be the first to know."

"ROLLY SKATED AWAY FROM HORSE GUARDS that evening, his head spinning with the events of the day. They all had to be sorted out and cherry picked. He hurried down Whitehall past Number Ten, turned left at Parliament Square, and up half a block to the street level entrance to the underground station on the District Line for a thirty-minute ride home to Fulham. It seemed to him that every government employee was packed along with him into the small, low-ceilinged ticket hall.

"That wasn't a pleasant ride in those days, Freddy. The District Line took the commuters to the outlying suburbs, where people enjoyed single and duplex homes double the size of the old row houses. Even though the trains had recently been electrified, little had changed in the harsh environment. Unlike the Tube, a cut and cover tunnel arrangement shared its track with some steam trains that vented the smoke and soot out through massive grates open to the sky. Yet the smell of the coal residue penetrated the stations and carriages. It was a familiar heavy scent which added more particulate to the coal fireplaces that heated every dwelling. While it blanketed London in the winter, it lingered on into the end of April. There was a residue of greasy black dust on the train seats. Rolly, like most, tore off the last page from his newspaper and placed it on the seat before sitting, trying mightily to keep his wool uniform trousers clean. A train change at Earl's Court was an added irritant that could delay him as much as twenty minutes.

"That day, your father reviewed in his mind Kitchener's diatribe on the shortage of artillery rounds and the tactics of the British Army. He had refrained from writing anything down for fear of detection. No notes meant no notes, and he wasn't going to be called out in such a distinguished assemblage or bring any attention to himself. That afternoon he was kept busy by Mildred back at his desk and following Uncle Hilly around the officers' club lounge, eavesdropping on conversations to get the impression left by Kitchener.

"Once off the train, a brisk two-block walk brought him inside the two sets of double front doors, which acted as a weather shield. The terriers, who had taken up their station the minute he passed through the underpass a block away, overwhelmed him with joy. 'I don't know how they do it, sir,' Mrs. Alberry said, shaking her head, 'but they've got you pegged before you come into view. You'll never sneak up on those two watchdogs. There is no dissuading; they know their master is on his way.'" Charlotte chuckled. "That wasn't very reassuring to a young man who was supposed to be a spy. But your father always stopped to play with his pals jumping and swirling around his legs. 'Yes, yes, I love you, love you both—come with me to see Grandmamma.'

"The dogs tangled around his ankles, twisting and jumping as he climbed to the second floor. The pair of square-faced, dingy white companions reached the top way ahead of their master and turned in disgust, peering down from on high as if they had won the race and now had to wait. Though Rolly trotted along up the double-level stairs, he was way behind. 'I'm a-coming, trooper; stand fast,' he called. Rolly had conducted an enlistment ceremony early that week for the dogs. Valerie was promoted to leading man, which she objected to on the grounds of gender, and Teddy was a private soldier. They were the only ones under his direct command, and he practiced his field commands learned at HAC in case he ever needed them.

"I could hear Rolly approaching that evening, and when he opened the door those two hellions sped through to tell me, most excitedly, that their master was home. Those dogs decided that we four were a gang and that the servants were retainers there to wait on us and put down the water and food. Since those dogs had the run of the house and led the way to the park, which was obviously for their benefit alone, they might have in fact perceived that Valerie was our leader assisted by Teddy. They saw Rolly and me as minor domestics or paid companions, I am sure."

Freddy couldn't repress a smile at this. This was the charming grandmother he had always known.

"I was ready at my writing table for Rolly to dictate a message. It wasn't as easy as we thought it would be. After an hour of scribbling and rewriting, we established two points. The first was that the change of tactics caused the shortage of artillery rounds. The second was that Kitchener was likely to be blamed and such high-level political unrest could result in a change of leadership in the government. Once we pared the message to its essentials, I gave the signal that there was a message imminent and Rolly took the dogs on their afternoon walk. The following afternoon I watched the clock for a rebuke over the wording of the dispatch, but none came. We were no longer amateurs, Freddy. We were spies."

"DESPITE THIS GOOD START, IN April and May, events took place that troubled Rolly's state of mind.

"In late April they got word at Horse Guards: FLASH, YPRES 22 APRIL, 1730hrs FRONT LINES OF YPRES SALIENT, DEFENDED BY THE PRINCESS PATRICIA'S LIGHT INFANTRY (CANADIAN) AND FRENCH MARTINIQUE REGIMENTS ATTACKED AT DUSK WITH POISONOUS GAS/MULTITUDE OF CYLINDERS FROM FORWARD GERMAN POSTIONS. GERMAN INFANTRY ATTACKED DRIVING BEF FORCES BACK LESS THAN THREE THOUSAND YARDS BEFORE REGROUPING. CASUALTIES HEAVY. SALIENT HELD.

"This was important news, Freddy. For the first months of the war, the battle line had shifted wildly, had flowed as near to Paris as thirty-five miles. But the line was now pushed north and solidified at twice that distance. Both sides had settled into deep trench defenses and dared the other to attack. Ypres, a wool town in the Flemish province of West Flanders, had become the focal point of the British lines. The Germans obsessed over the salient, the area around Ypres. It was a thorn in the side of the Kaiser's war operations. Deeply dug in, the British line held in spite of repeated disastrous German assaults. Both sides suffered.

"The communiqué at Horse Guards that morning was the first evidence of a new German strategy: the use of poison gas. Germany expected it to induce hysteria and lead to retreat, as well as to cover the withdrawal of a dozen German divisions that were being redeployed to the Russia front. Yet the first attack and many more to come only produced dreadful injuries to lungs and eyes. Lungs filled with fluid; eyes bandaged, they were walked to the rear in long chains, hands on the shoulders of the men in front. Hundreds died from pneumonia-like symptoms.

"Of course the British immediately denounced Germany, saying that the Hague Convention of 1907 prohibited asphyxiating gases. But the restriction addressed only artillery employment, which was not the case in Ypres. England lost no time in experimenting with gas and other counter measures itself. None of it made any difference in the end. Surprisingly the dimensions of the battlefield remain largely unchanged.

"Rolly was well aware of the continuing battles around Ypres from the daily staff briefings he attended every morning. That battlefield was known to the staff and troops as 'Whypres.' The British loved to Anglicize 'froggy' French words.

"Not long after, Rolly's state of mind was tested again. On the eighth of May 1915, the *London Times* shocked the readers with the latest war news: 'Yesterday HMS *Lusitania* was sunk by a German submarine as it entered the Celtic Sea off the Old Head of Kinsale. The count is feared to exceed one thousand passengers. The devastating attack from undersea failed to give the passengers and crew a chance to escape. Eyewitnesses in Ireland saw the ship, heard the explosions and launched boats in the direction of the tragedy.' Propaganda posters emerged showing a young woman sinking slowly into the depths of the ocean while holding her infant in her arm—very effective.

"Although the sinking was upsetting, of course, the outrage against the Germans was simply overdone. The ship was carrying war contraband and so of course it was subject to interdiction. The passengers had even been warned of it in the New York newspapers before sailing! And the contention that it was a passenger ship was simply not credible. The *Lusitania* was an auxiliary war cruiser. We know this, Freddy, because it was built with its power plant below the water line to prevent gun damage to the boilers. The British papers didn't mention this, but you can be sure my German friends did. Besides, the U-boats had been active interdicting ships bound for England since the start of the war. When possible the boats were stopped; crew and passengers were taken off, and the ship destroyed by cannon fire. That wasn't an option with *Lusitania.* No one complained when the Royal Navy home fleet sealed off the North Sea, starving German ports, or when they blockaded the English Channel from Central Powers trade." Charlotte spoke as if she had repeated this line of justification many times in her mind.

"Well," she continued, "in the end Rolly came to understand that violence is simply endemic to war, and the Germans were no more brutal than any other nation, including our precious England. It was all too convenient to forget the thousands of colonial natives around the world armed with dried grass and spears against bolt-action rifle bullets and high-explosive shells from field cannons flung at them by the Redcoats. But these battles provoked anti-German riots in Liverpool, Manchester, and London, which I'm sure delighted the English generals no end. Soon posters with ghoulish images of uniformed Huns grinning as Belgium women and children suffered under their booted feet appeared. It was no longer a war but a crusade. Lord Kitchener admitted as much; he was known to say in the corridors of the War Ministry, 'Young men all over the empire welcomed the chance to leave their boring jobs, nagging wives, and local responsibilities to go on an adventure.' He overloaded his mouth, however; wives and mothers were not happy with such frank comments even if they were quite accurate. Kitchener was much better off in India, China, Egypt, and South Africa, where he was reported on rather than seen or heard. A darling of the print media, his reputation was largely built on sensational exploits enshrined by talented reporters. He was not good at boardroom insight. He once said, 'Bad publicity, shaming the Germans is my best recruiter. . . . It was a jolly game and every boy loved to play games.'"

Freddy was becoming unstrung. His grandmother's delight, her feeling that she had been involved in a great adventure, was too much for him. "Grand-mamma, were you playing a nursery game? Espionage isn't Snakes and Ladders, but the lives of men and boys—your countrymen's children—for God's sake."

Charlotte came up on her haunches. "A game, never! I was saving the lives of German and Austrian men and boys, *my* countrymen's children. The German empire was besieged on all sides. The Russians and Italians saw their chance to ally with the French and English to break up the German people into a fractured mosaic of dependent principalities begging for handouts from the 'Entente.' No. The Germanic people had brought forth the great music and literature while the allies were jealous rivals determined to send them back into the bogs of Northern Europe. England gloated that the sun never set on the English empire. Why shouldn't Germany have her empire? And so it should have been were it not for that blundering Crown Prince and his wife at that backwater in the Balkans."

She settled back in her chair, looking at Freddy with supreme confidence.

WHILE CHARLOTTE CLATTERED ON WITH more detail, Freddy began to think that there was something not quite right about this whole affair. The information on Gallipoli was particularly puzzling. That kind of timely infor-mation could have a profound effect on the war. A warning of that dimension was of major strategic value to the Germans. The Germans were committed in the east and west. Intelligence regarding a British incursion in Turkey would force them to venture south as well. And isn't this what Churchill and Kitch-ener wanted—for the Germans to spread themselves thin? Was it possible that the British *wanted* Germany to anticipate a strike in Turkey?

For the first time since his grandmother had begun her tale, Freddy began to listen with something other than shame and horror. Charlotte was telling the tale of a traitor, but Freddy was hearing another story echoing in the back-ground. He leaned in, now intent on picking up those pings and waves, the faint transmission of the story behind the story. She may have been deceived and not the deceiver. If only *he* could talk to his father. His grandmother's tale, he now knew, was the coded version; he was determined to get back to the plaintext.

*Part II*

# PLAINTEXT (1915–1918)

## Chapter Eight

# London, May 1915

PAST WARS, AND THERE WERE plenty of them over the past one hundred years, were short, involved a modicum of resources, disrupted few lives, were fought abroad, and produced marginal rewards. That was then.

The second half of 1914 convulsed Europe, spewing chaos into every corner of the land and surrounding sea. What was fast and true in July became unrecognizable in August. What was intended to be a mere holding action on the part of the Germans against Russia suddenly gobbled up all the Kaiser's attention. The Imperial Staff's timetable, which had been created years before, slipped, shuddered, and then fell apart. Masses of troops intended to overrun Belgium and France in six weeks, according General von Schlieffen's 1909 war plan. It was rewritten on the fly, but no matter—the German Imperial General Staff had staked its reputation on it and somehow they were going to triumph even if it bankrupted the nation and killed off a generation.

AFTER A HECTIC MONTH ON the British Army staff, Rags took a Saturday afternoon off to go to his favorite pub, the Spotted Horse on Putney High Street. Leaving the dogs at home, he strolled across the rail bridge, turned right on Deodar Road, and walked at a casual pace under the yellow brick railroad arch, a block to the corner and left one block to Wandsworth Road. Rows of tiny neat front gardens were overflowing with flowers in stone planters by shiny green holly bushes. A quick step across put him in front of the parish almshouse, a long, low, yellow brick Victorian structure that provided a home for the local old-age pensioners. A dozen bright red doorways complemented the building and made them rather inviting. Each had its own entryway, making the dear old things feel they remained worthwhile members of the community. A clever design, he thought.

Another short block was the bus stop shed where ladies in cloth coats queued with bulging shopping bags that concealed fresh veg for their supper. At the High Street he waited impatiently for a line of snorting buses to pass. Once across he was left with a quick sprint, a hundred yards or so to his alma mater, as he called it. The venerable Spotted Horse Pub welcomed all who labored and many who didn't. Built in 1837, according to the gold lettering on the front of the mock Tudor house, it didn't look like a pub at all but a middle-size dwelling. What gave it away was the quarter-sized black-and-white heavy horse in harness standing on a platform above the double doors. The second floor was a bank of diamond-shaped leaded glass windows four feet high with timber frame between each. The roof carried two dormers in the same style flanked by rows of dark grey slates.

But it was the inside that beckoned. The single large room lined in dark mahogany paneling made him feel he had come home. He had downed his first pint there as an underage lad and that afternoon planned to spend the next four hours snug with his back against a shelter bench in heavenly repose. His favorite table against the back wall, near the loo, was where he planted himself for the duration. Miss Bundy, daughter of the proprietor, knew what he drank. They nodded to each other as he made his way past a few customers who raised their glasses to his uniform. "Go get 'em, lad" and "Here's to the army" was cheered in his honor. A quick comb and brush-up was in order before the festivities began.

Before serving the pint of bitter the waitress scolded, "Well then, uniform and all, Rags . . . to what do we owe the pleasure? It's been a while, thought you might have joined up like all the rest. But my father only laughed at my suggestion, 'Not that one, I'll wager.'" Rags only grinned and let it pass; he was the one entitled to laugh now. Gertrude (or Gert, as he knew her) was ten years older than Rags and served him from the start knowing he'd been underage. It was a common practice as long as he stayed in the rear of the pub and didn't call attention to himself. She was smart looking, with the latest hairstyle from the magazines and the reddest lipstick he ever saw. A buxom lass who wore her white blouse with the top button shamelessly undone for the benefit of tips. Her father encouraged her friendly ways—"good for business," he told his wife, who put up small cold meat pies for the hungry customers. The potted meat was mostly pork fat corralled by a thick, dry, overdone soggy crust. The pie was an acquired taste, best eaten with lashings of beer. Gert's father, the proprietor, kept an eye on her from behind the bar but favored her ability to sell beer with a wink and a squeeze.

"Thank you, my dear," Rags said in his new officer voice, "most welcome."

"I see from your pips why you've forgotten us lately. Been swelling at the officers' club with posh friends, have you? Too good for us down here with the muckers?"

"Been working like that plough horse over the door. Gert, my days and nights are filled with war work. There's plenty to go round. I fetch and carry and meet myself going the other way. I'm on holiday this afternoon; just keep 'em comin'. Ask your father to run me a tab. I've taken the King's shillings and will be leaving them here today." With that Rags downed a pint of best bitter in one go. With a playful little curtsy, Gert snatched up the empty glass and turned to another customer at the next bench to take his order.

"Can't help hearin' your troubles, Lieutenant. I was with that lot that went to South Africa some time ago. You're lucky to be on the home front."

Rags took offense, aware that the red markings of the General Staff showed to the world that he was a noncombatant. He countered: "South Africa, huh? Is that where you had machine guns and the enemy carried spears?" He turned away as Gert returned with pints for them both. Rags attacked his own with a ferocity brought on by his neighbor's jab.

"No, no, sir, I just meant that all soldiers were fortunate—lucky to be out of the thick of it . . . at any time. Sorry, I am a veteran of Omdurman and that business with the Boers. 'Twas wounded—kinda, slightly, my own fault, an accident really. I got typhoid . . . terrible stuff. They tell me beer is just thing to kill off those little buggers floating around in my blood." He let out a little cough, which had more to do with his age than illness.

Rags appreciated the man's honesty, not claiming direct enemy contact. Who would know if he told it the other way round to play the hero? "So did you see Kitchener in the early days? Ever meet him?" Rags was hoping to talk to a man who had looked into those murky crossed eyes.

"No, sir, 'twas in the ranks, corporal at the end, twenty-one years, East Anglians."

Rags' tone altered. "Well, your lads are in the thick of it now; I've seen the dispatches. Of course you're following the regiment in the newspapers."

The old soldier took a long pull at the edge of his pint glass. "Well, the lads down at the Legion Hall banter about the accounts in the papers, and I get a bit of it from them."

Rags realized that the man couldn't read. The corporal suddenly downed his pint and made his excuses. "Nice meeting you, Lieutenant, I'll be on my way. Hopin' all the best."

It was probably the first time in his life that the corporal had conversed with an officer, and he had run out of words. He didn't want to show his ignorance and knew that the officer had figured out that he was clearly out of his element. With a touch of his right forefinger to the brim of his cloth cap, his drinking companion's heavy boots executed an unsteady retreat to the road.

RAGS SETTLED BACK AGAINST THE high-backed bench and scanned the horse brasses linked one above the other on black leather strips attached to the support posts that ran down the center of the large but low-ceilinged room. Meant to spruce up the magnificent heavy horses in full harness in real life, they flapped and spanked the leather, adding to the rhythm of the hooves on cobblestone. Five inches square of thick bright metal, they all had designs engraved on them that reflected the political opinion of the owner or some family connection or industry. Rags checked off one length of eight. In the order of descent was Wellington, a wagon wheel, a shamrock, a lion, cross keys, a Maltese cross, a thistle, and finally a Christian cross. They were as mixed up as the times, he thought as he held his empty glass up to catch the eye of the very busy Gert. They came from the time when the horse was king. Nothing moved without generations of powerful draft horses. He thought of hundreds of thousands of hand-raised colts whose gentle ways would be transformed by the demands of war. Farmers lost half of their pairs, riding stables gave up the business to war department levees, and even the officer class had their trained mounts requisitioned. Rags was no horseman, but he felt for the poor animals who must have been confused and frightened.

The past turbulent ten months had transformed him as much as it had the poor colts. At the beginning of the war, he had been unconflicted—never gave the others of his generation a thought. He and his dear mother fully expected to be above the fray, not to be disturbed by anything so inconvenient as war. They would pack up and slip away to a cozy family life, protected by the mountains of Austria. But then the travel restrictions fell on them like a plate glass window, shattering their escape plans. Then, within days—in the blink of an eye, really—two war fronts swung open. Most unexpectedly, the Russians beat the Germans to the punch, occupying the eastern edge of Prussia while the British Expeditionary Force, or BEF, much to England's surprise, was stymied at Mons, Belgium. By the end of 1914, the dreams of both the Central Powers and the Triple Alliance for a quick victory had vanished. His mother, Charlotte, had read the papers each day, hoping to find a way they could circumvent the barriers of war to allow passage to Austria. Each night the two of them fussed over their luggage, trying to reduce it to essentials in the event that a clandestine fishing boat might allow them to make a dash across the Channel. But the Channel was crisscrossed with Royal Navy patrol craft; escape was impossible.

After those first months of all-out war, the *Times'* obituary column grew longer every week. Every lunch hour, younger brothers seated at his school's refectory table had read letters sent home from the battlefront, telling horror stories like the unexpected two-hundred-mile retreat. What should have been a massive clash of warriors at Mons turned into a stunning rout that drove the French and the BEF—40,000 strong—streaming down to Paris in bound-ing steps that had no precedent in modern military history. At assembly each morning the names of Charterhouse alumni who would be added the vener-able plaque in the great hall were read. It seemed to him that all alone the small British Expeditionary Force was taking on the entire German army. Where were the French? Wasn't it their war? The British Army was there to defend Belgium, not France. But as the months turned cold, two things became apparent to Rags: England was losing and the French were running, all the way back to Paris. Perhaps it wasn't such a bad thing, he thought. If the Germans took Paris, the war would surely be over and that would put an end to it. Then he and his mother could get on with their plans. He was sure that Lawrence Binyon was writing about his mates when he penned *For the Fallen*, just before that miserable Christmas, seven weeks after the start of the war:

*They shall not grow old, as we who are left grow old*
*Age shall not weary them, nor years condemn*
*At the going down of the sun and in the morning*
*We will remember them.*

His instructors, like almost all the figures of authority in England, had declared early on that the war would over by Christmas. The Germans would be overextended; their supply lines could not keep up with the front lines. The Hun would run out of supplies, bullets, and shell just short of Paris. They proved to be right. But what they didn't realize was it would take the destruc-tion of the British Expeditionary Force to do it. After Christmas, Paris was saved, but the BEF was decimated. England was rocked by the enormous loss of life. Kitchener came to the rescue with a new British army, built on a wave of volunteers that eclipsed the BEF in strength. His ubiquitous poster, show-ing the general pointing at the viewer with the words "Your Country Needs YOU," tapped the well of patriotism. Some 2,500,000 young men joined up, but a full 30 percent were not fit to serve. Those who didn't go to the battle-field were left to transform the landscape of England. Factories switched from making consumer goods to war work. Women became tram drivers, traffic wardens, lift operators, chauffeurs, bank tellers, even bricklayers. The sight of women in work clothes began to bother Rags. It was not right, he thought. They were the weaker sex and belonged in the home while men took on the heavy war work. What was happening to his country? The government was breaking all the rules, turning everything upside down, just to help the bloody French keep their bloody Paris.

As spring approached and the end of the school year drew near, he became convinced that his place was not the death trap of the trenches.

He was not going to be a statistic on the wall of Charterhouse. There was stalemate on both fronts, with the Russians in the east and the French and English in the west, and the Germans dug-in on both sides. The flat ground of northern France and southern Flanders had become nothing more than a graveyard. Speed of attack—so crucial in earlier wars—was replaced with weight of projectile and rapidity of machine guns. Artillery was all. Uncle Hilly and his cohorts reluctantly abandoned the horse cavalry when the British Army's Lifeguards gave up their mounts and took up machine guns.

The zigzag trench lines started at the edge of the English Channel and ended four hundred miles later on the banks of the Swiss Rhine. It was a line of men, nearly hand in hand, charging and retreating in an endless dance of demolition, destruction, and death. Nearing his graduation from school, Rags was reminded of the words of the ailing Pope Benedict XV: that the war was "the suicide of civilized Europe." That was when he decided that if he were to die, it would not be in a stupid trench for the stupid French.

Intervention was called for if he were to maintain his skin. Without it, the social pressure would propel him inexorably into the ranks of the doomed private soldier. Even a commission would not guarantee safety since junior officers died at an astounding rate. While the German structure called for three officers per infantry company, the British formation had eight and more to hand lead every patrol or platoon in the attack. His mother held the solution. Charlotte was a member of a powerful English family, and his Uncle Hilly was happy to oblige with a safe assignment at Horse Guards. His mother had plans of her own, but Rags had achieved his number one objective: to stay out of the trenches. And if the red tabs of a staff officer earned him the disdain of the soldiers he passed in the street, so be it.

THE NEXT MORNING RAGS HAD to lift himself off the bed without any assistance. He had slept late since it was Sunday. He would spend the rest of the day implementing a well-tested hangover recovery program devised by the clever Mrs. Jayson. His mother was gone to church and would be involved in good Christian parish works, leaving him thankfully alone until teatime. After drinking something that looked like tomato juice and devouring several racks of cold toast with lumps of clotted cream or tart orange marmalade, he dragged himself to the library to read the *Times*. He was used to bad news, expected it, and it could not have been worse. General French had let it be known he was ginning-up a grand push. Rags thought it curious that war plans were being leaked. Perhaps the old warhorse was trying to redeem himself after the annihilation of the BEF. The talk around the headquarters had been about the War Cabinet sniffing about for his replacement. French had few supporters at Horse Guards. It meant that Uncle Hilly would be in the thick of it.

That dreaded Monday morning Rags was committed up to his ears with the business of war. Telephones never stopped ringing. Staffers never took a breath. There was frenetic energy whirling around the room as doors opened and closed, visitors came and went, and schedules were discarded before the ink was dry. What seemed so simple in April was unmanageable in late May. The investiture of the Dardanelles was in place. Turkish forts were under siege. A naval blockade of Constantinople was expected. A small number of Commonwealth and French troops were being diverted to Egypt as a new ancillary theater of war formed. A major push by the Allies was looming in France due to the anticipation of German interest in Turkey. Troop units were being fielded by the battalion and married to their supply depots. Kitchener was building and training a new army. All of the decisions were being made as a result of the debacle of the previous ten months that had caught the army staff totally unprepared.

In the evening Rags was held at the office attending to Uncle Hilly in the mess. It was one of those nights when the senior officers were taking a break to play cards and get their minds off the pending morning briefing with their civilian counterparts who understood little of what they heard from the field. Rags was confined to a corner couch, alone, trying to stay awake. Big Ben marked 10:30. If he weren't relieved of duty, he would miss the last train to Fulham at 11:00 and be left to sleep in the cloakroom. He caught the boss's eye and a nod was given. Gathering himself together, he rushed down White-hall to the underground station that was nearly empty except for the nurses coming off shift from St. Thomas' Hospital just across Westminster Bridge. It was a welcome relief after the hours of sucking secondhand cigar smoke and watching portly generals swizzle snifters of cognac in their sweaty palms.

A dozen or more nurses, in their white caps and blue capes lined in red silk, chattered away in high-pitched voices. It was music to his young ears. He began to sort through the group as they descended confined in the wood-paneled elevator that clattered down just one level to the trackside. The station accommodated both District and Central Line trains, which meant the wait could be long that night. He didn't mind. His eager eyes lost half the bevy of beauties as they split westbound from east. Still, there were at least a dozen left over. He maneuvered near as they shuffled up to the edge of the platform when they heard the rails sing, a precursor to the arrival of the train. Around a corner the lead car burst up to the platform with a roar, and then came a screech of metal brakes like fingernails on a blackboard. "Mind the gap" came the call from the station attendant with the red paddle in his hand; "move right down in the cars, room for all." When the platform was cleared, "mind the closing doors—all clear." He swiveled the paddle to the green side. At the signal the train driver pushed the throttle slowly forward and a smooth transition was made to forward motion. In the interim, Rags had taken a seat facing the two side-by-side nurses who gave him a friendly nod, adjusting their legs out of his way in the cramped space.

As the train gathered speed toward St. James's Park, Rags made his move: "Evening, ladies. I've had a busy day, but I'll bet it doesn't compare with your war work. You must be overwhelmed the way the casualty trains are running."

"Oh, are you in the medical corps, Lieutenant?" the taller of the two asked while her friend rummaged through her purse for a cigarette, uninterested in what reply the officer might make in way of an introduction.

"No, I'm at Horse Guards; we see all the reports and recently the list of casualties has been alarming, you know, since there isn't a big show going on right now. I'm Rags—you know, kind of a nickname they put on me at Charterhouse." Rags knew this would put the young ladies at ease, would identify him as a well-bred, upper-class, safe candidate who might appeal to a pretty young lady of the same class. It was a popular gambit with the young people who were discarding conventions right and left in those uncertain and dangerous turbulent times.

"I'm Vivian, and she's Gracie." Her companion was still digging for her lighter at the bottom of her bag. Intent more on a smoke than a boyfriend, Gracie waved her hand, never lifting her head as she pulled out a handful of items and dumped them on her lap.

"Well, evening, Gracie."

She glanced upward with her eyes only, rather detached, to right a wrong. "It's Grace, not Gracie." She gave up eye contact and busied herself as before. Rags looked back at Vivian and was rewarded with a warm smile when the train passed through an open space and their world was rent apart.

Explosions were rumbling all around and the sky was lit with red flashes. The train rumbled forward, heading for cover in the tunnel, when debris began to strike the top of their car. "Zeppelins," Rags shouted as he stood up to shelter the nurses. Holding on to a strap with his right hand, he put his left over their bowed heads. "On the floor, ladies, below the seats if you can." They could and they did as the train disappeared into the tunnel before entering Victoria Rail Station. Other riders who had followed his shout looked to the young officer for direction. Rags found that he was the only person standing in the crowded car. "It must be the uniform," he thought. He hoped that the electricity on the line wouldn't be cut, as they were only a few hundred yards from the safety of the massive station. The two prostrate girls, tangled together between the hard seats, remained still even though the train had stopped next to the platform. When the doors popped opened, people froze, eyes wide, hoping from instructions. Should they leave, even though it wasn't their station? Or should they go on, trusting in the cover of the train and tunnels? What if the power failed while they were between stations? To detrain was highly dangerous in a pitch-black tunnel. If they got out now, where would they go? Was the station bomb-safe?

Rags took in all those eyes looking to him for direction. He helped the nurses to their feet and pointed the way. "Everyone exit the train!" The entire car followed his lead and emptied on to the platform.

The platform guard approached the car and confirmed his instinct: "Victoria Station, this train is out of service. Everyone off!" Fearing that the object of the attack might by the rail station itself, Rags led the frightened group up the steps and outside to the bus terminal.

"What now?" Grace at last had found her voice.

"Let's take our chances on the bus. This raid can't last for long, and the closer we get to the suburbs, the less chance we'll get bombed." He reasoned that the attackers were after commercial and military targets along the river. "Where are you girls headed?" Vivian was going to Richmond and Grace to Wimbledon. "I need the 97," Vivian said, looking at the rows of red and white double-decker omnibuses waiting in queues like metal pachyderms. The bombing had stopped for the moment, but smoke billowed through the air, giving the streetlights a soft yellow glow. Grace coughed and went back into her bag for a handkerchief. People on the pavements struggled to reach the open bus doors and climb aboard. Rags could see panic in their eyes as they squeezed between the throbbing coaches. Rags located number 97 and helped Vivian aboard. In a moment she was swallowed up and pushed down the aisle, never given the opportunity to say thanks.

"Grace, what about you?"

"I'm not going home. I'll be needed at St. Thomas'. They'll be overwhelmed."

Rags looked at the sky, then back at Grace. "You can't go back; there won't be any more trains. I think you should come with me to Fulham; there is an 86 over there and you can stop at my digs until this is all settled.

"No, Rags, I must go back; you go on. Thanks for all your help."

In the seconds it took for her to turn on her heels, he registered that she had called him Rags; she had been listening after all. God, she was pretty, and she'd called him Rags.

That was all it took. He heaved his satchel on his shoulder, yelled "Wait for me!" and set off after her.

## Chapter Nine

# Lambeth Bridge, 1915

"NUMBER 11 OR 24 WILL DO," Grace said. Rags had finally caught up with her retreating figure, taken her hand, and watched as she coolly assessed him. After a moment, she gave his hand a squeeze back, and now they were searching for a bus to take them back to Grace's hospital. The crush of the crowd slid them along the side of a greasy coach. Rags looked round and headed toward the lit sign that listed which buses were in the queue. Grace hung on as he pulled her along behind. There were half a dozen slipways each with several double-decker buses from which to choose. Dimly lit coaches were impatiently waiting with motors throbbing, blue noxious smoke rising. Choking on fumes belched out in spinning clouds that irritated his eyes, Rags could make out numbers 148, 24, and 211, which appeared to be eager to leave with or without passengers. A uniformed conductress hanging on to the rear rail of 211 rang the bell, and the driver lurched the bus forward, mashing the passengers inside into a sandwich of coats, purses, parcels, and bags. "The next one, I think—Grace," he called above the noise.

By the time number 24 approached, the station's lamps flickered and then failed, plunging the crowd into near darkness. The waiting riders moaned in unison. Only the headlights and the glow of the interior coach lamps provided a path to board. Explosions cracked too near, and a few more made impact some distance away with heavy thuds. They energized the riders to scurry forward, and Rags and Grace were swept along onto the coach and into the center aisle. The conductress was pinned against the rear stairs, unable to sell tickets. She managed to reach the control and rang the bell, alerting the driver to be on his way.

Number 24 vied with the other behemoths creeping forward toward the small end of the funnel that allowed them to diverge out of the confines of the terminal. Even though it was late in the evening, traffic was thick and ponderous. Masses of vehicles, fleeing the East End, headed west, presumed to be the only way out of the chaos. Explosions and fires had closed down several main routes. It seemed as if everyone was looking for a way out of the blasted city or to cross the river. Sporadic bombs were still falling ahead in the direction of the Thames, their route of travel. At last the coach turned out of the circle and down Victoria Street past Westminster Cathedral. The dean had thrown open its great doors to provide a refuge, and pedestrians were streaming inside. Rags wondered how many were practicing devoted parishioners. He thought a prayer from a sinner such as himself might not be in high order.

Though squashed in the aisle, Rags managed to secure a couple of coins and pass them back through helpful hands to the conductress, who gave her heavy metal ticket machine, hung around her neck on a broad leather strap, a ratchet. The paper receipt never completed the return trip. "No matter," he thought, "what could I do with it?" It was then that he had the first opportunity to really talk to his lovely companion. He turned toward her, ready to open with a stunner. But nothing came, so in desperation he said, "Grace, how are you then?"

Six inches shorter than Rags and fused tight against his buttons, she gazed up. "I'm all right—you?"

His chin was nearly touching the forelock of blonde hair that stuck out from under her white nurse's cap, "Well, it's nice to meet you; I'm a lucky guy, I guess." He was unsure exactly what that meant, considering the circumstances.

She smiled, looking up at the handsome young officer. "So am I, I guess." The crowd shifted as the bus swerved throwing them off balance against a seat-back, knocking a lady's hat askew. "Sorry, madam, sorry." Madam was not amused, and Rags and Grace quietly laughed at the nasty look he received.

His smile fell when he looked out the window. London was in chaos. Smoke, debris, and a general sense of panic tarnished the city. Though they had traveled a mile or two, Rags could see that traffic had now come to a standstill. Raising his voice above the din, he shouted to Grace, "We've got to get off. This bus is going nowhere. We'll have to walk. It's about a mile to the river. We're sitting ducks if this bus takes a direct hit." Others nearby looked his way with a sudden panic in their eyes and began to slide toward the rear platform. Arms and legs became tangled; packages and parcels were squeezed and nearly carried away. Shorter passengers were submerged as the masses crept to the rear. Politeness was maintained, however, everyone attempting to give way while at the same time maintaining their egress to the rear platform. They came off the step in bursts of two and three. Spun and twisted, each tried desperately to get their feet under them before shuffling off between creeping vehicles to the pavement.

Rags and Grace inched to the rear exit, and Rags gave her a sheepish look, feeling guilty for dragging her out to the pavement once again. "It's all right, I've walked it before," she confided. "Besides, I don't think my feet were touching the floor. I've been standing on your shoes ever since we got on."

A petite girl, he hadn't noticed. Like the others, they apologized their way to the rear with many "excuse me's," "sorry's," and "thank you's." Hopping off in the middle of the road, they slid between resting lorries, buses, and army trucks. Rags took his position on the curbside, a gentlemen's place to protect her from a vehicle mishap. Trapped several lengths ahead was a fire appliance, blue lights flashing and bell chiming. The clanging echoed off the masonry buildings in a piercing cacophony. "It's driving me mad," Grace cried covering her ears. The racket drove them off Victoria Street and down Greycoat Place. The soft hum of the side street was welcome. Walking was a relief, and they soon stopped in a shop doorway to catch their breath. "Just around the curve is Horseferry Road," Rags said. "I know Horseferry," Grace offered. "A ways up is the headquarters of Anzac. I go there often—I'm on their ward in the hospital."

She was communicating—a good sign. Rags said, "That'll take us across Lambeth Bridge and into the back of the hospital. I think that Westminster Bridge will surely be blocked, if not blown up by now." Grace smiled in the shrouded headlight cast by a passing vehicle. She took his arm and held on tight. "I agree, Lieutenant; let's go."

RAGS HAD KNOWN PLENTY OF girls in his school days. Charterhouse was twinned with several small girls' academies that provided escorts for dances and outings. Mamma was not keen on English girls and encouraged him to find "a nice German fraulein" during summer stays near Regensburg. He'd indeed done so, always careful not to make his mother's mistake of becoming too involved. He felt no such care now. Maybe it was only the danger of the evening, but with Grace at his side he felt excited rather than terrified. Grace was so pretty, and he liked the feeling of protectiveness that had come over him. Holding her hand tight against the dangers of that terrible night, he felt like a man. So this was what it was all about.

Gradually, as they walked toward Horseferry, the sounds of battle ebbed and were replaced with the din of civil firefighters and ambulances. A hospital van, desperate to get through traffic, drove up on the pavement, and Rags pulled Grace to him and into the recess of a shop doorway. Making its way around traffic, the careening vehicle nicked a royal post pillar-box, and Grace laughed to see the van bounce and skirt around obstacles; the driver must have been frantic. "Oh, I shouldn't laugh, sorry. But it's like the cinema shorts with mayhem all about!" she remarked, placing one hand in front of her mouth. "I must be more considerate of the poor patient being thrown about in the rear, in more danger in the ambulance than at the site of his mishap. I am awful, aren't I?" Rags couldn't care less about the poor patient, and he didn't think she was awful at all. There was an indefinable lilt to her voice that he had never heard from women he had come in contact with in his rather confined circumstances. He wished he could see her eyes better, but the light was poor. There must be a twinkle.

The two began the approach to Lambeth Bridge, which would take them to the south side of the Thames. The distinctive lamp pillars were dark. It could be a precarious crossing, for the five arches of the stone bridge exposed them for nearly a thousand feet. A lone brave police constable attempted to unsnarl the scramble of vehicles that funneled the pedestrians across the bridge past Lambeth Palace whether they wanted to go there or not. A friendly wave allowed the couple to sprint across the roadway and onto the pavement on the north side adjacent to Victoria Tower Gardens, the narrow green park below the Houses of Parliament.

As they approached Lambeth Bridge, for the first time they had a clear view of the landscape and the plight of the great city. Before, enclosed in the Underground, captured by the bus queue, crammed on a coach, or confined in the narrow streets against looming buildings, they had felt a kind of claustrophobic terror. But now, seeing the whole city afire, they felt something even worse, a despair at the size of the destruction. They stood motionless against the damp rail on the north side of the old bridge. It was the wrong thing to do, dangerous. Hot red embers passed by on the stiff wind generated by raging infernos downstream. London was on fire. Since childhood they had become familiar with the famous skyline, but it had never looked like this. The sky was orange, yellow, and red. Bright searchlight shafts swept the clouds, chasing looming zeppelins. Silhouetted by the fires were many familiar landmarks: Parliament's great clock tower, marking the time as if it were any night, and the cupolas of Scotland Yard. The river was crowded with motorized watercraft of all sizes and descriptions plowing upriver in a bunch, as if all were connected to one another, trying to escape. Smoke and stink drifted along on a hot breeze. The wide bridge vibrated underfoot as if it were overloaded, about to collapse. The throbbing boat motors mingled with the high revolutions of the vehicles, both giving off nasty fumes that choked the voice and burned the eyes. Poised at the iron rail for a moment, Rags felt stunned and Grace leaned in, against him.

"We better get going," Rags cautioned, as Big Ben rang out notice that it was 1:00 a.m.

"Yes, we must." Grace quietly agreed but didn't move. "It's awful, Rags. Our beautiful city. What do the Germans think this will do to us? We have been on this island for thousands of years; do they think that a few bombs will make us weep and give up? By God, they don't know what they are dealing with. This is England, not helpless Belgium. They will pay, if it takes all we've got. Bastards."

Rags felt his heart drop. *They*, Rags thought. *They* were the Germans— Grace's enemy. England's enemy. *They* was him. Those were his zeppelins floating over his home. Up until then he had thought of himself as a reporter, a mere clerk sending notes into the German ether. Since the day he began relaying secrets from Horse Guards, tucking them discreetly in the stones of Putney Bridge, he had reveled in the pride of his mother and the thought of his father's approval. But Grace's face did not make him proud; it made him ashamed. It made him feel anguish. My God, if she knew who he really was . . .

He put his arm around Grace's shoulder and began slowly walking her across the tangled bridge to the embankment just short of the traffic circle and then east along the river's embankment. It was late. He wanted to get her safely to the ward but dreaded leaving her. He should have been dog-tired, but he wasn't. There was an exhilaration brought on by the sight of the massive zeppelins, the jarring explosions and the heat of the roaring fires. They picked up the pace, and in another ten minutes they went through the hospital's back entrance and climbed the steps to the third-floor ward.

Once through the swinging double doors to her ward, Grace became another person. He saw her visibly straighten and her eyes become focused. "Rags, you should go, but here's my number." She scribbled down her phone number, stepped up on her toes, and kissed him on the lips. "Good night; be careful, my brave one." And off she went.

Back on the street Rags caught his breath. What a night! Getting home was a new problem. He must catch a ride. His home next to Putney Bridge was several miles west on the twisting river. While road traffic was surprisingly heavy at that time in the morning, he didn't relish standing in the dark attempting to hitch a ride. The river, that was the answer. There were boats a-plenty and they were all going his way. Energized now with a new prospect, he tramped down the embankment's stone steps to the pier. A naval launch had just docked to discharge a number of walking wounded from reaches below Westminster. It was obvious that they could not return east; the traffic and incoming tide were running the wrong way. He hailed the master and asked where they were going to put up for the night.

"Were headed for Reading. Where you bound for, Lieutenant?"

"Putney to be sure, Master; have a spot for the army?"

"Welcome aboard, army or no," came the reply.

So it was, a comfortable ride for a weary soldier. Facing to the rear, he took another look at London in flames, the same sight watermen had beheld during the great fire of 1666, and wondered if London would rise again as it did then. But that was one night, one day, one moment in history. This fire was clearly the beginning of many fires on many nights. How long was this war going to last?

CHARLOTTE WAS WAITING IN THE foyer when Rags got home, exhausted and stinking of smoke but at least intact. She had heard the air raid sirens and turned her attention toward the West End. The high beams were searching the sky for the zeppelins that were slipping in and out of the broken clouds. She saw the flashes before she heard the sound of the explosions, mostly clustered around the lower river. Experience told her that they were in Westminster. The rattle of anti-aircraft fire and a pall of smoke were carried up the river along with a line of small boats. She watched the sky turn red behind the houses in the east and thought of calling Horse Guards—she had a telephone, one of very few in residences—but doubted there would be anyone left in the office. So she waited, helpless.

It was two o'clock in the morning when the Westies alerted her to Rags' pending arrival. Valerie had been asleep in her basket, but the little one was at the door calling for his mother to join him. Charlotte stood, as nervous as the dogs. Finally Rags pushed opened the main door. The dogs did their usual twist dance as if it were six o'clock on a normal evening. He knelt down to greet the dogs, who sniffed and sneezed their way around him in opposing circles.

"My God, you made it home." Charlotte wrapped her arms around her only son.

"I'm fine. London isn't." Rags wrested his arms out of his coat, barely meeting her eyes.

"Come," she said. "Some hot cocoa and cake from the tin will do you good." She led him downstairs to the kitchen putting him at the long work-table while she filled the kettle. Rags rested his head in his hands on the table, exhausted. "Was Horse Guards hit?" she queried. "Have you seen Uncle Hilly?" He held the cup in both hands but remained mute, staring at his hands.

"There is a shelter there, isn't there? I suppose you all went down at the first bomb?"

"I don't know; I don't know anything. I was on my way home on the Tube and had to get off at Victoria; then I made my way by hitching a ride with the navy. It took a long time; everything is a mess, river clogged, nothing moving, fires everywhere. I just kept plugging along." He didn't mention Grace and their voyage through the burning city.

Charlotte watched him as he sipped his cocoa. She didn't care about Victoria or the navy, the mess, the fires. She cared about her son, and here he was, safe at home. If anything, she felt angry at London, angry that the city should have put him at risk. "Take that, England," she thought. "There is more to come."

Rags put the last bit of cake in his mouth and wiped his hands on a napkin, still not looking at her. "I'm going to bed—wake me in time to go do my duty. Whatever that may be."

Charlotte watched him retreat and felt an unexpected twinge of worry. She hadn't counted on her son's reaction. He mustn't be allowed to develop doubts. She turned back to his empty cup, taking it to the sink. She had to think. She'd write to Christian; he would know how to ward off Rolly's doubts, his weariness, any misplaced sympathy. He would provide fatherly guidance. Because this much she knew: the war was to pull England down. She would not let England pull her son down.

## Chapter Ten

# Horse Guards, 1915

LATE THE NEXT MORNING, AFTER Rags dragged himself off to Horse Guards, Charlotte had Anna, her maid, lay out her warm robe and then proceeded directly to the library. Though it was warm outside, she was chilled; she suffered from the shivers—all her life she had, just like her mother. It must have been the cold and damp of Yorkshire still settled in her bones. She was counting on Mrs. Alberry to prepare a proper tea in her best china.

Charlotte had tossed and turned much of the night. Rolly's behavior the evening before had left her in turmoil. She had seen it there in his face: the flickers of doubt, the cool distance, the tiny cracks in his fortitude that, if left unattended, could break her son's resolve. Possibly it was just shock from a frightening experience—he was, after all, still a teenager. But she could not simply hope for the best. They had committed themselves to spying for the Germans. Rolly had taken classified items from Horse Guards, information had been encoded and sent to Christian, and other German agents in England were involved. There was no going back, and for the first time, she couldn't ward off fears of being found out.

Charlotte's first footfall on the staircase alerted the housekeeper, who sent the cook, Mrs. Jayson, into action. The teakettle, which had been filled with cold water to ensure that plenty of oxygen bubbled through it, had been placed on the hot auger and brought to 208 degrees—never boiling. She poured it into the china pot, swirled it to warm the clay, and then dumped it out. Three level measures of Twining's English breakfast tea were cast in and the pot then covered with hot water. Mrs. Alberry checked the tray. Anna, dressed in a freshly starched apron, lightly knocked twice and entered the library with a tray laden with a Royal Worcester china service decorated with painted periwinkles. Four warm Welsh cakes, Charlotte's favorite, awaited on a matching service plate. The cup had been warmed and a spoon filled with sugar lay at its side. As a rule, an English lady added milk, not sugar, but the lady of this house was a rebel and defied convention. She liked it sweet. Charlotte nodded for the maid to pour. Anna knew better than to speak to the mistress early in the morning.

Once Anna had left, Charlotte turned back to her desk and contemplated the task ahead: to communicate her concerns about Rolly to Christian without causing Christian to panic and without tipping off any others involved—most notably the Bookers, who would up-sticks and disappear at any hint that Mistral was unreliable. At the same time, if the message was not explicit enough, Christian might not grasp the seriousness of the situation. In the end she wrote:

*Mistral shaken by last night's air raid. May require outside influence to nail him to the mast. Perhaps a father's influence.*

The message read badly, she knew, but under the circumstances it was the best she could do. She gave the signal to the Bookers that there would be a message to transmit that evening. For the first time, Charlotte would step out onto Putney Bridge herself, placing the message early at the dead drop before Rolly got home at six o'clock. Charlotte was nervous that a passerby might discover the drop during the four hours' wait before Booker retrieved it on his walk back from his local, the Eight Bells pub. There was also the chance that Rolly would come home with a hot piece of intelligence that would have to go straight out. If he found a paper at the drop, he would expect it to be a communiqué from Christian and retrieve it. She would have to derail any further messages that night for the Bookers.

Charlotte planned a diversion for the evening. She had a cousin who lived a few miles away in Clerkenwell. She would tell Rolly she needed to visit, claiming perhaps a female crisis that Rolly wouldn't ask for details about. But he would go along to protect her on the dark streets. Plan in place, she sipped her tea and prepared for a long day of waiting.

EXITING THE WESTMINSTER UNDERGROUND STATION that same morning Rags expected to see considerable destruction and disruption. As he climbed the steps to the street, the great clock tower came into view.

Amazingly, little had altered. The bridge was unmarked and the façade of the Houses of Parliament was intact. The pace of workers was unhurried. Only the boys hawking newspapers on the corner of Whitehall seemed disturbed by the headlines. "Zeppelin's Reign Over London." Rags knew a bit about the bombs. They were 250 pounds and mixed with high explosives, capable of great destruction. But although the bombs were powerful, they were also limited in number and London was a very large city.

Additionally, the London fire brigade had been preparing for this day. Shortly before the war they had invested in petrol-assisted electric-driven five-ton appliances. The appliances carried a crew of six and had a range of sixty miles at a speed of twenty-five miles per hour. Their agility on the crowded streets was quite extraordinary. The incendiary bombs mixed with high explosives had set many a fire, but the brigade drenched many of them before the fires spread.

Rags felt relieved. He had expected much worse after the harrowing evening. One of the government buildings on the south side of the street had lost its windows while its neighbor was still smoldering. A fire appliance was parked on the pavement while a small detachment of firefighters sifted through the ashes inside the damaged walls. The acrid smell of charred beams scented the air, a good reason to cross over to the Cabinet offices on the same side of the road as Horse Guards. But the landscape on either side of Whitehall was peaceful, as was much of the rest of the city. Most important, he was safe and Grace was safe. Rags recalled the burning sky of the previous night, the look of apprehension on Grace's face, and for a moment he forgot everything else. "Those bloody zeppelins . . ." He would make it his business to ferret her out before he went home that evening. He had tried the number she had given him the night before leaving that morning, but it was out of service. The hospital operator could get a message to her. There was a nice pub on the Vauxhall Bridge Road, the White Swan, a fifteen-minute walk from St. Thomas'. It would do nicely.

Rags went through the front entrance of Horse Guards and skipped up a couple of flights of stairs to face the crowd that always blocked the hallway. He struggled along the wall, finally popping into the central office to pick up Uncle Hilly's mail—his primary duty, morning, noon, and night. The ubiquitous Beryl, the pretty girl who had put him straight on his first day on the job, was filing. "Morning, Beryl! How was the show last evening?"

"Morning, Rags. I missed it, really. I spent last night in Reading and all we heard was fire bells as our department careened off toward the city and the docks. Your mother rang a few minutes ago. I told her you would ring her back. We talked; she seemed nice. General Hopewell's mail is on the table; there is something there for you from HQ." She smiled and lifted her eyebrows as if to say, "Are you in trouble?" "Didn't know you got mail as well; you *are* a dark horse."

On the top of the stack there was a large brown envelope addressed to him. "It looks official enough," he thought. His heart skipped a beat; he didn't think the army knew he was significant enough to send him anything. "Perhaps it's orders to the front. Uncle Hilly would nullify that for certain; he must!" He put the others aside and tore it open. A very grand, stiff piece of parchment was inside. In addition to the scrolls at the top and fancy printed letters, there was a center piece where someone had typed, *Roland*

*Agustus Grayling Stetchworth is hereby commissioned Lieutenant in the Welsh Guards Regiment of His Majesty's Military Service.* He looked up at Beryl. "My God, I've been promoted. I'm in the Welsh Guards!"

Rags knew it was an honor to be selected for the Welsh Guards. This fifth regiment of Foot Guards in the Household Brigade had just been formed in 1915, joining the Grenadier Guards, Coldstream Guards, Scots Guards, and Irish Guards. Since they were the monarch's personal military formations, they were considered the prime assignment in the regular army officered by the highest level of society. But they had fought in France from the beginning of the war as well.

Rags turned again to Beryl. "Uncle Hilly must have done this. I'm a Guardsman!" Beryl laughed. "There's a lot of that going around these days. Anyone can join the Guards after the loss of the BEF." In a way it was true. The casualties during the retreat from Mons devastated all regiments and included hundreds of young company-grade officers. Beryl gave him a peck on the cheek. "That's my boy. Fancy that: Rags . . . Guardsman."

Thrilled, he reread the inscription over again. "Beryl, does it matter that they misspelled *Augustus*? Does that nullify the promotion?"

"Ah no, some clerk did it; the colonel's signature at the bottom is just a formality. Someone in the Guards office signed his name as well. Correspondence comes through here all the time typed by gorillas; nobody reads it. But Lieutenant Rags, you're out of uniform. You better get to the stores and pick up some more pips and the proper cap badge. Mildred won't be as thrilled as you are if you fail to get the mail to her ricky-tick."

Down the hall Rags passed a lieutenant coming the other way and thought, "He's just like me." He was thrilled. As he had learned, second lieutenants were the running joke in every mess. Now he would be where he belonged and vowed to return the favor by harassing all second lieutenants. Passing his empty desk, he rushed into the inner office and greeted Hilly's secretary: "Mrs. Box, sorry I'm a tad late, just got some good news. I've been promoted."

Leaving the commission on top of the stack, he dropped the lot on Mildred's pristine desk. "Yes, I know, I had them do that. Can't have a second lieutenant traipsing around behind the general; it's unseemly. Off with you to the tailor and put on those pips. The general needs you to take him over to the Royal Society after lunch for a conference with some very important colleagues."

So that was it. His bubble burst. He'd been promoted by a secretary and dropped into the Guards, just like that. There was to be no honor, no well-earned authority. The other lieutenants in the mess would recognize another obvious case of nepotism, of which the British Army was full. And he would be just a slightly more prominent monkey scurrying after Uncle Hilly through the halls.

When Rags got back from the tailor in Jermyn Street, Mildred had a car waiting to take Hilly to the Royal Society for Improving Natural Knowledge. Founded in 1660, the Royal Society was the most distinguished group of scientists in the world. Its headquarters at Burlington House in Piccadilly, with its Palladian architecture and learned societies, was one of the most distinguished buildings in London, and Rags felt a sudden beat of pride as they approached. During past conflicts the grand gentlemen of science had kept themselves at an academic distance from the military, remaining aloof and, they supposed, above its tawdry exigencies. But the current president, John William Strutt, Baron Rayleigh, who happened to also be the chancellor of Cambridge University, had been appalled by the carnage in Belgium and France. He and his colleagues saw that the traditional weaponry and gentlemen's rules of past wars were worthless against the onslaught of German guns and gas. He, along with ten other Fellows, distinguished scientists all, proposed to form a working group to solve battlefield deficiencies through scientific investigation. The Fellows offered the weight of the Royal Society to Churchill, who was on shaky ground at the Admiralty after the initial debacle in the Dardanelles and landing at Gallipoli. Kitchener, who recognized the complexity of modern war, welcomed their assistance.

Rags followed Hilly into the east wing of Burlington House, where a military guard was securing the hall before seating the guests. Rags was confined in the rear along with Henry Segar, Kitchener's aide and long-time associate.

"Rags, you've come up in the world! Congratulations, well done. It suits you—very impressive, a Guardsman now, eh."

Rags was a little thrilled to see the impression the badge and pips brought, but chagrined enough to tell the truth. He confessed, "The boss's secretary did it. I wasn't aware I was so outstanding," laughing at his own expense.

Henry shook his hand. "No matter, all my glory is attached to the boss as well." They sat down and blended into the wallpaper. "This is going to be interesting," Henry said. "The boss thinks this is one of the most important meetings of the war."

Churchill took the stage and began to speak of the collaboration between the scientific community and the military. It had begun even before the declaration of war, when the British cable ship *Alert* left port on August 5, 1914, and steamed through the night to stand by off the coast of Germany. As the light from the east came up off the coast of Emden, Germany—six hours since Britain had formally declared war—it attacked five underwater communications cables. It dredged along the sandy bottom and grappled them on board. On deck they were chopped into pieces and dropped back into water, dead to the world. It took four hours of heavy work and was England's first offensive act in this war. Those lifelines ran across the North Sea and down the Channel to England, France, and Spain, there to be connected to North America and Africa. Germany could no longer send telegrams to its African colonies or America. All their vital communications would have to go by radio, which could be monitored and broken.

Churchill continued: "Great Britain had taken on a modern war that it was not capable of mastering without the help of scientists, mathematicians, engineers, chemists, and doctors. To win this war and maintain our position in the broader world, the academic community and the military will have to together break the enemy like they broke those cables." The war would be conducted in laboratories and scientific workshops as well as on active battlefields. Engineers would visit the trenches. Mathematicians would break the German security codes. England would beat Germany with its minds as well as its arms.

With his customary lisp, Churchill laid out Britain's most immediate concern: The wounds from shrapnel sprayed down on the men in the trenches by air-burst artillery shells was causing high casualties and low morale. The troops required personal overhead protection, a proper helmet like knights of old. It sounded simple but was anything but.

After Churchill spoke, the attendees began to consult with each other. Uncle Hilly kibbitzed with the men of science, whom he referred to as the boffins. It seemed that his uncle knew everyone. Rags watched him work the room, refreshing his drink for him as he walked and talked. As a Guardsman, he felt right at home among the distinguished company. His presence was nearly invisible, just as his Austrian father had predicted. He heard bits and pieces that could be useful, and he tucked them away to be transcribed later. The meeting broke up before tea, as expected.

Rags got in the car with Uncle Hilly as they were taken to the mess. Hilly explained the difficulty: "Royal Fellows working on armor plate. It might sound absurd; after all, our museums are chock-a-block with tin hats. The problem is made difficult by the high velocity of the projectiles. Light enough for a man to wear hour after hour, yet repellent enough to resist a chunk of steel traveling at hundreds of feet per second." Rags couldn't imagine wearing a steel pot on his head all day. Even the spiked picklehaubes worn by the cavalry in the last century were stiff leather. Those worn by the Household Cavalry were for show, very thin and shiny. They wouldn't stop a bullet. He thought of the ashes and embers raining down on London last night and was again thankful he was in Horse Guards rather than the trenches. But thoughts of London on fire led him to thoughts of Grace, and his sense of security wavered.

MILDRED BOX HAD ALREADY DEPARTED by the time Rags got back to the office to secure the general's case. In the empty office he dialed Grace's floor, the Anzac ward. After a short wait he heard her voice: "Nurse Moss-Jones, how can I help you?"

Rags panicked. Hearing her voice brought back her face, her warmth, the feel of her arm tucked in his. He couldn't think what to say.

"Hello, is someone there?" she inquired.

He pulled himself together. "Ah yes, it's me, Rags from the bus last night . . ." He grimaced to himself. "The, um, the zeppelin attack on the Underground, the walk to the bridge and hospital?" He left it hanging in the air, hoping he didn't sound as much an idiot as he felt.

"Oh, Rags . . . you got home all right? No complications, I hope."

Her voice calmed him a bit. "Oh yes, just fine. And you . . . how was the night shift?"

"Not as bad as we expected. Most were taken to Guys Hospital, so they didn't really need me. I went to the nurses' quarters for what was left of the night."

"I'd like to see you again, Grace, now that I know your whole name. Are you free anytime soon? I was hoping you could meet me for a drink sometime. I'm usually off by six o'clock or seven o'clock. Would you . . . ?"

"Oh yes, I'm on day shift, so I'm free any night . . . until something big happens, I guess."

"I know this nice little pub, good grub, on Vauxhall Road, just across the bridge in Pimlico. Anytime, even tonight, if you think that's all right." Rags cringed inwardly, afraid he was being too forward or babbling incoherently. But he could hear her smile through the telephone line.

"I'm game, Rags." Her lilting voice sent shivers down his spine.

"I could come to the hospital about six and we could walk from the nurses' quarters along the embankment. I hope they don't drop bombs on us this evening. Though we know what to do now, don't we?"

"That sounds fine. I am staying at the number 37 hallway stairs nearly on the west end across the road from the gardens. I'll be by the desk on the bottom floor. Do you remember what I look like? Wouldn't want you to pick up the wrong girl."

She sounded so wonderful, so full of life, not like anyone he had ever known. Before last night he had been surrounded by spotty schoolmates filled with gloomy advice about girls, how scary they were, how tricky to talk to. And his mother was no help, always steering him away from what she called "the wrong kind of girl"—which appeared to be any girl at all. But Grace swept him off his feet and dashed his fears.

"See you then, Grace."

RAGS HAD LESS THAN AN hour to make himself presentable and walk the half mile to the venerable hospital across Westminster Bridge. "Wait until she sees my new pips and finds she is to be escorted by a Guardsman," he thought. He hoped he wouldn't run into a fellow Guardsman since he knew nothing and no one in the Guards.

St Thomas' Hospital was a tangle of old and new structures. Shrubs masked the dark wooden door to the ground floor, whose only clue to its identity was an old bronze plaque saying "Original location of the Florence Nightingale School of Nursing and Midwifery, 1860." Now a dormitory, the dark red structure was showing its age, and Rags thought it looked like a fire trap. Looking at the well-worn wooden stairs warped by years of student feet, Rags could see that any money for improvements had been spent on the hospital and not the residence. The lobby smelled of dry, flaky paneling, unwaxed for sixty years. A long table with a large mirror leaned against the wall, covered with unclaimed mail. Two young nurses came up from behind, arms full of books, chattering away. They brushed by. He guessed they must be accustomed to seeing suitors anxiously waiting for some sign of their date at the top of the stairs.

Grace, late from her shift, was in a muddle. As a rule she lived at home and had little in the way of civilian clothes with her. After Rags called, she had rummaged through the wardrobe of her roommates in hope of finding something suitable. The search was fruitless. At least Rags had the good sense to pick a quick meal at a pub, nothing fancy, nothing requiring her to primp up. She would have to stay in uniform. She removed her cap, fixed her hair, and replaced the cap with a sly look at the mirror. "Well, that will have to do; after all, it's only Rags." She liked his name very much. It put her at ease. She left her borrowed room and plunged down the first three flights of stairs. Then she paused on the landing to get her poise back before taking the last flight in a slow, lady-like descent to the lobby.

# Chapter Eleven

# The White Swan and Woolwich, 1915

GRACE WAS AN ARMY BRAT. The Moss-Jones family came from Monmouth, Wales, near the border. Generations of naval officers, artillery gunners, and cavalry horsemen had put their stamp on the family. Her father was in the British Army, and she, her mother, and her five brothers had lived everywhere from India to Ceylon to Gibraltar while her father was off to war in South Africa. As a teenager she had been educated at a girls' academy near

London, followed by nursing school. She had finished her training that spring and the assignment at St. Thomas' was her first as a ward nurse. Like so many young British women, out of the home with paying jobs for the first time, she was enjoying her newfound freedom, flirting with the soldiers and sharing gossip with the other nurses. Surrounded by officers and doctors, many of them had strings of boyfriends and wild affairs, but Grace had always kept her head. She'd had plenty of offers, but she was a trained nurse in wartime; what did she need a husband for? Nonetheless, the young lieutenant from the previous night had captured her attention. He was handsome, to be sure, but there was something else, some mix of maturity and innocence, like he was just beginning to discover his own power and was a little frightened by it. And maybe just a little exhilarated.

And so she found herself strolling down the Thames promenade on Rags' arm that Wednesday evening. Due to the shortage of motorcars and rationed petrol, everyone was walking. Though the metropolitan Underground and bus system crisscrossed the city, there was always a concrete or cobblestone foot-pounding walk at the conclusion of every journey. Grace latched on to Rags' left arm, leaving his right to render salutes to oncoming soldiers and passing officers. They retraced their steps from the night before and glanced downriver as they crossed Lambeth Bridge. A steady breeze was in their faces, blowing the scent of ashes that remained suspended in the evening air, but neither mentioned the previous night's horror. It was another evening, and since the weather had changed over the Channel to storms and high winds, Rags was confident that while they might get wet, they wouldn't be killed.

On Horseferry Road once again, Rags took a quick left turn in the first block and they plunged down a narrow street named for John Islip, the Benedictine abbot at the time of Henry VIII, the man responsible for the reconstruction of Westminster Abbey. The abbot would have enjoyed the thick line of majestic chestnut trees that formed a green tunnel for blocks just out of sight of the Thames River. Expensive residential red brick apartment houses lined both sides and blocked the noise from heavy traffic on Milbank Road. The rain began to drip off the tips of the low-hanging branches, which added a little life to the evening shadows. Rags asked about her family and got an earful of stories about life in India and Ceylon, shopping for saris with her mother, learning to shoot with her brothers, and failed attempts to learn Hindi. Her fondest memories were of her father, an expert cavalry rider who taught her to hunt. "There are two kinds of girls, Rags, those who like horses and those who love them. We have always kept a string of polo ponies. They are my father's weakness, and I must say I am his daughter. John and Morgan, my two oldest brothers, and I spent our days abroad in the stables. They are both in the army, in my father's regiment, of course."

Rags had a nodding acquaintance with horses, mostly as he passed them on the street. He was a city boy. Was this going to be a problem? Was he going to have to take riding lessons? Or perhaps she could teach him to ride. No, he didn't want to appear that vulnerable; he would have to solve this one on his own. And as for the two older brothers, how much older? He conjured up two overprotective giant Guardsmen thumping him about the head and asking about his intentions. He looked down at the pavement. "What a family, what a childhood. I can't match that. I'm just what you see. I'll be twenty soon, fresh out of Charterhouse when I was about to go to university." That was a white lie, but it fit the circumstances and he could get away with it. He wouldn't be the first school leaver to expand on his education prospects. "But the war, well, you know, kind of captured me as well . . . like so many. I'm kind of on hold until this mess is concluded."

She looked over at him and squeezed his hand. "What is home like? Where is it? I really know nothing about you except you are in the army." Rags gave her a short staccato history, leaving out the part where his mother killed his stepfather and that his actual father was an Austrian aristocrat. Otherwise his family history would sound like a play on Radio Four. He also failed to mention that he was a German spy.

On the corner, three blocks along was a tobacconist shop, there was a poster next to the newspaper rack. In bold red letters it read "DAILY MAIL, £10,000 ZEPPELIN FUND," followed by a listing of payouts for relatives lost, possessions pulverized, and even limbs blasted off. Grace joked, "Let me look you over, you could be worth some money." She grasped his chin and turned his head from side to side. "Have you always had that little scar on your temple?"

Rags smiled. "Yes, courtesy of a cousin when he threw a Dinky toy car at me for pinching his dustcart lorry."

"Well, you'll have to do better than that." Surprisingly, the macabre poster lightened the mood and they turned the corner to Vauxhall Road. The traffic sounds drowned out their quiet moments, but no matter, both thinking what could have been last night, had they had worse luck. Within forty yards Rags opened the welcoming door of the White Swan pub on the corner across from the Pimlico Tube station.

With the rain it had become chilly, even for summer, and the warmth of the fireplace inside took away the damp of the evening. Low ceilings, dull wood paneling, and a raft of supporting old posts made the long room appear darker than it really was. Rags had scouted the room beforehand and picked a tiny table for two in the middle that was raised on two steps against a leaded glass window. It was secluded even though it was in the center of the room, across from the long bar. Customers ordering food and drink had their backs to the couple, which put them alone on opposing benches.

"What will it be? I hear they have great fish and chips; it comes through from the back door." He had to explain that there was a chippy next door.

Grace was hungry, having not had a thing since grabbing a meager tea from patients' leftovers before she went off shift. "Good arrangement, how clever. Make mine plaice, not cod, if you don't mind." Plaice, a lighter fish, would cost Rags a shilling more, but money was never a problem for a rich young lad with a generous mother who indulged him with plenty of pocket money.

Rags nodded as he took off his cap and put it under the bench. "I'm having a cider; it goes down a treat with the chips. Would you like one as well?"

"Cider, that sounds refreshing, and it should cut the grease. They don't like to serve cider in Wales, you know; the barmen say it makes men fight."

When he returned he found Grace reading a newspaper that had been left on the table. She read a passage sent by a correspondent from the beach at Gallipoli. "Tell me, mister general staff officer, what *are* we doing in Turkey? Don't we have enough war in France?" Her tone was light, but Rags felt underneath it worried her that the war was escalating and would take her father from one frying pan into the fire.

Rags had direct knowledge of that question and could have given her chapter and verse after sitting through meetings for days over the same query. But while he had passed that information on to the Germans, he felt he must not pass it on to his dinner companion. "I don't know. There is some concern about the Turks closing the Suez Cannel, I guess, though it seems far-fetched to me. All I know is that I won't be going out there. I couldn't take the heat and bugs. I'm stuck right here in good old Blighty." This was a bit of slang for Great Britain picked up from other soldiers that he thought made him sound more authentic, like a veteran. It had clearly not impressed Grace, and there was a long pause as she looked back down at her borrowed paper.

He tried again. "Notice anything new about my uniform, in addition to the promotion?" He glanced not to his shoulder with the new pip but more to his lapel to give her a hint.

Her eyes lit up when she recognized the Leek, the miniature regimental badge of the Welsh Guards. "But that's my father's regiment! Rags, how did you get in the Welsh Guards? My father's involved in the recruiting of new formations; have you been keeping something from me? He's down near Folkstone somewhere putting replacement battalions together." She stopped and fixed him with a gimlet eye. "Did my father send you? He has been watching my movements, afraid I will get swept up by some bad sort in London."

Rags didn't know her father and didn't want to give the impression that he did. Nor did he want to tell her that his elevation in rank was due to the kind intervention of one Mrs. Box, secretary extraordinaire. "Oh, the army moves in mysterious ways. Perhaps it was my guvnor—he's a Welshman, you know, Major General Hopewell. He's a distant relation of ours. I'm his aide-de-camp here at Horse Guards."

"Uncle Hilly! You're attached to Uncle Hilly!"

Rags' mouth dropped open. "You know Uncle Hilly? I mean, General Hopewell?"

"He's married to my mother's sister, Winifred. Why do you call him uncle? Is he related to your family? This could be embarrassing if we were first cousins!" she laughed.

"No, not actually. My grandmother was a Howard from Yorkshire, and one of her aunts married into the Hopewell clan. It was through my Grandmother Howard that I was schooled and later became acquainted with the Honorable Artillery Company where I got my commission. You know it's all 'good family' if you're to get anywhere in this country." To tone it down a little, he added, "I suppose it's the same all over. It's the system and we are the beneficiaries; I shouldn't complain."

"Well, that is just marvelous. I must tell my mother of the coincidence; she will be pleased. She's always after me to go out with the right sort of chap and there you are. She couldn't possibly complain about you."

Even as she said the words, it occurred to Grace that she really knew nothing about her companion. What could she tell her mother? That they met on a train in the middle of an air raid and his blue eyes and earnestness intrigued her? That his hand on her waist at the very moment the closest bomb hit made her want to hold onto that hand for the whole rest of the war? It was unlike her to be smitten, but even now, as he picked up his cider glass and sipped, she wanted to feel that hand on her waist again. She picked up her own glass and drank it in. She was right—the cider did cut the grease.

THE NEXT MORNING AT HORSE GUARDS Rags was as bright as a button. It was all going his way. He was secure in his safe post in London, far from the trenches in France. His new insignia gave him a certain swagger as he walked through the halls of Horse Guards. And best of all, there was Grace.

The night before, Rags had left the White Swan on cloud nine. Not only was Grace the prettiest, most lively girl in all of London, she was a daughter of his regiment. She was energetic and hardy, irreverent but with a moral core that radiated from every cell. And those eyes. And that slim waist that was so, so touchable. If Rags hadn't been raised by a mother who thought he was the center of the universe, he might have been too insecure to pursue her. But he felt his strength growing every time he saw Grace. In his heart he had decided to take her on.

So it was with chagrin that he learned, upon getting to the office, that fate had other plans for him than the delivering of memos and the pursuit of pretty girls. As he strolled in, Mrs. Box caught him and gave him the bad news: He and the general were to leave for Egypt and Gallipoli in a fortnight. "You'll be transported on a man-of-war from Deptford or Woolwich, not sure which at this time. Should expect a month, I should think, haven't set up the return at this date. It will be a fact finder for the War Office; you know Kitchener trusts our general, but few others." Rags looked at her, dumbstruck at his bad luck. She stopped and put her hands together on her desk, adopting a patient, if slightly exasperated, tone: "You've got a lot to do. Go see the Navy Board offices at Somerset House. They take care of VIP travel. You must go there to arrange it." She waited for a mute nod from Rags and then went back to her typing.

Rags spent the rest of the day starting preparations. A week in Egypt, and on the return voyage they would stop in Rome to concur with the Italians, who had come into the war on the side of the Allies. France had made overtures about returning Trieste to the Italians if they opened a new front on their northern border with Austria. Rags grumbled his way through the day, ruing the lost time with Grace. But it wasn't until he got home that evening that he realized the other complication of the trip: his communiqués with his father. That was how he had begun to think of those coded messages: as a form of keeping in touch with his father, the two of them professional soldiers, in the thick of it, trading stories and information.

His mother was as caught off-guard as he was. There was no way Rags could maintain the flow of information to his father away from the Bookers' radio link. That night, in the darkness, they left a short message with the itinerary and asked for instructions. Within two days Christian sent a short message: "Compile a detailed report of Hilliard instructions and observations." That was all; no alternate plans, no concern. Was something up? His mother fretted, but a small part of Rags hoped that the Germans had lost interest in his supply of information, that it was found to be of little use, not worth the risk.

For the next two weeks Rags was submerged in the wartime bureaucracy, as he was shifted from one office to another, from one supply point at the Navy Board to another at the Ordnance Board. A special launch had to be arranged from the pier at Westminster Bridge to the officers' mess at Woolwich for early in the morning the day of departure. Snatching two evenings from the jaws of work, he continued to treat Grace to poor food and warm beer within a radius of a mile of St. Thomas' Hospital. She was disappointed that he was leaving town for a "big show"—a term she knew from her father's military career—but was understanding. She traded shifts with girlfriends to see him when she could. And the night before he left they were to meet at the Clarence Pub across from Horse Guards for one last cider before he sailed. She waited, but he never showed.

It was unavoidable. At the Clarence he had made arrangements for a special table upstairs, which was known only to aides and their masters for quick, cozy dinners. Though it was only a fact-finding mission, Rags felt like a soldier going off to war and wanted one special evening with his girl, something more than the usual chips and cider. Mrs. Box had advised him here just as she had with shipping schedules and supplies. She knew that Hilly treated a particular lady to lavish dinners and overnights at the Clarence and told Rags just how to proceed. She seemed keen for him to become a wartime libertine like so many dashing young officers, but Rags knew that Grace wouldn't be pushed. And he wanted her for the long haul, not for a night or even a war.

But at lunchtime, Henry Segar left a message for Rags: "Need to see you in person—now!" Henry was not the kind to panic, so Rags did the quick step down Whitehall, entered the Cabinet Office door a block west, and charged down the stairs to the long corridor that had once been at street level before the fire of 1666. At the office of the prime minister's private secretary he met Henry, who took him by the arm back into the hallway. "The boss wants Hilly to accompany him this afternoon down to Woolwich dock for private talks before he leaves for Africa. Don't tell anyone except Mrs. Box. Horse Guards must not know. And Rags, keep your decorum, no tip-offs—understand?" Rags agreed and tried to hide his excitement. He wore Segar's trust like a badge and thrilled with pride at his insider status. The war minister wanted to talk with Hilly where no one could eavesdrop. With their immediate departure for Egypt, Rags had no way of passing on information about the meeting to his father, and he would have to try to cancel his plans with Grace. But this was big.

Under the instructions of Kitchener himself, all military personnel were to be seen in uniform for the duration of the war. Wherever Hilly went he was recognized, so the transit to the boat had to be quick. Rather than a staff car, Rags had a common taxi at the loading dock off Horse Guards Parade for a four-minute drive to the steps at the north end of Westminster Bridge. They boarded an unflagged, curtained launch. Henry escorted Kitchener aboard downriver at the Tower of London pier. It took an hour at slow speed, not to arouse notice, to reach Woolwich.

The Woolwich Arsenal was the headquarters for the third branch of the defense of the establishment. While the Royal Navy headquarters at the Admiralty was adjacent to the army headquarters at Horse Guards, the Ordnance Department was twenty miles south at the waterside town of Woolwich. Upon arrival the party was greeted by the master gunner of the artillery who commanded the arsenal and sat down to a table set with tea in his quarters. Rags, too low-ranking for the discussions, was disposed of on a tour of the gun-making factory. There he saw both naval and field gun barrels being forged in white-hot furnaces and pounded into shape. He watched massive boring machines hollowing out the tubes according to caliber; hot sparks went flying in all directions. At the gun yard the barrels were matched to carriages. Rags was given a quick course in sighting an eight-pounder before a test firing.

When Rags rejoined the group, Kitchener suggested they switch to cognac, though he abstained. The war secretary laid out their mission. He passed Rags a packet from Churchill, only a few days before replaced as First Lord of the Admiralty, which expressed critical concerns about the Royal Naval presence and the level of leadership on display, in particular that of the Royal Navy fleet admiral. Hilly was to keep an eye on several naval and army commanders and report back to him on their fitness for command. It seemed to Rags that the questions asked were more political than military. It had come to Kitchener's attention that things were going badly at the embarkation port of Alexandria, and he was especially interested in the French contingent. One-quarter of the force on the ground in Gallipoli was French, and Kitchener wanted to be able to give an evaluation of their performance to General Foch, the French allied commander, when they met in fall. Kitchener and Hilly generally shared the British Army's prejudice toward the "frogs," but they were dead serious on this day. The Gallipoli expedition was being conducted by Anzac—the Australian and New Zealand Army Corps, a newly formed force—and Kitchener needed a clear eye, as he put it, of their capability. Rags contained a smirk at the thought of a clear eye from a man whose eyeballs were clouded by years of campaigning in the desert of Egypt and Sudan. He glanced at Henry, who winked back at the joke.

After a final cognac, the three boarded their launch, which turned down-river to their waiting ship, leaving a slow wake behind. Rags had all of their baggage shipped the day before with instructions to the batmen to stow them on board HMS *Alexis*, a medium cruiser set up with state rooms for senior officials and their parties. Hilly was not the only senior official on board. Several brigadiers and generals, along with a diplomatic party from the Foreign Office, would help pass the ten-day voyage. It would have taken less time if the war precautions had not been in place. German submarines were sure to be in the Bay of Biscay and waiting around the constricted waters at Gibraltar. Rather than follow a compass course, the captain was required to zig-zag.

They left on the outgoing tide. To break up the voyage, a lecture was given as they passed over the site of the Battle of Trafalgar, a standard pitch on every warship that passed by. Though Rags commented to Segar, "Little to see—combatants were either sunk or sailed away in 1805," the Royal Navy never let the site of its most prestigious hour pass without a tip of the hat. And despite his showy cynicism, secretly Rags wondered if his war would be remembered for great moments—and if he himself would be remembered with those who left or those who sank.

## Chapter Twelve

# Mediterranean, Late June 1915

EGYPT IN JUNE WAS HOT, and Rags tugged at his collar as he debarked from the *Alexis*. Alexandria Bay was a beehive of activity as ships unloaded, staged, and reloaded cargo and troops. A forest of tall masts and belching smokestacks obscured the manic activity along endless docks and sweltering warehouses. The clanking of steam cranes and the swinging of cargo being dropped into steel-sided ships was deafening. Rags followed his party's way through narrow passages strewn with wet rope and cargo nets. Though they walked on the cool water side, the heat and humidity drained his energy and he longed to return to the ship.

Despite the exotic locale, he was discontent. He missed Grace, and, like many other young officers, he was wondering what the hell they were doing there. He had heard Churchill and Kitchener lay out their strategy earlier in one of those endless meetings—to distract Germany and draw them into another arena while improving Russia's maritime access—but Rags couldn't help but side with Admiral Fisher, who favored a second front on Germany's northern coast. Fisher pointed out that it was easier to land and supply an amphibious force protected by the Home Fleet operating in the Baltic Sea. There it could also engage the fabled German navy, shatter it, and blockade their ports at close quarters. Fisher pleaded: "Why else did we build the greatest fleet in the world—to hide it away in Scapa Flow? What are we afraid of?" Fisher was the father of the modern Royal Navy, so he would know. Rags agreed, but no one was asking him.

Hilly was his usual avuncular self, walking through the crowded streets as if he'd been born there. He couldn't help but recall packing up in the port for the excursion to the Sudan to right the wrong that had been done to Chinese Gordon. But Rags noted an undercurrent of worry that was unusual for Hilly. The general knew the German-sponsored states were pummeling French and

British colonies, and Enver Pasha and his Young Turks had thrown their lot in with the Central Powers. Beaten badly a few years earlier, they were hoping to regain lost territories from Russia. Oil had replaced coal as the energy staple, and it flowed like rivers all around the Turkish borders. Turkey also controlled the Bosphorus, the Sea of Marmara, and the Dardanelles, the strait separating the Sea of Marmara from the Aegean. The Allied forces had been fighting for control of the Dardanelles and the Gallipoli Peninsula since April with little success. Rags understood Britain's interest in the region, but why were *they* here? After a week in Egypt, they were due to steam onward to Turkey to do God knew what.

"Sir, there must be a serious deficiency out here. Why else would an inspector general of the army be dispatched to Turkey, in the middle of the European war, on a *fact-finding* mission?" Hilly was a nuts-and-bolts inspector whose motto Rags knew well: "Things screwed up from the top can't be unscrewed from the bottom, but it is at the bottom where problems are manifest." Hilly liked to be on site and see things for himself, but Alexandria in the summer was a little much.

Hilly replied with an all-purpose huff and pointed to the outdoor café on the veranda of the Metropol Hotel. "Rags, find us a table." He led them to a small square table and plunked down. "Let's take our malaria shots—gin and tonics all round!"

The canvas awning provided a bit of relief from the summer sun, and the view of ships cutting through the Mediterranean would have made for a lovely scene had sweat not been running down their faces. Rags wished he were wearing loose white cotton robes like the Arabs rather than the tight cotton uniform of the British Army. He lifted his hand to catch a waiter's attention and order their G&Ts. The waiter suggested some bits of chilled shrimp on sticks.

It was over this interlude that Hilly explained to Rags the real purpose of their visit: to assess the Allied leadership and recommend alterations. The Australia and New Zealander soldiers in the newly formed Australian and New Zealand Army Corps (Anzac), accompanied by both Indian and French formations, were being thrashed on Gallipoli, the peninsula right where the Sea of Marmara narrowed to the Dardanelles. Hilly was here to answer Kitchener's question: "Is victory imminent, or, in defeat, could their reputation be salvaged?"

THE NEXT DAY, HILLY BEGAN his assessment in earnest, here where Anzac had launched. He sought out the British Naval Board's harbormaster in Alexandria. He would have been the primary official to cope with satisfying the army's deployment demands. Commissioner PB Lax, a red-faced man who proved too outspoken, stood at the third-floor window of his stifling office overlooking the circus.

"Would it surprise you, sir, to learn that initially the troops and supplies had been debarked here in Alexandria for training nearby? In the desert? The troops were first intended for deployment in France, and someone decided that the cold, wet climate of England was not a suitable training site for these fellows." Lax snorted. "To my recollection France and England are less than a hundred miles apart, but the army said you can't expect soldiers from Down Under to perform in the harsh conditions of an English spring.'"

"Balderdash," sputtered Hilly. "Desert training prior to landing in France . . . what are they thinking?" Hilly turned to Henry Segar, who was to be his right-hand man on this mission. "You know, Segar, the War Office could have come up with a much better lie than that to cover the actual reason for their desert training. You see, the good harbormaster here thinks we're idiots. Not even the Turks would fall for that one."

Segar shook his head. "Actually, the government didn't want to have 100,000 jabbering Diggers and Kiwis cluttering up the southern counties. Housing and feeding them would have destroyed the economy, which is on tic as it is. Additionally, Kitchener knew it to be a good place to hide a reserve in case his recruiting program began to flag. He expected Germany to strike with the Ottomans sooner or later and take the Middle East by the end of the war. But you're right—the explanation that troops who came from summer conditions below the equator to another summer climate just north of the equator couldn't train in England was pure poppycock. Even the newspapers saw right through it."

Lax jumped in. "Well, you can't tell generals anything. When I challenged their logistics plan, they told me I didn't understand war and should leave it to the professionals. 'Just get us the men and supplies on their way as directed.' But the loading plan was a mess. They had the entire landing force of nearly 100,000 men, plus equipment and supplies, stopping at Lemnos. Debark there, put everything in combat order, and then reload and embark for Gallipoli? Foolishness. I found that the Expeditionary General Staff is mostly officers from India! They've never experienced an amphibious landing, or much else, I'll wager."

Rags could see Hilly wince at this news. No wonder it had taken so long to get the landings underway—and little wonder why the Turks were waiting in well-prepared positions when Anzac finally landed on the southern beaches. He knew that the mission's commander, General Sir Ian Hamilton, had been posted in India for far too long and was out of touch. But Hamilton was a good friend of Kitchener. Segar took note.

A FEW DAYS LATER, WANTING to arrive unannounced at Lemnos, Hilly asked Lax to find him passage on a freighter. Rags had transferred their kit first to the Hotel Metropol and then by cart to the *Ascot*, throwing off the escorts provided by General Hamilton. Reporting back that all was accomplished, still seated on the veranda, Hilly was letting his frustrations out a bit when Rags arrived. "You know, Segar, this is not first time the army has been here. The British and French staged military adventures in both the Crimean War and some years later the expedition to the Sudan, neither of which went smoothly. I was at the Battle of Omdurman, you know. But alas," the old soldier sighed and looked to God in desperation, "we never seem to learn. It's going to be a pig's breakfast at Lemnos, I can assure you, Rags."

The trio settled back and began to map out their lines of investigation. It was decided that the first step was to probe the decision to restage the men and equipment at the Greek island of Lemnos. Proper planning in Alexandria should have eliminated such a costly delay. A day on the island would be followed with a look at the invasion beach at Cape Helles. With that under their belts, they would go on to review the progress of the fighting before confronting General Hamilton.

Rags had been given his own set of instructions. He was to book the entire party at the Hotel Metropol under his name that night but leave shortly after dark for the *Ascot*, which sailed with the evening tide. Their arrival was masked by embarkation of a large group of Australian nurses who were to care for the wounded at the island's temporary hospital at the port city of Moudros, the main port of Lemnos. Rags went on board knowing that the posh days were over. One look at the freighter, lights reflecting rivers of rust running down its grey hull, told him that their comfortable sea passage had come to a sticky end. The freighter was small, perhaps three hundred feet overall. The upper decks were painted a muted cream with oak companion doors that hung on large corroded brass hinges. If they were traveling on the same transport as the nurses, it would be basic. Moudros promised to be no better, and it finally dawned on Rags that, for the first time, he might be headed to an actual battlefield.

IT SEEMED THAT THEIR BREACH of protocol—ditching their escort— was a delicate matter. Once the officers on the *Alexis* realized Hilly was gone, message traffic was sent to all concerned about their unscheduled departure. Hilly considered the subterfuge to be unavoidable. He knew that General Hamilton would not want him wandering around Moudros unsupervised and would know, in fact, that the arrival of an inspector general (more popularly known as an IG) indicated a major crisis. Hilly was determined to investigate the Gallipoli campaign without oversight or obstruction, from the ground up, at every step along the campaign's path. He wanted to hear from the field officers, sergeants, soldiers, sailors, and gunners. He knew the cooks, packers, grooms, and signalmen could paint a more accurate picture than Hamilton's staff. While Hilly's party was under escort, only one side of the situation would be revealed. The IG didn't want or need a minder.

That evening, General Hilliard, Henry Segar, and Rags were escorted through the narrow, dim corridors to quarters on the *Ascot*. The general went topside to bunk in with the captain, who would spend most of the night and the next days in a small cabin aft of the bridge, his usual place in dangerous waters. Segar displaced the first mate, and Rags was four decks down, below the water line, with the ship's engineer. In the cramped officers' mess, Segar and Rags lamented the loss of their comfortable chambers on the Royal Navy warship. "It smells like neglected oil rags that have been left in the corner of a garage," said Rags. "There is a sheen of coal dust on every horizontal surface. And a cracked ceramic washbowl and pitcher with an oriental design, which I think came from China on a previous voyage. Though I can't believe the *Ascot* made it there and back."

Segar described the pattern of paint chips that clung to the metal bulkhead next to his wet musty bunk. "I think they resemble a very bad portrait of the old queen. The hull is so thin I can hear the dockers loading barrels." His tone rose: "The cabin door doesn't fit the frame and won't lock. I'm not sure, but I think I saw a rat in the passageway on the way here. And I couldn't even complain to my shipmates: They are all Malaccans, and don't speak a word of the King's English."

The thudding of the engine coincided with the vibration in the deck as the ship creaked into action. They were off. It wasn't a reassuring sound to Rags' ears. Both men looked pensively at each other and went for the door, sensing that on deck was the best bet as the ship trudged past the breakwater and out into the deep darkness of a rolling sea. The submarine threat demanded that the ship run dark. It gave an ominous start to the voyage. Were they alone or a part of a convoy? They couldn't see their hands in front of their faces. The freighter began to loop, as the bow plunged into the unseen swells and rose up ever so slowly. Who could tell they even existed?

In the morning Rags breakfasted with the nurses in a small, low-ceiling mess hall, which served the meals in twenty-minute shifts. The ship was not designed for passengers, so the nurses, some twenty-five of them fresh from Australia and New Zealand, were forward above the chain locker in a compartment meant for the crew who had doubled up aft. The nurses had spent most of the war thus far treating soldiers—young men away from home for the first time—for the consequences of their frequent visits to the brothels of Alexandria. They were chatting about cases left behind in a most unappetizing manner. Rags felt they were used to the squalor of army hospitals and seemed unfazed by their bare-bones quarters on the *Ascot*. But Rags still caught in their faces a trace of the foreboding that mirrored his own. He stopped at the head of the table where there was an empty seat. With tray in hand he spoke, "Morning, ladies. I'm Lieutenant Stetchworth—Rags, for short."

He was eager to be the center of attention of half a dozen young pretty women. He missed Grace and thought he could use his acquaintance with one of their kind to break the ice. He baited them with questions about their voyage from Australia and the conditions of their passage. Eager to have an officer of the Guards from London express an interest, they opened up, one talking over the other with streams of chatter about leaving home and the great adventure that awaited them in the new hospital. He made note of their unit and said he would be sure to bring General Hilliard around to check the conditions. He was surprised how open and friendly these foreigners were. Rags, like many of his class, regarded Australians and New Zealanders with suspicion. After all, they were the progeny of criminals who had been transported there to make England safe. He chuckled at his own foolishness; they were no different from English nurses, even if they did talk funny.

The voyage wasn't long, but the wait at anchor was interminable. With Lemnos on the horizon, *Ascot* hove to in the shallow waters of a large bay several miles across. The surrounding lands gently slopped down to the water from brown, sparsely covered olive groves. To the east the view of the island was interrupted with rows of ships of all descriptions revolving at the mercy of the tides about their anchor chains, waiting for the lighter to be attached to the sides and debarkation to begin.

The bright blue sky and its resulting heat made for a cranky general. Livid that after three days a senior government official party was still waiting on ship, he sent sizzling messages ashore. Finally a Royal Navy launch plowed its way to the *Ascot*. Complete with the pennant of a major general on the prow, it hugged the side of the decrepit old freighter. A ladder was passed over the side, and Major General Win Carruthers hopped aboard. Carruthers was an old friend of Hilly's, obviously sent to calm the IG's frayed nerves. It seemed that Hilly's stealthy departure had worked far too well and he was being sought in all the wrong places. Carruthers apologized for the delay and escorted them down to the launch. Hilly and Segar were accommodated in the posh cabin and plied with cool drinks and light refreshment while Rags saw to the kit.

On board the naval vessel, Carruthers gave them the whole story. Hilly's plan to escape the HMS *Alexis* unnoticed had worked only for a few hours. Once the captain had noticed all three officers were missing, he had sent out an alarm. The army didn't know what had happened and feared they had been kidnapped for ransom. It was an old Barbary industry left over from the nineteenth century, so the fear was not unfounded. And in November of 1914 Turkey's caliph had declared not just a war, as other parties had done; he declared a jihad, or religious war of survival. Allied naval attacks, which began as early as February of 1915, stirred up profound emotions among Turks. The people viewed the attacks as a modern Crusade by the Christian world, led again by Britain and France, as they had been in the twelfth century. The Turks allied themselves with Germany, but they also feared becoming subservient to the Central Powers, cognizant of the old cliché: "If I am allied with a powerful friend, may they not protect me out of what I own." But the prospect of gaining territories in Caucasia from Russia was too tempting.

So while Hilly fumed on deck of the *Ascot*, thinking he was being taught a lesson for not traveling with escort, in reality the eastern Mediterranean was being scoured for the party's whereabouts by every Allied military unit between Turkey and Egypt. The Turkish rules of engagement stated that "enemy combatants would be publicly executed."

When the launch finally reached land, Rags was unprepared for the sight before him. Moudros was pandemonium. Having never been to a Greek island, the lieutenant was struck by the cramped harbor. Miniscule by any standards, it was a mere fishing village—no commercial craft—with hundreds of open boats devoid of masts tied to concrete jetties, waiting for the evening tide. Very colorful, each had been washed with vivid paint. With barely room for a crew of two or three in what were large, open rowboats, they worked to ready the nets for a night's fishing. Rags surmised that they fished the reefs near the island, never going into the open waters of the Aegean. The small two-story whitewashed buildings in the harbor seemed to cling to each other for fear of being blown away in winter storms. The swirling breeze in the cove was hot and humid in the morning sun, warning the newcomers that it was going to be a most fatiguing day.

Hilly took one look at the harbor and remarked over his shoulder to Segar, "This is no place to stage an invasion." Because of the shallow approaches to the Helles beaches, slow intermediate vessels with a shallow draft had been employed to debark the invasion troops on Gallipoli. That was months ago, and yet support elements remained at Moudros feeding in vital supplies of all kinds. Return trips brought wounded soldiers to the temporary hospital at the edge of the village. Every type of local craft and support vessel was shoehorned into the tiny harbor. Rags saw a pair of deep riding barges loaded with pale camels, crammed cheek by jowl, being tugged toward the breakwater; the two tight rows of the animals were all facing out toward the gunnels, tails behind swishing in unison. They appeared content and clearly commenting to each other about conditions in general. The port was a tuneless cacophony of steam whistles and bells echoing under a muggy blanket of groaning heat. On a bluff he noted scores of white hexagonal hospital tents, no doubt the destination of the gaggle of nurses. He feared they would be badly disappointed.

Opposite the docks were lines of whitewashed buildings separated by thin alleys that careened down from the hill. Clotheslines clipped with family washing formed a canopy for pedestrians. Garbage was stacked in messy piles on the corners where dogs and cats picked out meals. He could appreciate that before the arrival of the army it might have been a picturesque haven for holidaymakers. Outside a restaurant was a sign with a most disturbing picture of a fat boiled octopus tentacle on a plate, suckers on top. The war had pushed the tourism trade out, replacing it with hard work but higher wages. Like a stream of cutter ants, locals carried boxes and burdens on their shoulders in long lines that crisscrossed the lanes. The only bright spot was the full employment of every citizen. Moudros had never had it so good. With the scads of soldiers out of their hair, the lucrative logistical tail was alive and well.

MAJOR GENERAL WIN CARRUTHERS, THE operational commander at Moudros, was a comical-looking character: large red hawk nose, concave chest, spidery arms, and a voice like a bird of prey. His headquarters was near the docks where the troops and supplies were being off-loaded and reassigned to assault craft for the sixty-mile leg across the Aegean to the beaches on the Gallipoli Peninsula. He had taken over a boat-building shop with high ceilings that allowed air to pass through unimpeded. It was the coolest and most welcoming structure in the village. Once inside, Hilly's party was escorted to a meeting room and plied with ice water, lemonade, and cold fruit, while Carruthers' staff scurried to arrange a briefing. Map boards were scattered about on easels. Each briefer dragged his board into position in front of the party and handed out copies of notes the briefer was about to illustrate. Rags was happy to see these, since it meant he could skip some of the initial note-taking. Hatless in khaki short-sleeve shirts and baggy knee-length shorts above slipping knee socks and brown laced shoes, thin men—nearly all identical in appearance and demeanor—rattled off statistics from columns of unending numbers. It was a litany of supporting supplies consumed by thousands at a blinding rate of three meals a day and the expenditure of millions of rounds of rifle ammunition.

"What about drinking water? You left out water," Segar reminded one.

Carruthers broke in, "Yes, well done, sir. A major problem. There is no drinking water on the beaches, you know, and little can be trusted further inland. We expend a third of our craft to carrying water from wells here on Moudros. It is a major problem; everyone recognizes that." Rags noted that was a point in favor of maintaining this port some sixty miles from Gallipoli. In light of the tough going on the beaches, perhaps it was a good idea to have staged the invasion from here and not days away in Egypt. Rags was learning that being on the ground was superior to reading a map at Horse Guards. *That* was why Hilly was going to Turkey.

"So," Hilly began. "Tell me about the deployment."

Carruthers stepped up to the map board. "You must understand, I'm in support and am speaking out of turn about invasion tactics; for those, you should address your question to Sir Ian or one of the ground commanders. But, since you ask, in my opinion it went very well. Yes, we took few hard shots, but we drove the enemy up into the hills." The pride in his voice was to be expected.

Hilly pressed, "Any surprises, Win? Enemy strength, supporting fires, terrain, intelligence, those kind of surprises?"

"Yes, quite, those kind. We hadn't a chance to test the beach sand, no daylight reconnaissance was possible. Caught us off-guard, but we coped—after a fashion. Maps are nonexistent, and we didn't have any native guides. It is a desolate place, you know. There is no living off the land. No one lives there, no farmers, no forage for the horses, camels, and mules. All we could find was Turkish soldiers, and there were plenty of them, I can tell you."

Hilly could see he was asking the wrong fellow for details on the fighting and let him off the hook on that subject. He pressed on: "Have we had to curtail operations due to shortages of rifle bullets, cannon rounds, and correct calibers for the guns? Or is that just an unfounded rumor spread by the reporters to sell newspapers?"

Carruthers jumped to answer the question, which he had heard about daily in correspondence. "It's not a shortage. We fill at the rate in the books from previous campaigns. It's the tactics employed by the artillery. Those gunners have been blasting away with their rapid-fire cannons; it's no wonder they run out of ammunition. I tell you, there is no fire discipline." Hilly had heard the same response from the front in France. Carruthers carried on in the same vein: "The artillery shoot for hours at nothing!"

The inspector general said nothing but nodded to Rags to make a note. He would evaluate that criticism the following day when he met the ground commander. Hilly had no ground to argue at this point. In a way, the supply specialist was correct. The new field guns with automatic recoil mechanisms required more ammunition. The old firing tables supported muzzle-loading cannons that only fired twice a minute. The rate of fire from a French 75mm cannon, which was ubiquitous on this campaign, could fire twenty times in one minute. Like the new machine guns, the soldiers were burning up the battlefield with hot metal to keep the enemy off.

Hilly switched topics. "How about casualties?"

Carruthers took a deep breath. "We've converted one of the troop carriers, RMS *Aquitania*, to a hospital ship. And I believe that HMS *Britannic* may be on its way out here as we speak. No room on the beaches for hospitals; besides, the beaches are under threat of enemy artillery. We're bombarded every day at Cape Helles, you know."

Hilly cocked his head. "No, I didn't know. You mean that the enemy can still strike the beaches after two months of operations? Just how far have we moved up the peninsula since landings in April, Win?"

Carruthers touched the tip of his long wooden pointer on the standing map. "I should say a good four miles, about here."

He looked Hilly in the eye, waiting for an explosive reaction, knowing that the IG would be shocked. And shocked he was, since some of the Turkish guns had been taken off German naval vessels and could range ten-plus miles with ease. He stared back at Carruthers for a long moment. Hilly's face turned a bright red. Staffers came to the defense, offering up excuses. They insisted that every shortcoming was the result of poor planning on the part of the Naval Board, Royal Navy, or Horse Guards. There was the weather, insufficient direction from above, even acts of God. Finally, Hilly could hold out no longer and dismissed the staff. He knew his party's mission was not to defend the War Office but to determine what had happened. And, more importantly, whether it was feasible to continue the campaign in its present state, reinforce the troops, or quit.

"Win, you and I should talk privately."

A few hours later, Hilly, Segar, and Rags headed to the officers' mess. Tempers cooled down as officers slipped blissfully into their cups. It was a time-honored and wise procedure since what occurred in the mess stayed in the mess. The mess was a rather posh holiday hotel on the low bluff overlooking the harbor that had been taken over for the duration. Dinner consisted of barrels of local wine and mountains of fresh-caught seafood. Uncle Hilly was no lightweight when it came to dinner and dug in, transferring his anger to crushing crab shells.

THE NEXT MORNING, RAGS SUGGESTED a hospital visit. A lorry was commandeered for the short jog up the hill to the makeshift hospital. The commanding officer was a Doctor Harold Somerville, recently of Guys Hospital in London, who held a commission in the Army Medical Corps and had served on and off as required. Hilly tried to conduct the inspection in a low-key manner so as not to unhinge the poor staff who had been doing good work in the wards. The care was clean, prompt, and professional. What it lacked in structures was made up for in enthusiasm and genuine patient care. Hilly was struck by the number of head lacerations. When he inquired, soldiers replied that crouching down in foxholes left their heads subject to clouds of shrapnel from Turkish guns. Machine guns killed outright, as did snipers. There were wards of diseased casualties who acknowledged that poor sanitation was part of daily life. Too long in one place with far too many men crammed together in the open seemed to be the order of the day.

Rags searched for the girls from the *Ascot* and found one, Nurse May, who was scrubbing a wound while the victim bit his lip in pain. Rags introduced her to General Hilly, and the old man turned from laser-eyed critic to soppy old grandfather in a matter of seconds. He covered her hands with his warm, mammoth palms and dropped his voice into a whisper. He asked her about her experience and praised her work. Rags had never seen that side of the boss before. The general was a chameleon, a very good actor.

The party spent the heat of the day ducking under tent flaps and talking to the wounded men, most far from home for the first time. They were hurt, homesick, and questioning their mission. One lad asked the general, "Is it worth it, sir?"

Hilly dug deep. "The Kaiser wants to enslave us. If we don't stand and fight, he will succeed. It's easy for this old man to say yes, it's worth it. But you're young and on the battlefield; it's for you to decide if it's worth it. With your long life ahead of you, you must tell me."

The soldier peered down at his bandages. "I hope so, sir."

Hilly smiled at him. "Now that you're a combat veteran, you have to tell me. What should I do when up against those Turks tomorrow?"

"Keep your head down, sir."

*Chapter Thirteen*

# Gallipoli, Mid-July 1915

NOW APPROACHING THE SHORES OF Cape Helles on Gallipoli, Major General Sir Avery Hilliard Hopewell was about to tangle with General Sir Ian Hamilton, commander of the Allied Mediterranean Expeditionary Force, whose mission was to defeat the Turkish army on the Gallipoli Peninsula, thereby allowing the Royal Navy to clear the passage to the Black Sea. In late April 1915, the initial allied force of over 100,000, which included Australian, New Zealand, Indian, and French elements, landed on several beaches on the south and west shores of the peninsula and encountered stiff resistance. Hamilton had been surprised by the presence of a well-prepared Turkish army.

At that time there was no professional military intelligence element in the British Army to assist in the planning for the invasion. Trapped on the beach at Cape Helles, deprived of Royal Naval gun support, the invasion stalled and the force had taken heavy casualties. The enemy occupied the precipitous heights where, because of the restaging at Lemnos, they had had the luxury of time to dig in and register their guns. Additionally, the Turkish army possessed internal lines of communications, good roads, and railway lines, which allowed them to rapidly concentrate troops when and where they were required in a timely fashion. That allowed the Turks to defend Gallipoli with a much smaller commitment. The Allies, on the other hand, had to pack up each time they changed their plans, load sustaining supplies, embark on ships, and transit to another invasion beach to go through the same slog to the high ground, where the Turks were there in strength. Three months into the campaign, little had been accomplished while alarming casualties were mounting from snipers and daily artillery bombardments. To quote the newspapers, "they sat and took it."

It was well known that amphibious operations required meticulous planning, the most experienced officers and troops, supply in depth, exceptional coordination with the Royal Navy, and the use of intense logistic delivery systems. Those requirements were exacerbated if the landings were opposed. Once ashore, herculean efforts were required to sustain the troops unless they could live off the land. The other variable was terrain. Gallipoli was a hostile environment. The beaches were composed of soft sand that didn't support heavy artillery and transport well. The natural cliffs and escarpments were even better defenses than man-made fortresses, providing observation and cover for enemy troops in defensive positions who therefore enjoyed a four-to-one advantage over the offense. Gallipoli had become a quagmire the British Army could ill afford.

Hilly was well aware that Hamilton had been Lord Kitchener's chief of staff during the South African campaign and that he had to tread lightly. That is why Henry Segar, Kitchener's representative, was along with him. But the first stop was Major General Aylmer Hunter-Weston, commander of the 29th British Division, which had spent the last months being pounded on the shores of Gallipoli.

AT DAWN, WITH HEADS FEELING thick and twice their normal size from the splendid evening before, Hilly, Segar, and Rags walked along the dock in near silence. The motor launch taking them out to the waiting destroyer pitched and splashed into the white caps, jarring the three slightly green passengers who were wetted down with buckets of spray. Rags thanked God he hadn't joined the navy. The man-of-war *Dunluce Castle* was stoked up and rumbling as they dragged themselves up the wooden rungs of the rope ladder that had been hung over its camouflaged side. From its current position, it would be a sixty-mile sprint at twenty-four knots to the edge of the fleet anchorage just off Cape Helles. Rag's years spent at Charterhouse, where he had toiled over the translation of Greek mythology, prepared him for this moment. Feeling quite superior, he told his companions how the Hellespont was named for Helle, a young woman who was drowned there when her stepmother plotted against her, according to the story of the Golden Fleece.

Finally arriving at a rickety dock on Cape Helles, the small party put on their beige pith helmets. This militarized domed headwear, adapted from the Indian tophi version, was designed to protect non-native heads from the killer rays of the sun, but not from hot shrapnel. Hard as rock, with meager vent holes drilled around the suntan hatband, the helmets were ubiquitous in the hot climate of the equatorial belt. Rags commented that the party looked quite authentic as they stepped onto the loose sand at the waters' edge. Their army guide, a young major from General Hamilton's staff, offered Hilly a hand as they negotiated their way out of the soft sand and onto firmer ground. The general would have shunned the help, but as he was about to put it to the major, off he tilted sideways and was caught by the elbow.

"Nasty footing, sir; everyone has the same problem until you get used to it. Then you can scamper about like one of those green lizards." Hilly had noticed them darting in and out of crushed ammunition boxes scattered about the cratered beach.

Rags couldn't help but count the interlocking shell holes that pockmarked the landscape. He became nervous and looked to the sky for incoming rounds as if that would be sufficient warning. Pausing at the sight of the debris strewn all about, Hilly muttered, "Stockpiles of brand-new steel helmets were accumulating in English depots. Why aren't they here?"

The scene on the beach was troubling. There was wreckage of knocked-out vehicles, fragments of crushed wagons, trash, rubble, and rubbish in all directions as far as the eye could see. In the lapping water interlocked flotsam and jetsam, several yards deep, lazily swung to and fro. The smell of empty food tins and rotting, broken packing filled the humid air. Men in open-front tan shirts, baggy shorts, and sodden boots wandered about carrying burdens up to the Allied positions on the closest heights or down to waiting craft that hung onto the docks for dear life, like lost immigrants.

Hilly, searching his thirty years of military memory for a similar scene, was the first to speak. "My God—what a disgrace!"

The escort officer stammered, "Sir, there isn't any place to tidy it up. We barely have room for the incoming supplies and no manpower to clear away the spoils. We tried dumping it in the harbor, but the tide brought it right back in."

Segar and Rags struggled along in their boots, which sank into the loose edges of shell holes six feet deep. They made their way toward the sparse green foliage of stubby thorn bushes and coarse, tufted grass a hundred yards from the water, and paused to look back at the bay before climbing higher. The makeshift harbor was cluttered with provisioning vessels of all description, churning up the Adriatic to a fare-thee-well. A line of Royal Naval vessels was far enough out that it took field glasses to make out exactly which they were.

Hilly asked, "With the naval guns that far out, how can they reach beyond our front lines?" While the general could plainly hear the Allies' light artillery off in the distance, the Royal Navy was silent.

"That's a problem, sir," the major offered. "If our sailors come any closer, they risk being ranged by the Turks up on the heights just beyond our front lines. So we use our own light artillery that came ashore with the landing—French 75's as a rule. They're good boys, but it's a chore to feed them ammunition up these sandy cliffs on unimproved treks—goat trails actually, sir."

Now Hilly understood the shortage of artillery ammunition and the lack of heavier guns on the heights. Direct-fire light artillery could keep the enemy back, but it couldn't provide nearly enough cover for a frontal assault on the Turkish forces up on the far heights. They were stuck.

WHEN HILLY'S PARTY REACHED THE crest of the cliffs, flat ground spread out before them. While the enemy lines were still three miles ahead, tent cities with abandoned trenches and foxholes spread out to the left and right. Their first stop was a field hospital, where they were sure to get a drink of water, as parched and foot weary as they were.

Hilly led them to the half dozen large medical tents that gave off the noxious scents of medicine, wounds, sweat, and moldering uniforms. Used to the aroma of field operations, Hilly proceeded from one tent to another while the other two held back, taking advantage of the space between the wards to catch a breath of air that seeped up from the beach. A triage element clustered casualties by type. Open lacerations were tended to and stabilized before evacuation to the hospital ship. Broken bones were splinted and waited their turn to be carried by stretcher-bearers down the slope to medical barges. Those with diseases were quarantined and treated there on the cliff. Men with direct gunshot wounds were evacuated as fast as possible to prevent septicity.

Rags understood that soldiers were wounded and killed in war—of course he did. But that knowledge hadn't prepared him for his first look at trauma on the battlefield. Hilly had paused by a young officer with a HAC badge getting prepped for the operating room. The medics were unceremoniously cutting off his clothes. A massive midriff wound was gushing blood that pooled at his belt, and every time he coughed, blood bubbled out of his open mouth. The smell from the hot body threatened to choke Rags, and he concentrated all his powers on not letting it. When the young officer was taken to the operating room and his blood-soaked uniform thrust into a bag by an attendant, Rags reached down and took the Honorable Artillery Company badge from his collar. He didn't know why he did it and was a little embarrassed by the gesture. But he wanted to remember the man as more than just a body, and an ugly, bleeding, fetid one at that. He wiped the badge off and put it in his pocket, and he thought of his classmates in France whose names would be added to the great plaque at Charterhouse the next time he visited.

Hilly's face had gone dark, and soon they moved out into the burning sun. Rags was alarmed to see the ambulance wagon that would be taking them to the battlefield. Drawn by a pair of sweating mules, the small covered wagon did provide some relief from the heat, but the cloud of dust that filtered through the floorboards was nearly as choking as the hospital's atmosphere. It was a jarring hour before the report of the guns told them they were near. Hilly ordered a halt by a cluster of white hexagonal tents. A lieutenant general's flag and set of colors were posted in front of the one in the center. A pair of armed guards snapped to attention at the sight of the insignia on Hilly's shoulders.

They were led to the commander's tent, but Hilly paused for a good minute before entering. Rags could see the effort it took Hilly to shift gears. The commander of the forces was Lieutenant General Hunter-Weston. Hunter-Bunter, as he was known, was considered a classic donkey general—an incompetent bumbler who led "lions," the brave soldiers whose lives were too often shattered by their leaders' stupidity. It was said that he lost nearly half his men at the taking of the Hellespont beach, and he was quoted as calling the enemy's sinking of the Royal Navy battleship HMS *Majestic* "a marvelous sight." Just months before, during the third battle of Krithia, Hunter-Weston had committed the reserve to the flanks, instead of the enemy's weak center as requested by his field commanders, and it cost them the victory. Segar had informed Hilly that the Brigadiers in the 29th Division no longer took orders from Hunter-Weston.

Hilly's mind was preoccupied by the major general's appalling reputation and the morning's sights—the chaotic beach and the full hospital beds. But he knew he couldn't approach Major General Sir Aylmer Hunter-Weston, KCB, Laird of Hunterston, as the grim inspector general. Hunter-Weston's position in the army was primarily due to the friends he had made along the way. He had served on both General Kitchener's and General French's staff and was a personal correspondent with King George. An imperious demeanor wouldn't do. So by the time Hilly opened the tent doors, miraculously, he had transformed himself, all hail-fellow-well-met.

The commander of the 29th British Division was leaning over a map table with a number of officers when the party strolled in. "Hilly!" He strode forward and shook his hand. "Glad to see you have survived the Gallipoli sun." Hilly smiled broadly and shook his hand vigorously. "Doggy, how are you?" Hunter-Weston had been master of hounds at Staff College, and "Doggy" was yet another of his endless nicknames. Rags had began to think that a man's incompetence rose in direct relation to the number of his nicknames.

Hilly had the foresight to talk with Hunter-Weston without the major general's subordinate staff on hand. As they settled in, Doggy, always the optimist, began. "I know there is some talk at Horse Guards about my conduct of this campaign. But I can assure you that I have taken the utmost care. Tell those fellows back on the staff, this is no walk in the woods and these aren't a bunch of Dutch farmers from the veld of South Africa. These Turks are fighters aided by members of Germany's General Staff Corps. Their heavy gun support is most competent while our Royal Naval guns, which are supposed to be supporting me, lie off afraid to risk it."

Hilly knew that was all correct and said so. "Doggy, you're spot-on; I am going to see Hamilton next to winkle out the measure of the supporting fires."

"Hilly, I was hamstrung from the start. I warned that Helles was untenable because of the loss of the element of surprise and told Hamilton to call it all off. Right from the start, my men were spread over five beaches, none of which could contribute to reinforcing the other. My span of control was far too great, far too great." Hunter-Weston shook his bald head. He was tall and thin with a magnificent, bushy, army-style mustache, and he looked as if he could have come off a tobacco card. "I could only do for those on the beach directly in front of me; the others were on their own. When I went to see Hamilton on his ship I put on a brave face. I had faith in our troops to overcome any adversity. I know that some of my subordinates claim that they requested reinforcement and more ammunition, but I never heard from them directly. I was isolated there on the beach."

Doggy went on, more intense now. "Hilly, you must understand, old chap, this operation was bigger than anything in which I've ever participated. It was all push-push-push. I had to manage five beaches simultaneously. It was an enormous task, I can tell you. Communications were a cockup. It was a bad show."

Rags thought he could see something welling up in Doggy that he dared not admit. He was in over his head, and he needed a friend at court. Despite the nearly forty years of service under his belt, too much had been asked of him. He had always been the staff ape, following the lead of others. Now he was beset—indecision, the one failure not permitted in a commander, was creeping in under the tent.

Hilly must have seen the same thing, because after another few minutes of discussion Hilly stood up and shook the major general's hand. Rags and Segar followed. "So you're on your way to see Hamilton. Take him my regards and tell him that we will get it right soon. I will break through in spite of the anomalies that have dogged my effort here in this godforsaken wilderness. It has been great to see you, old friend. Be careful and stay safe. It is a dangerous place up forward, numerous snipers looking for a big kill."

AS THE PARTY LEFT THE tent, Hunter-Weston, head down, went back to his map table. The staff filed back, sheepishly averting their eyes. Rags thought the major general was fragile, emotional; he had never seen anything like it, certainly not among the stalwarts at Horse Guards, and wondered if

Hilly saw the major general the same way. He got his answer once they were outside and Hilly buttonholed the chief of staff. He gave him a hard look.

"What's going on, Colonel? Have you been taking care of him like you should, or is there something you want to tell me?" The chief pulled the party out of hearing range of the tent. "I don't know, General. Ever since he was elevated to Corps Commander there has been a marked change in the boss. I think he's overcome with the responsibility; he has lost his bottle. He dithers, seems confused at times, has lapses of memory over things he had a grasp of only hours before. He is uncomfortable with the troops and the staff, withdraws when he should be up at the front. He's becoming a different person, hard to get through to, changes his mind at the worst possible times and countermands decisions. Frankly, I am worried about his health. I see a stagger in his step and slur in his speech."

Hilly nodded. "What's the answer, Colonel? You see him every day."

"Sir, operations are at a standstill. We are taking casualties for no reason. We're unable to push the enemy any farther with the resources committed. It is time to do something else. We either reinforce in a major way or cut and run. I know you, sir; that is my reading of the situation."

Hilly paused, kicked a stone at his boot. Surveyed the command center and turned back to the chief of staff. "I understand. Thank you for your frankness, Colonel." Hilly stepped back, a signal for the colonel to salute and withdraw.

Hilly blew out a long breath and turned toward the waiting wagon. "Come on, lads, we have work to do."

## Chapter Fourteen

# Gallipoli, July–August 1915

WHILE HILLY AND HIS PARTY MET with Hunter-Weston, the staff major had preceded them off the heights on horseback and was waiting at the dock when the refreshed party arrived by wagon. He had also dispatched a fast motorboat to HMS *Queen Elizabeth*, General Hamilton's headquarters, advising that the inspector general was on the way and would surely be there for supper. He hadn't used a radio. As a result of an oversight, army radios were not compatible with naval frequencies. He hadn't had time to find the navy beach master, who could talk to fleet elements on his private communications link.

The wagon ride down the rutted trail had been rough. Now the party trudged over the wet, compacted beach and boarded the admiral's waiting launch that bobbed in the water as its cloud of light grey fumes rose in the humid air. They tracked a good deal of sand across the highly polished deck, but not a word was said; rank had its privilege. Once seated on plush, red-velvet-covered benches, the craft pulled out, sounding its horn in a series of beeps notifying all around that a bigwig was aboard. The *Queen Elizabeth* lay several safe miles out in the anchorage, where it was surrounded by lesser men-of-war. Rags had never seen a battleship up close before and found it was monstrous yet stately. A metal stair was fixed in place, an improvement over the destroyer's primitive ladder. Climbing slowly up the massive steel side, five stories, he was relieved to reach the open metal door carved in the ship's side.

Once they entered the *Queen Elizabeth*'s A-deck square, a line of dress blue–clad sailors were whistled to attention as the ship's captain stepped forward to greet Hilly in the best tradition of the Royal Navy. Carruthers' boys had moved the party's kit after they left Lemnos, and Rags was taken first to his own meager cabin, bunking with his escort in a nine-by-nine cell much like one found in His Majesty's prisons. Leaving his cap behind, he then proceeded to Segar's lodging, much posher than his own, and then on to the flag accommodations high up in a walnut-paneled stateroom to check on Hilly.

The inspector general was conferring with his War Office confidant over a cold, sweet pink gin. Invented by the Royal Navy in the early 1800s, the relaxing beverage was considered a cure for seasickness. It was just the civilized pick-me-up the party needed after days rooting about in the heat and hills of the Gallipoli Peninsula. As Rags and Segar joined the men and stretched out in the upholstered chairs, Hilly made it clear he wanted their honest assessment of the operation before he met with General Hamilton. Confident in his own judgment, he knew the value of letting subordinates talk freely, knowing that there might be some insight, some detail, that only they had noticed.

"Rags, my boy, tell me your thoughts. After everything you've seen together, what is the one thing that is absolutely undeniable?"

Rags didn't hesitate. "Gallipoli is a hell of a place to fight a war, sir. There is nothing in our favor. The heat, humidity, rugged terrain, bugs, disease, to say nothing of the sheer desolation. . . . It will be most difficult to relate that to someone who has never been here." Rags glanced first at Uncle Hilly and then at Segar for some hint of approval, in hopes that his comment was worthy of the level of discussion.

Segar put his glass down for a refill and leaned back. "I don't know how they do it, those soldiers, day after day, night after night. They must know in their hearts it's futile. How can they dash themselves against the wall while their comrades fall beside them in a relentless scrabble for a few yards of dirt? Yet they never falter; they obey orders."

Hilly muttered at his boots, "They're just boys. And we can't even get them those damn steel helmets rusting away in the London depot."

"I wonder," Segar continued, "what would their lives be like at home if they had never volunteered? Would they enlist again if needed? Twenty years from now, would they send *their* sons?"

"I have seen similar wastelands in the Sudan and South Africa and wondered, as you have, why anyone would want to fight for the place," Hilly said. "It would be far better to just leave it be. But there is a bigger picture, and we can't afford to miss the opportunity to sew up this end of the Mediterranean. What I can't understand is the amateurism of this whole fiasco." His voice began to rise and both his companions knew what was coming. They had heard bits and pieces of it for days. "Given the best troops, excellent weapons, and an armada at their fingertips, how could senior officers with years of experience and extensive education display such faulty, idiotic judgment on such a consistent basis? They don't seek intelligence on the terrain or the enemy. They appear detached from daily activities. At the command level they allow the chips to fall where they may as if the Turks will give up because of their mere presence. One brigade commander asked me, 'Why don't the fellows just give up?' I could have throttled him. 'Would you fight for the Outer Hebrides?' I asked. Damn idiots. What's happened to the British Army?"

"When do you meet with General Hamilton, sir?" Rags asked.

"All too soon—and not nearly soon enough," Hilly replied.

ONE HOUR LATER RAGS REJOINED the conclave in the war room. He had never seen so many brass hats in one confined space before. The lowest rank was colonel and there were only two of them. It seemed to him an entire platoon of generals and admirals were clustered around the map table. Hilly was conspicuous, still clad in his wilted suntans from the day's inspection among the dress uniforms of the other flag officers. Hilly had requested that they get right to it while he was fresh from the battlefield, and General Hamilton seemed put off by Hilly's casual dress. Hamilton was known for his fuss and feathers, and perhaps Hilly was sticking a finger in his eye, ever so gently.

Rags slipped in and took his place next to Segar, who had withdrawn out of the line of fire of the brewing battle. The operations director, Major General Bantree-Slack, was already his enumerating his excuses: "Sir, we weren't given enough men, materials or time . . . the only thing we have in quantity is Turks! And they are not accommodating our . . ."

Hilly was having none of it and cut him dead: "Is this a war or am I dreaming, General? Everything with you is *they are too many, these aren't enough, those are not my problems*—when are you going to take responsibility? My impression, General, is that the staff preparations, so vital in an amphibious operation, were misplaced, resulting in half measures carefully disguised with excuses. You are a staff college graduate, aren't you? Most unprofessional—you are responsible, not the Navy Board, not the Royal Navy, not even the War Office and certainly not the soldiers who you send to their deaths. If everything was not in place, you should've heeded Hunter-Weston's recommendation and aborted the plan then and there before you turned this into a colossal cockup."

The gloves were off. In the few months that Rags had sat at his boss's feet, he had never seen anything like this outburst. Back at Horse Guards and Whitehall, conflict was underplayed. It would have been bad form to lose one's temper in the courtly atmosphere of headquarters, where the golden rule was to never back colleagues into a corner, to always allow them to save face. One would yield, for the moment, rather than create a kerfuffle that would echo through the halls of power for months and damage delicate reputations.

Rags saw a slight curl of a smile at the corner of Segar's mouth. Hilly's tirade was directed not only at the expedition staff but also for Segar's benefit, who would pass it on, word for word, to Kitchener on their return. Rags was beginning to learn of and respect the depth of expertise of Major General Hilliard Hopewell. He was proud to be in his company and to share the experience. He thought how lucky he was while so many of his friends and schoolmates were mired in the mud of France.

The operations manager was shaking with equal parts anger and embarrassment, but Hamilton stepped forward with steam fairly rising from his ears. "Hilly, I don't think you've understood the true direction of my command. We admit to some miscalculations, but this is not France. It's a dark corner of the world we have not experienced before—we're groping our way forward. How dare you lob these accusations at us."

Hilly dropped his voice to a near-whisper, field rank be damned; no one talked down to the inspector general of His Majesty's forces, by God. "How can you justify the loss of one-third of your strength in the face of a tin pot army lead by mercenaries on a strip of land the size of Yorkshire? You've allowed the navy to put you off without a whisper, losing the most vital gun support that could have reduced the enemy to quivering peasants. You sat out here on your bum, out of sight, out of range, uninterested. You've handed command in the field to subordinates and then turned your back on them. I have yet to see anything that resembles a coordinated plan of attack, supporting fires or the re-entry of fresh troops or, most important, the follow-on of supplies. *Neglect* is the only word I can find to fit your situation." Hilly paused for effect. "General, what the hell *are* you doing on a battleship?"

LATE THAT AFTERNOON RAGS WAS about to enjoy his first moments of privacy the entire day. After his confrontation with Hamilton, Hilly had sat down with him and Segar and gone through the notes Kitchener had given to him on the launch, weeks before, off Woolwich Arsenal dock. Rags left for his quarters below the water line in the bowels of the great metal ship. Never paying a great deal of attention to direction, led by a crew member here there and everywhere, he suddenly found himself lost. Up one ladder and down another, around a corner down a companion way . . . they all looked the same. The Royal Navy jargon stenciled to the bulkheads was gibberish. He didn't know the top foremast from the lee waste deck. When he asked a passing crewmember, he pointed up and then down and around two decks to the fore companion way. Rags suddenly found himself on deck, where sailors were washing the rough planked deck on their knees with bricks. In desperation he climbed ladders to the flying bridge, where a young officer was practicing shooting the sun with a sexton. "Mate, can you give me a hand?"

"I'm not a mate, I am a midshipman! If you want a mate, you'll have to go below." And so it began again, this time with success a quarter hour later.

Taking advantage of the rare moments of solitude at last in his cozy cabin, Rags started to compile his impressions of the trip. He realized the Germans knew far more about the state of the Gallipoli campaign than he did, since they were actually on the field with the Turks opposite Hamilton's forces. But he also knew that his mother would want him to convey the state of the British command and the general lines of their thinking. The notes he made now would have to be meaningful to him but innocuous to anyone at Horse Guards who might come upon them. He knew that Mildred would go through everything, pigeon-holing any papers into the filing cabinets that lined her inner office. She regarded every piece of paper as if it were meant for the national archive. As he tried out phrases in his mind, he wondered, not for the first time, if his communiqués were making his father proud of him, if he got any pleasure from his son's service.

Rags thought there were three or four key points that would interest his father. First, there was the attempt to disguise the desert training as a distraction meant to throw off the German intelligence. Then the inadequate supply of artillery shells that turned out to be more of a transport issue than a manufacturing failure. It mimicked the problem that had surfaced in the London press about support in France. The lack of qualified staff officers from India and among the Anzac corps, and the eternal rivalry between the Royal Navy and regular army. It appeared most troubling to the war effort and the Germans could play on that. But what the Germans would most be interested in was Hilly's recommendation for future operations on the Gallipoli Peninsula, which had not yet surfaced. And that was a point of intelligence he would have to be very careful about.

That was the key, he thought; it must be handled with care. Rags was no longer a schoolboy, and he was dabbling in matters far beyond his comfort zone. Perhaps a real spy would have better performed the role in which his father cast him. He possessed no spycraft. He wasn't sure what a professional spy's report on a complex matter should be. Yet he must operate by trial and error, which was not at all what was required. Thrown into what seemed like a lark in spring, sneaking bits and pieces, was not enough in the summer of 1915.

HENRY FRASER SEGAR CVO (Commander of the Royal Victorian Order) sat at the ship's bar and savored the fine Portuguese port in front of him. He was surely on his way to a knighthood—a K, as those in line for one called it. Two years before, his elevation had come in recognition of distinguished personal service to the monarch. As a career officer of the English civil service, Henry advised the royal family on the care and investment of their enormous fortune. Some believed that the king might be the richest man in the world, if only they could count it all. Years before, a young Segar had been recruited right out of King's College Cambridge upon securing a first-class degree in economics. In the years since, he had shown that he could master any subject to which he turned. That was his great strength. Henry had a most inquisitive mind and he relished a challenge. Thus he had examined the royal family's holdings in Canada and presented a plan to consolidate farming and ranching assists in the provinces of Manitoba, Saskatchewan, and Alberta. As with the consolidation of the land in Scotland centuries before, a higher level of income resulted. Most British subjects probably had no idea that the Crown owned vast portions of western Canada.

For the mission with Kitchener's Ministry of War, Henry had been seconded from St. James's Palace, where he specialized in the collection and distribution of war funds. In particular, he was instrumental in the campaign to sell war bonds. Years before, he had become embroiled in the British government's management of its considerable interest in the Suez Canal. Now a senior member in good standing of the civil service, he held unique qualifications. Henry was a careful observer and sound advisor. He preferred his usual medium grey three-piece scratchy wool suit, but in the hot climate he was forced to become more conspicuous in a nearly white two-piece linen suit, white shirt with detachable collar and grey tie that hung loosely at his belt.

That afternoon his light blue eyes had darted about the room, sizing up the row of generals the boss was lecturing. Thin, one might even say gaunt, the bespectacled Scotsman sat upright with a portmanteau on his lap, taking notes. A Presbyterian, not particularly interested in food or drink, he never stopped counting the cost of war, in both men and resources. Henry had spent his time on the voyage to Turkey reading the three trunks of books he had put aboard on the Ottoman Empire's political, economic, and military history. From his analysis, he believed the Turks' military prowess was grossly underestimated. It was true that the kingdom had descended into corruption and was restricted from operating in the modern financial world because of Islam's restrictive usury laws. However, they still maintained a character of will that was far better focused than that of Western European thrones. Perhaps, Henry mused, the toll in this war will be taken from those thrones.

That afternoon he had inwardly applauded at Hilly's dressing-down of the navy command. He found the military to be showy, wasteful, indulgent, and pig-headed. Like Kitchener, he cared little for regimental tradition and had supported the minister's recruiting program that centered not on expansion of the regular army but on volunteers from the shires, formed into divisions that could easily be broken down after the war. He thought a new army, one free of a long, tiresome history, might escape the meat grinder of modern machine-gun war. Henry's demeanor was conservative, and he often thought his colleagues might be shocked at how radical his thoughts about the military actually were.

During the map exercise he concluded that the whole campaign was a fool's errand. Even the alternative approaches discussed after the meeting failed to take into consideration the enemy's intentions. Henry Segar was an experienced military aide, but he was also an academic, and he knew that the Turks and German allies constituted a highly educated warrior class. The British Army continued to underestimate them with every new plan they floated. As a civil servant, he tended to be dismissed by the military brass. As an observer, he tended to watch and listen. At least he would be able to bear testimony to what really happened when the history was written.

AS BEFORE ON LEMNOS, a cease-fire was called with the striking of the dinner gong. With the change of uniform into short crimson mess jackets, the mood had softened, but tension still hung over the company. Hilly was seated in the place of honor at Hamilton's right elbow, and they spoke of old campaigns and even older friends. Rags sat at a side table, along with the younger staff, like children at Christmas dinner. Segar had excused himself and was served in his cabin at his own request, feigning exhaustion, common among civilians, it was thought.

Rags used the time to question other aides about the effectiveness of the general staff. The scuttlebutt of aides, as ever, betrayed the higher-ups, despite their bars and stripes. Tonight the talk centered around one man: Hunter-Weston. Some had heard Major General Egerton, commander of the 52nd Infantry Division, say that there was no discussion of the invasion plan—Hunter-Weston had simply enunciated what Egerton called his "positively wicked" plan, full stop. Another had heard Hunter-Weston describe an action that took hundreds of casualties as "bloodying his pups." The aides traded snorts of derision and grunts of disgust.

A communications officer on Hamilton's staff said that Hamilton had little interest how Hunter-Weston and the staff were running the invasion beach, and all agreed that the commanding general was concerned with his reputation and future posts. He had, in fact, been looking forward to Hilly's arrival and planned to impress him, hoping to be moved to a more prestigious assignment, to the "real war." He had let it be known in the mess that Kitchener was a good friend who was looking out for his welfare and that he had been promised a command in France once this sideshow was concluded. The aides were dumbfounded by his overweening self-regard. In the midst of what was starting to look like the greatest disaster of the war, Hamilton had pronounced that "things were going bloody well, all things considered."

A FEW DAYS LATER, RAGS was surprised to see Hilly back in his usual high spirits at breakfast. Hilly turned to Rags and Segar, and the source of his good cheer became apparent. "You two intrepid hikers will be glad to learn that our toil on the heights of the Helles was not in vain. After our private talk yesterday, the commanding general found that Hunter-Weston has been suffering from—of all things—sunstroke and will be embarked aboard hospital ship *Mauretania* for treatment and evacuation. I expect he'll enjoy an honored retirement. It's sure to go down well with the troops." He smiled broadly, remembering Segar was a total civilian and, like most, had preconceived ideas of the army's practices from newsmen who shared Segar's uninformed status. "You see, Segar, the army isn't as daft as you might think, even under these trying times."

Segar smiled back but countered: "After convalescence, I wouldn't be surprised to find him back in harness—one grade higher, I would expect."

"Nonsense," Hilly scoffed. "Now up you go, lads. I've got news. Birdwood has plans for his troops, and we've been invited to observe. Let's go see our Australian cousins."

## Chapter Fifteen

# Gallipoli, August 1915

THE AUSTRALIAN AND NEW ZEALAND ARMY CORPS—familiarly known as Anzac—was a cohesive clan led by Lieutenant General William Birdwood. On April 25, 1915, the day of the five-beach landing of Hunter-Weston's VIII Corps at Cape Helles, Anzac had been sent farther north, on the Aegean side of the Gallipoli Peninsula. Birdwood intended to lead them across the peninsula at its narrowest point, Gabatepe, cutting east behind the Turks.

As with every operation at Gallipoli, the maps had been poor and the planning poorer. Anzac had disembarked at a small cove a mile north of their intended landing place in darkness. Waiting there was the Turkish 57th Infantry Regiment under the command of Lieutenant Colonel Mustafa Kemal. Segar's belief that the army had underestimated the Turks was never more spot-on. The Allies had been unable to hide their preparations at Lemnos, and Kemal was able to predict with frightening exactness their likely landing sites. He was a passionate commander who told his soldiers, "I do not order you to fight; I order you to die. In the time which passes until we die, other troops and commanders can come forward and take our places." These were the descendants of the dauntless Janissaries who raked the medieval world and conquered nation-states as far west as Spain. But the Allied commanders seemed to expect a cakewalk.

In the main attack on the Helles' five beaches—known as beaches V, W, X, Y, and Z—the Turks had been strong enough to contain, but not defeat, the Allied troops. At one beach, of the first 200 Allied soldiers to disembark, only 21 made it to shore. At W beach, 60 percent of troops were killed; at V beach, 70 percent. That morning, landing in the dark, Anzac had quickly become disoriented and scattered, and Kemal further chopped up their forces. Anzac lost nearly 2,000 of their 16,000 landing soldiers that first day. Like the other attacks, at dawn the next day they withdrew to the cove where they had landed, which quickly became known as Anzac Cove, and there they stayed for nearly a month.

In May the Turks launched a major attack of 42,000 against the 17,000 Anzacs dug in near the cove. No ground was exchanged, but the Turkish army took 13,000 casualties while Anzac suffered 468. From May until July fighting continued at a high pace with no exchange of positions while casualties from sniper fire and artillery never ceased. Attrition, for the British, was not a good game to play since their reinforcements and supplies came by slow boat a month away and the enemy needed only to board fresh troops on a two-hour rail ride. As a result, the Gallipoli campaign, intended to break the stalemate of trench warfare on the Western Front, had become yet another quagmire.

ON THE MORNING OF AUGUST SIXTH, General Hamilton escorted Hilly's party to the dock to embark for Anzac Cove. A massive attack known as the August Offensive was being launched that day, but Hamilton declined to accompany them to the cove. "I continue to believe, as the force commander, that my place is here in support, on board the *Queen*. We'll be steaming after you to get in position to assist in the whole enterprise, not just Anzac Cove." He said this forcefully, to emphasize his position as commander. "I'll remain with the naval bombardment Johnnies giving those Turkish louts what they deserve."

Hilly knew he needn't concern himself with the general's safety in the midst of eighteen battleships, twelve cruisers, twenty-two destroyers, and eight submarines. He was more concerned about the Anzac soldiers conducting the operation that day. Wanting to pin Hamilton down for the record *before* the battle, Hilly asked him, "Tell me, after four months on these hostile shores, what are your expectations for today's operation?"

But Hamilton hadn't gotten where he was by falling prey to the twin dangers of honesty and clarity. Hamilton side-stepped the question and deftly turned the focus: "I must admit I've been surprised by the level of grit in these Turkish fellows. Horse Guards hadn't an inkling of what we were to face on these shores. Only a few civilian tour guides briefed me while we were preparing back in Cairo, and the Royal Navy had bugger-all to show from flight reconnaissance. We were under the impression that the Turks weren't a modern, committed force. I sent word to the troops in the invasion fleet that the Turkish soldiers as a rule manifest their desire to surrender by holding their rifle butt upward and by waving cloths or rags of any color. An actual white flag should be regarded with the utmost suspicion, as a Turkish soldier is most likely to possess everything of color. Nothing white. Easterners, you know; they favor bright color combinations."

Hilly, with equal agility, a common trait among generals, turned the conversation back to the offensive. "I expect the troops will do okay. The commanders here have learned much over the last month. Defeat is always a good teacher." And with that the little party stepped on the boat to take them to Anzac Cove.

IT WAS A BRIGHT, HOT forenoon as the single-stack naval corvette dashed to the VIP dock at Anzac Cove. Rags had his sea legs and stood forward with a grip on the leading gun turret, knees like rubber to match the pitch and roll of the speeding craft. The vessel's young captain had lent his glasses to Hilly and Segar while he described the gun action that crackled all about.

Hamilton had divulged only the barest outlines of his August Offensive. Anzac would launch attacks at Sari Bair Ridge, while the IX Corps would simultaneously attack Suvla Bay to the north. Every soldier and sailor within the expeditions' realm would engage the enemy. Nothing was left in reserve. From their position on board the corvette, Hilly, Rags, and Segar could see Royal Navy shells being lobbed over the beach and into the Turkish hills beyond. The counter battery fire from the Turks rattled Rags as rounds passed overhead and splashed down between the lines of Royal Naval men-of-war.

Rags wished he were on board one of the low-flying naval reconnaissance biplanes above them. Instead he looked up at Turkish projectiles of consider-able size that were screaming down all across the grey line of Royal Navy ships lateral to the beach. Shells splashed down, sending plumes of white water that erupted into the air as if from a mighty whale. Rags expected at any moment for the enemy to find the range and strike a ship. Thick black smoke belched from the stacks of the phalanx of British warships, partially obscuring the ships' ever-changing position.

Ducking under the Turkish barrage, their craft, an insignificant dot in a boiling sea, sneaked to the beach. Rags had never heard the whiz of live can-non fire as it passed overhead at high speed. He couldn't see them no matter how hard he tried. His fears were assuaged a bit when the boatswain mate told him, "If you can hear 'em, they can't hurt you; they are already gone by. It's the one you never hear that kills ya." Rags smiled and said, "That's a great comfort, mate. Does that also apply on land as well?" The boatswain gave him a cheeky grin before setting off to supervise the ship's approach to shore. Soon Rags had disembarked on the beach and was watching the ship reverse engines to make its escape.

The three found themselves dumped on the sodden beach just below the Anzac main camp, where a young staff escort, armed with only a service revolver, led them to the commander's HQ. Hilly and Rags wore their light khaki field uniforms while Segar had dressed in civilian clothes in hopes that they might provide him some modicum of immunity. That was until their escort officer, who pointed them to the staff car, remarked, "Takes a brave man to wear a white suit on the beach today. Kudos, sir."

Rags was eager to meet William Riddell Birdwood. Birdwood had been born in India to a British military family and didn't set foot in England until he was a teenager. A graduate of the Royal Military College at Sandhurst, he secured a King's commission before his first posting to the northwest frontier of India. Birdwood campaigned with Kitchener during the Boer War, and he was known for his heroics in the field. Like so many Gallipoli campaigners never before in charge of a large formation, he was appointed to command in combat in spite of his lack of experience. Kitchener, wary of the unorthodox soldiers from Australia and New Zealand, just as he had been about the Welsh, felt it would take a vigorous, brave, and creative soldier to earn their respect. He chose Birdwood against the advice of both Hamilton and Horse Guards. Rags thought that Hamilton's opposition only burnished Birdwood's sterling reputation.

The car stopped halfway up the beach at a dugout where Birdwood's colors flapped in the wind along with his laundry. Prominent on top of his dugout, his washing was strung out on wire hanging between radio antennas. Birdwood evidently preferred to bivouac in the center of his formation, no matter how exposed or pock-marked and rudimentary the site. Rags felt an uncommon emotion at the sight of the commander's humble headquarters; he decided it might be respect.

Bouncing out of the tiny, dark bunker doorway, framed by leaking sandbags, Birdwood emerged with hand outstretched, waving off Hilly's salute. He was considerably undersized for a warrior, in Rags' opinion, though Birdwood's pressed uniform and shiny boots were a credit to his batman, given his surroundings. "Glad to meet you, General! His Lordship sent me a note from London about your visit, and how glad I am to have you here today of all days. We've got 'em where we want 'em. Right, boys?" He looked to Rags and Segar—a change from the usual indifference other flag officers showed them—and shook their hands in turn, shepherding them down into the underground bunker. He spoke with a strange accent made up of English, Indian patois, and Australian slang, and Rags' sense of respect started to break out into something very similar to *liking*. This was the first friendly meeting the party had gotten since arriving in the theater, and Rags chuckled inwardly at how rare the sensation was.

In the bunker there was the ubiquitous map board, dotted with colored map pins crisscrossed with unit boundary lines. Small portable field tables, in rows, were linked together with hand-printed signs arranged on the front. They organized the various functions of Anzac and were manned by shift officers around the clock. Field telephones were hooked with communications wire that hung like cobwebs from the ceiling. A radio crackled with reports while message clerks clattered by. The floor was made of thick planks with cracks wide enough to sweep the sand away.

Hilly was surprised to find the general's headquarters so close to the perimeter, well within range of even light enemy artillery. "Rather close quarters to the line, General. Ever take a hit?"

"All the time, old chap." He pointed through a gun slit over toward the bay and said, "See my swimming hole? Take a dip every morning and afternoon, you know. The Turks like it too. They shell me, a kind of friendly gun salute, you know. Haven't hit me yet." He winked. "Just don't tell the wife."

Soon the party gathered around the map board and Birdwood laid out the details of the day's operation. Scouts had stepped out of camp early while the sun was still low. Engaged on the slopes above the beach, where the terrain had defeated them before, things were looking good, according to the briefing officer. Hilly studied the map while half listening. He was disturbed at the overlay tracings of undulating terrain and deep gullies. Not only was there a steady rise toward the Turkish main line of defense but the ground was convoluted into cuts and ravines, traps—killing grounds. Hilly stopped the briefer. "Tell me about the undergrowth, Major. What do you see above the front blade of a rifle sight?"

The young officer was taken aback by the specificity of the question and hesitated. Hilly narrowed his eyes. "Have you been out there on the ground yourself?"

Birdwood, however, was too good a commander to let his staff be bullied or unprepared. "General, all my staff officers have served on the line, including myself. The terrain fooled us at first. It looked rather open, but it is anything but welcoming. In addition to the gorges and gaps, the cover provided by the scrub undergrowth favors the Turks. In addition, attacking uphill holds its hazards, as you well know. The Turks have dug in and are therefore hidden behind tall grasses, piled rocks, and thorny shrubs the height of a man. Yet they have to be obliterated—root, leaf, and branch." It was the last thing Hilly wanted to hear. Soldiers fighting for their homeland were always the worst kind of opponent, and it sounded as if the Turkish troops were primed. He pondered the advice given by Hamilton at the start of the campaign, that the Turks "surrender with rifle butts in the air."

The briefing officer jumped back in. "Sir, on the beach we have the advantage with our marksmanship and accurate naval gunfire. But up in the hills it is a far different story. They have a four-to-one advantage in their defensive array of trench lines, falling back in order, one prepared position after the other. The German advisors are expert at that craft. We've been knocking against it for months with little progress while sustaining high casualty lists. One very promising note is the high morale. It is the sergeants who are our backbone and sustain our resolve. But I must admit, it's like pulling on an elastic band: the Turks spring back time and again."

Rags couldn't help but admire the officer's analysis of the field conditions, so different from the amorphous generalities and excuses on board Hamilton's ship and on Lemnos. Hilly's even tone showed Rags that he felt the same, but the IG still pushed a bit: "How does this maneuver differ from the past ones, which have been so bloody and inconclusive?"

Birdwood took the pointer and indicated the main sites of the offensive on the massive map on the bunker's back wall. "Our troops have been stuck since April—Anzac at Anzac Cove on the western shore of the peninsula and the British and French at Cape Helles in the south. The Turks are holding us down from their position on Sari Bair Ridge, just north of Anzac Cove—it's the highest point on the peninsula, and they're picking off the Anzacs like pigeons. We have to take that ridge, Hilly, or we'll still be here a year from now. So—this afternoon my Anzacs will attack simultaneously at Lone Pine to capture the 400 Plateau and from the Fisherman's Hut just north of Anzac Cove to make their way to Sari Bair Ridge. Lone Pine is a diversion, and there'll be a second diversionary front in Cape Helles. They should prevent the Turks from sending reinforcements to Sari Bair. As well and most importantly, Stopford's IX Corps will land at Suvla Bay and attack north of Sari Bair after nightfall. If all goes well, Anzac will have the ridge and the IXth will have the hills around Suvla Plain."

Here Birdwood turned to Hilly. "You ask what is different, sir. We'll only have to contend with the force we know and not be concerned with the arrival of reserves. Our task is to our front." He snapped the tip of his long pointer hard against the map. "If we can break through just here," tapping the map at a crossroads, "and I think we can, at that point we can bisect the peninsula and cut the Turkish forces in two. God willing."

The main Anzac offensive was slated to start late at 2:30 p.m. Hilly wanted badly for this to work, but he was skeptical. The surprise offensive that turned out not to be a real surprise, the diversionary bait that failed to draw off Turkish forces . . . It all sounded too much like April 1915. "Kemal wasn't fooled the first time, General. Is it really worth trying again?"

Birdwood rested his hands on his hips and gave a long exhalation through his mustache. "We'll find out today, won't we?"

THE OFFENSIVE STARTED THAT AFTERNOON, August 6, with the troop movements at Cape Helles and Lone Pine. Rags and Segar, neither of whom were horsemen, remained at Anzac Cove with medical aid station workers while Hilly accompanied Birdwood forward with the divisions. Hilly had joined such long columns of troops many times before; it was a soldier's lot. The scouts, light as feathers, were in front, followed by trudging, over-burdened troops, and trailed by mule-drawn wagons, artillery limbers leading heavy cannons whose narrow steel wheels cut into the sand, refusing to follow willingly. A mile-high dust plume accompanied them and identified their intention to the Turks who watched from the heights, sun glinting off the polished lenses of their field glasses. Hilly knew what the enemy was doing. They were counting—men, guns, and ammo wagons—and identifying regiments, comparing it all to the order of battle they had taken from British newspaper reports. They had chapter and verse before the first frontal attack.

The armored Rolls-Royce that Hilly and the commander rode in had a small machine turret behind the driver and in front of their padded, open leather seats. A strange contraption, it was of little protection or use other than identifying its passengers as a high-value target. All uphill, the road became a track and then petered out at the base of a high ridge where the troops fanned out and awaited orders. Hilly left General Birdwood and struck out with Major Willis, the white commander of a Gurkha company. With the exception of the officers, the troops were all Nepalese soldiers in the service of the King. Hilly knew well their reputation as fierce fighters and believed his best chance of survival was within their ranks.

Back at the cove, Rags planted himself at the bedsides of bandaged soldiers to write letters home to mothers and girlfriends. While safe out of gun range, he heard its rattle and comforted the blooded veterans as best he could. Outside in rows like cordwood lay those beyond harm, covered in dusty sheets. Rags and Henry woke the next morning to the news that the operation at Suvla Bay conducted by the IX Corps had begun the night before.

Rags knew the IX Corps was intended to relieve the Anzacs and allow them to finish the job. But Segar was skeptical. At the helm of the IXth was Lieutenant General Sir Frederick Stopford, KCMG, son of the Earl of Courtown, Grenadier Guardsman, Knight Commander of St. Michael & St. George. Known primarily as a general staff officer in Egypt and the Second Boer War, his only previous command was as commanding general of the Brigade of Guards in London, responsible for the security of the royal family. Over the objections of General Hamilton, the sixty-two-year-old was appointed by Lord Kitchener to command the IX Corps at Gallipoli.

The full details of the Suvla Bay landing began to emerge as the day wore on. On August 6, as the IXth made their way toward the landing spot, Stopford had chosen to remain on board his command ship, the sloop HMS *Jonquil*, which was at anchor offshore. The IXth attacked after nightfall as planned, but this proved to be an inconvenient time for its commanding officer. Rags heard from his network of aides that Stopford had simply gone to sleep at his usual bedtime, leaving his soldiers and officers to their own devices. On hearing that disgraceful tidbit, Rags began his usual inward scoffing at the celebrated English military prowess, but then he thought of Birdwood, his morning swims and his unpretentious quarters. Those button-front shorts hanging from the radio antennas.

For two more days Rags and Segar watched the new casualties arrive and wondered if Hilly would be returning as one. They were beyond relieved when the IG trudged in on August 8. In his early fifties, Hilly had exhausted himself while attempting to maintain a position within the Gurkha ranks as they scuttled between the rocks like angry ants. He found he couldn't keep up and didn't dare get behind where he was alone and liable to be captured. It was a dilemma solved when a passing ammunition train of camels crossed behind their evening bivouac. Dropping their loads, Hilly climbed to his ten-foot perch and held on for dear life as they loped downhill to the base camp in the dark. His first words to Rags as dawn broke bright behind him were "Never again will I be able to look at a camel. The only way off was to fall off. You know, Rags, I would have rather stayed behind and been killed than to do that again."

In the morning a liaison officer reported that the IX Corps had not been able to penetrate the Turkish-held hills and were broadly engaged on the beach. Birdwood arrived back at base camp and confirmed the bad news: while they had had some success at Lone Pine, the Allies were taking heavy casualties and Hunter-Weston's corps were stymied, unable to increase his fires because of ammunition shortages. Worse news was to come: Birdman took Hilly aside to report that after Hilly had left, the Gurkha regiment had been accidentally targeted by a heavy Royal Naval gunfire barrage. "I must tell you that Captain Willis and the majority of his command are listed as casualties and that the regiment has been withdrawn with 60 percent dead due to friendly fire." Stunned, Hilly slowly wandered to the back of the briefing area where Segar and Rags were seated. He didn't speak but sat and waved off an orderly who approached with a cup of coffee.

"The Gurkhas are gone. What can I say . . . I have seen it in every campaign. The battlefield is a dangerous place; still we think we can manage it. All the schools, all the experience, all the valor, all the planning and good intentions, and yet we pay over and over with the lives of the innocent. Why can I never get used to it?"

Rags got out a few words of condolence, unsure of how to react to the stalwart Hilly's devastation. Feeling wretched, he looked at Segar for some direction, who took up the thread of conversation. "What of the IXth, sir?"

"The IXth is in tatters," Hilly said. "The liaison officer told me that the IX Corps was made up of Kitchener's new battalions from the shires. The shire soldiers are untrained and have no previous experience of combat. When the enemy pulled back, they simply stopped in place. Regulars would have pursued up the slopes and into the hills. But these lads had no idea what to do, and God knows that Stopford, napping away under his blankets, was no help." For a moment Hilly looked like he would say more, but then he stood. Without a word more, he walked to the nearest tent and found an empty bed.

OVER THE NEXT DAYS GALLIPOLI continued to defeat the Allies, as it had from the start. Division after division perished from all the same operational flaws that had dogged them from the first offensive in April: insufficient support, foolhardy command, ignorance of the terrain and of their enemy.

General Hamilton had remained impounded on board the *Queen*. Hunter-Weston's offensive was too little, too late. The main attack of 16,000 Anzac infantry yielded only a brief occupation of Lone Pine and Chunuk Fair. Losses were heavy, and at times both sides, low on ammunition, found themselves locked in hand-to-hand combat armed only with bayonets. Often the Turks attacked at night in massive suicide charges, screaming "*Allah!*" Worst of all was that, because of poor communications and coordination, Royal Naval gunfire had landed on other Anzac formations as it had on the Gurkha regiment. It was said that the Anzac troops, knowing they were being hit by friendly fire, "streamed off the hill like a crowd leaving a football match."

By the end of the offensive, the lines had returned to their original positions, with the Anzacs on the beach and the Turks on the heights. The Mediterranean Expeditionary Force—MEF—once manned by 410,000 soldiers, recorded 213,000 either killed or wounded. It was unprecedented in modern warfare. The Turkish losses were slightly larger.

By the end of August, Rags, Segar, and Hilly were on the hospital ships ferrying 22,000 of the MEF wounded to safety. Soon they would be bound for Egypt, Rome and England. Some were relieved and repaired while so many others could only look forward to a life of pain and disfigurement.

On deck watching Gallipoli recede from view, Hilly buried his head in his hands. "What am I going to tell Kitchener?"

Segar filled the silence. "Tell the old man the truth. That's why we're here. No one else will, you know that. It will be sugar-coated by Hamilton's staff. Even the newspapers won't touch it. It must be stopped. It is time."

## Chapter Sixteen

# Alexandria and Rome, August 1915

THE STORY OF THE MODERN steam-powered Royal Navy was written by one man, John Arbuthnot "Jackie" Fisher. A small man born in Ceylon to British parents, he was the dynamo that drove out the patrons of sail power and dragged the stagnant naval officer corps into the twentieth century just in time for the outbreak of hostilities in 1914. When Fisher joined the Royal Navy, it was composed of slow, wooden sailing ships, and he recognized that an island nation must protect its empire in the face of competitive countries that coveted their holdings. Since the sun never set on the British Empire, it was the Royal Navy that had to be ever vigilant to defend the colonies and the merchant navy that was England's lifeline.

When he became First Sea Lord in 1904, Fisher's first order of business was to sell off the navy's outdated ships and replace them with modern, fast warships. Dreadnoughts, battlecruisers, torpedoes, breach-loading guns, electric firing systems, submarines, and fuel oil all followed his appointment. Germany kept a close eye on Fisher, and soon the German High Seas Fleet seemed to be remaking itself in the image of the Royal Navy. When Fisher retired in 1911, he predicted that a war with Germany would begin in 1914. He also famously asserted that a single sea battle could determine the course of the war. He was correct on both accounts.

The British commercial shipping industry soon followed suit, applying the navy's innovations to ever-larger profit-making commercial vessels. New hull designs, construction methods, engineering, and propulsion innovation leaped from blueprint to shipyard at a fever pitch at yards in Ireland, Britain, France, Italy, and Germany. Maritime construction companies vied for the North Atlantic and Pacific trade.

Even more conspicuous to the public eye were the great passenger liners, the only method of mass travel in the Golden Age prior to the war.

Competition for the Blue Ribbon, awarded for the fastest crossing between Europe and the New York, garnered headlines, and the massive stately ships of Cunard, White Star, the elegant French and sleek Italian lines, and the heavy haulers of Germany plied the Atlantic, alight with luxury and gaiety until the loss of the *Titanic* cast its tragic shadow.

The RMS *Mauretania* was one of the most famous ships of this Golden Age of ocean travel. In 1906 Cunard and White Star constituted Britain's greatest luxury passenger lines. The British government subsidized Cunard's construction of the *Mauretania*, along with its sister ship *Lusitania*, in its ongoing competition with Germany, whose Kaiser-class superliners had eclipsed British construction.

The British bid was wildly successful. With the latest turbine technology, the *Mauretania* was the largest moving structure ever built, and it soon became the fastest. At 24 knots, it could conceivably outrun a submarine, and in 1909 it captured the Blue Ribbon for the fastest transatlantic crossing. The interior had been built to impress, boasting a multilevel first-class dining salon topped by an enormous glass dome. Its Edwardian design included beautiful wood paneling, metal grillwork, and the almost unheard-of inclusion of elevators. Nearly a thousand feet long, it had five passenger decks and a storied outdoor café on its promenade deck.

The British subsidy of the ship came with the proviso that it could be converted to an armed merchant vessel in times of need. And that need came quickly enough. But when Britain declared war on Germany in 1914, the navy quickly realized that the *Mauretania*'s enormous size made it unsuited for the job. For a year it sat in port. Then, in May 1915, the *Lusitania* was sunk by a German U-boat. Rather than taking the Lusitania's place as an armed merchant cruiser, however, the *Mauretania* was drafted to serve as a troop carrier for the British Army's new campaign on a small but significant stretch of land stretching into the Aegean called Gallipoli.

HILLY AND HENRY SEGAR TOOK their last looks at the battlefields at Suvla and Helles before turning toward the massive ship lying quietly off Cape Helles. Rags had arranged transport to the *Mauretania*, and no one would have guessed that just a few years before it had been considered one of the most luxurious passenger liners in the world. Its exterior of bold green crosses on white indicated its identity as a hospital ship, protected by international law. Its luxuries had been stripped away and put in storage. Furnishings were moved out to accommodate bodies. Its exterior was painted dark grey with black funnels. With its speed and experienced crew, the *Mauretania* could outrun the Germans—and it did, avoiding torpedoes and delivering troops on run after run to the Allied headquarters on

Moudros Bay. Now it had been called to Gallipoli to shepherd the wounded to safe waters.

Its interior had been gutted to accommodate the wounded, and the wounded were more than grateful for the spartan protection of its steel. Equipped with a number of operating rooms, no better care for the severely wounded could be found even in London than on the *Mauretania*. There were wards to accommodate 2,000 wounded of all categories. The medical staff of the Royal Army Medical Corps—experienced surgeons and nurses—had left their private practices to serve their country, constituting one of the finest medical corps in the world. The RAMC had been in existence, in some form, since the 1600s, and the unprecedented bloodshed of the current war was providing its greatest challenge yet. The promenades that had once hosted Edwardian ladies were strewn with soldiers, but an air of luxury oddly remained. The tapestries and octagonal tables were gone, but the hand-crafted paneling and towering sky-light dome stood as they always had.

Hill, Segar, and Rags boarded as the last of the casualties were loaded. The ship's captain reserved space on the uppermost deck for VIP travelers who enjoyed their own mess and wardroom. Hilly rubbed shoulders with flag officers returning home on leave, for medical treatment or reassignment. Some were accompanied by their ladies and older daughters, which added some civility to mealtimes. The ladies were a welcome relief to the inspector general, who preferred the company of women to men.

Henry Segar took advantage of the unwonted calm and burrowed in the ship's library. Now in his forties, he had recently married a minor member of the Grosvenor family whom he met during his days at St. James's Palace. Olivia assisted Princess Alexandra of Denmark, queen consort of the late King Edward VII and mother of the present King George V, with her voluminous correspondence. Having to write in both French and German, Olivia Segar was known for her charm and air of sophistication. Even in the waters of the Aegean the distaff knew of her and were more than eager to engage the new husband in gossip. But Henry had not reached his present stature by being blind to the lay of the land. He retreated and spent the next days with Rags.

Henry felt he had seen a new side of Rags while working with the wounded at Anzac Cove. He thought he detected in the younger man a good mind that should not be wasted in the army and hoped to encourage him to continue his education after the war, safe within the quadrangle of King's College Cambridge, a plan of conservative action of which Rags heartily approved. The *Mauretania* would land in Egypt in roughly three days, and the pair spent some hours together in the smoking lounge where Henry could puff away on his "disgusting log of a pipe," as Hilly called it, while Rags soaked up his insights.

"This isn't the first time there has been a war in Europe to 'end all wars,' you know. Jean Jacques Babel estimated that in 5,000 years of Western history only 292 have been without serious armed conflict. I blame a simple thing, a human thing—tribal jealousy mixed with an equal portion of greed. I am afraid we are all culprits; as you know, no other animal displays them, but humans possess them in spades. Germany wanted an empire like France's and Britain's; France wanted Alsace-Lorraine returned. Germany resented France's prestige; France wanted vengeance for the Franco-Prussian War. They all wanted their pride, and they all tricked themselves into believing a quick victory would be forthcoming. A bloody waste."

Rags was toying with a checkerboard on the table but listening closely. He found Henry's ideas to be disquieting. In his school years at a topnotch English institution, no instructor ever related any topic to the human condition. And certainly his mother harbored no such thoughts. But he was intrigued. "But Henry, that doesn't explain why England should step into the caldron. We were safe on our side of the Channel. And you know the English," he ventured carefully. "They hate 'those people' on the Continent. For them Europe is good for museums and rich food and comfortable accommodations." Rags stopped abruptly, hoping that Henry wouldn't notice his use of "them" to describe his fellow citizens.

Henry didn't appear to. "It's not that simple, Rags. We have to keep the markets open. Europe remains vital to our commerce. And what about the French, the poor arrogant things? Their military was relying on élan to win the war, for heaven's sake!" Henry shook his head in disbelief. "They assured themselves that the *spirit of the offense* rather than modern military hardware would defeat the Germans this time. Without our involvement the Germans would have overrun the place as they did in 1870." Rags, who had little respect for the French, didn't think that was an entirely bad thing, but he kept mum. "And now there's Italy. Mark my words, Rags, we'll have to divert our forces to prevent their defeat."

Emboldened by the privacy of the library and his new camaraderie with Henry, Rags ventured further. "I don't see how we can break the Germans, though. With their discipline, their equipment? Kitchener was the only one who knew it couldn't be over in a month or two. Then he added to the mess by sending the force to, of all places, Gallipoli!"

Henry shook his head and stopped to sip his tea. "Germany can't win. They're landlocked except for the North Sea, which can be closed off by the Royal Navy in an afternoon. Their food supply relies almost entirely on grains and sugar from North America, and their metal ore from Scandinavia. They have no numerical advantage, only seven million Germans and Austrians against the thirteen million that make up the Triple Entente. No, we've only to hold tight. We'll survive this round of history. Well, *we* may or may not," he smiled sadly, "but England will."

THE HARBOR AT ALEXANDRIA HAD not changed that fall, still hot and steamy. The *Mauretania* discharged the wounded and took on an equal number of soldiers who had been fighting their way across Palestine. The stay was over before it began and the great ship churned into the open waters of the windy Mediterranean, heading north across the widest portion of the crowded sea. The 700-mile voyage from Gallipoli had taken three days, and they were expecting to reach Civitavecchia, the port of Rome, a thousand miles north, in another four.

Rags was happy to be on board a ship full of young nurses again, and he once again ate his meals with them. His principal meal companion was Vivien Yates, whom he had met on the voyage to Lemnos. She was relieved to be seconded by the medical crew while transferring patients from her hilltop hospital. "We had hopes that your boss would return. The permanent buildings were never erected, and those smelly tents were awful. My ward was filled with amputees sweating like pigs. They kept promising things would get better, but no one up above cared."

Rags could see from her deteriorated state—her weight loss, scaly red hands, and hair in strings—that she had been pushed to exhaustion.

With a sigh, she continued, "What kind of state is that for young men who have given their all?"

The conversations were not good for digestion, but Rags eventually gave in and told his own stories of the hospital at Anzac Cove. He had fought being drawn into the drama of war for so long, had in fact hoped never to be near enough to actual soldiers to even risk it. But the nurses could talk of nothing else, and the pull of their shared experience was irresistible. As he spoke, it began to well up inside him and his voice began to break. He stopped and stuffed his mouth with grub, leaving the conversation to the nurses after all.

When they finally arrived at the port of Rome, everything going ashore was transferred to the litters and then on to smaller craft for the beach. While few passengers were exchanged, a mountain of medical supplies and a horde of food and fuel were loaded, part of the new deal with the Italians to supply the Royal Navy in the Mediterranean. Outside the harbor a launch had dropped off a Royal Naval commander from the embassy in Rome charged with escorting the party for the duration of their four-day stay. Rags was given a packet of information concerning their transportation, accommodations, and mess. He could expect a naval lieutenant and crew to meet him at the dock who would conduct all aspects of the visit. It included a fifty-mile drive in a small convoy of vehicles and accommodations in a hotel on the Vatican side of the Tiber. He was delighted, ready to leave the nurses and the memories they evoked behind.

Hilly was scheduled for talks with the government of Italy that didn't require Rags' attendance, which disappointed him. Instead he was given the time off, which, Segar pointed out, he surely deserved. The British embassy provided a local guide named Carlo to take him to see the sights. The first day, after a marvelous breakfast of truffle eggs, cold meats, and Italian toast, he was planted in the cramped front seat of a tiny car that Carlo drove like a madman through the back alleys to the fountains hidden in the plazas across the river. But the war had interrupted mass travel and, like the fountain, only a trickle was evident that early in the morning. Carlo explained, "They turn the water down when the tourists are not so many."

Rags was dropped off at the top of the Spanish Steps. "I meet you at the bottom in fifteen minutes. Take a walk; it's nice," Carlo insisted. Rags expected to be enveloped by photo-taking tourists, but there was just an old man with an ancient plate camera halfway down pleading in fractured English to pause for a picture. Charlotte had insisted that he have tea at Babington's tea shop at the bottom of the wide stone steps should he make it to Rome, and Carlo must have read his mind since there he was waiting at the glass door. The tea was a nice break, real scones and strawberry jam with clotted cream straight from Devon. His mother was right; it was a bit of home, which he needed at that moment. Across town they trudged the concrete oval midway up the Coliseum and gazed at the Diocletian Baths that had been transformed into the Catholic Basilica of St. Mary of the Angels and the Martyrs by Michelangelo Buonarroti and others. He marveled at the architecture—church after church devoted to saints who were quite alien to his own Church of England upbringing. He hadn't realized how good it would feel to be back in a familiar landscape, and he felt his mind was being washed clean of the blood and dirt of Gallipoli by the beauty of the Eternal City.

On the second day he and Carlos walked from the hotel a few blocks to the Vatican. They stood in front of the Basilica of Saint Peter, and Rags bought postcards and souvenirs for his mother, who had long since embraced the religion of his father. Lunch was at a restaurant across the bridge at the edge of the river in sight of the great fort of Castel Sant'Angelo. A tiny establishment that fit no more than a dozen small tables, the café's specialty was a bowl of pasta as big as his head. The owner treated Rags himself, grating parmesan over a dish that was already covered with at least four other melted cheeses. Rags marveled that just a few days before he had been surrounded by soldiers who were bleeding and dying, and here he was, enjoying the sun and bounties of Rome. It made him happy, but perhaps not quite so happy as it once would have. His happiness was great, but no longer unalloyed.

Carlo had gone back to his home for lunch, so Rags was sitting alone in the crowded restaurant. Though not the custom in England, he could see that sharing tables with strangers was common in Rome and was unsurprised when a tall figure approached his own. He reluctantly acquiesced and a black-robed monsignor sat across from him. Removing his broad-brimmed hat, the cleric looked over at him with steady eyes and Rags had a jolt. Monsignor Pieter Merchanti, his mother's old friend from Regensburg, whom he had met at his home so many months before, stared into his wide-open eyes.

"Lieutenant Stetchworth, I presume—is that you, my young friend? We were introduced by your dear mother last spring at your home in Fulham." Rags could only smile briefly at the similarity to Stanley's famous greeting of Livingstone before he coughed up his penne.

RAGS LURCHED BACK FROM HIS state of shock. "Monsignor," he stuttered, "I thought you were in London, at Westminster Cathedral. What are you doing in Rome?"

They were interrupted by the restaurant owner, who obviously knew the monsignor well and didn't bother to take his order. A bottle of red wine arrived followed by trays of steaming pasta, baskets of torn bread, and pots of olive oil sprinkled with herbs and garlic.

"Grazie, Manolo," the monsignor said. The proprietor gave a slight bow as the waiters scurried back to the kitchen. He turned to Rags: "I hope you like your lunch. It is my treat, of course, since I had you brought here."

Rags stopped twisting his fork in the bowl and looked at the priest. "The guide is from the British embassy. Carlo brought me here."

"The guide is from the Vatican. I arranged it, told them I was a friend of your mother's in London and promised to look out for you while in Rome."

"Does General Hopewell know that?"

The monsignor smiled. "No, no. General Hopewell has much more important matters to attend to. These are details he need not be bothered with. I can assure you that you will be back at your quarters before he and Mister Segar are finished. They will be dining with their hosts tonight, well cared for."

Rags was shaken. His activities until this time had been blessedly impersonal: taking notes and dropping off messages on the bridge. Now he was in a foreign country, in a public place, dining with someone he knew to be a German agent. Someone who knew where he had been, where a *British general* had been and when he would be back—knew who accompanied that British general and where they would be dining that evening. He had been moved from spot to spot and delivered—actually *delivered*, like a parcel—to his handler. Suddenly the rich sauce was heavy in his stomach, and he was aware of breathing in the exhaust from the buses and trucks going down the adjacent street. Not far from them the Tiber flowed past in a green mass of floating debris which had marked its walls with centuries of floods and droughts. Rags felt sickened.

Monsignor Merchanti seemed to sense his unease but continued eating as if nothing were amiss, the very picture of two strangers making small talk. "You have been enjoying your stay here in our city?"

"Um, yes. It's beautiful, of course."

"It is indeed. A bit different from your London, yes? But then you've been away from London for some time. I hope your travels have gone smoothly?"

"Um, yes. Smoothly, if war can ever be described without killing or maiming. Yes, smoothly."

Merchanti smiled at Rags' sudden loss of speech and took on the burden of the conversation. For another half hour they ate in leisure, Rags feeling ever more like a small animal being gentled or lulled. The initial shock began to wear off, and the vise round his head loosened. So when at the end of the meal Merchanti suggested a walk to the Castel Sant'Angelo, Rags was not only willing but intrigued.

It was no more than a fifteen-minute walk to the Castel, where a wave of the monsignor's hand garnered them salutes and passage from the armed guards. "Few tourists are interested in an old unused fort in the shadow of Vatican City. They are a religious crowd or visitors interested in the art collection. But here in the confines of these thick silent walls, I have something you will be most interested in seeing."

They climbed stairs, one flight after another, until they came out on the ramparts and looked down on the traffic and restaurant they had just left. It was a beautiful fall day. The terrible heat Rome was known for had abated. The city lay before him and Rags leaned on the crenelated wall as the priest pointed out the sights and church steeples he knew so well.

Standing a short way down from them was another black-clothed figure, rather tall, silent, looking through binoculars at the same vista. When Merchanti suggested a closer look, Rags asked the man if he could borrow his glasses for a moment.

"Of course you can—my son."

## Chapter Seventeen

# Rome, August 1915

THE PRIEST TURNED TO FACE the officer. Rags didn't recognize the face, but he knew the voice. It was the unmistakable voice of the man who told him about a stag jumping a chasm to escape the hunters in the Black Forest, so long ago.

Rags stared for a moment, jaw dropped and eyes wide. "You are my father." The black robes of the Catholic priest confused the issue. His father was a soldier, not a priest. He was at the front somewhere in France, not in Rome. Why wasn't he in a high, stern Prussian collar of grey-green piped in red and covered with rank laurels and medals, as he had pictured his father? Whenever Rags got a message from Germany, that is how he imagined a colonel in service of the Kaiser would be.

Christian looked at his son appraisingly. "Yes, Rolly, I am indeed." The monsignor stepped away, leaving the two men to talk privately. Rags felt self-conscious but mostly dumbstruck—he never imagined he would encounter his father until the war was over. To see his father looming there was intimidating, but the feeling warred with his memories of Regensburg, of childhood hikes in the Bavarian forests. "Father, *how long* I have waited for you" was all that came out. But it was heartfelt. If his mother had her way, the family would unite in Austria when the conspiracy Christian had hatched ended with a treaty leaving Europe at peace. Rags hoped the task he had taken on for both his mother and his father would help, somehow, to bring a happy conclusion to a very dangerous game.

Christian looked about the long palisade where a few others were walking in the sun and suggested that the meeting might be a little too public. He turned to Pieter for relief. Smiling, he beckoned to the monsignor to come closer. "Pieter, find us a place where we can be comfortable and talk. We have much to discuss."

161

PIETER HAD SECURED A CORNER of the German officers' mess where they could enjoy refreshments and talk with some privacy. Clad in misleading attire, father and son followed the jovial cleric into the lounge bedecked with regimental glories that dated back to the Roman army. Christian regretted the disguises, yet it was a necessity. If only they could appear as two German soldiers instead of costumed in the garb of the wrong countries. Seated in soft armchairs around a low, ornate, inlaid table, the party was partially concealed behind a bank of green ferns. The monsignor ordered a bottle of cognac, the first of a pair to be consumed that afternoon. Christian insisted on Courvoisier, which had an image of Napoleon on the label. He proclaimed vigorously, "It is the only brand a *soldier* should drink."

Soon Christian was sitting back swirling a cut-glass snifter in his hand to warm the amber liquid. "Let us speak in proper English in case we are overheard." His strong German accent made Rags cringe, certain no one who happened by would be fooled. Yet it seemed Christian was quite proud of his grasp of the language initially taught him by Charlotte over years of summer holidays. "A British officer should not be conversing in German, don't you know." Christian was practicing his English idioms. Rags raised his glass in salute, broadly smiling at the valiant yet comical attempt. "I didn't mean to confuse things, *my boy*, by masquerading as a priest but 'when in Rome, do as the Romans do.'" It was a very bad joke, but all three laughed. "I couldn't meet a British officer in a German uniform, could I? In *our business* you must always assume that you are being observed. If reported to your uncle in the morning that you were seen with a German officer, there would be some pointed questions you couldn't answer. But to talk to a priest in Vatican City on a sightseeing tour, now what could be more natural?"

Christian topped off Rags' glass. "Rolly, I must tell you that General Von Lobin-Sele, the chief of German intelligence, has praised your humble father for the service of his son. You must know that I am billeted in a most favorable position—I now occupy the international espionage desk. There I have found how fragile and time-sensitive information can be. It must be constantly renewed. What was vital today can be worthless hours later. I know I'm putting a great deal on your shoulders, but believe me when I tell you that we both will benefit from your stellar performance. The British would see us in our graves. They want to dominate Europe as their playground and reduce us to passive peasants there to entertain their decadent, privileged, and coddled upper class. We cannot let that happen. At the successful closing of the war, when the Wehrmacht has restored our place in the world, we . . . you and I . . . will wear the laurel."

The monsignor, who had been working steadily on the cognac, agreed. "Hear, hear. Liston to your father, my son, he speaks the truth. To victory for Germany!"

Rags smiled and drank, but said nothing. Although he had often imagined meeting his father again, he had always envisioned an emotional reunion, full of warmth and personal exchange. The speech his father had just given seemed rehearsed, intended to secure his sympathy firmly in the German camp. Perhaps he was wrong—Rags didn't know the habits of the Teutonic warrior class, and he had never experienced his father in a setting like this before. Still he wondered: Was Christian deliberately testing his reaction? Was he suspect? Rags was born and raised in England and chose to be German, but perhaps his father suspected it was only Charlotte's strong influence that made him accept the mission. Or perhaps, just perhaps, the father thought his son was purely driven by self-preservation. Could his father think that he might be a coward? Once challenged, it appeared that many British men were. Some even sought work down deep in the coal mines rather than serve in France. English women kept a supply of white feathers in their purses to present to any young man on the street in civilian clothes. As an officer, he remained safe in London away from trenches and those annoying women. But the lieutenant felt no guilt. He believed that a spy had to display a different kind of courage than that required to face a machine gun. Rags understood that Christian must be sure of his son's loyalty to the Kaiser, but he was equally confident that he had demonstrated his resolve as a German spy. Why should he be questioned?

Rags was aware that the Germans were more verbose by nature, more inclined to absolutes. In England they put down the enemy while at the same time calling him "Fritzy" and endlessly remarking about the first Christmas in the trenches when the two lines put down their arms and sang carols. The British saw the war as between monarchs, not populations. Like good Christians, the Brits were all children in the same extended family. While the cultures clashed, Rags felt equally at home in both because of the long summer holidays spent in the company of Austrian children in the fairy-tale land of pastures, cows, flowers, and good cheer. Then, of course, there was his craving for the indescribably delightful food, beer, and music. His stomach always balked on the return home to England's boiled beef and greasy fish and chips, though thankfully the beer was just as good. Rags knew how unique he must be, content—or so it seemed—in two opposing cultures at the same time. The lieutenant could forgive his father's strong views while embracing Uncle Hilly's and Henry Segar's friendship as he toiled to maintain his equilibrium.

By the time the first bottle was destroyed, Christian and the monsignor were well into their cups. A lunch would have moderated the effects of the alcohol, but none was offered. The arrangement of the seating, Christian in the center and the other two to each side, tucked into an alcove with planters on three sides, allowed right-handed Rags to pour more than half his drinks into the soil of the bedded ferns. Rags never liked hard liquor; it upset his stomach. Hadn't the Italians ever heard of beer? While the other two got very drunk, Rags maintained his stability and control of his tongue.

The monsignor fell in with Christian in rubbishing the British. "Christian, at least you don't have to live among the *Limeys* as I do at Westminster Cathedral. You should hear the moaning from the women at mass and their beloved fundraisers. Their concern is not for the soldier but for themselves and the privations the war has put on them. As far as they are concerned, all they want is more, more butter, more sugar, more eggs, flour and fat to stuff their mouths." Pieter took a breath and burped before twittering on, his voice ever higher. "I tell you another thing, they pray for an end to the war and the annihilation of the Bosch—that's us! The Kaiser this and the Kaiser that, I can't repeat the terrible words they use. They call us Huns and talk of us as barbarians. They make up horrible posters of our troops dripping with English and Belgium blood. I have to bite my tongue and say, 'Yes, yes . . . but that is not very Christian of you, madam. Christ implored us to love our neighbor.' It makes no difference; they go right on about how *we* started the war. It irks me no end that I am unable defend the Kaiser. It must be hell for you, Rolly, as it is for me, to be a cuckoo bird in the English nest."

Rags recognized that it was time for him to join in the criticism. "I find it hard to excuse the class distinction in England. As you are born, so you are to be. That can't be right for a person—it can't be good for the nation. It is kept that way by the hierarchy, the courts, the schools, and employers. How can any government seek war on a grand scale knowing there is no standing army waiting in the wings to back up their boast? They just throw lives away. Kitchener's recruiting program, his new army, depends largely on lads joining up with pals in a glorious romp to a battlefield they have been ill prepared for. In Europe, large standing reserve armies are comprised of men who have taken a year out of their young lives to train and embrace the military experience, before returning home to pursue a living. If called up for an emergency, they need only to be topped up before going into battle. I have seen it at Gallipoli, whole divisions from the shires landed and lost within days. It's criminal." Rags took a breath, overcome for a moment by his memories of Gallipoli. "My disappointment is with our government, not our soldiers, who I have seen in the field. Magnificent fighting men lead by incompetent appointees who should have been dumped on the dust heap years ago. That old man's Army Club . . . the bloody Club needs to be cleaned out." Rags realized that his voice was echoing against the hard brick ceiling vault and coming back to him in ringing tones.

Christian and Pieter seemed to be eating it up, so Rags continued with fervor. "The man on the street, shopkeepers, bartenders could give a damn about the lads returning all broken. Women goad their men into service with silly songs: 'We hate to lose you, but we know you must go, for king and for country.'" He was not known for his singing voice, but his companions swung their glasses anyway, urging him on. Pointing, passersby were amused by the three jolly characters. "That's right . . . Sometimes I think the 'ladies' are tired of the old men and just want new ones!"

Rags had to pause to recall what he had said. "There is an exception, though." The cognac was beginning to have an effect; Rags always got sentimental when he had too much to drink, and he let it well out of him. "I must tell you both . . . I have one ally who keeps me out of trouble. Advising me to keep a low profile to protect all our interests. Mother is a truly devoted Austrian. She fell in love with Father and Austria when a young lady. She is loyal to both. She never stops reminiscing about her days at the university and at your home, Pieter, her friends and the freedom of living away from English oppression. All I hear at meals are tales of mountain folklore from books she reads in German. I can assure you both that if British intelligence ever comes to camp in our library, they will immediately start plundering the bookshelves as signs of treason!"

AS RAGS PRATTLED ON, CHRISTIAN August Manfred von Thurn und Taxis Unterhart sat back and surveyed the young officer. He could report to his masters on the imperial staff that Rolly looked the part of a military man. He was straight and tall, shoulders wide and head up. Christian pictured him in a German uniform, an Aryan, no doubt. That British uniform his son currently wore turned his stomach. Great Britain was crushing the life out of Germany, and he despised the supercilious George V, whom he considered a traitor to his class. Christian was proud that he had willingly offered up his only son to the Kaiser's cause. Having Rolly billeted to an English inspector general was a fantastic gift that proved once again that the Fates were with Germany.

Likewise Rolly's report of the fervor of his mother was most pleasing. These were the words Christian wanted to hear, one of the reasons he had gone to so much trouble to be in Rome and host the meeting. But not the only by far. Christian felt warm and confident from the brandy and the enthusiasm of his protege. It was time to get details.

Christian smiled broadly and lifted his glass: "I see before me a young soldier of the Kaiser with iron in his heart. Rolly, you have done well. Now tell us . . . what have your little English friends been up to since we last communicated?"

RAGS WAS FEELING A COMRADESHIP with his two drinking companions he hadn't felt for a long time. On the job, he was a mere servant, a dog robber. Even though Uncle Hilly had been more than supportive, he was a busy, prominent man more than twice his age. Rags was mostly a hat watcher, making sure it was within easy reach as they moved from stuffy office to pompous mess. Rags had no friends of his own age and rank, and there would have been no time for young friends even if they had existed. He missed the school buddies who got into mischief and talked about girls. As an aide, it was all business every day. Soon his workload was bound to take time better spent with Grace.

Rags was proud of his father, a senior officer in a grand army, lord of a castle in a beautiful land. His mother reminded him constantly that he was an actual son, if illegitimate, of a Continental aristocrat, and it had always rankled to conceal his lineage. If planted in Austria, he could be claimed and ascend to his rightful place. It was one of the reasons he accepted the role as a spy for Germany. He had wanted to be worthy of his blood. Someday Rags might be a count.

Rags dragged himself from the past and remembered his duties. His father had asked for news of British strategy. Though he didn't have his notes with him, Rags felt he could present the most pertinent information to his father in a clear concise manner. He began with the mix-up at Alexandria and how the British expected to fool the Germans into thinking that the Anzacs were destined for France. Egypt was a jumping-off spot for Palestine and the underbelly of Turkey, which they planned to turn into a British colony after the war to protect the Suez Canal. Gallipoli was a Royal Navy operation gone bad that the army was tasked to clean up. The goal was to open up the Bosphorus to shipping for the Russians. Rags kept the tactics to a minimum but emphasized the pigheadedness of the British Army commanders on in the field and their lack of training and inability to handle large formations.

Rags warmed to his subject. "The army leadership and, I suppose, the Royal Navy as well are giant gentlemen's clubs. One hand washes the other and be damned with the troops. The generals are divided up into cartels based on previous operations. The leadership pool to pick from is littered with sycophants who have little to offer except loyalty. The only good soldier in the hierarchy I have found in these past months is my Uncle Hilly, but he's past his prime. He can only report to Kitchener, who I believe is of the same category. You have little to fear from the British general staff."

Christian preened at the savage assessment of the British military brass but noted a certain lack of detail, perhaps from Rolly's youth or inexperience. "Rolly, that is all most interesting, and I am gratified that I picked you for this mission. But what of the future? What will General Hopewell and Segar advise Kitchener and Churchill to do about Gallipoli?"

Rags took a deep breath. "I don't know because they have not openly discussed their findings in so many words in my presence. However, I think they expect the British Army to be successful if only the leadership positions across the board are changed. I was told of the importance of Suez, and even though the Royal Navy is unable to open the waterway to Russia, the British Army's occupation of the peninsula will continue to tie down the Turkish army, which means a two-front war for the Turks."

Christian looked meaningfully at Pieter. If accurate, this plan would mean the Germans would continue to be tied up modernizing the Turkish army. The General Staff would not be happy with the news. They were up against it in Russia, the Austrians were faltering, the Italians were menacing, and the Western Front had turned to a defense strategy. The continued diversion in Turkey would be a drain. "Well, Rolly, that's not good news, but it is better to know what's in store."

THE AFTERNOON LIGHT WAS BEGINNING to wane, and they were on their fourth bottle. Rags was beginning to feel a bit giddy and wondered about the wisdom of staying much longer. The cognac was doing its work, and Christian turned sentimental. The fire had gone from his tone, and he appeared sleepy-eyed and failed to turn his head to look Rags in the eye. "Spying isn't a comfortable way of life. I feel guilty for having thrust it upon both you and your mother. But I trust you to do your best for Germany. I know your hearts are with the German people. Remember, I too am a foreigner working for the German Kaiser. I was with Franz Joseph's intelligence office in Vienna when a call came to send a liaison officer to the famous German General Staff—a great honor. I was chosen because I went to school in Regensburg, and no doubt my family connections also brought me forward," he noted proudly. "There I found that the espionage office had been sending German agents into England who spoke the language like butchers and drill sergeants. All of them were caught and shot. Well, nearly all. Those that remained on the loose became suspect that the British had turned them to their own devices and were giving us misleading information." He touched Rags' arm and dropped his tone to a whisper. "I came up with a brilliant plan which has been recognized for its innovation and cunning. I told them about your faithful mother and her wonderful son. I may not know much about the English, but I know they believe no native son would ever betray the crown.

Pieter stepped in. "Your father is a genius, everyone says so. He will go far. I am proud to be a part of the operation, even though my part is merely negligible. Well, maybe a little more than negligible."

Christian agreed and put his left hand on the monsignor's shoulder and gave it a shake. "Between us all we will crack Horse Guards; they will never know what happened. Mark my words."

It was growing dark and the officers' club was beginning to fill up with the usual crowd of wiry workers.

Christian began to wind things up. "England has dealt you a terrific blow, separating our family because of some ancient prejudice and religious differences. We can't let them continue to split us up. You and your mother's loyal efforts will contribute to ending this awful war and unite us for the first time since your childhood. The work you are doing for Germany is so vital that I must continue to ask you and your mother to serve the Kaiser's cause. I place my confidence in you both and pledge my loyalty to our family. Don't let the danger defeat you."

Rags cut in. "Mother is anxious; the feeling never leaves her. She's ever vigilant, afraid for herself as much as she is for me. But I am trying, and I think I have the bit in my teeth now that I have experienced this long trip. I was scared at first, but now I can see that the faster we can bring the war to an end, the better for all concerned." Rags felt he needed to tell his tale of the zeppelin attack before the moment passed. His mother may have communicated his distress at the attack, and it was important to own up to his feelings, lest he give the impression of hiding his trauma. This time he didn't leave out meeting Grace, for she was central to the tale. It took him a long time to come to the point, for he feared to articulate to his father the anger he felt at the destruction of his city when in his eyes it was not a part of the war.

Christian couldn't hide his contempt entirely for what he saw as his son's sentimentality. "It is not a time to be weak, Rolly. You are a man, doing a man's job, and there is no place for hesitation. Reach down inside, remember your convictions, and stick yourself to the mission. It is war and people will die. Believe me," he reached across the table and took his son's hands, "I and your dear mother would never put you in harm's way if it were not terribly important. Your efforts, in the end, will bring a close to the madness of war and lead to a much better future for the whole world."

There was a great deal at stake here for Christian, a colonel in the Kaiser's intelligence corps. Rolly wasn't just his son but a key link in the effort to anticipate the direction of the British war effort. He had taken great care to get his son placed in a sensitive position, one that would be impossible to replicate. The information Rolly and his mother had passed had been recognized for its accuracy. To the colonel these two assets were precious and not to be trifled with. For insurance, he had one more ace up his sleeve.

"I know how difficult it is for you to maintain your perspective, living in the heart of the enemy, and believe me when I tell you that the Kaiser himself is aware of the burden we have placed upon your young shoulders. He would like to express his love and respect for you and has asked me to give you this." Christian reached into a leather briefcase that rested on the floor next to his chair. He handed Rags a folded black leather portfolio, which had the gold crest of the Imperial General Staff embossed on the top. Rags accepted it with wonder in his eyes. He opened it slowly. It was scribed in German gothic script. Rags had been commissioned: Captain in the Imperial German Army.

Rags looked up, stunned.

Pieter leaned over from his adjacent chair and offered his hand with a satisfied smile: "Congratulations, Hauptmann Stetchworth, and welcome to our ranks." Pieter vigorously shook the new captain's hand.

Before Rags could grasp the ramifications of holding a commission in opposing armies, his father pulled another rabbit out of his hat. "Hauptmann Stetchworth, His Imperial Majesty has asked me to present you with the Iron Cross, Second Class, in recognition for your personal service to the empire." Rags felt its power the moment it was taken from the ornate leather-covered box. Christian refrained from pinning it on his son's British Army tunic. Instead he placed it on Rags' outstretched palm, where it rested until the monsignor took it and put it back in its box, never to be recognized again while the Hauptmann was in British service.

Christian spoke of those in the fields of France who shared the honor and painted for Rags a portrait of Teutonic gallantry. He described Rags' efforts as equal to the men in the trenches who faced the enemy with bravery and love for the Kaiser. "Let this medal be a token of the honor and respect you have earned in this Great War. You have entered the Valhalla of Germany, there forever in the hearts of the empire." He shook his son's hand and embraced him with a kiss on the cheek.

## Chapter Eighteen

# Rome, August 1915, and London, September 1915

THE FOLLOWING MORNING RAGS WAS awakened by an alarmingly loud knock on the door. He dragged himself out of his hotel bed feeling stuporous, but it was only the porter with his breakfast. Hilly and Segar, he learned, had gone to the Italian Ministry. It was 10:30 a.m.

With the porter quickly whisked out of his room, Rags sat back in bed and looked at the tray placed on the bedside table. He nearly vomited. Bypassing the coffee, he went straight for the tea and huddled over the warm cup. He blamed the Italians. Why hadn't they ever taken to plain old beer? Cognac, whiskey, they made him sick, and he suddenly wanted nothing more than to be back at the Eight Bells Pub and the Spotted Horse in Putney nursing a pint of warm bitter.

The details of the evening before began to come back to him. The shock of the visit still thrummed in his chest, and he wondered if his mother had known of it. The commission, oh God, the commission. At least as an official soldier of the German army he couldn't be shot as a spy. Perhaps that was why his father commissioned him. But wait, he already had a commission— the King's commission. Which meant that *both* sides now had reason to shoot him. Worse than a man without a country, he was a man with two countries, both of which had grounds to put him in front of a firing squad. "Oh my God, I'm for it."

And the Iron Cross. Where was it? What did he do with it? He sprang on to the parquet floor and dashed to the wooden wardrobe that stood against the inner wall. Flinging it open, he rummaged through his luggage, finding the evidence stuffed at the bottom of his laundry bag. God, what a stupid place to hide them. He must have been more drunk than he remembered. The maid could have found them while he was asleep, and they would already be in the hands of the authorities. Some spy!

He returned to the bed with the commission in one hand and the Iron Cross in the other. Holding it was both frightening and fascinating. The Iron Cross was one of the most famous military honors in the world. It had its origins with the Teutonic Knights of the Crusades but had been resurrected by Prussia to reward individual combat service to the fatherland. Remarkably, both officers and enlisted were eligible for the decoration. Tossing it lightly in the palm of his hand, Rags appreciated its striking appearance: a black cross with four equal arms edged in silver, suspended from a black-and-white ribbon. Kaiser Wilhelm II made it his own by adding a black crown and the year 1914 in addition to a block "W" to the facing side of the cross.

After being presented with the cross at the officers' club the night before, he had agreed to follow his father out for supper. He recalled knowing that Uncle Hilly and Segar would be out at a diplomatic affair and he wanted a good meal at someone else's expense. Central Rome is small, a walking city slid between hills that have lost their identity. Every square inch is covered with colorful buildings. Like giant pastel-colored sugar cubes, they line every street, plaza and alley. For his benefit, he supposed, Pieter had selected a restaurant, Monopoli's, only a block from the central train station, which was a long, pleasant walk up the low hill from the Coliseum. Rags had complained earlier that he needed some exercise after the sea voyage. Evidently, Pieter was a patron of a particular establishment and a dedicated gastronome. Rags thought it was a good idea to be a little tardy so he could join the party already in place. At the door he was greeted the owner, Signor Monopoli, who apparently was waiting for him to arrive.

"Ah, this must be my lieutenant, you must be, so happy you come to my little restaurant, I am honored to have an Allied officer at my table. Your friend, the monsignor, told me of your arrival that was coming. This way, signore.'"
It was a greeting he had gotten everywhere he went since the Italians had joined the Entente. The proprietor's grinning face seemed a little put on. With the wave of his hand, they had threaded between crowded tables filled with boisterous eaters. Rags looked at the plates as he passed and noticed that the tabletops were concealed by copious plates and bowls of heaping pasta. The smell of the garlic, cheese, savory sauces spun in his head. Steam rose from the coffee bar next to the counter stacked with cakes, cookies and cannoli. He slid sideways into a corner table against the back wall near the kitchen door. Rags reckoned his father had selected the locale, suspecting that spies never sat anywhere else. Another tip for the neophyte.

This was Pieter's party. He had arranged an eight-course meal—banquet was a better title—where the first three courses were pasta. Rags never frequented the few Italian restaurants dotted around central London. His diet consisted of fish and chips or the conservative English meals prepared at home by Mrs. Jayson.

"Now Rolly," Pieter said as he examined the first course, "antipasto is our starter. Something light to go with a light wine. As you can see, it is like hors d'oeuvres in England—anchovies, cheeses, olives and thin-sliced dried meat in a light sauce. Very nice, brings out the appetite." Rags replied, "My appetite needs no direction; I am as hungry as a cart horse."

Within a half hour, Rags' wine glass was filled by the hovering waiter for the third time. He was planning on getting Pieter's money's worth. The appetizer had done its job, and Rags acquired a newfound enthusiasm for Italian cooking. He felt it was going to be a memorable occasion. What could be better—good friends in a good city with good food. What could match it?

"My boy," Christian alerted, "here it comes the primo, another appetizer. This should take some time, first the soup, rice, and some nice polenta to stretch the stomach. You'll like this." Rags did and ate it all while he listened to Pieter and his father tell war stories about incompetent contemporaries. The second course was the tipping point as Rags dug into first chicken fettuccini, then a small portion of shrimp alfredo. Signor Monopoli himself brought his signature dish of beef tips in wine over rice. Pieter praised the gesture, as did the entire party. Just when Rags was expecting a finish of lemon sherbet for dessert, the contorno—a platter of steaming vegetables—arrived along with more beef in rich sauce. Pieter complained that Rags wasn't doing his part and helped him by scooping more of everything onto a fresh white dinner plate. Finally it came time for dessert. Not a nice cool sherbet ice, but a pair of cannoli. One bite of the super sweet heavy cheese center nearly did Rags in. With eyes drooping and stomach touching the table, he managed to consume one and nearly a half before crying for mercy. His father reached across and slapped him on the back. "That's my son, he can put it away like a man." That was the last thing Rags remembered until the next morning.

What in the world could he do with his commission, not to mention his medal? His only idea for disposing of them was zipping down to the Tiber and tossing both into the river to mix with the other debris that chocked the stream. He found that the hot tea revived him enough to dress. Before putting the medal along with the commission into a heavy envelope he had been using for scads of papers gathered along the way, he opened the box and looked at it in the light of the window. He turned the cross over to see his name engraved on the back: Hauptmann Roland Stetchworth. A pal at school brought one to class taken off a dead German by his older brother. The boy had pinned it catawampus on his own shirt and paraded around the classroom in a mock military march. But for Rags this Iron Cross, his Iron Cross, was no joke.

Rags headed out the hotel entrance alone, or so he hoped, and wound his way through the tight alleys, backtracking now and then to shake off any followers. He stopped to window shop and jumped into a doorway for a quick look back. He was safe, he was sure of it. Just off Piazza Navona, round a narrow corner, he was drawn to a luggage shop display. It came to him: an attaché case of his own—just a small one that no one had reason to probe—where he could keep his schedules and reminders. That's what was needed. He knew he couldn't put his German commission and medal in his luggage. Cabin staff or room maids were always rummaging through his things thinking they could be of assistance. A carrying case of his own that would never leave his side and would not be conspicuous. Rags entered the shop confidently and was greeted by a North African clerk. The familiar smell of leather surrounded him and made him feel at ease.

"Ah, Lieutenant, what can I do for our allies, now that you are on our side?" Rags was unaware that the Entente had joined the Italians, thinking it was the other way around. But no matter.

"I require a light carrying case, for papers, orders, and the like," he said, keeping the requirement very business-like and official. "Something like the one in the window with the buckles and handle, over there against the glass." He motioned to the display and a handsome, medium brown case that didn't have a price tag.

The clerk praised his choice. "Very smart, just the thing for an important officer. It is made of our finest and most lightweight Moroccan leather. It is the grade we use for covering fine volumes fit for an English library." He kept up the patter, extolling the quality of the stitching, the buckles made from the brass casings of French artillery shells, the fine red silk lining. He picked up the case and ran his bony fingers over the inside.

Rags took it and felt its lightness. The workmanship was impressive, not at all like the heavy case he had dragged around London supplied by the quartermaster. At the mess, officers would think it too fine for a junior. When asked, he could tell them he picked it up in Rome from a Moroccan. It could raise his stock.

"Have you noticed anything peculiar about the lining or the case, Lieutenant?"

Rags probed the inside down to the bottom and back up against the three interior partitions. "No, very nice, well made."

But the man wasn't asking about the quality. The clerk smiled mysteriously and turned it over. The bottom, which was slightly wider than the top, slid away in his adept hands to reveal a secret compartment. "Just the thing for a spy, or a man of many talents with the ladies. Big enough for official papers or indiscreet letters, wouldn't you say?"

Holy mother of God. Rags saw white and thought he might faint for a moment, but he steadied himself. Did the Moroccan actually know he was a spy? Or were there so many spies in Rome that he merely assumed that all his customers were spies?

"I can see you like it, Lieutenant." Rags could tell the salesman knew his clientele and what they could afford. "It is most reasonable, a mere thousand lira." The price was within the officer's pay grade.

Rags gave it back. "Do that again, open the bottom; I didn't see how you did it." He wanted to sure that the device held it safely closed. It was a little tricky, and pressure had to be applied at two places simultaneously, thus preventing it from opening accidentally. When Rags was certain he had mastered it, he bought the briefcase. He knew he was expected to haggle, but he couldn't be bothered today. Everything was too much for him: seeing his father, getting the Iron Cross, wanting to rid himself of it but not quite being able to, and then seeing this beautiful case in which he could hide and treasure it.

He paid the price and walked away to a nearby stone seat at a fountain. Under cover of his coat, he placed both the medal and the commission inside and then checked the case from all sides to see that nothing was sticking out. He smoothed his hand over the beautiful leather and, confident, resumed the trek to his quarters.

IT WAS VERY LATE WHEN Hilly and Segar returned from their marathon talks with the Italian authorities. Rags had waited up, but the two gentlemen were worse for wear after a long dinner at the compulsory diplomatic event in which they easily overindulged. Rags remembered too vividly his previous night's ramble and concluded that eating and drinking on someone else's tic was never a good idea. All caution was thrown to the wind and he could see that his two companions had been attacked by the same spirit of excess. Fortunately, the car to pick them up the next morning was not scheduled until noon, allowing plenty of time to put everything and everybody together for the drive to the port.

The ship's departure was delayed and the itinerary changed. The hospital in Malta, where the *Mauretania* had been scheduled to drop off the wounded, was overflowing, another misstep in the pitiful naval and military planning. So they would bypass Malta and go directly to Liverpool, much to Rags' delight. He was opposed to any more delays, wanting to finish this business and see Grace. He felt changed by the last few weeks and wanted to see confirmation of it in Grace's eyes. He felt less like a young page. He had been to the field, seen the wounded; he felt a man, a soldier with a medal (even if he couldn't tell her about it).

The only change on the route back to England was the food. Fresh fruit and vegetables were added to the menu and the bully beef was no longer in evidence. Within days they were cruising at full speed headed for the Strait of Gibraltar. Sleeping in was the order of the day. Uncle Hilly was noticeably fatigued, as was Segar, and both were very tight-lipped about the two days spent in Italy. Mostly they quizzed Rags about his rubbernecking around the Roman ruins and the Basilica of Saint Peter. Rags mentioned in passing his encounter with the monsignor, explaining the connection between the priest and his mother from her days as a debutante at Regensburg. Never leaving his case in the cabin, Rags stuffed it with notes about the trip which he planned to deposit with Mildred. Box. When the ship paused at the great Rock of Gibraltar to take on passengers, Rags took the opportunity to climb about the island, exploring the fortifications hidden within the rock and feeding the Barbary macaques.

When he returned that evening, the ship's executive officer announced a briefing. In neat company uniform that could easily be mistaken for Royal Navy, he addressed the passengers as if they were about to see a play in the West End. "*Mauretania*'s destination has altered once again." The officer seemed disappointed, and Rags surmised that a port change meant that the young officer would not see his family. "We are no longer going into Liverpool since German submarines have been active in the Mediterranean, Bay of Biscay, and most importantly Irish Sea. In the last two weeks, in addition to merchant marine losses, the troop ship *Royal Edward* was lost off the Italian island of Kos, with 1,800 soldiers on board. *The Arabic*, a White Star liner sailing on the Irish Sea, and the liner *Hesperian* were both sunk as well. The voyage is now scheduled for 1,340 nautical miles, which should land us at Southampton near Portsmouth in approximately three full steaming days, at an average speed of twenty knots . . . considering weather and other conditions permitting, of course."

His matter-of-fact recital of these tragedies was rather off-putting; he treated it as if it were a weather report. But the passengers displayed less sangfroid. They were relieved to know an attempt was being made to safely conclude the voyage, but the thought of German submarines was one that struck fear in the hearts of the British at sea. The Germans had constructed the first really formidable submarine fleet for wartime, and they were known to patrol the entire British coast. Once British passenger ships had been ordered to act as auxiliary cruisers, no ship was off-limits to German attack, starting with the *Lusitania*. In addition, the Germans had abandoned the prize rules whose protocol was to allow the crew and civilians safe passage before sinking a ship. British civilians had seen the photos of the bodies from the *Lusitania* washed up on the Irish shore. A common poster in England was of a woman drowning with a baby in arms, with the title "Loose Lips Sink Ships." In addition, the harrowing tales of the sinking of the *Titanic* were well known: the freezing water, entrapment under steel decks, screaming passengers, the massive iron vessel sliding helplessly under the waves. These images gave them chills, even nightmares. But the *Titanic*'s sinking had been a terrible accident. The passengers on board the *Mauretania* knew they were being hunted by metal monsters sliding under the surface of the turbulent dark water. Even though their hospital ship was protected by humanitarian convention and lit at night, a hungry submarine captain, searching at night in poor weather, could still attack and sink the unescorted *Mauretania*. High speed was their defense, but then *Lusitania* had been nearly as fast.

Tamping down his anxiety, Rags conveyed the news to his party and was reassured by Hilly's equanimity. Landing only seventy-five miles south of London, with excellent rail connections, meant they could be home in a couple of hours. As they got closer to England, the tension rose until they entered the Solent and passed the old Napoleon-era gun forts between the Isle of Wight and Portsmouth Harbor. The anxiety on board among the passengers, who had endured so much on the battlefield and voyages on the hostile Mediterranean, was released at last. They had made it to safe waters.

THE FIRST-CLASS RAIL COMPARTMENTS, bound from the coast for London, were choc-a-block with jovial companions who broke out traveling bars containing ornate crystal decanters that were filled with cheap booze purchased in tax-free Gibraltar. The high-speed Great Western steam engine whisked them through Winchester and on to the capital city in 90 minutes. Once the baggage was tagged and put into taxis, along with Uncle Hilly and Segar, Rags was relieved of duty and told to spend the weekend with his mother and forget the war.

The dogs alerted the household when he paid off the cabbie. Two high-pitched howls from behind the thick wooden door to the great house at Ranelagh Gardens reverberated through the neighborhood.

Rags paused a moment to take in the warm and clear September evening. The smells of Egypt and Gallipoli—the rotting vegetation, the beasts of burden, open stagnant sewers and damp-fueled cooking fires, the sheer volume of bodies—faded from memory with every fresh breath of air. God, it was good to be home.

The Westies brought Charlotte to the door, and her shriek of surprise brought the housekeeper and maids. Rags had refrained from sending her dates because his schedule was so uncertain, subject to vagaries and whims. Charlotte had barely gotten her arms around him before she was driven back by the two terriers, who pulled at his trouser cuffs and begged him to kneel down and explain where he had been and how wicked he was for leaving them with an old woman who didn't walk them to the park. How could he do such a thing? Tied up in their own enthusiasm, they forgave him.

Rags felt only elation. As enthused as the dogs, he lifted his mother in the air and whirled her about. "My God, I have missed you. This house, my dogs, and England too." The taxi driver dragged his kit to the door and dropped them just inside, waiting patiently for an additional tip. He must have witnessed this ritual many times.

Stuck together like two kids, Charlotte and her boy shuffled to the library while the maids looked to the luggage and Mrs. Alberry went to put together an early tea. Out of habit, Rags toted his briefcase. The dogs sniffed about it for food. "No, no, you can't chew this one, pick something else," which Valerie did with no need for further encouragement. Of course, Teddy, no longer a puppy, wanted more attention from his master and followed Rags and his mother into the library, a room he was rarely allowed into.

"Mamma, the place looks the same. What have you been doing with yourself all this time?"

"Well, I've been looking for war work, if you must know. It is all the rage, even for women my age. But so far I haven't found a situation."

"Good for you—I have been doing war work as well!" They laughed together as they had before. All was well in the Stetchworth household. The dread that had accumulated in Rags over the past weeks—not just the fear and bloodshed of Gallipoli but the secrecy and duplicity of Rome—was dissipating with every passing minute in his childhood home.

In the last week the *Times* had published a five-column page of nothing but casualties from Gallipoli. Charlotte had pored over them with her heart in her throat, afraid to go on to the next name for fear it would be her son's. Now he was here right before her.

"Tell me, Rolly. Tell me everything you've done and seen. Don't leave out a detail; I am so interested in everything my boy has done."

Rags didn't want to scare his mother and, like all soldiers who experienced the war on the ground, knew he wouldn't be able to replicate it to someone who had no experience with the boredom and terror that work together hand in hand. Instead he concentrated on the trials and tribulations of Uncle Hilly and Henry Segar. There was little she knew about her distant cousin except for his rank. Rags was enamored with the man after watching him in action, and he tried to pass that on to her so she would know that he was not one of the "donkeys that led the lions." He also wanted her to know that in future ventures he would be kept safe by the inspector general. Hilly knew that this was no quick skirmish or colonial conquest of lands defended by spears and hope alone. This war was a long-term, ongoing tragedy, and he was going to do all he could to see to it that the donkeys in Whitehall knew what it was that they were doing to the British Empire. That was a mixed message for his mother, the German spy. Like so many others, she had clung to the official line—that it was going to be a short campaign resulting in a slap on the wrist for the loser. She assumed that soon all would go back to normal and she could move her household to Austria as planned.

Rags saw her mood change and lightened it with tales of Henry Segar, the out-of-place academic in his white suit on the beach at Gallipoli. His turned-up nose at the quality of the rations and his lack of stamina on the trek up the beach at Cape Helles. But somehow it soon turned to his story of writing letters for the boys in the hospital and then their wounds and the stench and the terrible, useless, unending assaults on the heights. Charlotte's eyes widened as he spoke. "How terrible for you, to see all that suffering." Charlotte hoped it hadn't changed her lovely boy who was so friendly and open. But more than anything she was furious at Uncle Hilliard, who had drawn Rags away from her and into the very hazards she had planned to avoid. She had intended to protect him in the cloister of Whitehall, where men talked big but did little, and Hilly had perverted her well-laid plan.

She changed the subject. "What was it like to go to sea? I haven't been on any real ships. The packets across the Channel were mere excursions, no luxury cabins or meals at the captain's table."

"Well, Mother dear, it isn't all beer and skittles on a troop ship. Although the warship on the way out to Egypt was pleasant, there was no luxury. The compartments for the likes of me were little more than a grey metal locker with steam pipes and electrics running up one wall and through the overhead. Uncle Hilly and Segar had it much better but still . . . rather dull, all business you know, ship shape and Bristol fashion. The *Mauretania* has a smattering of luxury on the top deck, where the VIPs cavorted with the ladies and families picked up along the way home. Food was good, once we left Italy. At the end, though, the threat of German submarines had everyone spooked." As soon as it was out of his mouth, he wished he hadn't brought up the subject of subs, as the German navy was racking up tonnage daily and the papers described the wreckage in detail. Somehow, too, it seemed wrong to talk of the Germans as the enemy to his mother.

Charlotte was well aware of the sea link and its importance to the availability of food at the markets. Mrs. Alberry and Mrs. Jayson often put in a jab about the shortages to ensure that Charlotte, who never shopped for food, was well aware that there was a war on. She had commented on the reduced sugar in the cakes and shortage of butter. Her bread and butter sandwiches at tea when company was expected were inferior to what they had been. She was also aware that the cook solicited—nay, demanded—visitors to bring items from the country when staying in the house. She had not actually seen a ration book, but the papers were full of controversy over who was getting more or less than they were entitled to. It was not a subject at her ladies' teas, with the exception of the state of qualified servants or lack thereof. The munitions factories were popping up everywhere, even in Putney and Fulham. While girls were joining the land army to keep food production up, country girls were flooding into the cities for better wages. Servants, most of whom could read and write, were prized. They provided the link between the male managers and the shop floor. Charlotte let Rags know that she was aware of the shortages of both food and labor. "Well, the rations have been hard on everybody. And you wouldn't believe the poor quality of applicants after my maids returned to Austria."

WITH TEA OVER AND DONE with, the plates carried away, and the sun warming the two in their armchairs, Rags changed the subject to the good news he had been saving until the coast was clear. "Mamma, I've been keeping the best story for the last. You know I was in Rome. Guess who I met there? I'll give you a hint. I met him at Saint Peter's.

Charlotte smirked. "You didn't meet God at Saint Peter's, did you? That's where my Catholic friends say he resides."

"Now, Mamma, we both know you don't have any Catholic friends in England, except for one, that is." He was teasing her and they both loved it. She thought again and shook her head.

"What if I were to say 'monsignor from Westminster Cathedral'? Would that help?"

Her eyes widened. "Pieter Luskey . . . is it Pieter? But no, he is in London, isn't he?"

"You got it in one, well done. But not just Pieter. He introduced me to another priest, well, a spurious priest at any rate. I was introduced to a man disguised as a priest on our tour around the Vatican." Rags couldn't hold it back another moment. "I met my father."

"Christian? You met Christian, at the Vatican?" Her delight quickly turned to dismay. "What on earth was he doing at the Vatican?"

Rags smiled at her confusion. "Father is still as he was, in the German army, but masquerading as a priest so he could meet me. He knew I couldn't send a completed report of all I had seen by radio message, so he arranged to wait for me in Rome. Your letter, the one with the photo of me in uniform that you sent about my itinerary through Pieter, resulted in them both being in Rome. You did it, Mamma—you are quite a spy yourself!"

The conversation plunged into a minute-by-minute recounting of all that was said and done at the meeting. Charlotte was captivated by every word, gesture, and embellishment of the epic engagement. It was everything she had dreamed of, the two of them working together at the highest levels, consulting with each other over the great task of restoring German-Austrian supremacy. Rags broke the news of his captaincy in the German army when he slipped open the bottom of his briefcase. Charlotte read the German text, in its ornamental gothic script, under her breath, ever aware of the new English servants who had replaced her Austrian girls. Handing it back to Rags for protection, she overflowed with admiration. "The Kaiser himself signed it, my *liebchen*, what an honor. It is no less than you deserve. Captain Stetchworth." She gave a little salute with her tiny white hand. "Must I stand at attention when I speak to you?" she said, amused.

"You could—I hold a commission in two opposing armies; who would know which you were saluting?" They laughed. "But Mamma, that is not all, it is just the beginning." Another probe at the case and Rags produced the leather-covered box. Cradling it in the palm of his left hand, he pried the top up with his right to reveal the Iron Cross, Second Class. "Do you know what this is?"

The peculiar scent given off by the red satin lining cleared Charlotte's head. Her eyes opened wide as she looked at the medal and then into Rags' eyes. She didn't speak, but clasped her two warm hands against her cheek in astonishment. "It's yours. Where did you get it?"

Proudly Rags proclaimed, "It's ours, Mamma, yours and mine. Father gave it to me . . . well, the Kaiser gave it to Father for me. You deserve it as much as I do. The Kaiser knows all about us. He told Father that we were indispensable to the war. He said I deserved it as much as those soldiers fighting in France . . . all over the world!"

Charlotte gasped, "Can I touch it?"

Rags was a little surprised at her admiration over the medal. He didn't think that women knew about medals. "Touch it, turn it over, read the back out loud."

She did in a hushed tone so only Rags and the dogs could hear it. "Hauptmann Roland Stetchworth; that doesn't sound very German. Dare we keep it? What if it were found?" She closed the box with a snap and looked toward the door. "I know, I'll put it in the cupboard." The cupboard was the name she gave her secret wall repository used for copies of messages exchanged with Christian. "Watch the door, Rolly." Charlotte rose and took the box and the commission to the space between two sections of the bookcase that lined one side of the large room. She took the cross that hung around her neck on a long chain and thrust the broad flat bottom into a recess in the molding, turning it until the door sprang open an inch or so. Checking the door to the hallway once more, she selected the top shelf and slid the items deep inside before carefully closing the hidden compartment. "There, safe and sound."

## Chapter Nineteen

# London, September 1915

AS IMPORTANT AS THE GROUND WAR was, by 1915 the naval effort had become just as important to both sides. Germany could not feed itself without imports from the Americas. With only Baltic and Channel ports within Germany's grasp, the Royal Navy stepped in early and closed them tight. The Royal Navy was the senior military service and pride of the nation. The Kaiser had overhauled the German navy at the turn of the century, fully aware of Britain's naval superiority, and was rewarded with a more modern and heavily armed complement of superior ships, which, if handled correctly, could seriously challenge the First Sea Lord's fleets. Churchill was not worried. He had hoped, in fact, that the Germans would opt for a major battle, confident the Royal Navy would take them out and cement its control of the waves. The British had a larger complement by nearly a third and were highly experienced in the shallow waters of the North Sea. It would be all too perilous for the Imperial German navy, as well as its merchant fleet, to make a break for the open waters of the Atlantic through the narrow passage between Iceland and the Hebrides.

The Germans were forced to change tactics. Early attempts to call out small portions of Royal Navy elements to be defeated piecemeal along the eastern coast of England had little effect, as did the shelling of coastal towns. So the Kaiser turned to a new strategy: the deployment of an unrivaled submarine force to prowl the North Atlantic and break up the effort of America and the empire to nourish and support the British Isles. The submarines—deployed on a large scale for the first time in wartime—were stealthy and deadly.

The functional submarine appeared in the United States after the turn of the century. Known as Holland boats, they were developed to scout enemy fleets and coastal defenses. Germany established the first fleet of twenty-nine subs before war was declared. The threat resulted in the adoption of the international Cruiser Laws, which provided merchant ships some degree of protection from the marauding subs. They stated that a warship could stop and search a merchant ship, and if it had arms or contraband on board, the crew and passengers could be legally removed and the ship seized or sunk. At first the submarine commanders complied, surfacing before attacking. But when the British armed merchant ships with deck guns the practice ceased. The fragility of the submarine could not withstand attack on the surface.

Within months of the start of the war, German submarines had sunk a considerable number of Royal Navy men-of-war and commercial ships carrying food to England. The underwater attacks were highly successful. In the Atlantic, two merchant ships each day were sunk. In addition to the torpedoes, submarines surfaced and fired deck cannons into helpless merchant ships, to save the few torpedoes available. The success lead Germany to declare unrestricted submarine warfare. German set a zone surrounding Britain where all shipping, to include neutral nations' vessels, could be engaged and sunk. The terror on the high seas reduced the availability of able seamen serving the industry, further restricting shipping. Extra hazardous duty pay did help with the shortage. Some submarines laid mines that were chained just under the surface outside harbors. These watchful sentinels of death sunk ships within sight of the land.

These attacks hardened the will to fight on in England and enraged the hearts of Americans against Germany. Unfortunately for the Germans, they failed to loosen the economic blockade that kept food from the New World from getting to German civilians. What internal food production there was in Germany was largely dedicated to feeding a two-front army of millions who ate three meals of 4,500 calories every day. The people of Germany—and of the territories it conquered—crept closer to conditions of starvation with every passing year.

RAGS AWOKE SAFE FOR THE first time in over a month. His own bed, kept just as he had left it, the crisp sheets, the model ships that convoyed across the top of his dresser . . . they all sparked in him a feeling of happiness they never had before.

He couldn't believe the adventure that had been thrust upon him. When constructing the model ships, he had never imagined himself on board a real one in a shooting war. Snuggling down in the blankets, he recalled the throbbing engines that had vibrated his bunk and the lights that flickered when the warship changed attitude in an effort to throw off submarines that were surely lurking. He recalled the appalling nights spent on the freighter *Ascot*, a rust-encrusted bucket so decrepit that submarines wouldn't waste ammunition on it. Every memory made his present comfort more precious.

As much as he wanted to luxuriate in his well-earned rest, the last month had changed him. He thought of the young soldiers facing another day on Gallipoli and the fresh-faced nurses ready to treat them, and he slid out of the sheets and into his army boots waiting by the bed.

At the office deep within the musty confines of Horse Guards, he sorted out his notes from his new briefcase—the secret compartment was empty now—and gave them to Mrs. Box. She hadn't said a word to him about the trip but went straight to work. "Wait a minute, come back, Rags; what is that word?" He paused at her desk and peered in wonder. He had no idea. His handwriting, which seemed legible when he wrote the report by the light of a field lamp or ship's glow, looked like a child's scribbling in the calm light of the office. "You'd better take these back and put them in the King's English. Thank God at least the general is literate." She was at him once again. There was always a little curl in her voice that told him he wasn't up to the job. He had gotten the billet because he was a family member; that was the way it was done in England. However, Mildred seemed to resent his presence and was inclined to come down on the side of merit and not heredity—a hurdle Rags hoped to jump before long.

Rags retrieved the sheaf of dog-eared papers and took them back to the outer office for revisions. Alone, except for Captain Howard Leggette, aide to Senior Inspector General Badington-Smyth—who was the boss in name only. Rags noted Leggette's total lack of activity, which was the hallmark of the army high senior staff. "How's it going, Howie? Boss still awake?"

Leggette jumped to his feet and crossed the open space between their desks there in the large anteroom. "Not so loud—you know it's morning nap time. He had a big breakfast this morning, so he's good for at least two hours on the couch." The senior inspector general reserved his inquiries to members of the army at his own level. As a lieutenant general, that left only generals and field marshals who were worthy of his attention, and that suited his nap schedule down to the ground. Hilly was more than happy to pick up matters of significant import while the remainder of the IG staff—a brigadier chief of staff and a dozen colonels—conducted the daily business of the army at home and in the field.

"Rags, I wish I had something to occupy my days," Leggette said. "I envy you, always on the hop, meeting the big wigs. It must be fun."

While Rags wanted to have a natter with the captain and tell him about his adventures, he was compelled to put him off. "Sorry, Howie, can't talk, must get these notes readable for her majesty."

Seated, he adjusted the desk lamp directly above the scattering of papers and began, "What's that word—*requffered*. Is that a word, an English word? Maybe I'm not right-handed. What do you think, Howie?"

The captain squinted through his thick glasses. "Beats me. Who wrote it?"

Not wanting to admit that he was the author, Rags covered. "Some idiot, I suspect." He had intended to make contact with Grace by now, but the dreaded Mrs. Box had put the kibosh on that. He gazed at the next page, hoping his penmanship might have improved. But he was stuck, and it was after lunch before he left a message for Grace at her station in the hospital.

Rags' notes included a list of the people the IG had met and a short description of their positions. Hilly freely admitted that he had no memory for names, just faces. Rags had scribbled hastily, rendering job titles of newly acquired acquaintances along with the name and title. But they had little meaning to him because his army jargon was not up to snuff. He was aware that his uncle often wrote notes back to people who had been of assistance as a gesture of his interest in their efforts. This was Rags' job now, and now he racked his brain to make sense of them all. Fortunately, he had kept the scraps of paper he had stuffed into his tunic side pockets during their days on the road. A combination of notes and scraps added up to a pretty fair memory, enabling him to finish the job before the duty day was up, and he dropped the English version on Mildred's neat desktop before she could complain to the general.

GRACE HADN'T RETURNED HIS CALL. In the late afternoon, as the light was beginning to fade that early fall, he walked down Whitehall to Parliament Square and went left to Westminster Bridge. He could see St. Thomas' Hospital when he crossed traffic and stepped onto the heavily traveled right of way. It was shift-changing time, and he thought he could catch her one way or the other. At the nurses' residence he stopped a girl coming out, and she said that Grace was just going up to her floor. "From the look of you, I'll bet you've been here before. You know her station, don't you?" Rags admitted he did back in July and inquired if she was still taking care of the Aussies. The girl gave him a nod and smile and added, "Good luck, Lieutenant."

He started up the worn wooden stairs that creaked on every other tread. On the top floor he caught his breath to find himself in the middle of a traffic jam composed of walking wounded, gurneys, dinner carts, and general confusion. No one paid any attention to him, so he shuffled down the center of the wide corridor in the direction of an overhead plaque that read "Nurses' Station."

Most of the patients were in ill-fitting blue cotton uniforms, which meant they had been processed somewhere else. To his surprise, he recognized one who crept along on crutches. He had talked to him on board *Mauretania* as they stood an amateur submarine watch on the rail of the top deck. Before Rags disembarked he had been informed that all patients were bound for Guy's Hospital across the river from the City. He stopped to talk. "How did you all get here from Southampton so quickly?"

The young soldier smiled to find someone he knew. "Well, sir, they dumped us on a medical train sitting astride the dock and we were on our way before two shakes of a lamb's tail. There was a trail of ambulances as far as you could see at the station, and we just took it easy and rode along, pretty as you please. Mighty big city, your London, never seen anything like it. The nurses are prettier here too. Sure beats Gallipoli, eh sir?"

Rags was not surprised by the glib assessment; it was pure Aussie. He had come to admire the Down Under spirit of a man with only one leg. "Hope all goes well, mate," Rags replied, giving the wounded soldier a tap on the arm. "Have to go; I just saw my girl."

"Grace!" raising his voice, "over here!" She was carrying a tray in the other direction but looked over her shoulder at the voice. She smiled, put the medical tray down on an empty stand, and pushed her way to his outstretched arms.

"Rags, it is you! I saw that you called and didn't know how to call back." He had left a message but forgotten to leave his number.

"Sorry, I wasn't thinking. I was so excited to be calling you. I thought of you every day I was away and hoped we could be together soon. And . . . here we are in the middle of the Australian army! I feel I've brought them with me. I guess I can't get away from a good thing." He was babbling, but she didn't seem to mind.

She hugged him, rested her chin on his chest and closed her eyes. In her heart she thanked God. "How is my brave boy? All in one piece, I see," as she stepped back to inspect the young officer beaming from ear to ear. "I thought you forgot me, not a line," she scolded.

Rags blushed. "I was rather out of pocket, you know, out there at the end of the world. I had intended to write, but you can't imagine the chaos and the confusion in the wilderness. I was either beached or confined on a ship; it was distressing and I didn't want to worry you with, well, you know, you see it every day . . . I only wrote to my mother—once."

Her eyes softened. "You're forgiven. We had a steady stream of Gallipoli casualties and I asked if anyone had seen a handsome Guard's lieutenant, but you remained anonymous. I was worried." Rags was flattered and relieved that the connection he remembered hadn't been his imagination or wishful thinking, that she felt as connected as he did. Grace nodded toward the station desk. "As you can see, we are rushed and Matron is giving me the eye. I go on break tomorrow. Can we meet somewhere?"

The following day Rags, confidently dressed in a new uniform his tailor had run up while he was gone, hurried over to the Clarence Pub across the street from the Admiralty on Whitehall. Rags was uncertain as to the exact time he could come free from his duties, but he didn't want to waste time walking the twenty minutes to St. Thomas'. Uncle Hilly was not in the office; Rags suspected he was at the Clarence as well, relaxing upstairs above the main floor. He'd heard Mildred on the phone making arrangements for a small party of two earlier that morning, followed by an order to the florist to be delivered that afternoon.

Rags crossed the traffic and noticed Grace at a small window table as he pushed through the double doors. She was as pretty as a picture, with the light behind her in what was surely a new red hat on her blond hair. Not knowing if the dress was also new, he stayed away from comment and instead praised her figure . . . always a safe bet. "Grace, you do look a treat. You're thin—I must take you for a good spread. I've made arrangements for afternoon tea at the Langham." She was pleased, he could see it in her bright blue eyes.

"How did you ever get reservations? So posh, and on a lieutenant's pay at that. My, my, Rags, you do spoil a girl. My mother took me there when I was a little girl and I remember it so fondly. You are a dear."

Rags accepted the compliment. "We must go. I'll get a taxi. Nothing but the best for us two." He was flush with cash, not having spent so much as a farthing in over a month. "What better way to go broke?"

In 1864, the Langham Hotel's Palm Court, just off upper Regent Street, had been the first restaurant to feature afternoon tea. Understated yet elegant, the brass and crystal doors were held open to welcome guests into a sequestered space that contained only twenty tables under a high canopied ceiling. The lights were bright to pick up the color of the Wedgwood china and the treats to come. Tall baskets stuffed with large blooms were dotted around a centerpiece featuring statues of Britannia in all her glory. The walls were masked with flowing brocade golden drapes held back with twisted black and gold cords to reveal elegant Victorian tableaus.

The concierge led them to their seats and took Rags' cap. Both had been thinking of what to say when they were finally alone. Rags thought Rome would be a good start and loosened the conversation up with the mischief at the Italian restaurant, but he substituted Uncle Hilly and Segar for the monsignor and his father. She asked, "What was the Vatican like? We're strict Chapel at home in Wales, so all I know about Rome is that's where the pope lives."

Rags talked about the museums and ruins he had seen, laying off the religious parts. He admitted that he wasn't much of a believer himself. "Religion is more my mother's penchant. She converted when she was a girl visiting Germany in her student days." Grace knew little about his family connections, so she steered the conversation to his childhood and home in London. Rags found that whenever talking about himself, he had to walk a tightrope. He wanted to be open with her, but the Langham was no place to tell her that he was an illegitimate son of an Austrian count, much less what had happened to his stepfather. His military service was a minefield as well, and he felt that his whole story was becoming a tapestry of misdirection and evasions that would be difficult to run up consistently if he failed to remember the order and context of his lies. He suddenly felt that it was rather a lot for someone trying very hard just to live to be twenty.

Valiantly he turned the questioning back to her: the hospital, her family, even music, which he knew she loved. He suggested they to go to a theater and see the latest show. Grace sighed. "You know I love the theater, but it's so complicated now. All the top German and Austrian musicians are interned on the Isle of Man for the duration. They even planned to present Wagner's operas in English until they had to cancel them altogether! Plenty of Shakespeare and Thomas Hardy, though, anything patriotic. But I live the war every shift and don't need it to be inserted into my evenings off as well. There are recruiters in every lobby, and every show ends with a performance of 'God Save the King.' I went with Rory Edgerton-Gray—you know him, he's a captain in your regiment—to see *The Enemy Amongst Us*, a play about German spies. The Germans were all vilified. They attempted to blow up a water-pumping station. Whenever the players mentioned the Kaiser, the audience booed. It was most off-putting and quite unnecessary, so melodramatic. It turned the play into a pantomime, and it wasn't even Christmas!" She stopped and smiled at her own rant. "I know, I know . . . there are worse deprivations in London right now. But I hate how the war has penetrated every segment of our culture. London theater has been spoiled by it. It's nothing but silly German stereotypes and tasteless jokes. I can't stand another night like that."

Rags pretended to be very concerned about the state of London theater, but his mind was stuck on Captain Edgerton-Gray. He had assumed Grace was too busy to be concerned with other young officers. He now suspected that they must be spinning around her like moths to a flame. He must step up his game if he was going to remain in the picture.

"Mother tells me much the same tale," he remarked. "She says it's childish to paint the Germans as vicious monsters. After all, she says, the war will end soon and we'll all going back to being civil and well-mannered when we travel back on the Continent. She's right, of course, one should keep a long view."

"Well, I wouldn't go that far," Grace broke in. "With what I've seen, I don't think the Germans can ever be forgiven."

Rags backpedaled quickly. "Of course, of course not." Finally, a safe topic popped into his mind as they finished the tiny sandwiches and went on to the sweets that were piled high on a three-tiered Wedgwood stand, topped off with two candies in the shape of Big Ben. He produced a packet of Murray's

Mellow Mixture and offered her a cigarette. He pointed to the advert on the packet: "Don't stop smoking because tax on tobacco has increased. It is your duty to the state to keep on smoking."

"Ah, it's my duty to take one." Amused, Grace admitted she smoked Mitchell's Golden Dawn because it showed a happy soldier smoking in a green field on the front of the packet. "Silly, isn't it, but it must be working. I took up smoking on the ward when the soldiers offered them to me."

Rags felt equally guilty. "I was issued them free with my rations and found them relaxing and not so much trouble as a pipe—loose tobacco, cleaners and all that," he admitted. Looking about, nearly everyone in the room was smoking cigarettes, holding them up with an air of sophistication. A cloud of pale blue smoke hung in the crowded room like some internal, self-generated London fog overwhelming the natural perfume of London's most celebrated tea.

AT HORSE GUARDS THE NEXT week Rags gathered together elements for a short executive evaluation to be the lead element of the study composed in concert by Segar and Hilly. The three would shortly be heading to Churchill's offices on the top floor of the Metropole Hotel, which had been commandeered by the War Office for the duration. Churchill, though he had resigned as First Lord of the Admiralty several months before and was soon headed to the Western Front, had kept his office as well as keeping his fingers in the pie. He and Kitchener were good friends, and both were being pilloried in the press for the unending disaster that Gallipoli had become. While adroit at the big picture, they were not much for detail and had left operations to the staff and field commanders. With the Gallipoli campaign it became apparent they were "good starters but bad stickers." In the midst of strife, they had turned to Hilly and Henry Segar to pick it all apart and provide direction to save the expedition and their own reputations.

The Metropole was within walking distance of Horse Guards, a couple of blocks down toward the river on a corner of Northumberland Avenue, and Rags was increasingly excited as they walked to meet two of the most prominent figures of the war. Churchill had established the war strategy for the Royal Navy and overseen its operations. He wasn't a sailor, but a Sandhurst-educated, experienced soldier with the reputation as an adventurer. He brought a certain panache to the office which was not necessarily appreciated by the War Cabinet. Kitchener, for his part, was an anti-politician. He had commanded forces in the Sudan, South Africa, and India and now was leading the British Army in its quest to defeat Germany.

As they walked, Segar told them of a particularly frightening article that had appeared that morning, lifted from *Der Spiegel* quoting a noted cavalry officer who distinguished himself in the Prussian victory over France in 1870. Friedrich von Bernhardi reminded Germans that "it is the natural law on which all other laws of nature rest . . . the law of the struggle for existence . . . War is a biological necessity." Segar found it vulgar, "just the sort of rubbish the Huns spew out that tangles logic and makes war obscene." Segar, like many Britons, started using "Huns" after the Kaiser bragged in 1900 that the Germans would "bring terror to the hearts of the opponents just as the Huns did."

The Metropole Hotel was grand. Immediately inside the bright, brass-framed glass doors and up three broad, black quartz steps was a round room of some size with a giant crystal lit orb eight feet in diameter that brightened the whole ceiling space. They were directed by an aide to a private elevator that took them quickly to the penthouse. Rags followed along behind his boss and Henry Segar to the northwest corner, where double doors were opened in advance and Churchill and Kitchener waited. Once warm greetings were exchanged, Rags distributed the final version of the report. The four principals enjoyed a brandy passed by a uniformed steward while Rags took his place in a leather chair against the paneled wall. Hilly checked his watch against the time on the clock tower at the Houses of Parliament visible from his seat near the high windows. Segar put his own notes in order, anticipating questions from Kitchener, who was always curious. Churchill and Kitchener did not suffer long and involved analysis. They liked it quick, dirty, and to the point—and the point in question was the leadership of the Gallipoli campaign.

Hilly began to speak before they finished reading. "You asked 'what about the leaders?' Indeed, we found it to a most profound question. It is the essence of our response. We found Hamilton to be miscast. His conduct prior to the move from Egypt was sketchy. Little attempt was made to study the terrain or the enemy. The decision to recast all the supplies and troop formations on a small Greek island was foolish. His view of the role of high command left him disconnected and moribund. He has and continues to hold himself aloof from his field commanders. What few decisions were required at his level were not addressed. As a result, good commanders remain good and poor ones remain helpless. The result is neglect, which leads to poor performance, misuse of resources, and bloated casualties, none of which can be tolerated. We recommend that the man listed be relieved of command and that," addressing Marshal Kitchener directly, "you and your selection for commander should go to Gallipoli and assess the situation on the ground in person as soon as possible."

Kitchener spoke first. "Well, Hilly, you never were much of a diplomat and I recognize Henry's hand in the written words. The fact remains, Mr.

Churchill and I personally selected Hamilton and the others. Could we be that inept or are you two pulling our legs?" Hilly hadn't expected his report to be taken at face value, knowing how much was at stake for the reputations of the two prominent gentlemen.

Prepared for questioning, Segar steered them to a number of passages in the body of the document and the four men discussed them in detail. It was plain to Rags that they were looking for a way out of the command structure while saving face. But too much blood had been sacrificed in this far-off land by troops from the wide expanse of the empire.

Churchill was intense. He was concerned about the naval role, not having abandoned his original plan to take the Dardanelles with a naval fleet and strike at Constantinople, the heart of the Ottoman Empire. He had already taken the heat from losing nearly a dozen ships of the line earlier and needed redemption at the hand of the army victory to reenter the fray anew. But there it was, and at the end of an hour, Kitchener caved in and agreed he must go see for himself.

So it was that sixty days of preparation, travel, reconnaissance, labor, and pure bloody hardship were reviewed and accepted, and they were on their way out the door when Kitchener buttonholed Hilly once more. "There is another matter, old chap, I would like you to shepherd through the staff. Cumming has a bee in his bonnet and I have sicced the old hound on you as his point of contact. Do what you can with him—he has my full support, you know. Take care of it, Hilly, in your own way, and keep me and only me in the loop. D'accord?"

SPYCRAFT HAD REACHED A ZENITH as the war went into its third year. The Royal Navy had set up listening stations around the British Isles and on special ships that accompanied the blockade fleet at the entrance of the Baltic and along the length of the Channel. Jersey and Guernsey had listening stations, as did Iceland and Norway. Code breaking was centered in the Admiralty building next to Horse Guards. With the increasing threat to Atlantic shipping, the Americans set up a station at Fort Monmouth in northern New Jersey in aid of convoy operations. With the airways filled with Morse code, code breaking and the need for security was becoming a field with a great future. The regular British Army establishment did not establish an intelligence branch, detailing officers on short loan to interrogate prisoners of war and, in a haphazard manner, to gather general information on the enemy's intent. Spying was left to the Royal Navy's Captain Mansfield George Smith-Cumming and his band of misfits and oddballs to hotfoot around and meddle in everyone else's business. It wasn't gentlemanly work, a bias that had plagued Britain throughout its preparations. Prior to the war, the navy had agreed to build only three submarines—despite the Germans' hundred or so—because sneaking about underwater was unseemly. The original British anti-submarine strategy, when the high seas fleet was threatened by German subs at Scapa Flow, was to send sailors into the harbor in rowboats; when a German periscope was sighted, they were to strike it with a large mallet.

The Royal Navy soon realized the threat, fortified the area and began a serious intelligence effort which lasted the entire war. Central to that effort was Cumming, the first director of a new department of government known as SIS, or in some quarters MI6, early in 1914. That year he had been in a serious road accident in France in which his son was killed and he was injured. The captain described it himself on many occasions, saying, "I amputated my own leg to free myself from the wreck to cover my dying son with my coat. Though my boy, who was the driver, died, I was found nine hours later unconscious."

Recovered and walking on a wooden leg, the captain, who had been medically retired from the Royal Navy in 1885, had a flair for intrigue and a weakness for spycraft. A large man with thick, rounded shoulders and an oversized personality, he stood uncomfortably as a rule in a dark, double-breasted suit with pale pinstripes. The source of his abrupt manner (some would say a loose cannon) was his wife's great wealth, which she showered upon his solo work, indulging his love for eccentric spy accoutrements. Experts hired by Cumming perfected codes, cameras, and miniaturized film years ahead of commercial production. With meager support from the government and the military, who considered themselves to be focused on the "real" war, he had single-handedly begun to build an espionage agency that operated throughout central Europe in both Allied and enemy countries. He was particularly interested in Russia, which, as he put it, "smelled of revolution." Only a few knew of his alliance with Sidney Reilly, whom he ran in and out of Russia in anticipation of the revolution. A personal visit from Cumming would not be welcome by any of the Horse Guards' staff, but especially not by Rags. Even his father knew of Cumming's canny reputation and had warned him to stay clear of "Old Captain C."

IT WAS NO SURPRISE WHEN on return to Horse Guards a perturbed Mrs. Box was waiting at the door to the inner office. "General, there is an odd person waiting for you in your office. His credentials are quite unusual and he pushed his way in without a 'by your leave.' I fear he may be a foreign gentleman to boot." Her general, however, was not surprised then, nor had he been when Kitchener raised the topic. Rags was waved into the meeting ahead of the general and realized that he had seen the man before. Yesterday, when he met Grace at the Clarence, that man had been climbing the narrow steps of the pub leading to the upper rooms. He wasn't carrying flowers, so he wasn't the delivery man he had overheard Mildred phoning. Suddenly the mysterious and alluring upper rooms of the Clarence took on a different sheen. Hilly was happy to let one and all believe that he entertained lady friends there, but now Rags thought of all the reservations at the Clarence leading up to their trip to Gallipoli. There was no paramour at all—Hilly and Cumming had been working together, were in cahoots and had been since June, at least.

The gentleman had seated himself in a soft leather chair and was content resting his left leg on the ottoman. "Lieutenant Stetchworth, I would like to introduce you to a most remarkable naval person, Captain Cumming, of Cambridge Circus," Hilly said. Rags didn't let on that he had seen Cumming before or that Kitchener had warned them of the visit.

Making no attempt to stand, the captain nodded but didn't extend his hand to the junior officer. "Can we get right to it, Hilly? I walked the halls as conspicuously as possible to let them all know that something is afoot. Whenever Cumming is in the area things happen, and they know it." He obviously enjoyed his own outrageous reputation. "I say, in the newspapers today a woman reported to authorities that she saw four German spies dressed as nuns in Brixton. I thought it noteworthy to see nuns in Brixton, let alone spies." He was amused by his own joke, and Rags found it unusual for a man of his eminence to be so congenial.

Rags was relieved when the chief of spies ignored him, treating him like a piece of furniture, which he was becoming used to. It allowed Rags to take his time observing him back. Cumming was heavy in the face and neck with small eyes. His hands seemed meaty from the heavy use of the stick he kept next to his chair. It was said of him that when interviewing prospective agents, he would suddenly thrust a sharp letter opener into his wooden leg. If the man flinched, he wasn't material for MI6.

"George, I'd be surprised if there were nuns left anywhere in England outside of Westminster Cathedral," Hilly retorted with a smile. "But speaking of German spies . . . you have something to report, do you not? Everyone knows something is afoot if you appear outside your lair."

"Hmm, indeed. So many—Kitchener included—think that it's impossible that an Englishman could spy for the Germans. Un-British, you know. But you and I, Hilly, we know better. And our instincts were right. I've heard from my boys at Kiel: There is a mole here at Horse Guards."

## Chapter Twenty

# Horse Guards, September 1915

THE DEFENCE OF THE REALM ACT—popularly known as DORA—established on August 8, 1914, was a batch of authoritarian measures put in place by a government at war, as governments at war had done for centuries. It consisted of mostly typical wartime restrictions: It banned speech deemed harmful to the war effort, altered factory production, controlled land, rail, and sea movement, and placed formidable restrictions on the press concerning the conduct of the war and daily combat operations. Young pacifists were being jailed under DORA simply for opposing the war.

These risks were much on Rags' mind as he walked to the underground station near the Houses of Parliament. DORA prohibited bonfires, kite flying, the feeding of wild animals, and the purchase of binoculars. He felt safe there. Nor was he bothered about the government's right to requisition his home, though he was hugely opposed to them watering down his pint. Most of all, however, he was tortured by the provision that any person "communicating with the enemy or obtaining information for the purpose to jeopardize the success of the operations of any of His Majesty's forces or to assist the enemy . . . could be sentenced to death." *The enemy* most certainly would include Hauptmann Stetchworth.

Already several violators had been caught, tried, and shot. Mindful of the Iron Cross hidden in his home—which the Crown had every right to requisition should it be deemed necessary—Rags felt vulnerable in a way he never had before. He was relatively confident in his mother, but there were also the Bookers and that weak link, the hand-over between the two parties on Putney Bridge. And what of poor Valerie and Teddy? *Walkies* wasn't a crime under DORA as yet, but there was no doubt the Westies were deeply complicit in communicating with the enemy. He chuckled inwardly, but still: If he were to be caught, those night-time walkies were where it would all come apart. He decided to tell his father of the new threat and ask advice.

At home that evening, the terriers played in his bedroom at their turned-over toy box. Valerie jumped up on the bed and lay on the pillow watching Teddy chew on an odd slipper, having destroyed its twin. She was content to watch and wait for her master to prepare a note, knowing they would deliver it to the dead drop and then go on to Wandsworth Park. It meant the walkie was guaranteed, even though it was pouring down rain. A loyal supporter with a keen mind, she very well knew what was going on. Ruffing up her short, coarse white coat, Rags chided her, "Perhaps *you* are also a spy, huh? You do look guilty, Miss Valerie."

He would write two short messages that night. The first concerned Kitchener's upcoming trip to Gallipoli. Standard intel there. The second, however, was crucial. Did his father know that Cumming believed there was a mole at Horse Guards? What should he do? How did Kiel know about him? Or was there another mole at Horse Guards? Rags worried that Booker would panic when he saw the content. He gave it a test run by taking the messages down to his mother's salon and having her read them before he took the dogs for their evening walk.

All was well until the moment she read the second message. Her face darkened, she sucked in her breath and placed one hand in front of her mouth in shock.

"Rolly, what does this mean—do you think that we are suspected? Could they have seen you in Rome?"

She looked at the dogs, ready for their nightly outing, and back up at her son. "Don't go; wait a few days, see if anything else happens. Go to work and come home and . . . and we do nothing for a week or more."

It was odd for Rags to see his mother so fearful. She had hosted Pieter Luskey in her own home and then turned around and had the ladies auxiliary over the next day. When had she ever shown the least bit of doubt? It was unnerving, but Rags took the role of comforter this time: "No, no, I don't think they know. It's just a hunch they have." He gave the assurances he was hoping to hear himself.

"Rolly, I'll stay at the window and watch to see if anyone is patrolling around the house . . . day and night if need be. We should shut down for a while. That's what we'll do. Maybe they just have suspicions, no real evidence. We never see the Bookers. The messages don't get tampered with before Booker gets them, do they, Rolly? Do you think they're picked up, copied, and put back before Booker can retrieve them?"

Rags realized he had no idea what happened in those few minutes between drop-off and pick-up. But he put on a face of certainty. "No, we'd know. I think Booker can see the drop from his top roof window; he would know."

Rags was rattled now and looked for an excuse to delay the drop-off. Lightening the mood, he went to the cord and gave the kitchen a ring. "A nice hot cup of tea, that's what we good British need," he said wryly.

As they waited for the maid, he returned to his mother's side. "If they know already, there is no way out, Mamma. No matter, I must get this message transmitted. Kitchener is leaving soon and my information will be overtaken by events if we hold it too long. Germany might have to plan something and will need early warning of his visit." He gripped her cold hand. "If it's to be, then we have failed and it will be over. In a way I'll be glad to have it done with—finished." He was surprised how true those words rang for him. "They'll never know you were involved, I promise. And after all, I'm just a kid, not even twenty. Maybe the act doesn't apply to a minor. It will be all right. After the war you can leave the country and go to Austria to be with Father, like you always wanted."

His mother became steely at his words. "Rolly, I *will* tell them that it is all my fault; you didn't want to do it and I made you. I am to blame, not you. You are innocent, just trying to obey your mother like a good son." She beckoned him to sit next to her on the settee. Rags, seated next to her on the pink brocade couch, felt her fear morph into resolve.

"It will all be fine in the end. These are the British, after all. How sharp can they be?"

THE GREAT OLD HOUSE REMAINED very quiet the remainder of the evening. The dreaded cold rain stopped before 9:00 p.m., allowing for a welcome dry and uneventful late walk. Teddy found something to eat in the grass which Rags tried unsuccessfully to pry from his strong jaws. He had a routine drop-off at the far end of the bridge. And other than feeling the chill that foretold the miseries of the next few months in soggy Wandsworth Park, nothing happened.

The next morning he was back at Horse Guards, shaken but not stirred from his resolve. He and Howie prepared the anteroom for the weekly morning staff meeting, held every Tuesday. A refectory table was pulled from against the wall and placed at one end of the large, high-ceilinged chamber on the top floor of the great old headquarters. An ancient discolored crack across a corner plaster molding of the outer wall was dripping rain rhythmically into a metal bucket, only one of many deteriorations in the building. The damp got up everyone's nose and the mold betrayed the neglect of the physical plant. Three cushioned armchairs were placed between the back wall and the near side of the table. Hard wooden armchairs that normally lined up against the wall were dragged across the parquet floor and arranged in rows. At the head table the Inspector General, old Lieutenant General Badington-Smyth, would be installed, with Hilly and the chief of staff, Brigadier Kenneth Kimberly, seated comfortably on either side. Mrs. Box had established an agenda that would be strictly observed. Rags and Howie would distribute papers appropriately to the body of the staff, which was composed of a couple dozen colonels and lieutenant colonels seated on the hard chairs. Hilly would be the second to speak and was the one to drop the morning bombshell.

"Gentlemen. As I'm sure you have seen, our good friend from the navy, Captain Cumming, is on the premises this morning. You all know what that means . . . trouble. Cumming believes that we could have been betrayed, here on the Army General Staff, with an insider working for the Germans. We've been tasked with examining the daily work done here—across Horse Guards—to determine if Cumming is correct. I don't know, and yet I must be assured that our business is not known by the enemy. The chief of staff will be in charge of the program to identify any and all breaches of security within every department and to recommend changes to staff procedures. Additionally, we will reorganize *this* department to ensure that secure procedures are strictly followed. As a result, all storage of classified documents will be consolidated in this chamber. Documents will be checked out by signature with time restrictions in place. No classified documents will leave this department without scrutiny. I will turn this matter over to the chief for assignments. If need be," he shook his finger, "we will place guards at the doors to inspect every outgoing container." Hilly peered around the room to get their reaction but didn't solicit comments. He was pleased to see the staff appropriately shocked. "One more thing: Captain Stetchworth will be tasked with the establishment of the Classified Library and will keep the staff informed of its progress."

Rags hadn't heard anything after the first few words of the last sentence. He looked to Mrs. Box, who was seated against the side wall next to her office door. She never twitched. As the meeting broke up, no one except Howie seemed to notice the promotion.

"Well done, old chap! Captain, well and under a year's service; you must know someone," he teased.

Rags couldn't laugh, but he smiled knowingly. He went directly to Mildred, who had left the meeting and was seated behind her neat desk. Rags placed the morning notes in front of her. "*Captain*—an uncharacteristic typing error, Mrs. Box?"

"You know, Captain, that there is no such thing in this office. You've been promoted . . . again." Failing to look him in the eye, "Well deserved—I'm sure." There was an obvious note of sarcasm in her tone. Rags rolled his eyes, not knowing how to react to what was a very important announcement. A captaincy in the Guards was highly sought after by prominent families. It opened so many doors to a young man's future. He knew it was a matter of privilege and influence, but he was glad for it all the same. He was a bit suspicious, though, since his last promotion was less than two months before. "What's happened, Mrs. Box?"

Acerbic as always, Mildred replied: "It is quite simple: Loos happened."

THE WAR HAD NOT FOLLOWED the plan cooked up between the French and the British in the aftermath of Germany's invasion of Belgium. When Germany had invaded first Luxembourg and then Belgium in early August 1914, the understanding was that a regular British expeditionary army of 40,000 or so would cover the left flank of the massive French army, which in turn would hold the Germans near the border of the Rhineland while a French strike force would counter across the Lorraine. The British intended to march unopposed across Belgium to its eastern border and dig in.

The Germans, for their part, had implemented the Schlieffen Plan, which had been developed for just this situation—simultaneous war with Russia and France. The Schlieffen Plan called for a quick victory over France while the Russians—lacking railroad transport—made their way slowly toward Germany. The Germans hadn't counted on the British entry into the war, however, and the intense mobilization required by the plan took a severe toll on German soldiers. The German army hammered the British Expeditionary Force at Mons, but they were unable to reach Paris, having exhausted their troops and outrun their logistics. From that point the French and British pushed slowly north in a series of outflanking moves to the west until a line was formed across northern France that touched the English Channel just inside Belgium. The British field force at Ypres, Belgium, formed a bulge in the German lines, and trench warfare became the alternative to mass movement that had characterized the first year of the war.

A little more than a year after the opening of hostilities, in September 1915, the British "New Army" attempted to break the deadlock on the Western Front and attacked the German army in Loos, France. It was not a success. Within just hours of going over the top, the reports of carnage were terrible. The first attempt by the British to use weaponized gas resulted in a high level of friendly casualties. Loos was the first time in their history that the Welsh Guards had entered combat as they attacked as part of the Guards Brigade in direction of Hill 70. They never made it. The twelve attacking battalions in the brigade suffered 8,000 casualties out of 10,000 men in four hours. Nearly a fifth of all British casualties in 1915 occurred at Loos.

An unexpected result of Loos was the tremendous loss of officers from the Welsh Guards brigade. This was due to the organization of the infantry company. The British Army's ratio of officer-to-enlisted in 1915 could be as high as eight officers in a company of 200, while the Germans, who suffered many fewer officer casualties, fielded only three officers in the entire company of the same size. Their sergeants led the platoons for the most part.

The sudden loss of so many officers was well known at Horse Guards, so Rags was left in no doubt as to the meaning of Mrs. Box's proclamation. Loos meant that the Guards needed officers and fast, and here was Rags to step into the gap. "You're out of uniform, Captain, and, furthermore, loitering in front of *my* desk. You have to brief the boss on how and when you intend to implement his directions. When would the Captain like to be put in the diary?"

AFTER BEING DISMISSED FROM BOX'S office, Rags took a brisk walk across the gravel of Horse Guards Parade and up Birdcage Walk. He returned the salute of the gate guard at Wellington Barracks and went down the stone steps into the Quartermaster's cache in the cellar. There he purchased a number of shoulder stars for his various uniforms. Taking off his tunic, he laid it on the counter and pinned one more star to each shoulder strap. But when he lifted it up, the sergeant on duty seized it from him with impatience.

"Captain, they need to be in a straight line, spaced properly and just the right interval from the shoulder button—like this. We are the Guards," he said, raising his voice. "Can't have our officers looking catawampus." The supply clerk had plainly seen many new captains come through in the last weeks and was disgusted with what their inexperience might mean for the reputation of the regiment. The clerk barely concealed his attitude with a polite "There we are, sir, right as rain." The Guards were plainly not the Honorable Artillery Company, where life was a little more relaxed. Rags took some umbrage, thinking that the lack of a proper batman to take care of his uniforms put him at a distinct disadvantage. He wasn't entitled to a low-enlisted aide as most serving officers expected. Aides-de-camp didn't have aides. Nonetheless, dressed as a genuine captain, he walked a little taller on the way past the back door to Number 10 Downing Street and in through the officers' club entrance of the army headquarters.

He sat alone for lunch in the junior officer mess. He was expected to organize a new functioning department. What did he know about departments? He was a dog robber, plain and simple, not a staff officer with work to do and things to be accomplished. His library would be on display each morning when Uncle Hilly passed through to his office. After cod and chips (a thinking man's meal), he came up with a brilliant scheme.

Back on the top floor of the old headquarters, he stopped in the staff office of the IG Department. There he sought out pretty Beryl Roberts, the girl who had shepherded him on his first day nearly six months ago. He had kept up a nodding acquaintance with her in hopes of taking her out for a drink if he ever had the time.

"Rags, here you are again and with another new pip on your shoulder; well, I never. Who was killed this time for the promotion?" It was an ironic comment; of course she was referring to his last promotion when she had handed him his commission in the Welsh Guards as a first lieutenant before he left for Gallipoli. Beryl was a very pretty girl, just taller than Rags, with jet black hair and smoldering dark eyes that enchanted every prowling soldier on several floors. Rags had offered to take her for a drink on several occasions, but she was in high demand. Plus, she was a little too pretty and he became unusually timid in her presence. But since the arrival of Rory Edgerton-Gray into Grace's social circle, he felt he needed a back-up and decided to make his move. "How do you like working here in this mainstream of confusion?" He didn't give her a chance to answer. "I'm in charge of the reorganization of the IG office and am about to reposition all the classified documents into my office." The introduction of "my office" was a slight exaggeration, but it gave his proposal gravitas. "I could put you in charge—chief clerk—and secure a promotion for you . . . in time."

Beryl was from Camden Lock in the east end of London, where plain speaking was the norm. Quick on the pick-up, she asked, "When did you get such power, my lad? Or is this just a come-on to get me to go out with you?"

"No, this is legitimate. I've never assembled a library before, and I need someone to put it together and run it. I'm still the aide; you would be the boss. You could get a bunch of your girlfriends to help you out, maybe three or four, under you, of course. I'm sure I can get them to spring for a step increase, couple of pounds a week at least. You're already doing the work here; it would be an expansion for you right across the entire IG office. What do you think?"

"This isn't some kind of wind-up, is it? You putting me under you, so to speak. I'm not expected to give you any special privileges, am I?"

"Oh no, I think you will be working with Mrs. Box; you know she is on the up."

"I like Mildred; she is my kind of mate. A little old, but we could get on. Yeah, I got some friends. We can do it. Besides, I would like to see the back of this lot. You got a deal, Rags. When and where?"

"I'll get the ball going with the general and move the furniture, so within the week, I should expect. Don't burn any bridges before I give you the word; keep this under your hat, Beryl." He touched his nose with his forefinger, indicating that it was all a touchy matter. People were always wary of a new office, anxious about losing staff and therefore power.

Within the week things began to move. There were new desks and filing cabinets, plus the various "donations" that other departments wanted out of their offices and found useful to dump in the new library. Rags had his hands full arranging them in some sequence that was pleasing to the eye. A barrier and counter were arranged across the hallway door where Beryl and her girlfriends accumulated, catalogued, and stashed away all the classified material and maps from officers within the IG department. Rags' desk was turned sideways and pushed against the wall at Mildred's door. A number of telephone lines were hung from the ceiling, which only added to the cluttered look of the big room. But in short order it began to function. It also meant that there was no one looking in Rags' office for a German spy, which was a good thing.

When he got home that evening, Charlotte informed him that there would be a message from his father to pick up on the bridge. Later Rags returned home with wet dogs and a message that was most informative. There was another German spy, but in the Admiralty. Rags was advised to keep clear of naval matters and Churchill's office in particular. Rags couldn't have been happier to do so.

JUST AS RAGS WAS GETTING his classified library in shape, he got a call from Grace, asking to meet him at the White Swan across Vauxhall Bridge, the same pub where they had their first dinner. The call sounded urgent. When he arrived, Grace was already there drinking a Pimm's No. 1 Cup; it may have been her second from the tremor in her voice. "I'm going to France. Rory has been wounded and I have volunteered to join Queen Alexandria's Imperial Military Nursing Service at Château Chenonceau south of Paris. Oh God, I hope he is all right. Father sent me a note to tell me of his condition and told me that civilians, families, are not allowed to visit the wounded. You see, that would add more chaos to the Channel traffic, which is so dependent on replacements and supplies. I knew that nurses are in short supply, so I applied through a family friend to get into the nurse corps, and they said yes. I don't know if I can get to Chenonceau, but I'll do my best. Have you got any pull to get me to his hospital?"

So that is what she wanted—his help to get her to Rory's side. It was obvious that he was number two, or perhaps three or four, in her love life. "Well, I can go to the office of the surgeon general and make inquiries, see if we have a direct connection with that hospital. Sometimes the IG is a formidable presence and can open doors. I'll go tomorrow and let you know. What if we meet tomorrow night back here for dinner?" She didn't respond to the proposal; her mind was clearly in France with Rory. Rags bent his head down to catch her eye. "We both have to eat, don't we?"

She gave a quiet smile. "Oh Rags, you are such a dear. I won't forget you for this."

Breaking away from the spy search that afternoon, he was going to make an effort on behalf of Grace and Rory. He was obliged since Rory was a Welsh Guardsman and therefore a brother in arms, even though they had never met. The surgeon general's office was not at Horse Guards but in a building near Guy's Hospital across the river. A Tube ride away, he was there after lunch when the manic business of the day had subsided. He quickly discovered that Chenonceau was a new venue and was in the process of being staffed. It was reserved for officers of the Guards division, and if Grace's information was correct, Rory was likely to be there or on his way there. Rags went to the staffing office with a proposal. The billeting officer was relieved to fill a billet with a name rather than a number. Rags flashed his credentials from the IG office, the best grease at hand to procure a named replacement order for Grace Moss-Jones. All he needed was a transport document. He was sent to Somerset House, back on the other side of the river, to fleet transport, where his credentials triumphed once again with the aid of a small white lie. Promising to fill in his name on the blank order, he left before anyone could question the unusual request. It was all done in a matter of an afternoon. With that bit of chicanery under his belt, he prided himself that he had learned a great deal more about the army and navy than he realized. He was a natural at this dog-robbing business.

He was pleased with himself as he waited for Grace the next evening at their table at the White Swan Pub, watching the heavy traffic lumber over the bridge and hoping that there would not be a zeppelin raid. Earlier that month the zeppelin had reportedly followed a tourist map of the city and attempted to hit St. Paul's, where more than twenty men and women and six children were killed. The newspapers called the Germans "baby killers."

Grace came dashing in from the rain and plumped down at the table. Her red cloak dripped a circle around her chair. "What news, Rags? Could you do anything for me?"

Rags took the lead. "I can do everything for you, Grace." He hesitated dramatically, looking her straight in the eye. "You're a lucky girl. You picked the right Samaritan." He pulled the transport order form his tunic and turned it around. "Print your name here on that line, and you are on your way in three days to France and your billet at Chenonceau. It's all done, free of charge, of course."

"That's impossible! They said it would be at least a month before anything could be done. Are you sure it's the hospital at the château?"

"Of course! The inspector general is never wrong; that is why I am an assistant to the inspector general."

# Chapter Twenty-One

# Horse Guards, September 1915

TOWARD THE END OF 1915, these was little enthusiasm among British men for joining their countrymen in the trenches of France. British soldiers returning on leave, which was offered according to rank and time on the line, spread stories of carnage that made strong men scurry to the coal mines instead. There were military exemptions offered to farmers, the police, and fire service as well, and a considerable number—perhaps up to 40 percent—of male volunteers were too undernourished to meet the standards for military service.

Nonetheless, some two million men had become soldiers, and holes remained in essential services. The result was an enormous influx of British women into the public workforce. Housewives and women in domestic service came forward, leaving their homes and great houses to take up gainful employment. At first it was shocking for Victorians to see female bank tellers, omnibus or tram drivers, and conductors in skirts. Willing women became bricklayers, welders, news press operators, magazine editors, chauffeurs, ticket inspectors, barrel makers, carpenters, railway porters, optical instrument makers, lift operators, telephonists, stokers, hedgers, and even ditchers laboring on the streets. Women volunteered to demonstrate that they were just as eager to labor for the nation as men. Some would say it was a relief to walk away from domestic toil and earn their own money. There were 23 million women of work age in the British Islands; 7 million would become employed outside the home by the close of the war. Count Bernstorff, German ambassador to the United States, said, "It is the nation with the best women that is going to win this war."

They rushed to the Red Cross in significant numbers, overwhelming the organization. There weren't enough uniforms, and often the volunteers were solely identified by miniature enameled red cross pins made up in the thousands by London jewelers and worn with pride on hats, scarves, and collars. Their movement was also a declaration of freedom, one that could not be questioned in the street, only applauded. Additionally, poor army pay meant many housewives had to work outside the home to make up for their husbands' lost income. Men had also been known to join up to get away from the family, leaving them destitute.

Queen Mary inaugurated the Work for Women Fund in response. "Employment is better than charity," she said. "My objective is to provide employment for as many as possible of the women of this country who are out of work. I appeal to the women of Great Britain to help their less fortunate sisters through this fund." With the money donated, she hoped to assist families while women sought employment. The time-honored Victorian fashion industry suffered when the French corset design was changed to a less restrictive foundation garment, doing away with stays and ties, providing mobility and great relief to working women.

Casualties flooded in from France on long trains from the Channel ports each night to be unloaded track-side in Charing Cross Station. The cavernous station hugged the north side of the Thames in the West End a hundred yards from Trafalgar Square. The walking wounded were served hot tea, coffee, cocoa, and Bovril along with sandwiches and cakes by a large body of volunteer women. Dressed for the cool evening, many wore the purple, green, and white of the suffrage movement to show their solidarity. They provided writing paper with envelopes in addition to cigarettes, socks, comforters, and, in the cold months, mittens. Midsized chintz bags, with a square of tracing paper stitched on for the soldier's name, were made by the ladies. A soldier could put his little treasures (old letters, cigarettes, matches, and souvenirs culled from his uniform pockets) in them when he went off to hospital. Convoys of motor ambulances, bumper to bumper, strung out toward Grays Inn Road and the new Royal Free Hospital, which was staffed almost entirely with women. Stuffed with stacks of stretcher patients and spattered with blood from leaking bandages, the cloth-topped ambulances shook along the cobblestones at a snail's pace. The bandaged and hobbled crept to waiting lorries, where they were assisted by corpsmen up into the back bins and seated tightly shoulder to shoulder. Under dim street lamps, there were no screams, but plenty of sorrowful moans that slipped out of hanging heads as the brown vehicles with red crosses on a white circles jockeyed into position and waited once again to start on one more sorrowful leg of their ghastly journey.

Women from the upper classes answered the call as well. Mrs. Pankhurst suspended the suffragette movement and urged her followers into nursing and support roles, saying, "Every woman who puts her shoulder to the wheel releases a man for the forces." The International Women's Suffrage Alliance was formed to assist women who were leaving home for the first time in the early wave of patriotism and assume a legitimate role in commerce. They expected to earn the right to vote through their intrepid service when the war ended.

CHARLOTTE STETCHWORTH WAS NOT OVERLY fond of work. Born into a family of privilege, her happiest times had been summering in Austria and spending languid afternoons with her student friends. The parents whom she so despised had provided a cushion of wealth that shielded her from factory work or farm labor or work as a governess to bratty, unappreciative children. As was only right, in Charlotte's eyes.

However, Charlotte Stetchworth was rather fond of public regard. And by September 1915, it was no longer enough to be a member of a prominent and wealthy family—one must be a member of a family who worked for the war effort. Who was selfless and patriotic. Doing one's part. Anything less would be looked upon askance.

And so Charlotte had begun to make inquiries. There would be no bandaging dirty wounds and writing letters for pathetic farm boys for her. Her place was at Horse Guards, she believed, and she looked to Hilly to find her a position appropriate to her stature and intelligence.

Having just sent off Grace to France, Rags found himself scurrying once again to secure female employment. Concerned that his mother could be drawn into some enterprise where she might inadvertently stumble and reveal their highly sensitive conspiracy, the newly minted captain requested an appointment with MI6 to review the security procedures he had incorporated in the classified library. It was an excursion to be expected as Rags expanded his duties. Naturally, Uncle Hilly applauded his initiative and opened the doors to Number 96 Cambridge Circus, an annex for clerical workers at the intelligence department. Just inside the five-story brick- and stone-clad Victorian building, across from the Cambridge Pub, Rags registered with the clerk behind the glass partition with his name, office of assignment, and phone number.

"Mr. Cable will be right down, Captain. Haven't seen you around here before—joining our little family, are we?" The old fellow was filing away the captain's face for future reference. Rags noticed that the white-haired sexagenarian jotted down a note next to his name in the duty book. No doubt he would call Mrs. Box to check. Security was tight here—a note to put into the back of his mind if the spy search of the army staff got ratcheted up.

"Perhaps you'll see more of me. Can't tell which way this war is going to go, don't you know." Soon Rags heard someone clamoring down the worn wooden stairs on the other side of the transparent door to the tiny lobby.

"Captain Stetchworth, I don't wonder. How are you, nice to have you with us. Come through, won't you?" Mr. Cable was a very tall thin man in his early thirties, all angles and dark-rimmed spectacles. There was no lift in the building. Slightly out of breath, they emerged together on the top floor. Rags had a hard time keeping up with Cable but didn't want to let on. Turning over his shoulder, Cable said, "Sorry about the stairs, old chap. I'm used to them."

Panting, warming up inside his wool tunic, Rags passed it off with a wave of his hand, since he was quite unable to speak. Mr. Cable occupied a corner next to a window that fronted to the Palace Theatre across the circus, where *Bric-A-Brac* was playing. "It is so popular that they have featured matinees all summer. Had a chance to go, Captain? You and your lady friend been to see it?"

"No, I've been away all summer at Gallipoli. There's quite a show on out there as well, but it runs day and night."

The comical comment caught Cable off-guard. "Sorry—naturally you've got better things to do than we civilians." Then, a little embarrassed and quite unsolicited, he added, "I'm exempt . . . you know, essential war work." Both men glanced at the mountain of papers spread out in the near vicinity and chuckled. "It is fun to sit up here and watch the crowds. I haven't seen the play myself, but plan to before it closes."

Rags got the feeling that not much was happening in Cable's office. The captain got right to the point and explained the creation of the classified library. Cable reacted with an upward twitch of his head and raised the thick black eyebrows that protruded above his enormous eyeglass frames. "Sounds interesting. Can I have a copy of your standing operating procedure for our files?"

Rags was gratified; he could tell Madam La Box that he had impressed the expert. With this official bit of business concluded, he then moved to the real purpose of his visit. "I'll bet, with the increase of activity in France and Gallipoli, you're looking for people who can translate German."

"That's so, we're always short of help. Hard to engage specialized assistance. Risky as well. Intelligence is a game that is played by both sides. Germans are always seeking a chink in our armor and we in theirs."

Rags thought of the rumors of a mole and wondered if Cable knew of it. That's the problem when dealing with intelligence folks, he thought; you're never sure what they know. He pressed on. "I have a family member who is seeking war work. I know that somewhere you must be screening unclassified materials . . . like international post, foreign magazines or publications for tidbits."

"Not my department, second floor, Rupert Mannering. He's expanding now that we have subscriptions to every periodical in the German empire.

Better him than me," he laughed. "Those Johnnies at MI5 shifted it over to us."

"Would you be able to introduce me to Mr. Mannering?"

"That I can. I'll give him a bell right now and send you down. I would go, but I've had enough of those stairs for today. Don't mind if I don't go with you?"

Rags could tell that Cable wanted to be rid of him and get back to watching pretty girls across the street. "No, no, not at all. Just tell me where to find him; this place is a labyrinth, seems like someone stuck two or three buildings together." While Cable dialed several numbers, searching for the elusive Mr. Mannering, Rags chuntered on in the friendliest of tones, hoping for a good result.

Hanging up, Cable jotted down the room number. "He's waiting for you. I think you'll get a good reception."

With that encouragement Rags skipped down the warped steps to the lower floor and asked a clerk loitering near the malodorous latrine for assistance. After a number of twists and turns, up and down levels, he was directed to Mannering's office in the rear corner of the fragrant old building which had many uses before the war. One of which must have been a tanning factory. Rags thought that rising damp had come here to die. Through the opened door he saw a rotund, bald man leaning back in a squeaky swivel chair, reading a German newspaper. After introductions, Rags settled into a scuffed, leather-covered chair, one leg a little shorter than the other three.

"I am inquiring about war work for my mother. She's a German speaker." Then added, "Not an old woman at all, very much in tune with the times. Learned the language as a student in Bavaria, Regensburg, back in ninety-five, went back every summer until the war. War work has become the thing to do, you know, for so many well-educated women." He was subtly making the point that she was of the upper class and didn't want to be improperly situated. "She's been involved with the Women's Institute rolling bandages, making up relief packages, and so forth. But now that the war is here to stay she wants to make a real contribution, and I thought, after meeting with Cumming this last week over at the Army Staff . . . well, I thought she might fit in here. She's a close cousin of my boss, Major General Hopewell, the deputy inspector general. I'm his military aide." Name dropping was most relevant; both Rags and Mannering were well aware of acceptable procedure.

"Well, Captain, you've come to the right place at the right time. We here at the Registry are seeking translators, in particular readers, of German. We're overwhelmed with copy. Finding searchers is most difficult; many German speakers don't want to be identified for fear of being branded as spies. And the native Germans we've placed on the Isle of Man are not trustworthy."

The press was beginning to question the selection process that sent thousands to internment rather than deportation. It was as though Rags had touched a nerve. The round little man rose and pointed toward the opposite wall. There, he sifted through a stack of newsprint and magazines heaped on a long side table.

"We have renewed the subscriptions of the detainees at their old addresses. But now we are inundated with material. The position I can offer your mother would be as a search clerk. Of course her bona fides would have to be impeccable. We would need to do an interview, test her skill, see if she is suitable for the work. How's her eyesight?"

"My mother is in excellent health, no problem there," he assured the bureaucrat.

"That's our biggest problem—tired eyes, you know. All day in a dingy, dust-filled room. I've asked for better facilities, ones with good lighting, clean, like a library, but I'm ignored. They say, 'There is a war on, Mannering; take what you can get.' They also tell me that my work is classified, you know, making it harder to find a proper facility. My sources aren't classified; they are open, over-the-counter publications, but no matter." He sighed and looked up at the celling in frustration.

Rags nodded his head in agreement and sympathized with the chronic frustration boiling under that bald pate, even as he smiled inwardly at the man's flamboyant distress. "When and where would she be required, Mr. Mannering?"

"I would fit her in with our office at the Admiralty. There's a reading room there that is interested in the goings-on in Atlantic convoy protection. The hours would be mornings and afternoons five days a week. She would be reading German publications, ones oriented around shipping and naval matters. Dull, but we do pick up a considerable amount of information from local newspapers about sailings and dockings that are a small part, a fragment really, of a larger picture of enemy activity. Is that what you had in mind for your mother, I hope?"

"Seems top hole, sir; she could come and go with me. The Admiralty is close enough for us to have lunch together, time permitting. Most agreeable, thank you, sir."

His mother safely ensconced nearby, reading shipping columns in her favorite language? Most agreeable indeed, he thought.

THAT EVENING IT WAS UP to Rags to sell the position to his mother at dinner. He waited until a good meal of pheasant with roasted potatoes had settled and coffee was being served. It had always been her favorite; game was sent down on the train from York with a servant who was in London to bring his mistress's personal laundry to be done. Such goodies were payment for giving the man a bed for a couple of nights in the servants' quarters at the top of the house. "Remember, Mamma, you mentioned obtaining war work? You know, to make us look good, above suspicion. Well, I have found just the thing."

Charlotte looked up from her cup, skeptical. "Oh yes. What have you done for me, Rolly? More bandages for me to roll? I think I've handled quite enough sphagnum, thank you very much."

"No, no, I went to Cumming's office, something official for Uncle Hilly, and found that they are desperate for translators to scan unclassified German materials, hometown newspapers, magazines and business journals, looking for items that might tip off the war office about troop movements or unit locations, war production and labor problems." He filled the sentence with items that would intrigue her. "Soldiers' stories from the front might give a clue to something important. It would place you above suspicion, and you might learn something that could interest Father. You would be working every day at the Admiralty. It would get you out of this mausoleum. We could go to work together. Wouldn't that be exciting?"

Charlotte put down her spoon and raised her eyebrows. "Rolly, I would like that. No one could criticize me for remaining on the sidelines and I would have a good excuse for giving up my acquaintances who go on about the terrible Germans, baby killers, and all that tripe. I tell you, sometimes I have to bite my tongue when they trash our people. I am afraid someday I am going to blurt out my feelings about the great British Empire, and then I will be for it. I accept." The remainder of the evening was filled with happy thoughts. Rolly had not seen her that content in years.

Charlotte arranged a tea for her female acquaintances the very next morning. A half dozen idle ladies, in morning attire of the highest-quality couture, pre-war from Paris, sat in a circle in the spacious drawing room. It would be a morning of one-upmanship. Charlotte quizzed each concerning their war effort and the condition of their men who were connected in one way or the other to "most vital" war work. "I am sorry to tell you that I won't be presiding over our morning tête-à-têtes any longer." She paused to let it sink in and to be questioned.

"My dear, what has happened? Is Rolly going abroad once again?"

"No, Phyllis, I've been offered a position with the Admiralty, Registry Office. Well, that is the cover name. They sought me out for my language skill, from university."

"My dear, I never knew you went to university."

"Oh yes, my mother and father were very progressive that way, sent me to do fine arts at Regensburg before I married. Now I have a chance to use my education in an effort to help win the war." She smiled at the clever ambiguity of this expression. "Rolly is so proud of his mamma. We will be working nearby and can travel to work together and lunch at the mess. I am so lucky. So you see, I just don't have the time for our little morning coffees any longer. You'll have to carry on without me."

The ladies probed the nature of the work, but Charlotte only hinted about the corner of the war apparatus to which she had committed. She would admit it was *for the empire*. Charlotte was bursting inside as she read the avaricious expressions on their face. She had held the best for last in case they could pick apart her extraordinary opportunity by changing the subject. She had saved Rolly's promotion for the final blow. "I must confess, it was not all my doing. My son, Captain Stetchworth of the Guards, used his influence to secure the position. I am so blessed." She smiled demurely as she sipped her tea.

Her lady friends smiled as well, perhaps with something other than pure delight. "Well," one of the ladies, who was as overstuffed as the chair in which she was sitting, remarked. "We are so happy for you, Charlotte dear."

WITHIN A FEW DAYS ROLLY reported that Mr. Mannering's people had reviewed Charlotte's application for the position of search clerk. She was invited to appear at ten that morning with a statement from her doctor concerning her health at 16 Charles Street, Haymarket. With the document in hand, Charlotte and Rolly arrived on the dot at the lobby entrance around the corner from the Burberry store. The open iron cage elevator clanged as the scrawny old operator slammed the accordion gate closed, allowing him to engage the ancient winding mechanism to yank them up four floors to the top of the building. He struggled with the unlocking handle before allowing his passengers to alight. It was a disconcerting experience for Charlotte, who had spent her years in comfort and was rarely exposed to the grimy buildings and antiquated infrastructure of the real world. The corridor was long and dark, and she was glad she had accepted Rolly's offer to escort her, which she had originally dismissed as unnecessary. The agency offices were cramped with filing cabinets pushed against every wall, partition, and desk. When they inquired where to go for an interview, people—at least they looked like people—popped up at all angles. It appeared highly unorganized, but that was the charm of intelligence work, Rolly assured her. The process, which they presumed was to sit through a comprehensive interview, turned out to be short and to the point.

"Ah yes, Mrs. Stetchworth, is that your doctor's certificate?" the smartly dressed young man with a cane concluded. The name plate on his desk indicated that he was a naval officer, medically retired. "We are most gratified to have you on board and hope you will enjoy your time with our office in the

Admiralty. Here is the room number; it is in the second cellar down at the Mall entrance. Thank you for coming." It was clearly an invitation to leave.

Charlotte looked almost offended at the perfunctory nature of the interview, being treated much like a laundrywoman being hired at a great house. She opened her mouth to comment, but Rolly interrupted. "Thank you, lieutenant. Most enjoyable to meet you. We'll be on our way, then, if you don't mind." The officer waved his hand and sat down, turning to the papers cluttering the top of his desk.

As they turned into the dark hallway once again, Rolly said, "What did you expect, Mother? Bulldog Drummond and a loaded revolver? You'll find that the work here is tedious, mind-numbing, and dull. But then perhaps there will be one moment that will change the war, and it will be you who are responsible."

Rags had not been in the Old Admiralty building that faced Horse Guards Parade, but he admired the large brick structure with the opposing stone towers capped with corroded green copper-domed roofs. But it was too late in the morning to make the walk from Haymarket through Admiralty Gate to the far end of the headquarters. Besides, his mother was dressed in her finery. There was always the Clarence Pub just halfway and the prospect of a good hearty meal. They entered through the side door off Great Scotland Street. It was early and the pub had not been inundated with hungry workers from Horse Guards as yet. Rags recommended the fish and chips, and his mother chose the soup and sandwich.

Their meals had just arrived when through the door came Uncle Hilly on his way to the narrow steps leading to the rooms above. Rags tried to distract his mother so as not to recognize her cousin, but Charlotte was quick to notice. Raising her voice as he passed close by, "Hilly, just the man I wanted to see. I was hoping Rolly would take me up to meet you before this extraordinary day ended, and here you are."

Rags saw how Hilly allowed himself only a split second of annoyance before turning on his charm. "My dear Charlotte, if I knew you were about today, I would have insisted that our new captain bring you up for a glass of sherry. It has been many months, wouldn't you say, since I enjoyed our talk about our captain's future. And as you can see, I am a man of my word. He is a credit to you, Charlotte; he's all you said he was and much more." Taking her hand in both of his, "Thank you, my dear, for giving him up to my service." He winked surreptitiously at Rags, who bowed his head with a smile.

"Please sit with us, Hilly. I must thank you for all you have done for my boy."

"I would love to, my dear, but I have a party waiting for me up above."

"Is it dear Winifred? I haven't seen her in ages."

"No, sorry to say, she is down in the country this time of year; won't be long before the shooting starts. You know how she loves her guns and dogs. Come down with us in October, won't you? Rags knows who I am lunching with; aides know everything. Mustn't be late, you know."

Charlotte didn't care for Hilly calling her son Rags, a nickname she detested, but Rags was too panicked to notice. He had been dumped headfirst into coming up with a reason for his uncle's rather abrupt departure and could hardly use the usual cover story, that Hilly was having a private lunch with one of his many women. Even less could he tell the truth, that he was meeting with Cumming. A well-known MP would do. Someone who, for unknown reasons, Hilly could not be seen with in public.

With lunch behind them, Rags took his mother across the road and up to his office to show her the progress he had made and to introduce her to Mildred Box, who had been merely a voice on the phone coordinating her son's movements. The first person they encountered, though, was Beryl, who stood sentry at the double doors to the IG's office and classified library. "Who's this, then, Captain? Your mother?" she said carelessly.

"Yes, as a matter of fact, this is Mrs. Stetchworth, my mother and niece of General Hopewell."

Charlotte's mouth made a moue of disgust at the girl's casual treatment, and she swept by silently to Mrs. Box's door. Mildred rose and extended her hand with a much more satisfying formality.

"Mrs. Box, thank you so much for keeping me in the loop during Rolly's trip to the Mediterranean. It was such a relief to a mother who was reading the awful accounts of Gallipoli on a daily basis." They spoke cordially for a few minutes before Rolly led her over to her new workplace.

It was a beautiful September day as they strolled across the sand of Horse Guards Parade and bore left to the old naval headquarters. With clear markings on the bulkheads, naval ship terms were stenciled on the passages, and they were directed down ladder number 8 to the second deck below. Along the subterranean passageway, they came to compartment D-8, which looked just like any other office. A considerable number of women—young to old and in-between—were seated at small folding military field tables, sifting through stacks of periodicals and newsprint spilling out of cardboard boxes on the floor. Charlotte turned over her paperwork and was introduced to the leader, Chief Petty Officer Marks. Clad in navy blue, he wore his rank insignia on his left arm, a Killick anchor in gold surrounded by a full laurel wreath topped by a crown. Rags thought how military personnel could be rather daunting to some civilians, but his mother bore no trace of discomfort. Marks was a well-fed sailor in his forties with a number of gold slashes on his sleeve to indicate considerable pre-war service. He addressed Rags.

"Sir, what can I do for the Captain?

"I've brought you a new recruit, Chief, fresh from Mr. Mannering, well vetted and ready to go to work for God and country. I hope you will take good care of my mother; this is her first adventure into war work."

"Well, sir, we can take care of that. The Royal Navy, our King's senior service, welcomes you aboard and wishes you clear sailing."

"How charming. May I call you Chief as well? I'm not familiar with the protocol."

"Yes, ma'am, that is correct, but the other ladies call me Chubby when the hatches are closed. And as you can see, it fits me down to the ground. May I take you over to Mrs. Rodney? She is our trainer and will be your sponsor while you are with us. Thank you, Captain, for presenting your mother. She will be ready for pick up at 4:30 p.m. each and every day."

## Chapter Twenty-Two

# Horse Guards, September 1915

IT WAS DISCOVERED, DURING THE Battle of Loos and other adjoining operations with the French, that the Germans were leaving behind agents who appeared to be Belgian peasants to conduct themselves as refugees and request asylum in Great Britain. These spies could disappear in the large numbers of transients into the general population of England for the duration, there to be housed with British families and blend into the population. Then they could get jobs in the munitions industries and other war work, or as translators to disrupt production as fifth columnists. Overt and clandestine, they, in groups or as individuals, could undermine those with whom they came into contact. It was surmised that they would communicate by letter or get their instructions from publications.

Captain Mansfield Smith-Cumming, who founded and led MI6, was the spirit behind the new intelligence branch known as MI7. However, it was not exciting enough for him to dabble with, so he handed it off to a bureaucrat who had always remained cloaked in secrecy. Its mode of operation was contrary to the British feeling of fair play and smacked of foreign ways. To be a sneak and pry into others' private affairs was un-British. Public schools personified the right to a private life, and it was regarded as bad form to meddle in assorted snooping. Yet in wartime Cumming and his betters agreed that the time had come to protect the nation and that things done in the name of total war were an exception.

The Intelligence Section number seven, or MI7, was therefore created and subdivided into four functions. They were MI7-a, censorship; MI7-b, foreign and domestic propaganda; MI7-c, translation and regulation of foreign visitors; and MI7-d, foreign press propaganda. The cover name "Registry Department" was provided to MI7-c to enable members to identify where they worked if asked by the general public. Of course the workers knew nothing of what the other departments did, since everything was guarded on a need-to-know basis.

The Army, Navy, and Ordnance Departments each had a branch of MI7-c. The naval extension of the Registry Department had taken on the most time-consuming task of the internal war effort. In addition to reading unclassified publications, they tirelessly perused lists of names, addresses, occupations, travel rosters, and suspicious acquaintances and read letters from overseas prior to delivery, hoping to find connections with would-be accomplices that might threaten the homeland. On each of two dozen tables were typed lists of watchwords to aid them in their quests. They even read police reports, which sometimes listed a unit or ship. If a police statement showed several men from the same unit, that meant that unit or ship was off the line or in the dock.

"MRS. STETCHWORTH, I'M BUNNY RODNEY, one of the girls; I know we will get on."

Charlotte looked at the smiling, open face with outward equanimity and inward disdain. Bunny was hardly a girl—she looked to be middle-aged and was still wearing her hat indoors, probably the better to flaunt the suffragette colors adorning it.

"Yes, I am Mrs. Stetchworth." She gave a quick perfunctory hint of a smile. "I really shouldn't be here, in the basement, you know; I am in rather delicate health. But anything for the boys, after all. My son, the Guards Captain, arranged this venue. My knowledge and facility with the German language came from summers as an art student at the University in Regensburg. I was just a girl but quite talented, they said—poetry, of course. So language and its deeper meaning is my forte."

"So nice to have you join our little team. Let me show you where we work." Bunny led her through the dark basement room toward a cleared desk on the far side. "It's a little dank down here—we call it the trenches. Makes us feel the war isn't far off and that we are contributors in residence. Here you are—your desk for the duration, with pencils, blotter, paper. Everything you should need to get started. Just have a seat for the moment and get settled. I'll be back to explain the work in a few minutes."

It was more of a table than a desk. There were only two large drawers, both on the right side, that were stuck from the damp. Charlotte gave the lower one a kick, but it didn't help. "Bloody navy," she cursed. The corners were rounded off, as if something had been chewing on them. The top was scarred, gouged and stained where an ink bottle had been spilled during a violent storm at sea. It rocked slightly when she put her purse on the corner. One leg was decidedly shorter than the other three.

Charlotte hung her coat on the hook by her desk and smoothed her skirt before taking a seat. For the first time in her life she was going to be paid by the hour—who could have ever imagined such a thing! She was an *employee*. Or at least that's what the Registry Office thought. She looked around at her fellow workers—a dozen or so ladies hunched over, paging through papers, making notes, and casting off piles of newsprint into bins for disposal. Low talk reverberated off the beamed ceiling, setting up a strange echo. Sailors roamed the chamber, bringing in more papers and hauling away the chaff. Against the wet foundation walls were rows of card catalogue stands soaking up the moisture. The ladies got up now and again to compare their documents with cards from the long, thin drawers of the card catalogue, to add a new card or scratch out a false connection. Charlotte was gripped by an intense urge to look into the drawer for "S" but forced herself to keep seated. Just in time, Bunny was back to start her orientation.

Bunny took her to a table with a light bulb suspended over it on a single cord. Arranged there were stacks of magazines, sailing notices, and, to her surprise, German police reports that turned out to include names of servicemen who had been arrested for drunkenness and disturbing the peace and, occasionally, the unit or ship they served with. "Our job, Charlotte, is to read through every bit of mail, newsprint, report, or correspondence that comes our way and to glean from them any bit of intelligence that might be helpful to our boys in the field." Bunny turned to a blonde young woman at the far end of the table. "That's Helene—she is one of our most experienced contributors and specializes in reading mail sent from Europe. She's going to work with you today, show you the ropes. Who knows—maybe you'll have a big find today. Good for morale, that."

Charlotte took a seat next to the young woman and waited primly while Helene finished resealing a handwritten envelope. Once the letter was replaced in a mail bin, she turned to Charlotte with a quick sigh. "Charlotte, so nice to meet you." She put out her hand, which was ignored in the midst of Charlotte's surprise.

"You're not English," Charlotte exclaimed.

Helene smiled and put down her hand. "No, I'm Swedish. I know most of the languages on the Continent, so they stuck me here. But it is all right, most interesting; would you like to help me?"

"Yes, yes, of course." Charlotte seated herself next to the young woman, who was opening a scented letter with long delicate fingers.

"Charlotte, you can be my steamer. If you would take these," handing her a pack of personal-size letters, "over to the tea kettle and steam them open, that would be a good start."

Charlotte needed no further instruction. She had secretly steamed open dozens of letters addressed to Rolly and could open and reseal them as if she had been working at the Registry Office for years. She found herself engrossed, reading bits of each letter as she steamed the next. When she had steamed several stacks and ferried them back and forth, Helene had her sit down to read her first batch. "Before you start reading the letter, Mrs. Stetchworth, record the address and postmark for identification purposes. We might get a series of letters from one address. The envelope may tell us more than the content. The opening salutation is important, as is the farewell at the close. The level of intimacy in the body should be noted on your review along with any suspicions you might identify. Here, you see?" Helene was holding up the review of a piece of correspondence she had just finished.

Charlotte was not accustomed to being told how to suck eggs and responded curtly. "I catch your meaning; elementary, I should think. We aren't building a dossier, just reading letters."

After another hour of joint instruction, the ladies broke for lunch. That afternoon Charlotte returned to the kettle for several more batches of letters, but eventually Bunny took her aside to learn the card catalogue. Charlotte tried very hard not to let her excitement show as Bunny opened the catalogue and began to explain what type of information was listed on each card, how the cards could be used to build a picture of its subject, and how all the facts and bits could begin to tell a story to the woman who was canny enough to notice.

As Bunny left her to familiarize herself with the cards and cross-reference some of Helene's names from the morning, Charlotte felt an elation she hadn't experienced since Rolly had gone to Egypt. The work could not have been more suited to Charlotte's goals. She knew she was a shrewd judge of communication, both verbal and nonverbal. And the evenings she had spent with Rolly crafting their communiqués to his father had been among the most exhilarating of her life. They had conferred for hours on how to be clear and opaque at the same time, what behaviors might arouse suspicion, what "tells" might give away their game. Now this was the great game, she thought, and the British navy was training her personally to become even more master-ful. It had everything Charlotte craved: intellectual challenge, utility, and betrayal.

The afternoon went quickly, and Charlotte was surprised when Chief Chubby announced that the workday was over. "Time to wrap it up, ladies; the sun has passed over the yard arm. Those wanting to join me in the enlisted mess for a drink and meet the boys of the good ship HMS *Never-sail*"—the readers twittering here at the nickname for headquarters building—"are invited to follow me to the upper deck, where we will all share in a cup of good cheer for a day's duty well done."

It was easy for Charlotte to beg off. "Most kind, but I must meet my son the Captain at Horse Guards. He'll be waiting for me." Finding her coat, her nose wrinkled at how damp it had become, and she decided to wear it tomorrow rather than hang it on the sodden wall. She made a mental note to dress warm even though the fall weather was quite mild. As promised, nothing—including warmth—penetrated below decks.

Bunny slipped her hand around Charlotte's elbow. "I'm heading your way; my husband is in the army map room. He's a brigadier (not general) and a plotter. I call him the plodder. He doesn't get the joke; terribly serious, you know. Where is your captain's room?"

Charlotte had a chance to identify her place in the social structure for the first time. "He's aide-de-camp to my cousin, Major General Sir Avery Hilliard Hopewell KCB, deputy inspector general. I trust your husband is familiar with him?"

"Hilly? I should say—he is married to my cousin Winifred! We are practically related, my dear! My old brigadier served under Hilly in South Africa. I knew you were quality the moment I saw you; we're going to have a good time, you and me and the Admiralty. We'll show the navy what's what."

Charlotte had nearly accepted Chief Chubby's invitation for a drink, thinking it was the smart thing to do under the circumstances. She was so glad she had refrained—what a poor choice that would have been. Bunny would never had linked up with her if she did. The two ladies walked gingerly in their block heels across the expanse of the sand-covered parade ground, which was filling with uniformed men breaking free to go in all directions . . . a pub, a flat, a night out.

Pub hours were one of the many aspects of British life that had changed because of the war. To mitigate the chances of drunkenness among workers in munition factories and highly classified positions, new alcohol license laws limited pub service from noon to 2:00 and from 6:30 to 9:30, seriously reducing their profitability and causing customers to drink as fast and as much as they could within those hours. The public adjusted. This also led to lock-ins, a practice of locking the outer doors of the pub, blacking out the windows, and incarcerating favored customers until the police had gone to bed.

Once at the inner door to the army headquarters, the two parted amiably, leaving Charlotte in the best of moods. Even the push of foot traffic opposing her as the offices emptied could not dim her elation. She made her way up the center staircase to the Office of the Inspector General and its closed double doors. Charlotte feared she had missed her son, but a push on the heavy brass plate was all it took to gain entry. She strode over to the service counter, where a receptionist was packing up her purse.

"We're about to close, love; are you sure you are in the proper office?" she asked.

Charlotte recognized the girl and the common voice with a moue of distaste. "I'm here to meet my son, Captain Stetchworth."

"Ah, yes, I remember you. He isn't here, Mrs. Stetchworth, and neither is Mrs. Box—you just missed her." She took a quick look over her shoulder. "Haven't seen Rags, but his cap is here, so he must be coming back. Come in and have a seat at his desk."

"That is most kind of you . . . Beryl, is it?" She hadn't met many Beryls in her life, so the name came flying forward from her short-term memory and her visit just after lunch. Whatever her faults and coarseness, the girl had *umph*—a popular new term for the energy of those bright young things Charlotte read about in her weekly copy of *Women's Chat*. Beryl was dressed in the loose clothing style like so many young women who had begun to shun the French fashion that had dominated Charlotte's life. *Women's Chat* magazine was filled with the new fashions and cartoons roasting older women with sophisticated clothes made prior to the war. The heat of the workday and the cool comfort Beryl displayed convinced Charlotte to remodel her wardrobe. She was no stick-in-the-mud like her mother, and she would never be one of those pitiable women whom colleagues and younger girls mocked behind their backs for dowdiness. Her new friend Bunny seemed to be rather smartish. She would probe where she shopped at lunch the following day.

Beryl followed her to Rolly's desk and hopped up on an adjoining table, showing far too much leg for Charlotte's comfort. "I'm ever so grateful for Rags' help in getting me this position. He's promised me a promotion if I do well. You know, if I catch the spy, then I'll be a hero. You can tell him that I'm on it . . . keeping my ear to the ground and all that. He is ever so charming, your son. Has he got a girl? You can tell me, I won't let on. He's asked me out several times, but I've been putting him off. There's no good in making it too easy for them, is there?" Beryl had the audacity to actually wink at her.

Charlotte was aghast. "Well, my dear, that is most admirable—I mean about catching the spy. I'm sure we will all be grateful for that accomplishment," she said drily. "As for Rolly, he's awfully busy now; I doubt he will be able to spare much time for you. The general is keeping him hopping, as you know better than anyone." Beryl smiled her pretty smile and did not look very worried.

But Charlotte was. A pretty girl could easily turn Rolly's head, but Beryl certainly wasn't the sort of girl Rolly should be seen with in his position and given her background. Charlotte had already picked out the type of girl Rolly should marry—a young, demure, sophisticated fraulein that his father would find for him in Austria once the war was over. It was also worrying to have someone in his office searching for the spy right under his nose. If he were to make a mistake, she would be right there to pick it up and follow the trail right to her son. Beryl would need watching. Charlotte would take it upon herself to keep an eye on the girl.

BREATHLESS, RAGS CAME THROUGH THE double doors and apologized for his tardiness. "Been with Uncle Hilly in the mess and those old farts. Couldn't get away. Sorry, Mamma."

"Language, Rolly, really! And in front of Beryl as well."

"I don't mind—the building *is* full of old farts!"

Beryl hopped down from the table and sauntered out with a flirty wave, while Rags gathered his coat and briefcase. "Shall we go to dinner here in the West End, Mother?"

But before they could go further, the phone rang. It was the general. "Good, you're still there. Can you find that report on Gallipoli and bring it down to the mess? I have had a request. Mr. Churchill wants to compare it with a note from his brother Jack, who is serving with Hamilton. It seems Jack agrees with our assessment. He echoes the same condemnation of the commanders' hands-off style. I'm going to meet him at the Naval & Military Club. I'll need a car. You needn't come along unless you wish."

"Sir, I have it in my bag. I'll bring it down as soon as I can arrange transport. Mother is here; we were just going out to supper." Rags nodded toward his mother to let her know she was in the conversation in case Uncle Hilly wanted to speak to her.

"Well, that's perfect—we can all dine at the club after I see Churchill. Bring her in through the ladies' entrance on Half Moon Street and I'll find you two in the ladies' lounge when I finish. It won't take long; he's in a bit of a hurry."

Rags and Charlotte made their way west to the Naval & Military Club, only a 15-minute walk even with the foot traffic at its height, and found their way to the ladies' lounge. Naturally the wait was longer than expected. The plush pastel furniture of the ladies' lounge made the wait tolerable, but the other ladies waiting in similar circumstances all seemed a little miffed at not having the run of the club. The Naval & Military Club was one of the most exclusive gentlemen's clubs in London, a masculine fortress with draconian rules concerning any accommodation for women. The club members' entrance was in the center of the carriage court on Piccadilly, where the two car gates were labeled "IN" and "OUT," which lent the club its nickname—the In & Out Club. It was renowned for its dozing chairs in the smoking lounge, where a warm fire kept the cold out. The long bar that overlooked Green Park was a favorite watering hole for senior military officers, both active and retired. It also boasted an ornate massive banquette hall for balls. That night the excellent menu would be front and center. The complex of buildings, Cambridge House, had been the residence of Prime Minister Lord Palmerston and was converted in 1862.

Charlotte, in her newfound expertise, struck up a conversation with the women about the state of daywear suitable for war work, delighted to be the center of attention and praise. She put on her best accent—"We *must sacrifice* for our boys in uniform"—enjoying as always the equivocal semantics of her words. The conclave was broken up by a liveried servant offering a note on a small silver tray, which notified her that Hilly was waiting in the smoking room. Charlotte had difficulty in tearing herself away from her admirers.

While the original residence was spacious and opulent, it was interconnected with service structures by long, red carpeted walkways. A small three-story hotel was attached on a side street that didn't appear from the outside as integral to the club. A carriage house had been converted to a gymnasium, originally used as a school for sword and pistol. A bank of climbing ladders covered the far end, and an ancient leather vault horse was in the corner along with a rack of Indian clubs. The walls of the venerable club were covered with paintings of admirals, generals, and British victories that were simply priceless. In the center of the building complex was a small, secluded garden filled with nude bronze statues of young women, which seemed to Charlotte more pornography than art. The smoked Scottish salmon from Fraserburgh, fifty miles north of Aberdeen, however, was to her liking. Hilly had joined them in the dining room, and Rags passed on the notes from Gallipoli.

"My dear niece, how good of you to come along to the club." Charlotte was not convinced that she was welcome within the walls until she heard his reassuring voice. "I imagine this will be your first of many visits since I have put Rolly up for membership. Guardsmen and their families are always welcome at the In & Out."

"Uncle Hilly, I do treasure your sponsorship and all you have done this year for our Rolly. You are too generous with your patronage." Uncle Hilly was nearly a generation older than Charlotte and not to be trifled with. His good will, so important to Charlotte, could be withdrawn at any moment, but that was highly unlikely. Naturally Charlotte asked, "How is my favorite aunt? Is she still in the country preparing the house for the shoot?" The conversation turned to family matters and discussions of sisters, aunts, marriages and balls. The subject of the war was off limits, as was business and especially money.

After the salmon and the duck and the crème brulée, Rags and Charlotte took their leave, ready for the two-block walk to the Green Park Underground station. When they emerged from the ladies' entrance, the searchlights in

Green Park across the road were on full blast. In the distance they heard the thudding of bombs. Rags had taken Charlotte's arm and started toward the station when the anti-aircraft guns in the park opened up with a fusillade. The trees were shaken, and dry curled chestnut leaves blew across the traffic on Piccadilly. Charlotte grasped her son as the barking Charlies pounded the German aircraft above.

Rags was of two minds. They could easily go back into the club, but it was a very old building and, if hit, would fall like a house of cards. They could run for the station, but Charlotte was not dressed for speed. He finally landed on a third option: to head to St. James's Park, just a few minutes' walk away. The park's lagoon had been drained at the start of the war because its waters reflected the moonlight and pinpointed the location of Buckingham Palace. With that marker hidden, the park was a relatively safe location, and soldiers were stationed there in sandbagged bunkers that could shelter a civilian or two in need. Rags took his mother's arm and headed that way.

German zeppelins had been attacking Great Britain since May 1915. Although the damage they inflicted was moderate, the psychological toll on the British people was enormous. The airships were large and out of reach, seemingly able to roam the skies with impunity. The short summer nights had limited their usefulness for the Kaiser, but now that September had arrived, longer nights and clear weather emboldened them. Also, the zeppelin captains had changed tactics and now were attacking from above 10,000 feet, where no weapon system could reach. They were in the clouds, yet could still come quite near their targets. Each airship deployed a cloud observation car on a cable a thousand feet long entwined with a telephone wire. Riding in the observation car, being swept along under the zeppelin at eighty-five miles an hour, was a lone artillery spotter who was calling the shots for the Germans.

It was just as Rags was making his way toward the park that one of the beams caught the strange craft as it passed by. The parks were all used because you need space to swing the guns. The streets were unusable because the buildings only allowed a small window to the sky. They also cut down all the trees. Rags changed his mind. He turned his mother around and hustled her down Half Moon Street to the Chesterfield Hotel, where he knew there was an air raid shelter. Breathless, with Charlotte coming out of her shoes, they arrived with a number of other pedestrians and dove into the hotel's small entrance as a bomb landed in Shepherd Market a block west. The blast wave helped propel pedestrians through the door and into the tiny lobby. Down the stairs the frightened fled to the safety of the shelter.

The following morning, Charlotte reported to work, shaken but determined. Her son walked her across the parade ground pockmarked by shell holes from the night raid. Crews were out transferring wagonloads of sand

and smoothing them out for the horse-mounted guard. Even though the attacks only occurred during the hours of darkness, Charlotte was nonetheless glad to be working underground in the "trenches" of the Naval Registry. Once there, Charlotte spoke to Bunny of nothing but the raid the night before. The newspapers reported that some 660 tons of bombs had been shoveled out the side of the four zeppelins in the course of the night, and it was suspected that 20 percent of the bombs had failed to explode. Parents were advised to tell their children not to touch one if found but to notify the police for the bomb disposal squad to come and render it safe. Bunny attempted to calm her down by noting that London was the biggest city in the world and a few bombs weren't going to amount to a hill of beans. Charlotte straightened and reminded her, "That may be so, Bunny dear, but last night I was standing next to that hill."

THE FOLLOWING WEEK, CHARLOTTE ARRIVED at the Registry to stares and raised eyebrows. Her first days of work had been spent in high-collared, buttoned blouses and long heavy skirts, all purchased from the exclusive studio of Madame Roulet in Haymarket, as were all of Charlotte's clothes. But between her first and second week of work, Charlotte had taken one of those bold steps on which she so prided herself and traveled to the new store of Selfridge & Co. on Oxford Street. By the next Monday she was no longer the pitiable older lady in neck-high, tightly buttoned shirtwaists. She was *au courant* in a blouse with a modestly open neckline and a looser skirt with an ever-so-slightly higher hemline. Bunny exclaimed out loud: "My dear, you have been reading the fashion pages of the *Guardian*!" Charlotte lifted her chin in pride but countered: "Bunny, I read the *Times*, exclusively. But I am not a country squire's wife—of course I know the fashions of the day."

Thereafter Charlotte and Bunny rummaged through the fashion pages nearly every lunchtime. They critiqued and analyzed the soft drapes of orientalism and the lowered waists of the Russian peasant dresses, the new alternatives to corsets and the wider, higher hemlines of the war crinoline. They debated purchasing a sailor blouse. Charlotte recalled having to scurry for cover during the zeppelin raid and considered how many inches of hemline she might be willing to sacrifice for mobility. She was still a good-looking woman, and she had great confidence in her calves.

The morning after the bombing raid, the *Tattler*, a glossy women's magazine devoted to fashion, advised the purchase of "women's smart pajamas for wear during a zeppelin raid." The illustration showed a slim young woman dashing outside toward a bomb shelter while a searchlight illuminated a zeppelin high in the sky. Charlotte was not prepared to go that far, excellent calves or not.

THAT FRIDAY UNCLE HILLY HAD taken to the country for a long weekend, and Rags invited Charlotte to come across to lunch. Charlotte asked Bunny to join them in the junior officers' mess, where cottage pie was always the best choice. Her lunch hour was limited now that she was paid for her time. But she wanted her new friend to meet her son and her son to appreciate how she fit in and found those of her own class among the chaff.

Arriving at the IG's office a few minutes past noon, Charlotte waited for Rolly in Mrs. Box's office along with Bunny. She was surprised that the bespectacled private secretary was also interested in the latest fashion even though she was clad in the usual Edwardian duds. The addition of the classified library had cost Mildred her waiting room, so the soft leather chairs in Rolly's office had been moved to Mildred's desk to seat visitors, and the women chatted a little more freely than usual.

"Mrs. Stetchworth, your Rolly is becoming quite the ladies' man," Mildred proffered. She leaned in conspiratorially. "Please do not tell him I said so, but he and his young secretary have plans Saturday night—dinner and the cinema, I believe." Mildred raised one eyebrow. "You'll have to keep an eye on that one."

Before Charlotte could voice her dismay, Rolly walked in and greeted them. As they left Mildred's office for the mess, he commented, "By the way, Mother, before I forget: I won't be able to go to the theater with you on Saturday evening. My regiment is having a dining in at the Wellington Barracks and it will go very late, I am afraid. I'll be spending the night at the bachelors' quarters. These things can get very raucous and it is best to stay the night."

Charlotte flattened her lips and looked him straight in the eye. "Not to worry, Rolly. I have plans of my own."

# Chapter Twenty-Three

# London, Early October 1915

PRIOR TO 1914, THE REGULAR British Army fought colonial wars against native populations who were small in number and armed with light, traditional weapons. No serving British officer had ever commanded on a broad front with 100,000 infantry backed by hundreds of artillery batteries discharging rapid-fire cannons, augmented by thousands of mounted cavalry. And it showed: The first year of the conflict in Belgium and France was painful, with the British Expeditionary Force—made up of soldiers from the regular army and the so-called Territorials—advancing only to be beaten back by the Germans and forced into a bloody stand-off.

The British knew that the BEF—known proudly as the "Old Contemptibles" after the Kaiser disparaged the Brits' "contemptible little army"—could not succeed alone. So while the regular army languished in the trenches, the British set about creating two new forces. The first was Kitchener's New Army. Secretary of War Kitchener was determined to create a separate army that would be trained in modern methods and fight alongside the regular army but not be integrated with them.

In addition, a new logistical force known as the Army Service Corps was put into place. Britain had seen a long line of divisions dedicated to supply and logistics come and go over the last century—men in uniform formerly known as *the trains* or *waggoners*. The ASC was determined to succeed where their predecessors had failed, and with recruitment at an all-time high, their numbers increased a hundredfold to 325,000. They soon proved their mettle. They prepared the routes to deliver everything to the front and took away the wounded to hospitals they established in France. Known to the fighting soldiers as *Ally Sloper's Cavalry* (after a popular comic book character known as a lazy schemer), the ASC performed magnificently throughout the war. They supplied food, equipment, ammunitions, horses, fodder, motor vehicles, maintenance, railways, waterway transport, and prodigious feats of logistics. They supported the medical community with ambulance columns, tent construction, operating room equipment, drugs, medications, and bandages. They provided the soldiers with clean clothes, shower baths, latrines, and kitchens. Their laundry line pastures flanked the roads for miles—uniforms, sheets, and underwear flapping in the breeze. Simply stated, the army could not move, shoot, or communicate without their daily and nightly support, since they never stopped.

On September 29, 1915, the British attempted to put their new divisions on the offensive. Up to that point the Allied armies had been fighting a defensive campaign along the Western Front—a 400-mile-long stand-off that stretched from the border of Switzerland in the southeast to a small hold on the Belgian coast of the English Channel in the northwest. Nothing like it had occurred in Continental warfare ever before. For two long years the armies had faced down each other in utter misery and futility.

The Battle of Loos was to be the Allied offensive that would shatter the German defenses and break out with horse-mounted cavalry into the open plain of Belgium. French General Foch and British General French planned the massive offensive, which included days of preparatory artillery fires assisted for the first time by gun target spotters above in Allied airplanes. The land attack by Kitchener's New Army that would follow could not fail due to its breadth and weight.

The battle began on September 29 with high hopes that almost immediately turned to despair. The Germans—confident behind stellar defensive entrenchments—were able to sweep the battlefield with machine gun bullets at a distance of a thousand yards. They cut down the marching British regiments like a scythe reaping wheat. Within four hours, the first wave of twelve attacking battalions suffered 8,000 casualties out of 10,000 men. The generals sent in more to take their place. The British employed chlorine gas for the first time and found to their dismay that it blew back into their own ranks, wounding the troops as they came forward and destroying the morale of following formations.

The reports of massive losses were horrendous, dominating the newspapers and panicking the nation. The commander of the BEF, Field Marshal John French, was relieved of duty and replaced by Douglas Haig. Over the three weeks of the offensive, 59,247 Allied soldiers had been killed, including the son of British prime minister Henry Aisquith.

IN THE AFTERMATH OF LOOS, Hilly was once again tagged to lead an investigation. The news of the new mission for the Office of the Inspector General sent Rags into a spin. He hadn't expected to have to return to the battlefield after Gallipoli, believing that the spy scare in London would occupy the IG for a considerable time to come.

Plus, a new interest had overwhelmed the young officer. His vibrant assistant had taken over his thoughts during work and his hours outside work. Beryl was pretty and, most of all, *fun.* They went to her local, the Champion, and played darts and drank. He frankly couldn't believe he was spending so many evenings in the East End and so many nights at the boarding house where Beryl had a room. It felt exotic, making love somewhere so shabby and outré. He had to lie to his mother, telling her he was spending the night at the bachelors' quarters at Horse Guards, but he knew that tack couldn't last for long. Besides, he was going off to the battlefield. Saying goodbye to sweethearts was a time-honored ritual for young men at war, and Rags wanted to know that feeling, that drama. He fixed on telling his mother that night, when they walked the dogs.

THE NEXT MORNING AT WORK Charlotte was strangely elated. She confided in Bunny before the gong about her fears of Rolly going to France. They sat on the bench under the coat rack and changed their shoes. The rough concrete would scuff a neat pair in a matter of hours. New shoes were not available since all the leather was going to army boots.

Bunny was full of advice. "The first thing you must do is take your son to the army/navy store and kit him out. He should have the best of everything. Make him a part of the field army and hope to God that he never hears a shot fired. Like the Prince of Wales, there but not really there. It will be good for his ego, make him one of the boys and put him on a higher plain. Plus, it will get his mind off that awful girl."

Charlotte smiled with what she hoped was modesty and detachment. "Do you really think that a change of environment will take him out of himself?"

"It's not a simple change, Charlotte; it is a life-changing experience. Like Gallipoli, but on an unimagined scale. I was there scouting for the Red Cross in Paris, and my dear, it profoundly affected me. It worked for Roger, my youngest. Now he is back in his depot with a broken heart while she has latched on to another poor unsuspecting soldier. Think of yourself at his age. How did you snare Mr. Stetchworth? A young pretty girl, may I say, consumed by the vapors, rebellion surging, sees a lovely simple boy uncertain about his future yet growing in anticipation. That helpless fool was mere putty in your hands, wasn't he?"

Of course she was right. But it wasn't Mr. Stetchworth, but that beautiful young student in Regensburg that she latched on to. He didn't even struggle. My God, she could see Beryl in her reflection.

After work the two made their way to the Army and Navy Co-operative. It was housed in an old brewery on Victoria Street where it was doing a poor business until a War Office contract boosted sales and made it profitable once again. The business was begun by a group of army and naval officers to supply their members deployed throughout the empire at the lowest cost. Colonial families tried to maintain standards in Africa and India by filling their quarters with goods from home. The store expanded according to requests from frantic members stuck for years in a faraway place in the days when transport was uncertain. Their catalogue, one found with each and every overseas family, contained Goodwin's toilet soap, Riders' snuff, alcohol in many forms, draperies, women's wear and foundation garments, furniture, shaving and grooming kits, toys and much more. And they offered services such as estate agents, contracting, tailoring, shoe and boot making, and banking. School arrangement for children left behind was of particular use, as was ship passage and transfer of whole households.

Bunny accompanied Charlotte on the rounds of the departments in the expansive store. The four-story industrial building experienced a rough conversion. While the staircases were new, the elevators were left over from the brewery's time, large enough to carry a dozen shoppers as it clattered up and down at a slow pace. The scent of hops still lingered, which was quite pleasant. Floors had been sanded and finished, and smart oak counters, hovered over by well-dressed clerks, catered to military families.

The Blick featherweight typewriter in a stout wooden case caught Charlotte's eye. She remembered Rolly complaining that he couldn't read his own handwriting on return from Gallipoli and thought that the machine would be a perfect item. Bunny suggested the folding triangular lantern or the Brighton Buns brass lamp, which she had bought for her oldest boy, who was in the trenches at Ypres. Knowing that Rolly would not have a batman, with which other officers of his rank were supplied, she wondered about the Bayler dressing case. "Perfect, my dear," Bunny agreed. "He has to look his best around all those 'brass-hats'; unkempt beard and nails would not be allowed in the mess, even if it were in the field," she assured her companion.

At home that evening Rolly was very late, yet Charlotte waited up with her treasures. When he came in, the dogs sniffed and sneezed as they jumped at his knees. It was a sure sign that Beryl's perfume, very strong and common, had set them off. "Well, Mother, it looks like we'll be off after lunch tomorrow. It'll be the three of us again. Henry Segar put in a strong bid to accompany Uncle Hilly and me. He said that a civilian's eye is most important in view of the discontent in the nation over the treatment of their sons. I suppose he is right . . . Asquith thinks so."

Charlotte insisted that he sit and eat the hot meal that Mrs. Jayson had kept warm. On the dining room table were the field items she purchased for her boy. He picked at the plate of food that cooled at his place while opening gifts. He loved surprises and these boxes looked a treat. "Now, Rolly dear, I want you to have all the best so the other boys can see how well you are cared for by your family. I wouldn't even mind if they were a little jealous."

Rolly dove into them like a boy at Christmas. The typewriter was a hit. "Mother, this is jolly good; I wish I had this on my last voyage. Segar will be impressed; I'll be just like a correspondent . . . Churchill in South Africa!"

When the morning arrived, Charlotte made certain that Rolly would remember home while he was in France, and not simply the pretty assistant waiting in his office. He was quick to the breakfast table and was waited on dutifully by the house staff. The room had been brightened up with flowers. A centerpiece of fat yellow blooms overflowed from the wide mouth vase in the center of the heavy wooden dining table. The curtains were spread, letting in the morning sun that early October morning, which warmed the carpet near the sideboard. It was a good day for crossing the Channel, according to the *Times*, which featured the weather on the front-page banner now that the war was on and many crossed the Channel every day, one way or the other. His kit had been brought down and stacked by the front entryway, waiting to be collected by a driver. Charlotte and her son would not be taking the Underground that morning. The dogs swirled around Rolly's chair, heads cocked waiting for the inevitable crumb to fall or hand to ruff them up. Rolly was explaining to Valerie in words of few syllables about his departure and sure return. Teddy was too young to understand English, so Valerie was expected to translate later after he had gone. He could see in her undivided stare that she was not happy with the cautionary tone in his voice.

Rags directed the car to the Mall end entrance to the Admiralty, stopping just long enough for his mother's parting embrace and words of love and devotion before leaving her to wave while other workers passed by in silence, eyes on the ground. He was on to the boat-train from Victoria Station, where the other members of the party would find their way on their own. He knew that Uncle Hilly would be in the Military Transport VIP waiting room and hoped that Segar would not be late. He was a brilliant man but helpless. His wife was with the royal family shooting in Scotland—never a good sign, for Segar was not good at organizing and highly dependent on his man, Croff, who would no doubt be found at arm's length. The first two cars at the head of the train were reserved for first-class passengers; Segar, in civilian clothes, would stand out like a sore thumb.

The train was very long, twenty cars. Rags popped in at the lounge to content himself that the general was there. He was cloistered with a half dozen senior officers over a second breakfast served by stewards in short white jackets. The smell of brewed coffee was in the air; Rags would have killed for a hot cup, but he was not invited. After making himself known, he left to shadow the luggage, which he was happy to see included Segar's kit, but the academic was nowhere to be seen. Electric carts, with drivers preciously perched on the front step, zipped up and down the long concrete platform while steam seemed to slip out from everywhere. Troops were formed up on the far side of the platform nearly the length of the passenger cars. Dressed for combat, laden with packs, folded shovels hung on their backs, wide straps over each shoulder, they stood with one foot in place at rest, Enfield bolt-action rifles resting on the butt plate. All had been issued the new Brodie steel helmet, which the sergeants insisted they wear to get used to two pounds of metal on their heads. None looked happy. They were allowed to smoke, which was a good idea. The free cigarettes handed out by the Red Cross calmed them down. Of course it made an unholy mess of the platform in spite of the cleaners, with short broom and pan, who never stopped cleaning up. A black smoke–belching engine, pulling an ambulance train from Dover, pulled in behind the troops and opened on the opposite side. As the wounded were off-loaded, the moans and cries from the victims of the battle of Loos caught the undivided attention of the men about to leave for France. Through open windows the soldiers silently viewed the evacuation of the train and hoped they would not be on it in the coming days.

Rags was happy to find Segar drawing contentedly on his pipe in the first-class cabin reserved for the party. The kits for all three men were stacked on the opposing bench and strapped down securely. That left four conjoined seats facing forward with plenty of room for comfort on the three-hour journey. Hilly preferred the window and Segar the companion way side, leaving Rags in the center, boots propped up on the luggage. There wasn't much conversation except for the weather and sea conditions in the Channel, which were always uncertain. The tea cart also sold postcards of their steam ferry with torpedo boat escorts on both sides. Meant for the troops to send back home when dropped off at the canteen in Calais, it was intended to show how safe the passage had been.

The transition at Dover was as smooth as silk. It had been accomplished a thousand times since the BEF went to France over a year and two months ago. A year is a long time in war, and this was no exception; it seemed like a lifetime since these same ferries had taken happy holidaymakers across to enjoy the wine and cheese of France and the beer in Belgium. No longer were there happy, expectant faces peering out for the coastline, only ranks of uniformed men wondering what was in store for them in what was once a peaceful land.

That day they enjoyed a serene thirty-mile voyage that took in excess of four hours. Rags had never seen the prodigious volume of traffic on the Channel before on his annual summer excursions. The steamboats belched black coal smoke that lingered and formed a haze over the stream of craft passing each other in long grey lines. The fresh sea breeze he had looked forward to was tainted with the smoke and the scent of war streaming off the Continent. The churned-up deep green water never had a chance to settle before a vessel going one way or the other tossed its tops to foam once again.

They heard the war before they saw the shoreline. Heavy, unending patter of outgoing artillery and the thud of incoming that must have been fifty miles off. He would write a few lines to Beryl and mail them at the first canteen they paused at.

NOT LONG AFTER ROLLY LEFT for France, Charlotte had left a pair of messages for pick-up. It was the first time she had acted alone and wondered what Christian would think of her, an agent in her own right.

That afternoon she requested to leave an hour early, not feeling well after sending her only son off to war for the second time. Chief Chubby didn't bother to dock her pay and let her slip away. She went directly to Rolly's office at headquarters. She wanted to establish a line of communications with Rolly through Mildred Box as she had before. There was no telling how long his work would take, and she wanted to remain close to the office in case there was a development, rather than learning of his condition in the newspapers. It seemed that no one was immune to injury, and the only reliable source of information was the postings in the papers. But most important, she had to be there before Beryl left for the day.

Mrs. Box had errands to run in the absence of Hilly's aide, which suited Charlotte fine. She found herself alone with Beryl as she was locking up the office. Sweet as she could make herself be, Charlotte inquired about Beryl's family and got a running account of the principal members and their daily activities. As long and fast as she talked, Charlotte only caught every third word mangled by Beryl's strong East End accent.

It was during this incomprehensible rundown that Charlotte appeared to feel faint. Taking a seat, she alarmed the young woman, who went out into the hallway to seek help. The passageway was empty. The closing bell on a Friday afternoon was like that at the Ascot races: the building emptied in record time.

"Missus, don't worry, I can help. Got any smelling salts in your bag?"

Taking short breaths and hyperventilating, Charlotte waved her hand to indicate she didn't. Beryl ran into Mrs. Box's office to get some water from Hilly's decanter, but his secretary had emptied it for the weekend. Beryl knelt down on one knee and patted Charlotte's cold hand. "It'll be all right, Missus, just you never mind."

Charlotte put a sentence together. "This has happened before; I'll be all right in a few minutes. I expect it's a result of my son leaving so suddenly.

You mustn't mind me, my dear. Thank you for all your kindnesses. If I can just get to Whitehall, I can take a taxi home. Can you help?"

"I can see you are getting better—not so peaky. Let's try standing up; I'll help. Upsy-daisy then!" Charlotte was not a large woman, but she wasn't helping, which added to Beryl's burden. Finally the two women managed their way to the hall and ever so slowly down the stairs, emerging arm-in-arm out the main entrance of Horse Guards onto the pavement. Steadied by Beryl, a taxi was hailed by a stranger, who assisted Charlotte into the back seat.

"Can you come home with me, my dear? It won't take long, and then I will send you back to Camden in this taxi."

"'Course," Beryl said. She didn't really want to spend more time with the old lady but knew she should take the opportunity offered to be of service and soften her up.

Friday traffic was brutal. The combination of lorries, army trucks, horse-drawn carts, private autos, omnibuses, and taxis all seemed to be going toward Putney Bridge on the King's Highway. Just before the railway arches, the taxi swung left for a hundred yards and stopped in front of the old mansion. Tall, yawning windows framed the first and second floor below a top floor pierced by an eight-gabled roof supported by ornate corbels. Charlotte was sure, as she took in Beryl's wide eyes, that the young woman was imagining herself grandly dressed, peering out through the glass one day, mistress of the house. Beryl supported Charlotte's arm as they entered the hall. She dismissed the driver who aided the two women to the door. "That a girl, take it easy now, almost there." He doffed his cloth cap and was gone.

Steady now, Charlotte didn't want to alarm the staff and was greeted by Mrs. Alberry, who called for the maids. "Get the tea and take it to Madam's chamber, quickly, girl."

Beryl was left in the library while Charlotte was escorted upstairs. She craned her neck at the grand high ceiling of the oversized room with heavily draped windows and antique furniture unlike anything she was familiar with in Camden Market. She walked around the room slowly with a bit of a swish like a grand lady touching this and that and fondling the *objets d'art* on the mantelpiece of the glowing fireplace. She puffed at her hair theatrically in the long mirror and laughed at herself. Crossing to the river side of the room, Beryl parted the heavy blackout inner curtain and noticed that the weather was closing in. A heavy steady rain was falling, which gave her a chill.

Mrs. Alberry opened the double doors and two rambunctious white terriers romped in. "Madam is most grateful for your assistance, as we all are, and would like you to join her in her chamber; follow me."

"Yes, ma'am," she said, as she tried to pet the dogs without letting them make ladders in her stockings.

They went out into the center hall and up the red carpet of the winding staircase to another set of double doors. Mrs. Alberry opened them to reveal Mrs. Stetchworth freshened and seated on a divan for two. "Come here, my dear, and sit by me. I *am* so indebted to you for caring for me when I had one of my turns. I am feeling much better and have ordered dinner for us both. We can have it on trays. I see the weather is dreadful; we just missed it. Can you imagine the two of us on the pavement at Horse Guards in a deluge like this in my condition and trying to locate a taxi on Friday evening?" Charlotte chuckled. "The shipping forecast, Mrs. Alberry tells me, is that it won't last long. Please, come sit."

Beryl's instinct was to run from the haughty mother and the starchy staff and all of that old, old stuff everywhere. But she liked Rags—a lot. He had a spark and was fun and he liked her too. So she smiled and sat down. Dinner didn't come until eight o'clock, and she herself had had no tea. But Beryl persevered, took the sherry on offer, and tried hard to respond to the stilted conversation with appropriate comments. By nine o'clock they had dessert and coffee and had found one topic of mutual agreement: fashion. Beryl was passionate about the shorter hemlines and looser fit and, above all, the firm rejection of corsetry. Charlotte found herself treated like a contemporary, a like-minded, forward-thinking role model in this regard, and the two found themselves laughing at the notion of battlefield nurses and ambulance drivers trying to do their jobs in bone corsets. It was when she found herself reaching out to the young woman to touch her arm as they laughed that Charlotte caught herself, almost shocked at her forgetfulness.

"Do you like dogs, my dear?"

Beryl had seen the way Charlotte had pulled Teddy up on her lap and rubbed his pointed ears. "Yes, I do like dogs. We keep a few to guard the yard. Big brutes—they scare the bejesus out of the neighbor kids who are always thieving around."

"These two are my companions when the Captain is gone," Charlotte countered, "and I find that now I am working I miss them so very much. I like to take them for a little walk at night, but I'm feeling a little unsteady on my feet still. Would you accompany me before you leave?"

"Yes, Missus, I can give you a hand," Beryl said. She surprised herself at truly not minding. The old lady, while still haughty, had turned out to be rather modern and assertive in ways she hadn't expected. She thought of the woman going to work for the first time at her age, so confident despite her inexperience. Beryl had thought Charlotte to be dry and mean and old-fashioned, but she had turned out to have an energy and determination Beryl related to very much. "Formidable," she thought.

At the front door the two women girded themselves for the weather. By the time they exited the front door, the rain had stopped and the moon had come out. It turned out to be a fine night and the dogs were their usual excited selves as they pulled the women down the lane to the bridge steps. Valerie led as usual, with Beryl holding the short lead. Teddy pulled against Charlotte but stopped every few yards to check out what Valerie had found. It was a slow process and the women chatted about the bridge and the trains that rattled across every ten minutes. Negotiating the wet steps was a tangle of leads, paws, and shoes, but they all made it successfully and began the long walk across the bridge toward Wandsworth Park, which Charlotte pointed out across the water through the gloom. "If it wasn't for this war, the park would be lit. At least here on the bridge the shrouds on the lights keep the zeppelins from seeing us and we can make out the flooring." Beryl could barely see the treads and was hesitant as the dog, who had no trouble seeing, dragged her forward.

At the middle of the bridge there was a bulge in the structure, and a dark figure of a large man was visible coming toward them at a slow lumbering pace. "Let's pause here, my dear, and let that fellow pass. Here, squeeze in against me." The man in the trench coat and dark brimmed hat closed in, now twenty, now ten feet away, now right before them. With his left hand he tipped the brim of his hat, and with the right he plunged a foot-long ice pick into Beryl's stomach just below her sternum. He held it there for a moment before withdrawing it and then flipped the bloody pick into the water below.

## Chapter Twenty-Four

# London and Calais, Early October 1915

ONE, TWO, THREE PUMPS OF her wounded heart, and it stopped, all over. The noise of a passing train, only feet away, had muffled her startled scream, and her lifeless body slumped in her murderer's arms. And then was gone, tipped into the Thames' dark waters.

For a moment, Booker turned and looked Charlotte in the face, impassive. Then he was gone, and Charlotte was left alone on the bridge with Teddy and Valerie. Charlotte was dumbstruck with the speed and brutality of the attack. She looked around her, not knowing whether to move forward or back, not quite believing that passersby or policemen weren't running toward her in anger. A life had been snuffed out right in front of her.

In the sky to the east, the searchlights beamed while the sound of zeppelins sputtering above filled the chill air. Bombs were exploding upstream near Westminster once again. The ancient river would cradle many victims that evening—who would care about one more corpse? Having lived on the bank of the Thames most of her adult life, Charlotte was well aware of the thirty-foot tidal surge which was running out to sea that time of night. At three and a half knots, the body would be in central London before the tide began its turn six hours later and brought it back west a mile or so. The following night it would take the corpse as far as Woolwich before it was carried back to Tower Bridge. If it were not discovered by the following night, it would pass the Medway channel and go out to the Thames estuary and finally the Channel and North Sea.

The zeppelin attack was no happy coincidence. Charlotte had asked Christian to arrange the attack before 10:00 p.m. to drive people inside and provide cover. At first she feared that the persistent rain would call off the German raid that night. Visibility had been poor. But the night sky had cleared just in time for the zeppelin commander to spot the moon reflecting off the Thames like a beacon. If the body was found, the zeppelins would be blamed for her death. The small penetrating wound would not raise suspicions. A flying bit of shrapnel, no doubt.

She looked around once again and took a deep breath. The dogs were silent, sitting still at Charlotte's feet, ears alert. The next train clattered across the bridge, sparking and banging as it had done minutes before as if nothing had happened. Charlotte wanted to go straight back to her house and turned to follow Booker, whose image was fading under the dim shrouded lights. The puddles from the earlier rain splashed to his heavy steps. But she knew she must go on to the park, where she'd be expected by others engaged on the same nightly chore. There was a nodding acquaintance of owners as the dogs crunched past on gravel paths. It was an unofficial club and her absence might be noticed. She gave a light tug on the leads. Her voice broke. "Come now, boys and girls. Walkies."

The anti-aircraft guns scattered about the grounds were silent. Although it had been a four-ship attack, the targets never came within their range. On the return trip she mounted the wet three-tiered concrete steps on the Putney end of the rail bridge and trod slower than usual. The dogs were in no hurry to go home and sniffed at anything to prolong the journey. As they reached the center of the span, she stopped to see if anything had been dropped, a clue, a torn piece of cloth that might recall the violent murder of a young woman. She shivered as she peeked over the rail, afraid the body might be caught on the protruding concrete foot of the pier to be found in the morning by a railroad inspector. But it was dark, the clouds once again covered the moon, and the rain started ever so slowly to fall. The rush of the running tide slapped against the stone abutments. It was over—not a trace. Taking a deep breath, Charlotte said, "We better get you two home before you are soaked to the skin and Mrs. Alberry will have to take you in hand before beddy-bye."

On return to the house, she would claim that Beryl was frightened by the bombing and sought the safety of an Underground ride home to Camden, where her station was very deep and used as a shelter. No one at the inspector general's office had seen Beryl leave with Charlotte, and certainly no one would guess that she had invited the lowly clerk home to dinner. The next morning Mrs. Box would report Beryl to the authorities as missing. She would be added to a list of hundreds of other poor souls that were lost in the air raid the night before. It was all too common. Charlotte would search the *Times* for the girl's name to show Rolly on his return. She expected Rolly would mourn the girl and then, as so many had before, move on. Wartime is both slower and faster than regular time. For some it will never end and they wake up each morning of their life with the loss. For others it goes by in a burst and is forgotten in the light of the next horror.

As she went to bed that night, the crime rested easy on her mind. She still felt good about her murder of the loutish Mr. Stetchworth all these years later. She prided herself on the time it took for him to die, in fact—rather clever, she thought. He hadn't a clue that she was at the bottom of it. She had expected to feel the same sense of satisfaction over the scheming upstart bent on snaring her Rolly. But the girl's laughter and fashion talk after dinner—and the gleam of admiration Charlotte had caught in her eyes for a fleeting second—nagged at her. And when she finally got to sleep she found herself dreaming of a hideous decomposing corpse floating face up on the dark surface of the Thames, eyes wide open. Cold and clammy, Charlotte bolted awake and sat upright in the big bed afraid to close her eyes. She couldn't quite identify her emotion, but she thought it might be despair.

ON THE FAR SIDE OF the Channel, at Calais, Captain Stetchworth sought the soldiers' canteen to post his card indicating safe arrival to Beryl. Across a muddy staging area, an aproned woman called to him and waved her hand to attract his attention, "Captain, over here! I can post that card in your hand." He smiled to see one of the comfort stations that society ladies had set up in Calais. While British women could not visit France, these wealthy ladies sought to serve the country in any way they could. At their own expense, they established stations to launder clothes, take care of little tasks to ease the soldiers' burden, and offer comfort food. Only here could you see society women with their sleeves rolled up, working as washerwomen and waitresses. Spattered with mud, the woman who called to Rags was a beacon of civility and a picture of what the men were fighting for. "Stop and have hot tea and a cake. I doubt the ferry ride offered you very much." Rags accepted the kind offer as he pushed his way clear between tightly packed murmuring soldiers. "Would you take a cup to Hilly . . . over there?" she pointed to the general. "Tell him Mercedes Trout-Waring wishes him good fortune." This reinforced Rags' contention that England was more of a club than a country.

Waiting for the IG in Calais was Major General P. E. J. Hobbs. Hobbs had brought an open motor car, which could be evacuated in a hurry if a German plane appeared. Uncle Hilly, true to form, greeted him as another old friend. Was there anyone in the army he didn't know? "Poppy, my dear fellow, I didn't expect to see you here. A car would have been sufficient. How are you, and how is General French? Busy, I expect."

"Hilly, things are at sixes and sevens with this Nurse Cavell kerfuffle." He grimaced. "I think the Huns are going to shoot her as a spy." Edith Cavell had been in the news for months. The daughter of vicar Frederick Cavell, the thirty-five-year-old nurse had moved to Belgium to become a governess to a French family. At the start of the war the nursing school she had been associated with was taken over by the International Red Cross. When the Germans overran Belgium, Cavell began to shelter British soldiers and aided in their escape. She'd hidden the troops in the hospital, protecting over two hundred British and French servicemen. Cavell was arrested by the Germans in August and found guilty of treason and sentenced to death. England was inflamed when it was widely reported that German Count Harrach remarked that his only regret was that "they had not three or four old English women to shoot."

Hilly and Henry Segar climbed in the car for the two-hour drive to the BEF HQ, where Hilly would begin his investigation into Loos. Rags directed the stowage of their kit into the back bin of a small lorry, mounted the left side of the front seat, and settled in to enjoy the gently rolling French countryside. The Army Service Corps driver supplied him with the London *Times*, which had just come off the boat. "It's all about us, sir; ain't we the lucky ones? They tell me all's well and we're on the up, but not where I've been, I tell you that, Captain. We are gettin' the hell knocked out of us by *Herman*. I've been on ambulance duty for the last months, and finally the guv'nor put me on this run to calm me nerves."

The paper was folded to an article: "Loos, Just the Beginning." Rags attempted to read it as the vehicle bumped and lurched on the beat-up road that headed inland.

*Rush of good news from France has necessarily been followed by less stirring dispatches. But there is no sign of a setback. A dispatch received late last evening from Sir John French records further progress of the British offensive east of Loos, while the inevitable counter attacks have been repulsed elsewhere with 'heavy loss.' The same apparently holds true for the French. Meanwhile the dominating factors must be constantly borne in mind. There have been tremendous storms of rain which may check the advance. Again, the second and third line of German entrenchments have to be treated with respect. It will take time to get the heavy guns into fresh positions, and we may be certain that the Allies are not going to throw away their new opportunities by impetuous recklessness. The present operations may last for several days. The first stages must not be overrated, nor must we speak of the prologue as though it constituted the entire drama.*

Rags found his school French allowed him to pronounce the village names as they motored at a slow pace, sinking into the rutted tracks left by the heavy guns on the muddy lanes. He could see his party just ahead jolted out of their rear seats as the staff car rolled precariously ahead. Not a young man, Uncle Hilly's bones would be rearranged by the time he rested in his quarters. Parties of wounded soldiers trudged along in small groups headed in the opposite direction. Their mood was most somber. He passed bivouac sites every mile or so. He could smell them before they came into sight. Charcoal cooking fires, the odor of boiled beef, and just a hint of latrine-slit trenches brought back the scents of Gallipoli. Unwashed troops in the field gave off a smell that was impossible to describe and equally impossible to forget. Artillery parks were ubiquitous. Limbers, sunken in the soft soil as they waited in neat rows to be dragged in trains behind heavy horses, were covered in brown canvas to keep them dry. Red-capped military police with white cross belts directed traffic and sought help to unstick an overburdened vehicle that blocked an intersection. Rags didn't complain; the rest was welcome.

Within the hour the lead car swung off the road and up a tree-lined approach to a chateau in Saint-Omer provided by the French government for the BEF headquarters. The clutch of honey-colored stone buildings was dominated by the main house, large enough to accommodate visitors in style. There were scattered buildings, stables, and an oval courtyard parked full of open staff cars with miniature flags on the front bumpers to declare the importance of the owner. The military police were required to memorize the holders and provide priority access to them on the road network.

The chateau was just one of a number of military complexes that took over the small provincial village. The Australian hospital subsumed the old convent, and wards were set up in the local churches and even the nave of the cathedral. The BEF staff numbered at least a hundred, most of whom were storemen, spudbashers, room clerks, sanitary orderlies, and pump waiters for the officers' mess. Only about thirty of the group wore the red collar tabs, hat, and arm band of the General Staff. A vast number of vehicles tangled through town, creating a constant cacophony of sputters, clangs, and bangs. A line of London omnibuses, filled to capacity with infantry troops and still sporting advertisements for hair tonic above the windows, blocked the road at the bridge to the railway station. Heavy horses dragged enormous guns from the port through the town center. Turning by the cathedral, a long protruding barrel snagged the corner of a building as the battery turned north toward the front line, half a day's slog away. Officers' chargers, belonging to the General Staff, were standing saddled in the stables sweating from a reconnaissance run. Only a beehive could have housed more confusion. In the north heavy guns boomed, bringing the war ever closer.

Housing for Hilly's party had been arranged in a small chateau—a misleading name given to every structure with more than ten rooms in France. While most of his party was housed upstairs, Rags assumed a servant's room near the back stairs. Segar told him to feel lucky. "On field operations the aides were expected to sleep at the foot of the general's bed on the floor in a blanket roll. Be glad you have a bed." He smiled at the joke.

Hobbs's aide took Rags in hand and provided introduction to a half dozen of his own kind. All were young men from top schools and good families, some of whom wore gallantry ribbons won in the first year of the war. Rags noticed most were somewhat invalided from their experience and sidelined for the present. Captain Stetchworth, to his surprise, was a celebrity. He was the only one present who had been to Gallipoli and Egypt, voyaged on ships, and run from submarines. As the center of attention, he fielded a dozen questions—a new role for Rags.

"What are the eastern women really like? Did you see any belly dancers in Cairo? Tell me about the harems; did you get a chance to see one, from the outside at least?" These young men didn't want to talk war. It was the mysterious east they had read about in schoolboy libraries where pages had been marked and creased. Not wanting to burst their bubble, Rags told about the market in Alexandra and spiced it up to satiate the mood. He wasn't going to miss his chance to tell a tale, even if he did make it up.

IN THE MORNING RAGS, THREE paces behind Field Marshal French and Major General Hopewell, followed along on a stroll through the formal garden. Not like a proper English garden: the plants were in strict rows, clipped into odd shapes, and laid out like a bright glass kaleidoscope. It was not to his liking, preferring to let nature have its way. But, then, what did he know about gardens? What did he know about war, for that matter? He wasn't a participant in either, just a casual observer, but with a mind of his own. He made a note to tell his mother all about the conformity. She didn't like the French, but, then, who did in England? Remaining discreetly out of hearing distance, Rags was happily sent away at the end of the walk and joined Henry Segar, who was poking about in the library of the chateau. There was no one around, since the staff was off on assignments.

"Professor"—a title Segar often responded to—"what can you tell me about the field marshal?" He expected a short history told with Segar's usual disdain for military authority and got it.

Segar had an opinion about everyone and everything. As a rule, he based it on what people did, not what they said. "French, he is our great leader, some would say, but not above criticism here and in London. A competent soldier, who started out as a midshipman and transferred to the cavalry. Rather strange, don't you think?" Rags nodded as expected. "He is fancied as a considerably successful ladies' man. He made his reputation on the Chinese Gordon rescue mission that failed. A year too late, he brought back Gordon's mutilated body, if you can call that a rescue. He served in India in the 1890s and returned under a cloud for a messy entanglement with a jealous husband. Redemption came in the form of a victory in a little battle near Ladysmith in the Second Boer War. You would be interested to know that he was the inspector general prior to Hilly. In 1912 he was made chief of the Imperial General Staff. . . ." Henry saw Rags' blank look and clarified. "That means he was the head of His Majesty's forces. A great favorite at court, he has been known to influence public opinion by planting favorable stories about the conduct of the war with his friends in Fleet Street. On the tactical side, he is a champion for horse-mounted cavalry, insisting that to charge with drawn sabers and then to dismount and fight on foot is the best employment of the cavalry. No doubt a hangover from his youth. He doesn't believe in machine guns; they use too much ammunition. No diplomat, he made a hash of the Irish question over Home Rule. He has a reputation for being rather quirky, mercurial. Known for violent mood swings. Frankly, I wouldn't trust him farther than I can throw him. I caution you, Captain, General Hopewell believes him to be a bad egg. Of course, he is correct." Rags recognized that "bad hat" or "bad egg" was nearly the worst epithet to be attached to an English gentleman by one of his own class. Only "card cheat" could be more damning.

The following morning, October 13, the talk in the junior officers' mess was of the German firing squad's execution of Nurse Cavell. Her dying words the day before were, "I realize that patriotism is not enough. I must have no hatred or bitterness toward anyone." In England the streets were taken over by crowds of angry women demanding that the government step up the war and destroy Germany. It was the last straw. Since the fall of 1914 the nation had suffered unheard-of numbers dead while witnessing horrific battlefield wounds which were paraded on their hometown streets. The sinking of the Royal Mail Ship *Lusitania* was unforgivable. Now the murder of Edith Cavell, a humanitarian, generated throngs of rioters attacking anything that had a German association, burning shops, vandalizing property and proclaiming that every man in England had a duty to join the army for king and country and kill the Hun.

The newspapers, taking a note from the spontaneous protestors, joined in the frenzy. *John Bull*'s Horatio Bottomley stipulated in an address at Speakers' Corner in Hyde Park, "I call for the vendetta—a vendetta against every German in Britain— whether naturalized or not. . . . You cannot naturalize an unnatural abortion, a hellish freak. But you can exterminate him." Within the week a branch of the government Registry Office printed a poster which was widely distributed depicting the female figure of Britannia brandishing a sword, with the broken body of Nurse Cavell visible behind her. The bold words read "TAKE UP THE SWORD OF JUSTICE." The papers also took the opportunity to print a story they had under wraps. Communist agitators had spread the impression that it was only the poor who died for king and country while the aristocrats remained safely in the rear. To set the record straight, the media announced that it was not just the common man's family who had suffered. The *Guardian* stated on the front page that among the 685 named aristocratic families listed in Debrett's, 1,500 members had been killed or wounded. Eton, the school of the governing class, reported that of the 5,650 alumni serving in France, one-quarter had been killed and two-thirds of those remaining had been wounded. Thirty-two peerages and thirty-eight baronetcies had become extinct. The *Times* proclaimed that the nation had bonded together in the all-out war and would not stop until Germany was on her knees begging for mercy.

AS RAGS FINISHED HIS BREAKFAST in the junior officers' mess, Hilly was strolling in the garden with Marshal French. Hilly disclosed his mission to look into charges leveled by General Haig that the initial casualties and counterattack by the Germans were the result of the unemployed reserve which had been promised but in the end was withheld at the most crucial moment. The catastrophic losses of 48,000 killed and wounded, combined with 10,000 more as attacks continued the next day, were of vital concern to King George, who asked for an inquiry into the discrepancy between the accounts of the two commanders. Both French and Haig were favorites of the king, but he was deeply disappointed in their conduct of the battle, which was intended to break through the German lines and end the war. Fifteen minutes in, French became defensive and stormed off, leaving Hilly thinking the worst.

That very morning, October 13, the generals had ended the failed twenty-day offensive. The forward temporary headquarters, occupied by Marshal French on the opening days, had been dismantled. The records of the major elements were arriving to be catalogued by the staff of the BEF adjutant general's staff. While Poppy and Hilly worked together interviewing eye-witnesses, Segar poured over the after-action reports, orders, and message traffic; he excelled at picking apart the wheat from the chaff. Rags was sent to casually interview the junior staff and keep his ear to the ground about the crucial events of the first and second day as the guards' brigade was employed in battle. He was expected to go forward to the Welsh Guards, his own regiment, where he would be welcomed, and interview officers on their first days in combat.

He was provided with a motorcycle dispatch rider who plunked the captain into the cramped sidecar seat. The Royal Engineers Signal Service were heroes of the war. Disregarding the hazards of German artillery that registered every intersection and supply route, they got through when the telegraph lines were disrupted. That sidecar, which was normally stuffed with communiqués or homing pigeon cages, was equivalent to a bucking bronco as they sped forward past opposing traffic returning south into bivouacs. As they closed on the reserve trench, Rags was surprised to find that the regiment was engaged. The British offensive was over, but the Germans continued to press the front lines for gains of their own. What he had expected to be a tranquil pick-up of flotsam and jetsam in the aftermath, like his carpet battles with toy soldiers when the dinner gong was rung, was not reality. The dispatch rider drove into a large bunker covered with beams and sandbags to refuel and perform maintenance. A runner from the Welsh Guards guided him through a muddy field and down into a communication trench that led to the battalion command post. A hundred yards from the reserve trench, it was not immune to the odd over-shot from the German guns. Rags was taken in hand by the adjutant who mistook him for a replacement at first, for he was short on officers. The red tabs and arm band soon became apparent when Rags confided that he was aide to the IG, which put a glint of fear into his host's eyes. No one in the army was glad to meet an IG, and the welcome melted. He had seen it before, the quizzical look that said, "What the devil does he want with us?" But what he heard was, "Well, you better meet the CO."

Lieutenant Colonel David Moss-Jones was reclining on a camp chair, boots up on an empty ammunition box, in the corner of the command bunker. A shabby underground structure with duckboard floors smelled from the stagnant water trapped under his scuffed boots. Rags could see that his batman had done his best, but the last twenty days had taken their toll on his footwear. The colonel's uniform, though the mud had been brushed off, had lost its color. His Sam Browne leather belt, complete with black Webley revolver, was hung on a spike behind him. There too was a wooden rack of a bed where his scraped helmet lay. His greying hair needed looking after by a competent barber. Dry lips peeked out from under a thick army mustache. Rags noticed a tremor in his hands as he reached out to pull himself erect. He managed to stand without assistance but was clearly distressed from some underlying injury. Or perhaps it was just mental and physical exhaustion. Rags reported in the most military manner, partially from his training but mostly from admiration at meeting his first Welsh Guards regimental commander. He could plainly see that he was in the presence of a warrior, first class.

"Captain Stetchworth, I know that name. You are the young man who went to great lengths to see my daughter safely to France. Thank you, my boy; it has meant a great deal to Grace and the whole family. I am clearly in your debt."

"How do I do otherwise, sir? Grace is a beautiful and charming girl and a tribute to you and your lady."

"She was right, you know. Rory was there—at Chenonceau, where she is attending to his wounds, which are quite grave, I am sorry to say. Shrapnel, you know. Awful stuff, we take casualties every day even though the war is static once again." On cue, German heavy artillery began to interdict the area. The colonel didn't miss a beat; it was as if he didn't hear the impact only a hundred yards away. "She informed me that the inspector general can do anything. Perhaps you can do something for me. Find out who authored this disaster and have him shot."

"Yes, sir, that's why I am here."

*Chapter Twenty-Five*

# Loos, Early October 1915

WARS AREN'T CHEAP AND RARELY turn a profit. Within a month of the assassination of the Archduke of Austria in June 1914, the financial markets began to quiver as one county after the other sought to stabilize their gold reserves. On July 24, the day after the Austrian ultimatum sent to Serbia to submit, the continental countries demanded the release of their gold reserves held in London. Over the next two weeks, foreign stock markets began to close as the nations of Europe mobilized their military forces. Russian bonds in particular fell precipitously. Only the London and Paris exchanges were open for business. Paris closed the second day of August, forcing London to follow suit. First Russia and then the other nations stopped paying in gold. Banks withheld credit and everywhere things ground to a halt.

Hoarding was in the wind. Concerned customers requested liquidation of their accounts in gold. The British banks paid out in five-pound notes—too large to spend. Recipients took the notes to the Bank of England in exchange for coins to live on until the restrictions were lifted. With that, the English banks panicked and some collapsed. In Germany the Reich Bank set up loan banks—Darlehenskassen—which offered loans up to 50 percent of the value of goods and 75 percent on stocks and shares, just enough to maintain the financial system. Germany sent all of its gold reserve to Spandau Castle in Berlin for safekeeping. For the first time, Great Britain's Treasury issued single pound and shilling paper notes. Chancellor of the Exchequer David Lloyd George believed that all was secure since the City held much of the world's debt. Allowing enough time for the emergency to cool, he reopened the banks on August 7. It was not industry that was the problem but international financial management that was at the heart of the unrest. However, the British stock exchange did not open again for trade until early January 1915. Cash only, not cheques, were in use throughout Europe.

The dreadful Battle of Loos, which was touted as the "Big Push" that would break through, caused the general public to realize that the Great War, for that was what it had become, was going to last. In Britain two million more workers, now men and women, were earning a wage in war-related industry high enough to pay taxes. Lloyd George had also increased the consumption tax. Britain's takings at first were sufficient to pay for the new army and fighting navy. But as the costs escalated the Exchequer realized that higher taxes paid for only a quarter of the nation's outlay. The chancellor then began a war bonds program in which British citizens could buy long-term interest bonds that could be redeemed years later at a profit. That, combined with the foreign borrowing and imperial bond sales, mostly to the United States, made up the wartime budget.

The American banker J. P. Morgan agreed to broker the scheme since England bought food, ammunition, and war machines with the proceeds of the financial instruments from the United States. It also provided jobs for American laborers, who in turn paid taxes. It solved Great Britain's money problem in exchange for more long-term national debt. In the spring of 1915 Lloyd George had become minister of munitions, spending the money where it was needed. But at Loos there hadn't been sufficient artillery stocks to implement the plan. Men and the first use of British poison gas had to substitute for guns.

CAPTAIN STETCHWORTH CONFIDED HIS MISSION to Lieutenant Colonel Moss-Jones. "Sir, General Hopewell, my boss, acting on behalf of the War Ministry, is remaining at BEF headquarters to conduct an inquiry into the conduct of the Artois-Champagne overall campaign. He has sent me to seek your help in his investigation. In particular, he would like to know your experience and that of the regiment in the first few critical days of the offensive, sir." Lieutenant Colonel Moss-Jones lowered his newspaper and began to listen. Rags took a deep breath before continuing. After all, this was Grace's father. "I've been briefed on the overall layout of the battle. My general's review of the offensive indicates that the Loos front witnessed the most significant fighting. Here the army took twice the casualties, leaving Horse Guards and Whitehall to wonder why. He's concerned that the written record and interviews of the General Staff at Saint-Omer will give us a distorted picture of the action on the ground. Can you assist in our inquiry, sir?"

The colonel seemed interested, could see this was an opportunity to get his point of view into the official record. His battalion had been at the end of a long string of bad decisions, and the Guards had paid a very high price for blunders at a much higher level. "How long have you got, Stetchworth?"

"A day or two, sir. I know you have substantial responsibilities, but if you agree—if you could allow me trail along as you go about your duties—might

I trouble you for a first-hand account? I think I could do you and the regiment justice." Rags felt that if the commander was given a chance to enter his views at the highest level, they would be taken seriously. He could see in the man's eyes that he questioned the captain's ability to judge the situation. "I'm no beginner, I have been in combat before, in Gallipoli for a fortnight . . . wouldn't be a bother." He doubted his record impressed the colonel, but it did show that he wasn't just a desk soldier from London. While the colonel was a veteran of many a battle, the fledgling Welsh Guards had been bloodied for the first time just weeks before. "Besides, sir, I do wear the 'Leek'; it's not as if I am an outsider." Pointing out the Welsh Guards insignia on his collar was his strongest gambit yet.

The colonel was cautious. "I see, so that's Hilly's game, is it? The two of us go back a ways, you know. He was my mentor at Sandhurst and I served under him in South Africa."

It had happened to Rags once again. The old man had sent Rags on an errand knowing it would produce exactly what he needed but failing to tell his young aide what he had up his sleeve. This battle was the first time Kitchener's New Army was engaged en masse. The Welsh Guards' performance in particular, the newest formation in the Household Brigade, would be near and dear to the King. There was more to this mission, but Rags concealed the other agenda. He hadn't forgotten about Christian, who was waiting for a message. He needed to send an evaluation to Germany as well, where they would compare the battlefield exploits of both sides.

Additionally, there was a personal attachment not even Hilly would recognize. There was no better place for him to meet Grace's father, who was also his regimental commander. Rags had been hurt and a little embarrassed by the way Grace had left him so abruptly for Rory. But getting close to Beryl had changed all that. The camaraderie during the day at work. The lovely long nights at her flat. Just the thought of her sparkle made him smile. Grace had seemed the perfect fit—she was beautiful and educated and from his own class. But Beryl felt like a fit for *him*, not just a fit for his mother or his class or his ambitions. Nonetheless, he wanted to meet Grace's father. He was an important man and could be a valuable contact.

The colonel was not a friendly man, but a professional one—he was deeply engaged with his duties as a battalion commander in combat. Nearly a thousand men depended on his skill to preserve their lives. He felt their weight and that of their families waiting at home and counting on him to bring their sons home safely. He had signed too many letters home when their identity discs were put on his table. He had made up his mind to participate in the interview. "I'll see you at stand-to this evening. You can walk the trenches with me and see for yourself the lay of the land. The countryside is wide open, that's the problem. You have to see it to believe what we were asked to do. Till then the adjutant will find you a spot." The commander turned his attention to the lap desk he picked up from the dirt floor and opened it to take out stationary and uncap his fountain pen.

Rags followed his guide between the fortified huts to a dugout. It was a smelly hole covered with damp logs, a couple feet of insect-filled earth, and a layer of sandbags that drooped over the dark entrance. Another captain, whose blouse was hanging on a protruding board, was asleep on the only other cot in the eight-foot-square chamber. The escort whispered, "You catch a kip whenever you can, you'll see. You can expect to be awake much of the night. Sleep is precious in the trenches. Never stand up when you can sit down, and never sit when you can lie down, that's my advice. I think the Boche are up to something. Mind how you go."

THE BOCHE WERE ATOP HILL 70 while the Welsh Guards were stuck in the trenches below. Looking up from a plot of sodden land, with the destroyed town of Loos a few hundred meters to their back, Rags could make out the German position in the gloom. He had been briefed that on the 25th of September and late on the 26th the might of Haig's force had overrun the hill but had been pushed back to where the Welsh Guards, a part of Foot Guards Brigade, was dug in. The Germans were looking right down their throat.

The stand-to was standard operating procedure. Evening nautical twilight was the time when there was enough light remaining for the attacker to move but it was dark enough not to be detected. It was a dangerous moment. The troops loaded their weapons, put Mills bombs in their pouches, and occupied forward positions, while the officers inspected their rifles and ensured that ammunition was clean and at the ready. Fires were put out under the dixies, and the last hot meal of M&V had been distributed. Rags was awakened by the harassing impact of creeping jimmy, a high-velocity shell, that whizz-banged into the area without warning. Even though there was no enemy ground attack, every day enemy artillery, fired at random, could fall on troops as they went about housekeeping activities, killing at a surprising rate. Bucket carriers, like ants, were always busy in communication trenches on daily chores, vulnerable to flying shrapnel. Rags heard the crack of a body snatcher—a German sniper—plying his trade during daylight. The opposing trenches were only three hundred meters apart. Although there was nothing to do but wait, there was plenty to do in preparation for the evening patrols preparing to go out into no man's land. The BEF generals believed it was important to keep the men active during the long stalemate of trench life and required patrols and raids to take place nearly every night by small bands of volunteers who risked life and limb in an absolutely futile endeavor.

Tonight's mission, according to the adjutant, was to have each of the three line companies capture a German prisoner for interrogation at brigade head-quarters. The idea was to assess the enemy morale, identify unit formations, and question the prisoners about conditions and future plans. As a rule, men would be lost or wounded on these nightly incursions since the Germans had their own patrols and raiders out on the same ground in the dark. Artillery star shells, like bright candles suspended on tiny parachutes, lingered in the light breeze and exposed groups of creeping soldiers scattering for cover. It was a nightmare.

As stand-to approached, Rags reported to the colonel, tin hat on, Webley revolver loaded safely in his leather holster. Before approaching the com-mander, the adjutant paused and straightened Rags' tie, hard for him to do with no mirror in his digs. This was the Guards and standards had to be main-tained. The colonel motioned for Rags to join the small party as he descended six feet into a communication trench that led toward the setting sun in the west. Rags was surprised by the quiet as he passed by parties of men mov-ing slowly forward past grubby earthworks that had once been German. The attack of September 25 had not been a total failure: they had advanced a bit, but not far enough to make any real difference.

Rags was surprised, the farther forward they progressed and changed to fighting positions, how deep down they were. It was a good ten feet deep by the time they stopped at a company position made obvious by the scaling ladders leaning against the forward reinforced wall. The men were lined up shoulder to shoulder in combat trappings, standing as near to attention as the footing would permit. It had been raining and the exposed white chalk soil hung on their boots in sticky clumps. Wooden-slatted duck boards ran down the center of the floor in some places. But as the trench zigzagged, gummy mud dragged the inspection to a crawl. The light rain had been falling without let-up, and the party sank into the goo nearly to the top of their riding boots. It sucked them down as enlisted men held out their rifles for them to grasp and pull themselves upright. "Didn't expect this, did you, Captain?" the colonel laughed. "Sometimes it takes me two hours to get to every forward position." It was not only time-consuming but fatiguing, and Rags found himself huff-ing and puffing with every step, which embarrassed him no end.

"Here, climb up on that firing step and take a look through the periscope and tell me what you see." Halfway up the shaky ladder, held by a lieutenant who had surrendered his watch position, Rags saw the silhouette of the now famous Hill 70 and the vague outline of the redoubt along its horizon. He turned the device from side to side, scanning the nearly flat open plain spi-derwebbed by rows of barbed wire and twisted pickets. The movement of the glass at the top of the scope reflected what little light was available, a telltale sign that did not go unnoticed by the German sniper on duty, who promptly took a shot that ended up buried in the dirt above Rags' head. "Active, aren't they?" the lieutenant chuckled. "They don't often miss; we lost a Guardsman yesterday as he was bucking up the wire." The officer's voice showed no fear or remorse at the loss. It was routine.

Rags climbed down and saw the colonel seated on a wooden ammo box. The colonel caught Rags' eye and pointed with his engraved swagger stick. "You know that the initial attack on Hill 70 was successful and the line divisions took it and were fighting on the other side when they encountered heavy resistance. The reserve divisions of the 21st and 4th were called for. We were rallying a few hundred meters behind for the past two days but were ordered some significant distance to the rear. Half a day's march, at least. We tried to cozy up through the village of Loos, which was a smoking ruin, but were held back just when we were needed. It wasn't until the third day when the reserve who had finally been engaged the evening before began to come through our lines, leaving us to face the counterattack of the Boche. Every time we popped out of the captured German trenches, where we had sheltered from the enemy artillery, we were driven out with heavy casualties. As you just saw, the ground is wide open; only shell holes and bombed-out trenches provided any cover. We made little progress, but we gave it our all. In the confusion our own artillery was falling on our positions. Officers nonetheless got up and led the lads into hand-to-hand fighting out there."

Of the survivors, he looked at the Guardsmen nearby, who could just make out the sound of his voice. "I must admit that these civilians turned soldiers are the finest I have ever led in my twenty years. I couldn't ask for more, but if I did—if I had to go over the top once more—they would be with me all the way. Tell Hilly that the new army is better than the old; he will know what I mean. However, the leadership from above is not there and he must do something about it." The old man rose and continued down the line as darkness nearly obscured his fading image.

Rags followed, gathering images and starting to form words for his report. It was another hour before they entered a communication trench that led back to the vicinity of the battalion headquarters. The time for a German attack had passed, and he pressed against the dirt walls as men began to slip around once more, carrying all manner of matter from garbage to buckets of stomach-turning night soil. Back in his digs he pulled out the portable typewriter his mother provided and put down his impression of the terrain, natural and man-made. He tried to capture the tone of the battalion commander's narrative as well as the facts. The soldiers had been strangely silent, but that was only natural in the presence of the colonel and other officers. The adjutant had provided some statistics for him: "forty-three officers were casualties and three times that came from the other ranks." Along with the figures he added, "I wouldn't be surprised if the old man asked your boss to second you to the regiment before tomorrow is up!"

The next morning did indeed come with a request from Lieutenant Colonel Moss-Jones. At breakfast in the headquarters dugout he passed the previous night's hospital report, and Rags saw Rory Edgerton-Gray listed among the dead. He had been wounded by shrapnel but not so severely as to require his immediate return to Blighty. Once in the hospital he seemed to be mending, but an infection had taken hold. Moss-Jones knew Grace had been at Rory's side and watched helplessly as he began the inevitable slide to the end. "Captain, she must be in distress. I think a visit from a good friend could be of enormous solace. I think I can justify your side trip to see our wounded to get their impressions; Hilly could see the logic. I'll get clearance for you on the next train to the hospital. The adjutant will take you to the railhead. Leave your kit. A day or two will not matter—we aren't going anywhere, I can assure you."

## Chapter Twenty-Six

# Chateau Chenonceau, October 1915

CHATEAU CHENONCEAU SPANS THE RIVER Cher near the village of Chenonceaux in the Loire Valley south of Paris. It began life in the 1300s as the feudal home of the Marques family, only to be bought, sold, torched, and rebuilt many times over the years. In 1547 Henry II gave it as a gift to his mistress, Diane de Poitiers, who built extensive gardens and constructed the arched stone bridge connecting the chateau to the Cher's far shore. When Henry died, de Poitiers was forced to yield the chateau to Henry's formidable widow, Catherine de Medici, who expanded the gardens and turned it into a glittering social site. The first fireworks ever seen in France were set off there in honor of her son's ascension to the throne.

After Catherine de Medici's death, the chateau continued to bounce between aristocratic owners. Aristocrats love castles but tend to accrue debt. It went from master to master, from the Duc de Vendome to the Duke of Bourbon, who sold off most of its furnishings, many of which ended up at Versailles. Under the care of Louise de Dupin, Chenonceau became a gathering place for Enlightenment figures like Voltaire, Montesquieu, and Rousseau. During the French Revolution, Louise de Dupin saved the chateau from destruction, citing its importance for transport and commerce.

After many owners, the chateau was bought by a chocolatier named Henri Menier in 1913. It was Menier who set up the chateau as a hospital for the Allies. No better site could be found in all of France for a medical complex to care for wounded officers. The ancient remnant of the roadway that still dominated the first floor provided a wide bed ward with four large anterooms set up for specialized care and an operating theater. The second and third floor mimicked the first, allowing separation between the patients of the five regiments. The circular tower adjacent—the only original medieval building to have survived intact—provided rooms for the medical staff as well as cellars for medical supplies. On the extensive grounds an operating farm of several hundred acres was capable of growing copious crops and grazing livestock, making the field hospital nearly self-sufficient. Even in times of constant rain the chateau remained dry, constructed as it was well above any river surge.

The beautiful chateau was adjacent to the main road to Paris and not far from the main rail line in the village, providing easy access and egress for ambulance trains. In addition to the ample facilities and medical supplies, the picturesque Loire pastoral countryside, far from battle noises heard near Pas-da-Calais and Bayonne, allowed the convalescent community to recover peacefully before being offered up once again to the battlefield.

RAGS WAS STRUCK BY THE quiet of the Loire countryside after the noise of Paris and Flanders. Moss-Jones had procured him passage on an ambulance train that was stopping at Chenonceaux, and then he was to hitch a ride a few miles to the estate. It only took him a few minutes before being picked up by an inbound ambulance and delivered to the front entrance of the chateau-made-hospital. He got himself settled in the visitors' quarters located in the tower and checked in with the hospital commander. Rags' official mission was to interview soldiers wounded at Loos. He was cautioned not to interview any who were suffering from facial and head wounds or those who had been under heavy sedation. The most critically wounded had been stabilized and sent directly to England. Those with broken bones, multiple bits of shrapnel, and direct gunshots were good candidates. The most stridently offered advice was not to disturb *Sister's* routine or he would pay the price. Anyone who had any contact with nursing sisters understood the discipline demanded within the ward system established by the legendary Florence Nightingale from the days of the Crimean War.

With a ward clearance in hand, he would start with an inquiry about Captain Rory Edgerton-Grey. He left the tower, walked over the old drawbridge, and proceeded past a pair of sentries at the double wooden doors. They were dressed in combat attire, armed with loaded rifles and shiny fixed bayonets. The weapons were brought up in a snappy salute, which the captain returned in smart fashion. He was immediately confronted with a long room the width of the old river bridge which must have been the original road bed. It had kept something of its old character but was wrapped in a marble floor and high walls topped with a painted floral ceiling. Beds in four neat rows stretched the great length of the ward. Some were masked with folding screens covered with white cloth. Men in blue hospital garb hobbled between beds, while orderlies and nurses moved quietly among the cots. There was a mixture of scents—lavender, carbolic soap, medicine, and the horribly memorable smell of putrefying gangrene that he recalled from his voyage on the hospital ship.

No one paid attention to him until an orderly directed him to an office on the second floor. When he mentioned Rory's name, the ward sister was surprised at his interest. "Are you a relative, Captain Stetchworth?"

"No, Sister. He was a member of my regiment," he said carefully. He made sure to imply an acquaintance without stating so directly.

"I see. Captain Edgerton passed away yesterday from his wounds. His body has been readied for burial. He will be taken to Loos-en-Gohelle and buried at the Dud's Corner cemetery, where all those who died during the campaign are buried by regiment. Do you wish to accompany the body along with the guard of honor?"

"No, Sister. I am here on a mission to interview participants in the battle for an official inspector general report to the War Ministry and can't leave at the moment."

"I take it that you have clearance? I would remind you that these men are under my care and you will have to conform to my rules and timetable. You may visit those who are well enough to be bothered with army business, as long as you advise me in advance of your schedule and the men with whom you intend to concur. Is that understood?"

Rags stepped back in submission. "Yes, of course. I'm not here to interfere with their care, which I can see is in your capable hands, Sister."

Sister sniffed while suppressing a smile, well aware of but not immune to Rags' endearing charm. "Well, then, young man"—purposely leaving his military title aside, firmly believing that in the hospital rank had no privileges—"you may go about your duties and I will go about mine."

Dismissed with a wave of her head, Rags exited to the hallways and buttonholed a passing orderly with the day's mail. "Corpsman, are you familiar with a Nurse Moss-Jones?" He was directed to the nurses' station down the second-floor corridor. The ward, in the same arrangement as the floor below, was open clear to the far end of the chateau. He doubted Grace would be on duty so soon after Rory's death. There must be a nurses' quarters on the grounds and the ward nurse could direct him there. Passing by the ends of the occupied beds, he envisioned himself lying there and thanked Providence that he had escaped the fate of many of his school friends. At the nurses' station he found a nurse with her back turned, buried in papers and charts. "Miss, are you acquainted with Nurse Moss-Jones?"

Not looking up, she turned slowly, still holding a chart in her hand, her eyes never leaving the page. "I should think so. I am Nurse Moss-Jones."

THAT EVENING THEY MADE THEMSELVES scarce with a trip into the village and dinner in the Restaurant Rousseau. The tiny rustic auberge paid tribute to the time Jean-Jacques was a frequent visitor to the chateau. "Here you go, Roland; take the menu but order the lamb. It's the best they have." That afternoon Grace had taken to calling him "Roland" after the knight in Charlemagne's court. "Rolly, you always pop up when I need you. First the night of the zep raid, then when I had to get to France to be with Rory, and now, once again, here you are. My hero." He smiled broadly, liking how the word "hero" made him feel, but he didn't miss the sadness in her eyes, which stung a bit.

At the restaurant, he inquired gently about Rory. She paused and took a bit of wine. "Rory's family and mine have served together in the east and on Cyprus, at home and South Africa. Our fathers were in the South Wales Borderers Regiment at that time, on and off through our early years. When I became a teenager, while he was away at boarding school, I asked my parents if I couldn't go to a finishing school nearby in Harrow on the Hill. We became an item; the families knew it, everyone knew it. We were expected to marry and live the life of our parents, roaming the world at government expense. I liked the idea of all it entailed. But this war, this hideous war, has shattered my dreams like a plate glass window, into a million pieces, and I can't see beyond today." She paused abruptly, the words stuck in her throat. "Well, that's our story and now I must close the book." Tears washed over her blue eyes as she looked up at him.

Rags was a bit at a loss in front of such deep grief, but he did the best he could. "I'm so sorry, Grace. I didn't know you were so close. I had thought, back in London . . ."

"I hope you don't think I led you on, Rolly. I so enjoyed your company and felt a bit . . . connected, I guess . . . after the zeppelin attack."

Rags nodded and surprised himself with how at peace he felt. "Please don't worry. I have someone myself now. But you . . . I'm just so sorry, Grace. You're not alone . . . that's about all I can offer. I am so glad I came at this moment. It was a fluke, really—I'm interviewing the soldiers about Loos, and only after speaking with your father did I realize you were here."

"I thought he was past danger, you know." Grace looked off as she recalled the past weeks. "At first he improved. The shrapnel that was embedded in his face was removed a little at a time and he was able to take nourishment. I fed him five small meals a day and he responded. We were lucky that it was just his jaw and face that was peppered with tiny black fragments. The face has a great deal of blood flow and heals faster than any other part of the body." She took a long gulp of wine, draining the remains of the glass. "But we didn't know that he had a rather serious concussion. A week ago his speech became impaired and he had paralysis on his left side. It got worse each day. The doctors trepanned his skull to relieve the pressure as the brain swelled. The end came quickly then and . . . oh Rolly, I can't stand it—he's gone." This time she began to sob—shaking inward.

Rags got up from his seat then. "Come on, Grace," he whispered as he bent to hold her. "Let's go home."

THE FOLLOWING MORNING, WITH GRACE busy in the ward, Rags conducted several interviews, which were not earth-shaking, in order to write a report no one cared about. He and Grace ate lunch and dinner together and made a solemn promise to stay in touch and to meet again back in Blighty when the war became history. Grace said she intended to remain at Chenonceau until the end and then go back to St. Thomas', where he was sure to find her. In the meantime they would write.

On the train back to Saint-Omer Rags relaxed for the first time in a week. It would take longer than usual to get to Paris. The medical train was filled with wounded who were in no hurry but happy to be going home at last. In the city he transferred to a regular service to Calais and hitched a ride to Saint-Omer, where Henry Segar brought him up to speed on the events of the past few days. Since he had left for Chenonceau, all hell had broken loose, and Hilly was embroiled in a war of will and words with Marshal French's chief of staff.

No talk with Segar would be complete without brandy and an easy chair, along with a roaring fire if at all possible, so Rags was happy to join Segar in his room to partake of all three. "Rags, you would not believe the last few days. While Hilly was interviewing all his old chums here and at General Haig's headquarters, he sent me looking into the after-action reports, which are filed daily before the end of day regardless of the heat of battle. Well, as you know, that is what I do best, ferreting out what some might want to hide. It turns out there was a bit of a disagreement over who said what and who did what. The whole battle settled on one factor." He hesitated for dramatic effect and refilled their snifters with the twenty-five-year-old Courvoisier. He took a sip and waited for Rags to do the same. He held the cut glass beaker up to the light to admire the amber color.

"The plan, Haig's plan, hinged on the agility of the reserve force made up of two infantry divisions and the Guards division to report at the crucial moment to drive home the attack and rout the Germans before they could organize to counter-attack. That moment came late on the first day when Hill 70 was breached. Marshal French agreed to have the reserve positioned but disagreed as to how far the reserve should be kept safe to the rear. When Haig called for the reserve, French hesitated and then brought them forward at far too slow a pace to be decisive. As a result, Haig's attack failed—in fact, turned into a massive loss of position and catastrophic loss of men and equipment."

He leaned forward. "Here's the rub. French altered the record to cover his reluctance to live up to his word. Hilly is confronting French as we speak.

If I were you, my boy, I would pack up my kit and get ready to leave in a moment's notice for London. Hilly wants his report in the hands of the War Ministry immediately."

Rags was confused. "Me, just me? I don't see that you're packed. You made the discovery—why not you?"

Henry sat back and took another slow taste of the finest cognac in France. "You are young and travel fast. We are a couple of old duffers and it takes time to get us off. We'll see you in a couple of days. The report, as I have drafted it, is complete and needs no clarification. It will blow the lid off the BEF, and the boss is not sure he wants to be in London for the explosion. For me, I am just a humble civil servant. You are the messenger, and since they might shoot the messenger I suggest that you drop off the report off at the War Ministry for Kitchener and go home to your mother, where you will undoubtedly be safe."

## Chapter Twenty-Seven

# The Channel and London, October 1915

AS EXPECTED, HENRY WAS CORRECT. No sooner than Rags finished packing up his kit, which was strewn over a wide area of their rooms, than Hilly arrived in a huff. He called out for them both and plopped down in an easy chair. "Well, they don't buy it—not the chief, not the field marshal. Silly old duffer. I showed them their words in black and white, their own bloody written words that condemn their actions. Marshal French refuses to take responsibility for the needless deaths of thousands of loyal soldiers on that disaster of a battlefield. They say I'm interpreting it for my own purposes. My own purposes, I'll be damned—who do they think I represent? There is no plot. I reminded them that the inspector general is an independent authority. They said I was in Haig's pocket; by God, I'll show them whose pocket I'm in—I'm in His Majesty's pocket. Rags, you're packed, I trust. Get on the road, my boy."

Segar, who predicted the explosion, had secured a passage for the captain on the authority of the IG. He handed Rags an official red travel pass, the kind that ensured no questions would be asked. "There now, that should do it, Captain."

Rags stood to attention. "Yes, sir. I would like to catch something to eat—missed dinner, traveling all day, you know, sir."

Hilly handed the report to Rags, not appearing to hear the request for nourishment. His tone became slow and deep as he looked directly into Rags' blue eyes: "This is vital, the most important thing with which you will ever be entrusted. Take it directly to Kitchener—no one else, mind you." Turning away, "You can get dinner on the ship; off with you."

Rags forgot his empty stomach, took the file, and placed it in his Italian briefcase. Segar rustled up an orderly to carry his kit. A car was summoned just as the sun was setting. No sooner were they on their way than the nightly

German artillery fires on the roads begin. Highly inaccurate—fired by map coordinates, not observation—they let loose on likely targets with large-caliber howitzers. The guns were surprisingly lucky, even though the few British heavy guns sent counter battery fire into the atmosphere. It was more show than effect. The order of the day was, "Don't stop moving and get off the bull's-eye as soon as possible." The old army saying applied that evening: *There are two kinds of soldiers: the quick and the dead.*

Under that evening's blackout conditions, the long and uncomfortable daylight drive to the port was even worse. The open car jolted its way along rutted tracts, nearly ejecting Rags several times along the way. The vehicle was stopped only once to tie down his kit. Rags held the briefcase tight against his body the whole way, so much so that his arms ached and he could barely unfold them when they stopped at dockside, where a four-stack destroyer waited in a swamping rain. On either side mercy ships were loading wounded from the medical trains, which were lined up head to tail for a mile. The destroyer's captain had been alerted to Rags' arrival and was waiting impatiently. From the flying bridge, he shouted through his megaphone at the young officer, "The sea's rising, Captain; quickly now and we'll be underway." Sailors stood on either end of the mooring ready to up rope and allow the ship to sail.

A steady rain began to sheet down, obscuring the warning lights on the jetty. Maneuvering slowly past other craft, the thin hull of the warship cut its way into open water. Once secure below decks, Rags was directed to the wardroom for his long-awaited dinner. There, across the table that was bolted to the floor, he met Major J. R. M. Chard, a septuagenarian far too old to be a fighting man. His uniform was impeccably tailored. His chest held two rows of rather faded ribbons. The first was still deep red: the Victoria Cross.

His fellow traveler didn't bother to introduce himself. That may have been because he assumed everyone knew Chard of the Zulu Wars, where he had distinguished himself at Rorke's Drift. "So you're the Johnny that has been holding up the show . . . must be someone important, but you don't look it, my boy. What's your business, lad?"

Rags' voice took on a boyish quality. "Sir, I'm aide to the inspector general and he's sent me to the War Ministry with a high value report."

"Has Hilly, indeed?"

This time Rags was not surprised to find that he was seated with another old campaigner of General Hopewell.

The major smiled, surely remembering the good old days with Hilly on some forgotten track in a place far, far away. "Well, that's most interesting. We're birds of a feather, both off on king's business, then. I'm one of His Majesty's messengers. And while your boss was busy with French, I've been with Haig. I might guess that we have similar positions. If this ship sinks, we two will have ruined the show, I expect." He placed his index finger up against the side of his nose and gave a knowing wink.

Rags paused from shoveling down his long overdue meal. After running the German artillery gauntlet en route to the docks, he had considered himself safe. But the English Channel was far more dangerous than the open road.

"King's Messenger"—Rags was aware that there was a very small number of highly trustworthy men who wore a silver greyhound badge, *The King's Messengers*. He examined once again the uniform of the major and looked to the hat rack, but there was no silver badge. Could it be on his dispatch case next to the old man's chair? His regimental badge, a laurel wreath with the letters SWB, was that of the South Wales Borderers. Rags was curious but didn't quite know how to ask more. Besides, he was very hungry.

Noticing Rags' search for his identity Chard offered, "I'm a Welshman through and through, but the badge is honorary, given by the regiment. I served with them at the Drift, but I am an engineer by trade. I was tending the ferry when it all went upside down."

The ship was underway and began to roll in the choppy Channel. They felt the engines thrust as it reached full speed. Chard asked about Rags' days with the Welsh Guards at the front and how the new regiment fared. Rags mentioned Moss-Jones and goaded the old officer into telling stories of Welshmen under fire as far back as the Zulu Wars. It made his long-awaited meal even more enjoyable than it really was. It was going to be difficult to keep it all down in that bloody sea. But the stories flowed freely as the major recalled campaigns and amusing stories of men Rags had met over the past year. Rags knew the story of Rorke's Drift—every schoolboy had played him in the backyard defending a makeshift fort of scrap wood and sand-filled burlap bags. Rags himself had made a wooden sword and painted it silver with a red tip since, as a ten-year-old, he had no blood at hand. Schoolmates girded themselves with dried grass skirts and bent spears to charge the flimsy ramparts. But the miniature Zulu warriors never breached the British walls, just as the Welshmen had defended the Drift in Africa.

They left France in the dark and arrived at Dover in the dark. In an attempt to avoid detection and a shot from a German gunboat, the destroyer had serpentined along the way, making the thirty-mile journey much longer but increasing their safety. The poor visibility and angry sea meant nothing to the sailors of the man-of-war; if anything, it protected the voyage from marauding German patrol craft. The weather turned foul as they reached the Dover breakwater, and it took two attempts to breach into the protected harbor. The quay was uncovered, and damp passengers waiting for the return voyage clambered up the narrow gangway while Chard and Rags opposed them on the way down. Rags rubbed shoulders with Major General Hunter-Weston, whom he had met in Gallipoli. While Generals Hamilton and Stopford had been relieved and retired, the worst of the three, old Hunter-Bunter, was—unbelievably—on his way to command once again. Rags would not relish having to tell Henry Segar that his prediction had come true—that "You can't keep a bad man down when it comes to royal patronage."

There was a fast train, as it was known, pressed into service just for the occasion of that evening's mission. It waited, puffing between the tunnel openings at Dover Station. Only two passenger cars in length, both first class, it was the best the South Eastern and Chatham Railway's rolling stock could manage. The engine, *Harbinger*, was a four-six-two wheel arrangement, which made it the quickest on the line. Shined and polished, her black elephant-ear air deflectors, fastened to the sides of the smoke box, made it look fierce as steam escaped, hissing in anticipation of an epic run to London.

As the sun rose over Victoria Station the two messengers emerged from the crowded passageway that led to the busy street. Rags was hailed by the driver that Segar had arranged and offered Chard a lift as well. "I think, sir, your meeting with the King trumps my appointment with Field Marshal Kitchener." It seemed that the IG office was more efficient than the palace, for there was no car waiting for him.

Chard smiled cannily. "Well said, Captain; you have a wisdom far beyond your years. I won't forget your generosity."

Of course, the palace was on the way to Horse Guards and it was only logical to accommodate Chard, but Rags made a point of deferring. The car delivered Rags to the front portico of the old headquarters before eight that morning. Climbing the polished steps to the War Minister's office, he was not surprised to find that Kitchener was available, though most of his staff had not yet arrived. Hilly's name turned the trick, and he was admitted to Kitchener's chamber overlooking the parade ground. Early on Rags had been nearly paralyzed with awe in the presence of the distinguished personages. Now he was used to it and simply presented his report and stood at stiff attention awaiting instructions.

The report that Kitchener held in his hands was short—only one page long. It contained a brief summary of the Artois-Champagne campaign and French's failure to support Haig in the manner they had agreed upon, backed up with a number of quotes that Segar had lifted from the after-action analysis at Marshal French's headquarters.

Kitchener looked up. "What part have you played in all this, Captain?"

"Sir, I was detached to the Welsh Guards' regimental headquarters, where I spent time with Colonel Moss-Jones on his rounds. He suggested that I interview officers and Guardsmen first-hand while offering his own experience.

Then I was fortunate enough to travel to Chateau Chenonceau, which is now a hospital for the officers of the Guards Regiment. There, likewise, I conducted interviews with the wounded."

"Did you come to any conclusion, Captain?"

"My thoughts are reflected in the pages of the inspector general's report in your hand, sir."

Kitchener turned back to the report for a moment and then tossed it on his desk. "Go home, my boy, you don't look well." In fact, he was, well, just exhausted.

BEFORE HEADING HOME, RAGS WENT to the IG's office to find an early morning Mildred Box on the job. He had planned to leave a note concerning the other two party members. Instead, he told her of their decision to remain behind and that they would follow in a few days as soon as the dust settled. He noticed that Beryl was not at her post and asked if she might be in soon. That was the one thing that had been on his mind ever since he left the ship.

Mrs. Box took a deep breath. She was aware that Rags and Beryl had worked together and were friends of a sort. "Captain, I have some bad news." She told him that Beryl's family had reported her missing the night of a particularly menacing zeppelin raid. She never came home that night after work and hadn't been seen since. "The raid was centered on the East End and the Thames Bridges . . . perhaps she had been caught in the open, visiting friends or going to that pub she liked so much. Silly girl—why couldn't she have gone straight home and sheltered as she should have?"

Despite the harsh words, Mrs. Box was clearly upset by the young woman's disappearance; while Beryl's low origins would generally have created an unsurpassable gap between the girl and Mrs. Box's middle-class sensibilities, the war had flattened the infamous class consciousness of Britain ever so slightly. War work and mutual sacrifice created strange bedfellows.

But her sadness was nothing compared to the yawning black hole that opened up in Rags' soul. He felt his heart thump hard one, two, three times, and his head sway. "No. It can't be."

"Captain, I'm sorry."

He staggered into the hallway and slumped against the wall. "It can't be," he repeated. But his head knew that it was all too possible. Civilians died every day, even ones as young and lovely and full of life as his Beryl. He made his feet move, made his legs take him to the Tube station, and soon found himself on Putney Bridge, staring into the Thames and dreading going inside with the death of Beryl so fresh on his mind.

The dogs were the first to recognize him as he rattled the front doorknob and dropped his kit on the polished floor of the open foyer. The morning chores had enveloped the great house, but his mother was nowhere to be found; he had forgotten to call when he heard the news of Beryl's death. He was glad to be able to simply go upstairs to his room and lie on his bed. It hurt, worse than the hunger he had come to know in Gallipoli. The pain was in the same place, the pit of his stomach and sometimes in his heart. And he thought, "This is what she must be feeling—what Grace must be feeling about Rory. We are war widows, the pair of us."

CHARLOTTE TOOK THE NEWS PHILOSOPHICALLY. At the breakfast table the next morning, she said all the right sympathetic phrases, which surprised Rags. His mother encouraged him to eat, for she could see his cheekbones standing out and his sunken eyes. He had little to say about the mission to France, and she reminded him that his father would be waiting for a report. But first a hot bath, it was agreed. The scent of France followed him about the room like an unwelcome guest.

A good feed, a tub of hot water, and a clean, dry bed were luxuries long forgotten during his time in France. Sleep had come and gone now, but the pain remained. He picked himself up and met his mother in the library to work on their next message for the German high command. He stayed away from the mundane—morale, troop movements, material shortages and over-ages, and the general care and cleaning of the field army. He zeroed in on the medical care, explaining concisely the efficient system of transport and care from the trenches to London hospitals: the triage which began just behind the line, the passage by ambulance on roads specifically designed for medical care and treatment, the quality of care at the chateau. The medical trains to the south coast and Saint-Omer were organized in advance by injury and staffed accordingly. The average Channel crossing was far better than his rough ride with the Royal Navy. In Dover he regretted that his fast train might have impeded that of a standard fourteen-car express directly to Charing Cross Station, where a caravan of ambulances waited regardless of the time of day or night for the fallen. Why couldn't the fighting war reflect such excellence? All this would not fit in a short message, but Rags and Charlotte attempted to convey in a few phrases the importance of the British system of coordinated medical care to the war effort.

The Germans would be only so interested in medical care, however. So he appended to that description what he knew the Imperial Staff wanted to hear. "Marshal French failed to deliver reserves at Artois-Champagne. Forged records. We expect he will be relieved and replaced by Haig."

## Chapter Twenty-Eight

# France, March–August 1916

IN ADDITION TO THE INCREASE of troop formations from nearly element of the British Empire, the war could claim brush fire copycats among the client states of Africa. Germany, Britain, France, Belgium, and Portugal ruled over African colonies and from their populations drew troop formations to France during the war. Additionally, cadres of military officers and sergeants were sent to fortify colonies by raising small fighting formations that clashed in set piece battles. Little attention was paid to their campaigns or losses.

The zeppelin, poison gas, quick reloading artillery, mass formations—all were an attempt to get the upper hand and end the war decisively and, of more importance, quickly. None had an effect as the casualty lists stacked up. In an attempt to gain the upper hand, the British Ordnance Department finally acceded to Churchill's idea of a land yacht. A mechanized combat vehicle, cocooned in steel plate, mounting a cannon or machine guns that crawled like a bug over rough ground and busted in and through enemy trenches. By early 1916 a prototype was developed, which would be disguised as a larger water tank, thus giving the Mark 1 its common name. When eventually deployed, the Mark 1 tank—thirty-two feet long, eight feet high, with a metal caterpillar treads wrapped around both sides and propelled by an internal gasoline engine—was a curiosity to the troops and enemy alike. Manned by a crew of eight who entered through a small armored door on the side, the men were exposed to exhaust fumes and heat, limiting their hours of operations. It was deployed in small numbers in selected areas were the ground was smooth. The shock was immediate, but soon the Germans learned to stop the new tanks with accurate artillery fire.

IN LONDON, THE COLD AND damp winter had closed in. The Office of the Inspector General spent its time seeking Cumming's mole, without result. The Royal Navy was more dedicated and continued to press on.

The cold and damp suited Rags just fine. He settled into his old London routine, nestled safely in the bureaucracy at Horse Guards, watching internal events and reporting to his father items that might be of interest. In France, the stalemate deepened with the winter, but the casualties—of artillery, snipers, accidents—kept coming. A second Christmas and New Year came and went without a resolution of the war. All the certainty of a quick finish had disappeared, and Britain began to understand what a long and fruitless slog was ahead.

One felt it on the hard streets of the capital. The day wearied and faded by four in the afternoon as darkness fell in that northern clime. Office workers emerged down cold, clammy steps, picking their way along the dim streets. With auto headlights blinkered to a thin slit, traffic crawled and giant buses and lorries seemed to be moving at the same pace as the people on the pavement. Pedestrians stumbled, careening into each other with half-murmured apologies. So dense was the darkness and chaos that more than 40,000 accidents involving pedestrians had been recorded since the fall of 1914. Some private park fences had been removed to allow war machinery through. Piles of tan, flat sandbags lay where ornate wrought-iron benches once beckoned. Uniformed men shone a massive cylindrical spotlight into the black sky, sweeping across high clouds for zeppelins. Rags felt the city's despair in his bones, but that was just fine with him as well. If he suffered, why shouldn't everyone else?

Grace was the first to write in the new year—a short note that ended with a poem by Rudyard Kipling, no doubt a reflection on the loss of his only son at Loos:

> *That flesh we had nursed from the first in all cleanness was given . . .*
> *To be blanched or gay-painted by fumes—to be cindered by fires—*
> *To be senselessly tossed and retossed in stale mutilation*
> *From crater to crater. For this we shall take expiation.*
> *But who shall return us our children?*

To add to the despair, the Military Service Act of January 1916 established conscription. By spring men would be inducted into what had been an all-volunteer army, just in time for Germany's latest initiative. Lieutenant General Wilhelm, crown prince of Germany, led his Fifth Army into Operation Judgement, a gambit intended to "bleed France white" centered on the forts and main citadel around Verdun. The Germans believed that if they took up position on the heights above the citadel, they could rain artillery down on the French army, establishing a war of attrition. The Germans were aware that many of the big guns and troop concentrations at Verdun had been stripped from the forts to support other French fronts farther west. A single road behind French lines known as the "sacred way"—*La Voie Sacrée*, or *La Route*—supplied the scattered auxiliary forts with artillery ammunition and reinforcements. With reduced firepower, the Germans believed troop reinforcements would come pouring in, which they could decimate with their own firepower.

Wilhelm's Fifth Army had disguised its build-up of troops in the thick forests north of Verdun. On February 21, 1916, it attacked the bulge on the northern edge of the French line, which rested on the Meuse River. Massive artillery fire, amounting to 80,000 shells for an area less than a thousand yards' square, was loosed on the surprised French line. Taking advantage of their position on the heights, the German infantry swept down across the river and drove the fleeing French before them. German aviation played a special role accurately spotting for the guns. Within three days the German army advanced four kilometers, to the shock of Marshal Joffre, commander of the French army, forcing him to alter his entire strategy.

But it was just the beginning. By the end of February, the Second French Army under General Philippe Petain deployed massive amounts of artillery in support. The battle of the great guns took over, smashing both lines to a standstill. Eventually twenty divisions, each of 15,000 soldiers, were added to Petain's force to defend in depth as they constructed forts and earthworks at a feverish pace. By late spring forty-five French divisions were in place, rotating in and out of the battle area. Still with no hope of holding Verdun, Joffre called on the left wing of his army to combine with the British Expeditionary Force to relieve the French army by attacking the Germans on a nearby front and drawing their forces away from Verdun.

Joffre's call found General Douglas Haig, now in command of the BEF after the departure of Field Marshal French, eager to prove himself worthy. Haig's plan called for artillery barrages prior to massive infantry assaults across an enormous twenty-mile front along the river Somme. This time the big guns would roll their fire several hundred yards ahead of the advancing infantry and move further into the German lines as they were taken. A former cavalry officer, Haig's plan called for mounted cavalry to charge through the breaches caused by the guns and the infantry.

July 1, 1916—the first day of the British attack at the Somme—was the deadliest day in the history of the British Army. Some 20,000 British soldiers were killed and another 40,000 injured. Haig's plan was an utter failure. It had not taken into account the terrain, the weather, or the likely German strategy. His outdated reliance on cavalry was disastrous. When subordinates had questioned the effectiveness of horses against fixed machine gun fire, Haig had dismissed the machine gun power as "overrated" and unable to track cavalry as they passed through. He insisted that the breakthrough of mounted formations would ride roughshod through the rear areas and destroy the support mechanism, bringing the German army to its knees.

Haig was quite wrong on all these counts. In addition, the telephone and telegraph were the only way to keep up with the changing field situation, and those wire lines were very fragile. The guns had to be moved as the infantry advanced out of range as well, which took a great deal of time. Guns had to be attached to horse-drawn limbers, put out on poor-to-impassable roads, and registered before they could shoot again. Yet Haig pursued the same strategy day after brutal day, callously remarking that the massive losses were to be expected. His confidence in his own ability defied description, and no amount of lost life deterred him. Throughout the summer, the corpses piled up and the Battle of the Somme grinded on.

IT WAS AUGUST WHEN MRS. BOX CHEERFULLY presented Rags with a set of orders. Rags had been secure in his duties in London but morose after Beryl's disappearance, never returning to his characteristic energy and spirit. Hilly saw that he was confronted with two problems that could solve each other: He needed eyewitness information from the frontlines at the Somme, and Rags needed change—badly. Something to take him out of his nihilism and recall him to the historic fight in which his country was engaged.

Packing his kit once again at his home on the Thames, Rags tried to console the inconsolable Charlotte. "I know the work might keep me busy, but I can't help but lose my concentration, worried that your name might appear on those horrid newspaper lists. Just last Friday Bunny Rodney revealed that her son was missing in action. I felt so happy that you were here safe in London." Tears filled her pale blue eyes but seemed to come from a kind of anger and sense of injustice more than simple grief.

Rags interrupted his packing and knelt beside her chair. "I know it's terrible for those who wait, but I'm not going to join the lads as a member of the battalion. I'll be there for a few days, get an impression of the goings-on, and leave to write just one more analysis for Uncle Hilly. He doesn't expect me to engage in the fighting; no going over the top, I assure you. It's nothing but a little jaunt across the Channel, and I'll be back in a week." He felt confident in his ability to take care of himself, but he also felt a faint excitement that he was careful to hide from his mother. Whether it was a sense of purpose or just the thrill of danger, he didn't know. But he was not nearly as sorry to be leaving London as Charlotte was.

There was a car waiting. The dogs were not at the front door but remained sequestered in the kitchen, their favorite room. Mrs. Jayson gave Rags a packed lunch for the Dover train. "The railway food is not fit for a stray cat, master Rolly; you fill up on smoked salmon sandwiches, and there is a stray sweet in there to boot." Gratefully, he took the brown package wrapped in string. The dogs were more interested in the smell of the lunch than their departing master. He gave them each a head rub. "Now Teddy, take care of your mother. Valerie, don't eat too much—you are looking a little on the porky side. Mind Mrs. Jayson, and I will bring you a macaron from France." Then he was gone.

"Orders was orders," and Rags found himself repeating the journey to Saint-Omer to get a track on the Welsh Guard's battalion. He reported to the commander near the village of Carnoy, where the battalion was digging in support to the Grenadiers. There wasn't much time for sweet hellos, so Rags sought a corner of the command post where he could set up his typewriter and stow his journals. As an official observer, he had no unit responsibilities, but he had no desire to sit in a bunker all day. So the next afternoon he trailed Colonel Moss-Jones down into a forward trench line to ascertain the extent of the damage from the morning's fighting and the efforts to restore the position before nightfall.

With the colonel in the lead, Rags kept up as close as possible, stumbling over freshly dug-up roots; the duckboards were not yet in place. "Rags, keep your head down; this trench is not deep enough if the heavy guns get our range." Moss-Jones dug his walking cane into the soft soil to maintain his forward progress—a hard wood cane had been sent by his wife to replace the useless swagger stick he had always carried.

Enemy sniper fire was beginning to find the range, and rifle bullets snapped over his head, forcing Rags to waddle more than walk. Yet he felt oddly at home, calm, eager even. Stopping next to a British sniper, who was potting at the enemy line, he rested as the colonel gave direction to the company commander on his defenses. The sniper was up high on the firing step and protected with a three-foot-square steel plate in which there was a hole, larger than the muzzle of his bolt-action Enfield rifle with a spotting scope. The opening was just below center. Rags watched from below as the sniper got off a couple of aimed rounds and cursed his target. "Bloody Herman. Pop up again, mate, and I'll have you. Captain, come on up and take a look through the periscope at that kraut just to the left of the machine gun. He's going to be mine in just a minute." The sniper talked at his target in low tones. "That's it, my laddy; just raise up a little bit more."

As Rags raised the box head of the periscope over the burm, the light reflecting off the top mirror caught a German sniper's eye, and he put one round straight through the lens, knocking the device out of Rags' hands. His hands were stung by the force of the bullet that sent a bolt of lightning up his arm. The British sniper beside him laughed. "Got you, did he! That's great, Captain. I see him now." He squeezed off one round with a bang, rocking back slightly in his standing position, and crouched down again with a satisfied smirk. "Got the bastard. That'll teach him to fire at my officer. Come up here, sir, and take a look, one down."

For the first time in months, Rags laughed. This was it. This is where he belonged. All this time avoiding danger, avoiding dirt and guns and sweat, and he had never known such a satisfying moment as when his fellow soldier smirked and said, "Got the bastard." Without even knowing it, he had outgrown Horse Guards, outgrown his mother, outgrown the secrecy and dispatches and spycraft. Outgrown safety. A feeling of energy that might have been purpose shot through his veins, and he stepped up to firing step. But before he could get a look through the hole, he heard a loud sound and felt a piercing sting in his head. He felt the blood running down his face and fell into the mud at the bottom of the trench.

HE WOKE UP TO THE welcome sight of Grace's face. He must be at Chenonceau. He was conscious but not able to speak. His eyes followed her as she changed his bandage and inspected the wound.

"Ah, you're awake, soldier." Grace smiled, and Rags knew he would be all right then. "You've looked better, I'll admit. Your nose is broken, you've got lacerations down your face, great big patches of swelling in the loveliest yellows and purples you'll ever see."

Rags barked out a laugh that immediately made him wince in pain. But he didn't care. He had never been so glad to see anyone in his life.

## Chapter Twenty-Nine

# London, September 1916

CAPTAIN STETCHWORTH'S VISION BEGAN TO CLEAR very slowly from the morphine haze that had settled all around him, but the first thing he saw was a welcome sight: Grace leaning over and cleaning his cheek.

"Nurse—Grace—is that you?" His right eye peeked out joyfully from the corner of the wrapper. "Am I at the chateau, or is this a dream I have conjured up?"

She smiled and squeezed his hand. "It's true, my dear, it is your Grace, your very own Grace, and you are safe and sound at our chateau. You're going to be fine; doctor has been in."

"What happened? I don't remember anything. I was in France with the Guards. How did I get here?"

"Well, my dear, you had a little accident, cut your cheek—but that's about it. That was three days ago; we were worried about a concussion but that's passed. I imagine your face is throbbing, maybe a sharp pain where your cheekbone was fractured, but it will heal. It won't be long and we'll be on our way home. I am going with you, back to St. Thomas' and you back to Uncle Hilly. Everything is arranged." She stood over him and took both his hands. They were a little too warm. She was afraid he might be running a low fever. As she stood there, he drifted off with a curl of a smile at the right corner of his dry mouth.

When he awoke again that afternoon, he recognized his surroundings, but Grace was gone and another friendly face announced in a high strong voice. "Well, Captain, let's change that dressing and give you a comb and a brush-up."

The wounded Captain had only one thought. "When will Grace be back on duty?"

"I'm afraid she's a little busy. An ambulance convoy has come in and we're all doing double duty. Can you get up on your elbows so I can undo the dressing and we can start afresh?" She unwound a yard of gauze. "Well, that looks good. Those stitches are very pretty. Doctor took extra care with you . . . didn't want his handiwork to turn you into a monster, did he? When they come out, you'll be a real looker." She held up a hand mirror. "Bit of a scar that will drive the ladies crazy, I shouldn't wonder. You'll look like one of those fencing masters, or a pirate from the pictures. A real war hero." The nurse smiled, but Rags was appalled. He didn't recognize the image that stared back at him. Red and black and even blue, swollen around his left eye while his cheek appeared as if he was eating a large plum, whole. There must have been ten black stitches from his closed eye to the corner of his mouth. The thread ends were ragged and stuck straight out.

"I'll bet those tickle. I'm going to leave the bandages off so things can dry out a bit; you'll be more comfortable that way."

Evening arrived without Grace. The hospital was a flurry of activity and he felt neglected. An orderly brought him dinner on a tray and helped him to sit up. From his confinement on the far end of the long ward, he saw others gather in a swirl of white near the stairs, hovering over strings of newcomers. He hailed a passing attendant, who paused briefly.

"Things are bad to worse, sir. They're coming in like a herd of cattle. They tell me the Welsh Guards were in the thick of it. Big German push. Outside they're stacked up like cord wood. Can't stay long, Captain; need anything else?"

Though Rags didn't know it, he had reason to be concerned. Among the casualties was Lieutenant Colonel Moss-Jones. His battalion was included in the center of a German attack that had drawn his formation up to bolster the Grenadiers. The battalion had become intermingled with the enemy in the fighting as the trench systems were enveloped. Once the line was stabilized the enemy infantry pulled back, and in came a mighty barrage of heavy artillery which fell on the Welsh Guards. The colonel was taken down by shrapnel from a bursting shell directly over his open trench. His hand ran with blood from his badly shredded left wrist and arm. His batman, Private Stack, tied a tourniquet above the elbow and found his first aid kit, a soap dish–sized silver box from the colonel's web gear that was caked with mud. Inside he passed his dirty fingers over the selection of ampules. Pure ether, Stovaine, sparteine, ergotine, camphorated oil, caffeine, and morphine. Morphine, that was what he was looking for.

By evening Moss-Jones had been triaged and stabilized north of Paris and could have been sent directly to Blighty, but he insisted he be taken along with Stack, who was concussed, to the chateau. He knew how bad his injury was and didn't think he could make it all the way to London. His best chance, he thought, was to get to Grace. After surviving the jolting ride that seemed to take forever, he was with her while they prepped him in the operating room. There was no question—the left arm would have to come off. Gangrene would already be at work, and there was nothing else for it. Grace stayed with her father until the intravenous injection of heroin was administered. Then the matron sent her back to her duties. "There is nothing more for you here, my dear; back to the ward, we'll take care."

Grace withdrew reluctantly but didn't go back to the ward. Instead she went back to her bed and laid down. She couldn't stop thinking about Rory. Over the past eight months his powerful memory had begun to fade, lost in the daily care of hundreds of stricken soldiers. And now, in the dim light provided by the hurricane lantern that swayed slowly in the draft above the bed, she could hardly separate her two wounded Guardsmen. Their disfigured faces blended together, both partially covered with blood-stained bandages. With the passing of Rory, she had lost a childhood mate, a family connection, and a lover all at once. There had never been anyone but Rory in her personal life; now, suddenly, there was only Rolly. Would he too slip away before her eyes? She told herself that she wasn't strong enough to go through watching another of her men die. "If only, somehow, the war would take me as well," she thought. A prayer came to her lips, for her father and for Rags, the same one she had said for Rory. Could it work this time? Could God hear her? Did He care? Exhausted, she got under the covers and let sleep take her.

It wasn't until late the following afternoon the Grace made it back to Rags' ward. She looked drawn, older, and it wasn't just the fading light in the great stone-vaulted ward. She sat next to the head of Rags' bed on a hard stool. Her white uniform seemed to droop down on her shoulders, bending her forward and dropping her chin to her chest. "Rags," she gulped, "Father came in yesterday with a wounded arm and it was amputated below the elbow." Rolly rolled toward her and reached for her hands that had been folded in her lap. "He's going to be fine, made it through the night, no shock, no fever, and he is awake. But the pain, the pain is wearing on him . . ." She had seen so many amputations the previous year at St. Thomas' and knew that the operation was just the beginning. There Dr. Marmaduke Sheild had objected to the guillotine method of amputation that left exposed nerves, causing both stump pain and a poor chance for a good prosthetic fit, but the method was still common at Chenonceau. Then there was the phenomenon of phantom limb pain—and the danger of overprescribing opioids and of addiction.

Grace arranged for her father's bed to be placed next to Rolly's and sat between them as dinner was served. Private Stack, still a little off-color, served them both. They kept him on the hop. He brought lavender bags to hang over their beds to reduce the myriad bad smells that accumulated in the stagnant air within the chateau's stone walls. Both men began to find their appetites. While the field hospitals were short on many things, food was not one of them. On order was tea, bread, fried bacon, boiled bacon, boiled ham, boiled mutton, potted meat, rissoles, cheese, jam, butter, soup, roast beef, meat pies, sea pie, stew, cauliflower, mixed vegetables, cocoa, rice pudding, biscuits, and suet pudding. Not only did his two charges eat well and gain weight, so did Private Stack.

Within a few weeks the hospital commander stood at the foot of their beds with three tickets to Blighty. The three packed their bags with a mixture of relief and sadness and joined the phalanx crossing the chateau's drawbridge. Rags, hatless, was back in uniform, while the colonel walked slowly along on Stack's arm, the left sleeve of his tunic pinned to his chest, blouse unbuttoned. The little party made its way, with Nurse Grace in the lead, to board the train to the coast. The impatient black engine built up steam and gave out a high-pitched whistle to remind passengers that time was a-wasting. The uniform coaches were painted a dull khaki with block red crosses conspicuously on white squares on the top and sides. The last car was reserved for wounded officers. Other cars accounted for patients in order of mobility from walking to assisted movement and ending with patients on litters.

The train was the express to the dock at Boulogne. The lead car had a modified operating theater if needed en route. It was the army's best show, flawless. All rail traffic waited on sidings for the express to pass. The ship that was tethered to the dock mimicked the careful rail arrangements. Here the most immobilized patients were on the top deck in case of emergency evacuation. It was true—the Germans had attempted to sink medical ships on occasion. The journey, which might be long in time, was short in distance as the mercy ship serpentined to avoid detection. It was seventy miles to the coast, another fifty miles across the Channel and eighty miles to Charing Cross Station as the crow flies. Yet it took hours before the morning light of London streamed through the fogged windows.

Henry Segar met Rags at the exit of St. Thomas' where the patients from Chenonceau had been deposited upon arrival in London. Segar was visibly concerned with the young officer. "My boy, what have we done to you?" Rags was surprised at Segar's attention, as if he was somehow personally responsible for the whole show. Segar had always seemed oblivious to his surroundings and detached from intimate feelings when it came to anything other than his job and his wife.

"The boss is up in Scotland, or he would have come in my place. Mrs. Box has prepared a cake for you." He thrust a large flat tin into Rags' free hand. "We are all most concerned; it could have been so much worse. Anyway, you're here now. I have a car to take you home. I called your mother as well—she knows you're on your way."

The traffic was gridlocked until they crawled past Hyde Park Corner. At the door of the great house in Fulham his mother stood, handkerchief in hand, waving as they arrived. There was no sign of the dogs; she must have put them away in an effort to maintain quiet for her wounded soldier. They could come later when he was put to bed. Stopping him on the threshold, Charlotte cradled his scarred face in her two soft hands. "What have they done to you, my pretty boy?"

Safe in his old room, the servants hovered around while his mother first opened and then closed the large tall windows, talking out loud to herself the whole time. Rags had never seen such emotion in her in his whole life. It had been just a month, but they treated him as if he had been gone a year. There was nothing else for it when the dogs arrived. "Put them on the bed, Mamma, or we will never hear the end of it."

THE NEXT WEEK HE REPORTED to Horse Guards sporting a neat scar on his left cheek. In the office he found Mrs. Box in a much more receptive mood. The tone of disdain that had couched itself in every phrase was softened, nearly cordial. "Welcome back, Captain. The general has missed you. I've put up with that weedy Howie from across in Badington-Smyth's office far too long. He'll be glad to see you back, I dare say. The heat is off, for the moment, over the spy . . . the navy had one. Well, we shouldn't be surprised. They are a scruffy lot, those sailors. All talk and no fight. We're going to have to win this war while they sit on their backsides in the wardrooms, larking about the world, pretty as you please."

Mildred was no fan of the Royal Navy. It was said that she was once known to be in the company of a chief petty officer at a previous assignment. "Your files are in your desk. There is something going on with Churchill. The general has it all locked up in his safe; I'm not even privy to it. I suggest you stay off the subject. It's on a need-to-know and you don't fit the profile." That made a great deal of sense. Something big was going on. Christian's inquiry about the land yacht, as the tank was sometimes known, was serious. Just then, Hilly returned in a rush, but he calmed down when he encountered Rags in his outer office. He greeted his young aide with a firm handshake and pat on the bicep and, along with Mildred, examined the wound on his face. "Does it hurt, my boy? It looks rather angry, rather red and puffy, I should say. What do you think, Mildred?"

Mildred took a hold of Rags' jaw and turned the scar toward the light that hung over her desk. Putting on a show of seriousness, she said, "He looks fit to me, General. Send him back to the line, I should think. It's a good place for a real soldier." She smiled.

Hilly laughed. "Not yet—I've missed my good left arm. And I've plenty for him to catch up with while I'm down on Salisbury Plain for a week or so. You can camp here, Rags. Spend some time with your mother, she needs you. She took your wounding very hard. Had a deuce of a time consoling her, don't you know. She drove poor Mildred round the bend with updates. Glad to have you back if for nothing else than quieting her down."

Rags tried to mitigate his uncle's position and volunteered to go along; they might be testing alterations on the tank. But Hilly waved him off. "No, no, you stay here and rest up. That's an order!" It was no use; the trip was hush-hush.

In an attempt to gather anything of interest for his father, Rags paid a visit to Henry Segar's office down the block in the Cabinet basement. It was at street level back in the days when Whitehall was a palace, before the fire of London in 1666. Up to his ears in books, maps, and paper clips, the pipe-smoking Segar greeted him with bravado. "Rags, I've been meaning to come by and see what you're up to, but I am over my head with the Russians. They're a miserable lot, but you knew that. Intrigues a-plenty. It seems the Germans have put the cat among the birds and that feline is having a meal, don't you know. Wouldn't be surprised if the Russian government is carried off any day now. I'll have to make plans for the czar to come here and live with his cousin. The King, I am told, is fond of 'Nicky' and we'll be stuck with the whole bloody court here to sit out the war." He jammed more rough shag with his forefinger into the top of his overflowing pipe. "That's my prediction, but no one here wants to hear it."

Rags was a little impatient and couldn't give a toss about the Russians. "What about the war, sir—how's it going?"

Segar stopped, paused, and turned his head. "What war?"

Rags just looked at him quizzically and pointed to the scar on his face. "Remember?"

Segar stood up, apologetically. "Oh, that war, no change, just banging ourselves against a brick wall. It's all of no consequence. The Russians, on the other hand, will have a profound effect on the economy if they take themselves out of the conflict and go their own way. Powerful stuff, Rags, revolution, and who's to say it will stop there. The communists have a powerful idea. You can't fight an idea with guns; mark my words, England could be on the brink. Lots of discontent in the working class here. Read Karl Marx; he is buried here in England, Highgate Cemetery, but his words are alive."

Rags changed the subject. "What does the government think of putting all that money into the tank after its debut at the Somme? I hear it was a bit of a napoo and the blokes inside joined the suicide club." He was trying to pry out a few words in an unguarded moment from Segar when he wasn't looking.

"Not my purview, Rags. I am working on a higher level, thank God."

## Chapter Thirty

# London, October 1916

A MONTH LATER RAGS was perched at the bar at the Eight Bells Pub, watching a group of soldiers at the large communal table in the corner. He had returned to Horse Guards after a month of recuperation at home, but he didn't feel like someone who had escaped into safety. He felt empty. He couldn't remember being shot at all, yet he could see in his mind's eye a hole in the center of his brain where it should have been. A dark spot was the only way he could express the cavity.

He saw that emptiness in the soldiers too. They were not boisterous or happy to be home. Hands clutched pints while eyes stared into space, unfocused on their mates across the table or at the cluster of empty glasses—hours misspent. Remnants of white foam lingered on the rims. Why weren't they laughing? They had just escaped Flanders Fields. They got what they wanted—to be home where everything was calm.

One of the party, a corporal, walked over to order more pints and noticed the miniature Leek insignia on Rags' collar. "Been to the Somme, sir? I see you have a souvenir there on your cheek."

Rags responded quickly, glad he had been recognized. "Yes, Corporal; I was there for a short time, until I was pushed off to the hospital."

"Me too, sir. I guess old Herman wasn't such a good shot after all, was he?"

He didn't ask Rags to join his mates at the table—that was unthinkable—but Rags appreciated the small moment of camaraderie. Looking straight at each other's dark spot seemed to make it close up a bit.

Rags much preferred a few hours at the pub, where he might get that momentary relief, to any amount of time at home, where his mother's calculations alternated with continued delight at their safety. With her son back home, Charlotte was nearly manic with ambition. Christian had asked for information about the tanks used at the Somme, and her constant prodding wore on him.

She was even more excited at her own progress. That fall she had been promoted to supervisor of the collection of suspected German collaborators and was moved from the cellar of the Admiralty to comfortable offices on the top deck overlooking Trafalgar Square. The collection she managed contained names, patterns, and even paraphernalia of captured enemy spycraft. There were books with pages stuck together that contained messages, invisible writings, codes, message traffic that had been picked out of the radio airways.

Charlotte's excitement was evident, but even Rolly didn't know the extent of it. The new position had made her see how she could become a spy herself. Until that moment she had been the catalyst, putting Christian and Rolly together; she was a collaborator, not a spy. With her new position, Charlotte could tip off Christian when the British were getting close to identifying one of his German agents. At that point he could withdraw them before they could be arrested. Most importantly, Charlotte believed this would further endear her to Christian—and maybe even the Kaiser.

His mother's smothering enthusiasm also contributed to Rags' almost constant yearning to be with Grace. Grace spent nearly all of her time at St. Thomas', either working or tending to her father, who underwent a second amputation when gangrene threatened once more. Lieutenant Colonel Moss-Jones desperately wanted to keep the amputation below the elbow; it would allow him to articulate a prosthetic wrist and hand. But Grace was adamant: "We must think about what will happen in the next twenty-four hours, not next year. Father, I have seen this before. You must allow the doctor to save your life, not your elbow." The deed was done, the arm was cut off above the elbow, and healing began. The throbbing pain of the phantom limb was agony, and it took "two bloody months" before he could see over the wall.

After surgery, the lieutenant colonel was sent to the Star and Garter Home, a hospital in Richmond, to convalesce. The hospital was a converted hotel where officers of the Household Regiments were tended by Harley Street's finest physicians under the watchful eye of the aristocratic families of the land. Once her father was ensconced there, Grace was able to spend more time with Rags. They sat at the Eight Bells or Clarence downing pints and sometimes took advantage of Hilly's favorite upstairs room. The combination of physical pleasure and their shared time in France made them an irresistible refuge for each other. She visited him at work, where he would take hold of her tiny figure at the hips and lead her to the junior officers' mess for lunch.

She teased him about the Military Cross he had been awarded: "Something new to go with the handsome scar on your cheek? Most fitting, I should say, Rags. You really are quite a Whitehall warrior." She smiled at him and he laughed back. It was a joke, both recognition and criticism. How in the world did a Horse Guards' staff officer get a Military Cross for being shot while on a field visit? He had gotten the honor just a few days before, not with a troop formation in a dedicated ceremony but, of all things, in the mess hall. He was having lunch when the chief of staff, Colonel Kimberly, appeared at the table next to him, asked the company to stand, and all eyes turned to him. Rags thought, "Uncle Hilly must be at the bottom of this." In a loud voice Kimberly began, "His Majesty, King George of England and the dominions beyond, expresses great confidence and fidelity in Captain Roland Augustus Grayling Stetchworth here by awarding the Military Cross for his gallantry during active operations against the enemy." Cheers of "hear, hear"—albeit with a certain unsure air—rang out as the colonel pinned the silver cross suspended by a white and purple ribbon to the left side of Rags' tunic. It wasn't the Military Cross that crossed Rags' mind, but the German Iron Cross that was concealed by his mother in the secret cabinet in the library wall. Would they cheer if they knew that?

Calling him a Whitehall warrior was one of Grace's favorite ways to tease him, but Rags didn't mind. She was getting her sense of humor back. So many hadn't, but they mustn't be blamed. While outsiders dwelt on the carnage of the war, those who fought it dared not. It was plain: they intended to move on as quickly as possible.

MOVING ON FOR RAGS MEANT moving out: for the first time, he left his mother's house. He leased a townhouse, complete with two ancient servants, in Sussex Gardens, a block from the Lancaster Gate Tube station across from Rotten Row in Hyde Park, where he could exercise his horse. He could ride to work past Hyde Park corner, Green Park to Birdcage Walk and Wellington Barracks. A stable in the mews came with the accommodation for his horse, groom, and new batman, Private Stack, borrowed from Grace's father. Stack enjoyed the new billet, sharing with the groom their own quarters above the stable in the mews, until the two terriers arrived on site and became his responsibility. They were rather badly behaved after all that coddling by the household staff at the house on the river. With no garden to engage them, they demanded trips to Hyde Park and boisterously pursued the squirrels, who were obviously neglected. Stack learned that "walkies" was a four-time-a-day mission, rain or shine.

For her part, Grace had found her calling. Several days a week Grace took the bus to St. Thomas' Hospital, where groundbreaking work was being done in the new medical field of war neuroses. In the evening she relayed her experience to Rags, hoping he would join in the topic. She began fitfully, "I can't believe the statistics. Did you know that 80,000 shell-shock cases have been reported? That is one-seventh of all disabilities. I know you told me of the mania brought on by the day-and-night shelling, but there is much more to it than that." She was heating up as if Rags was responsible. "On occasion, soldiers were ordered not to take prisoners. One boy I saw has records that show he shot three unarmed wounded Germans who tried to surrender. Another was said to have been buried in a trench after a German barrage and was dug out days later. I spoke to a sniper who has hysterical blindness. While I was speaking to one, he glassed over, stood up, and withdrew an imaginary bayonet from an unseen enemy. Others are afraid to go to sleep for the nightmares. The men try to repress the experience, but the images are painfully explicit."

Rags had heard the stories and believed them to be true. The little he had seen in Gallipoli and France was etched into his mind as well and he would try to help Grace to cope. He had been more detached than most from the action, yet believed all she said. She reached for a cigarette and Rags lit it with his gold Dunhill lighter. Taking a puff to ensure that it was properly lit, she continued. "I'm attached to a doctor's service from the British Psycho-Analytic Association."

Rags seemed skeptical. "Perhaps you should help out with the rehabilitation of traumatized bodies rather than minds. You were so helpful with your father's coping with his artificial arm. There the work can be so much more rewarding?"

Grace didn't hesitate. "I'm not asking for your advice, just your ear, darling. No, no, now that I have engaged with the service I can't walk away and leave them so alone." Rags could see tears well up in her eyes. "There is so much to be done and so few who want to do it. I'm hooked, I am afraid. I'll try not to bring it home, really I will."

Rags reached for her hand across the little dinner table. "I don't mind. I see soldiers every day in the Guards who I think have pushed themselves too far and will ultimately end up in your care. Maybe you can instruct me how to deal with them."

The couple's lives began to take on a rhythm: lunch when they could, drinks after work, the cinema on the weekends. They'd walk the streets of London in the evening, appreciating the simple air of home, the cool misty breezes, the warm feel of each other's hands. They liked to go over Lambeth Bridge to the White Swan Pub in Pimlico. It became their place, the busy corner where they had first huddled together during the zeppelin raid a lifetime before. They sometimes made their way to the Star and Garter to visit her father. They were each other's best, nearly only friends.

One evening in October Rags walked Grace across the mansion's terrace. The long, slopping, open plain of the park allowed them to view the silhouette of the dome of St. Paul's, spires (miles away) in the City of London, the reflection of the Thames and Westminster towers until the blackout made the city disappear. It was the best panoramic view of the wartime capital.

"How did we ever survive?" Grace wondered. "I feel I've been trapped in a nightmare." Rags knew she was thinking of Rory. He felt loss too—of what might have been with Beryl, of those moments before he was shot when he felt he had found his place in the world, of the sniper who had joked and shared the trench with him . . . Where was he now? Was he alive? Rags realized he had felt more camaraderie with that unknown soldier than he had with any of his schoolmates, more than with his well-pressed colleagues at Horse Guards, and God knows more than his mother, who he saw now had only been keeping him for herself. They were gone now: his school chums, his girlfriend, his unquestioning devotion to his mother.

But Grace was here. He squeezed her hand and they leaned up against the balustrade, and Rags felt his heart swell. So many were gone, but she was here—and he realized he wouldn't be able to bear it if she were gone too.

"So I've been thinking, Grace. . . . I know you have your hands full with the, well, impaired of mind at the hospital. But do you think you'd have room in your life for one more?"

"Have a cousin with no limbs and a rattled brain, do you, Rags?" she said as she watched the moon begin its transit across the sky.

"I was thinking rather of myself, actually. And whether you might be persuaded to marry me."

Her head swiveled to him quickly, eyes wide. For a moment she seemed undecided, almost frozen, and Rags' heart gave a great thump. It was only when the corner of her lip turned up in that classic Grace smirk that it resumed beating normally.

"Sir Roland, my ever-present knight in shining armor, I'd be honored."

THE COUPLE WALKED THE PARK pathways with a sense of giddy wonder, dazed by the shafts of piercing light that swept the London clouds looking for enemy aircraft—and by their own daring. All they had known had been shattered, but now they had each other, a rock in the storm—solid, reliable, known. The sirens of the fire appliances sang out their warning, but the couple was now safe on a ridge near the center of the city. The sky hosted four mammoth German airships dumping tons of bombs that blasted the city. Rags and Grace caught their breaths and watched red and yellow fires breaking out under the paths of the floating behemoth flying—no, floating—slowly at 1,200 feet. They saw the flashes miles away and waited for the thuds, sure to follow. Occasionally British biplanes could be seen splitting the shafts like moths in the light as they climbed in pursuit.

There had been more than forty such attacks over the helpless city over the past two years. Thousands had been killed and injured. Buildings, homes, factories, docks, and families had been destroyed, but no zeppelin had ever been touched, no matter how the flying fighters and anti-aircraft guns tried to bring them down to earth. German crews were merely amused by their efforts, and disdainful. But that night it happened. The military had been developing a new combination of exploding and incendiary machine gun bullets. And that night a lone British fighter sprayed them across the outer fabric skin of the zeppelin, allowing oxygen to mix with the airship's hydrogen. The lethal combination ignited the gas bags with a display of pyrotechnics never seen before. Quick as striking a match, the ship turned into an inferno. And from great height the zeppelin, falling slowly like a giant feather, was transformed into a dying planet, blazing all the way down to the ground.

# Chapter Thirty-One

# Europe, 1918–1920

RUSTED HELMETS, BROKEN RIFLE STOCKS, bent barbed wire pickets, twisted fins on unexploded bombs, discarded mess gear, piles of extracted machine gun castings, and white bones from forgotten corps had been the landscape of France and Belgium for four long years. The unrelenting stalemate that had begun with the First Battle of the Marne and its establishment of the Western Front finally began to give way as the Americans entered the war in April 1917. At their helm was General John "Black Jack" Pershing, a Missouri native whose accomplishments included the design of the "Pershing boot," made with better waterproofing for trench conditions. On the right flank, Pershing fought his way through the Argonne forests in the biggest American military operation to date. Hostilities ceased on the 11th hour of the 11th day of the 11th month of 1918. In a controversial move, the Germans were allowed to sign an armistice rather than surrender.

When the Paris Treaty talks convened in January 1919, thirty-two countries sent delegations to lay blame for the war on the aggression of Germany and its allies. It was expected that each would extract their pound of flesh. An executive council consisting of France, Britain, Italy, and the United States would dominate deliberations. Soon, Prime Minister Orlando of Italy absented himself. Lloyd George, now prime minister of Great Britain, led his delegation, which included eminent leaders from across the empire and a select few from his military corps. The negotiations were expected to take six months.

The clerical staff and most of the advisors were to be installed in five small hotels clustered around the Hotel Majestic, just off the Etoile. Cooks, brought from Britain, provided English fare of porridge, eggs, and bacon for breakfast, meats for lunch and dinner, and questionable coffee all day and night. The PM didn't want the alien and bizarre French diet to debilitate his delegation, making them unavailable. Lloyd George didn't trust the French; therefore the hotels were staffed with British workers and a courier service was established by the Royal Mail to prevent the French from rummaging through their post. Scotland Yard detectives provided access and egress via photo badges and insisted that all wastepaper be hand-shredded. The staff was cautioned about the casual use of the telephone since the French were known to bug the phones. Wives were not to remain overnight. The Majestic's no-tab bar was intended to reduce the amount of drunkenness among the staff—a forlorn hope in postwar Paris, where wine flowed like the Seine. No pets were allowed in the hotels, and cooking in the room was out of the question. A medical suite of a doctor and a bevy of nurses was available day and night. There was a billiard room and a winter garden for outdoor entertaining. Autos were allocated to the delegates by arrangements. In all, it was as spartan as it could be in the City of Lights. An English patron provided a luxury apartment nearby in the Rue Nitot for Lloyd George while his primary staff were billeted on the upper floors. The flat was made homey with chintz curtains and overstuffed English furniture.

Talks took place in the great staterooms of the French Ministry of Foreign Affairs in the Hotel Quai d'Orsay on the rue du Bac, a sprawling light grey stone complex of classical structures dated from the mid-1800s. Unlike single nations such as Belgium or Italy, with a handful of delegates, the British delegation needed room for India, Australia, New Zealand, and other worthy members of the empire from their ranks. The handsome stone buildings embellished with internal ornate decorations were most fitting for the monumental reordering of the world. The great state rooms could absorb the crowds of diplomats with ease.

Underneath, what worried the delegates was that Germany was still intact. Its army had not been defeated and was gathered on the eastern edge of the Rhine River. A quick read of the German citizens would have allayed their fear. Germany had scuttled the imperial fleet at Scapa Flow while the Royal Navy watched in disbelief. It had given up its merchant marine, which had been held intact in the Baltic Sea, to the Allies in hopes that food could once again flow from the Americas. While capable of attack, as the Junkers would have it, the understructure—the willingness of the citizens to continue—and the new government's desire for peace had crushed any thought of continuing the fighting in the field. And though hostilities had ceased, the German suffering had just begun. Food shortages and the effective British blockade had culminated in the Turnip Winter of 1916–1917, when meat and even potatoes were in such short supply that the population survived almost entirely on turnips, which until then had been only barn fodder. A year later the deprivation became critical. Bicycles had wooden wheels, and what sausage there was

was nearly all sawdust, since the zeppelins used the intestines of 250,000 cows to make gas-proof bags for one airship. K-Brot was made from lentil flour while butchers sold dog meat. That year rickets was found in 40 percent of the children. Scurvy, tuberculosis, and dysentery, aggravated by malnutrition, caused 425,000 civilian deaths.

The coal mines of central Europe, abandoned for lack of labor, flooded. Essential to life in the early twentieth century, coal in all forms would be sorely needed in the freezing winters to come. Train service was sporadic in Germany, hindering the movement of food. People ate coal dust, wood shavings, and sand. Others who survived on beets alone suffered from mangel-wurzel disease, which sent crystalline deposits to joints and organs that could not be dislodged. The Americas had food of all kinds to sell, but the Kaiser's submarines had sent a considerable number of merchant ships to the bottom of the Atlantic. There was a critical shortage of medical supplies. Pneumonia and flu became epidemic. Doctors recommended smoking as an excellent preventative. But these privations were not the concern of the Paris delegates. Every country expected Germany to be stripped of its empire, and they all had their hands out. British daily life was still quite difficult: food was rationed, petrol was rationed, trucks and buses reduced operation, and a shortage of coal and its byproducts was a burden. But the Treaty of Versailles was signed on June 28, 1919, and Europe let out a sign of relief, certain that this had been the "war to end all wars."

RAGS AND GRACE WERE WELL aware of the privations and tensions of postwar life, but they were isolated by his family's wealth and her father's connection with the Palace. The Guards Brigade shed their khaki threads for scarlet, and the changing of the guard once more became the spectacle it deserved. Now the tunics were marked with rows of medals and orders. Rags took his turn every few weeks at the head of a contingent of Welsh Guards that secured St. James's Palace.

By 1920 the newlyweds had settled into Rags' rowhouse in Sussex Gardens off Bayswater Road in a lovely tree-trimmed street just around the corner from the Swan Pub. The newlyweds busied themselves furnishing their home in Sussex Gardens by daily visits to the multitude of markets and warehouse sales. Greenwich furniture market provided several armoires for the closetless bedrooms. Prewar double beds were in fashion and the old gaslight fixtures were electrified, along with the cooker. The small coal fireplaces in nearly every room were cleaned and made effective as fall began to creep in, leaving pavements strewn with great crackling leaves. The Westie terriers crunched them on walks to Hyde Park. They thrust their gruffy faces into holes as they trudged along, pulling toward the trees where squirrels hid.

Grace became fond of Valerie and Teddy, who were both overfed by the staff. She had never had pets other than her father's gun dogs who lived outside the house in Wales.

Rags and Grace dined at the Swan often, eating battered plaice and chips. It was a charming old Victorian building with dark wood paneling and deep red carpets on the upper level, where they commandeered a table at least twice a week. Grace thought it cozy and warm, away from the bite of London's wind and rain that assaulted her short walk from the bus up the busy road plied with omnibuses destined for Oxford Street, blocks east. If the weather was less challenging, they could nip through traffic to the fountains just inside the spiked iron gate and watch the ducks on the Serpentine.

After obtaining Lieutenant Colonel Moss-Jones's permission for Grace's hand—celebrated with two snifters of cognac and a wry, ominous "Good luck to you, Rolly"—the two had married in 1919 at the little Church of Saint James-in-the-Fields, where she sang in the choir. Designed by Sir Christopher Wren in 1672, a gem in the recovery from the Great Fire, the diminutive red brick church was dressed in Portland stone and rang its bells for the bride and groom. The triple-story stained glass window depicting Christ on the cross caught the morning sun as they recited their vows.

By 1920 their lives had become much different. Horse Guards was quiet, and Rags began to wonder if Henry Segar's exhortations to join academia might be the right direction to go, though he had also kept in touch with Major Chard of the King's Messengers. Most important of all, though, was correspondence with his father, which had come to an abrupt halt with the signing of the armistice in November 1918 with the message: "Cease operations, send no more messages." Quicker than it had begun, he was no longer a German spy.

The relief was emancipating. Rags could unclench his insides. He feared being exposed; often he could taste it when he had retrieved messages from Putney Bridge. The hair on the back of his neck had bristled when he saw a figure coming toward him, and for the hundredth time he'd quickly rehearse a cover story about walking the dogs. He worried about the Iron Cross with his name engraved on the back; he couldn't explain it. But then he knew there were safeguards. To use a German phrase, the mission was *kaput*. And he could not have been more relieved.

His one remaining concern was the Bookers. That winter, in the cold and damp, he had walked briskly to Putney High Street and their stamp shop. At first he walked past, not stopping. At the Spotted Horse Pub he sat next to the frosted window where he might watch people looking in the Bookers' shop window at the collector stamps and new offerings. Activity was high now that minds turned at last to other things. "Booker must be doing well," he guessed. He'd expected to see a going-out-of-business sale or a shuttered shop. Rags imagined they would pack up and head for the coast, where they might be evacuated by a German patrol boat. Then he remembered, what about the radio? Wasn't it bulky to carry with them? No, certainly they would destroy it, throw it in the river, perhaps, as they panicked and burned the ciphers. No one would think it odd for smoke to be coming out of the chimney that time of year. And then a more disturbing thought: What about us? Might Booker want to silence us to cover his tracks? What kind of order did Christian send them? He surprised himself at this line of thought—how plausible it seemed that his father would order his and his mother's murder.

After several pints of best, Rags began to feel courageous. He was suddenly cavalier; beer was known to have that effect on him. One more pint of bitter down and curiosity took over as he stood straight and stepped down the High Street at a measured pace. Ignoring the colorful window display, he pushed the heavy glass and wood frame door open, which jangled a bell rather loudly. "Shop," he called as he glanced about at the show cases. No other customer was about. Mr. Booker came through the curtain from the back and stopped dead in his tracks. Speechless for the moment, he took his hands from his pockets. With trepidation, "Yes, sir, may I be of service?" Rags, now a little unsteady, looked about for other intruders. There were none behind him and he felt safe. "Well, Booker, my old mate. It's been an eon since we met."

The philatelist had little choice but to answer. "Yes, Captain, haven't seen you in dogs' years. How was the war for you, sir? Do some interesting things, I expect?"

"You know I have, matey. I thought you might be on your horse by now."

Booker had been ordered to stay put, a sleeper once again, but he kept this to himself. "Well, you know, sir, we are quite busy; with the end of the war, business has picked up. Can I get you something—would you like to look at our continental stamps perhaps? We have a new shipment of German and Austrian your mother might find interesting. They are popular now that the war is over. Will you and your mother be traveling to the Continent in the wake of all that has taken place?" With that two small boys came in with their parents. "Excuse me, sir, while I wait on these boys. I think they have their pocket money burning a hole and I would like to be of service. If there is nothing else for you, sir, I will say goodbye, for now. We are planning a little holiday but will be back directly. Hope to serve you another time." Confused and a little cloudy, Rags left the way he came, returning to Sussex Gardens and hoping never to see the Bookers again.

IN LATE 1920 RAGS AND GRACE TOOK a long-delayed honeymoon to France. Flanders Field was now covered a profuse number of bluebells and red poppies, but the couple avoided Chateau Chenonceau and other sites that brought memories of heartache and loss. Paris was a much better match. They shopped and ate, ate and shopped, and enjoyed a respite from the demands of home: the bureaucracy for Rags, the shell-shocked soldiers for Grace, the requisite visits to the house in Fulham every Sunday.

A mild afternoon found them holding hands on a bench in the Bois de Boulogne. Grace seemed distracted. "You're not missing your men back at the hospital already, are you? I know I've seen better days, but I hope you're not tired of me already," Rags said with a smile.

Grace smiled brightly but without looking at him. "Not at all. I was just looking at that pram the nurse is wheeling on the path there." Now she turned to him with mischief in her eyes. "I believe I would like one just like that."

WHILE RAGS AND GRACE AND the rest of London floated in a kind of happy delirium, hardly able to believe they didn't have to put up blackout curtains or watch the skies at night or send another son to the trenches, one resident found herself increasingly bitter. Charlotte Stetchworth was safe and warm in her mansion, surrounded by servants and material goods many would give their right hand for. Her son was not only alive but honored, respected, and married into a distinguished family. They had carried off daring acts of espionage without being detected. But inside she seethed.

Charlotte had been as excited as Rags to receive Christian's message to cease operations, but for entirely different reasons. She saw a bright future: shortly she could make final plans for them both to leave England. She would marry Christian, the man of her dreams. She would be honored in Austria for what she had done for the fatherland. How long she had waited.

In this spirit and with these hopes, she had invited Monsignor Pieter to luncheon. He had been her only private contact with Christian through the Vatican diplomatic post. Two years before, she had converted to Catholicism in order to use the confessional at Westminster Cathedral rather than the Putney Bridge drop. There she would leave messages for Christian about the British pursuit of German spies. Safely, she left or picked up the traffic from under the seat in the dark cubical for her confessor. Seldom did she find it necessary to confess her sins since she had none.

Now Charlotte found it so refreshing to be able to meet with Pieter in her home like civilized friends. Once the servants were out of earshot, she joked with him about passing items in the confessional. He laughed in response.

"My dear Charlotte, how wonderful it is to be in your home once again. It's been years, terrible years, but now we can be friends for all to see." Luncheon was served in the library, the warmest room in the house, at tea tables next to the wood fire.

Charlotte relayed her plans for her move once the treaty was signed, which was expected for June. She offered a letter for Christian explaining her detailed plans to be placed in the diplomatic pouch to Rome. She counted on a joyful answer. The post to Austria was still suspended during that tense winter and spring. The borders were not yet open and troops were moving in all directions. The lands were quite unsafe, as deserters and rogues moved through the chaos of postwar relocation.

Pieter surprised her by not reaching out to take the letter from her hand. "My dear," he hesitated, ". . . I have heard from Christian. Things are very different on the Continent than you recall. Society has been dealt a debilitating blow by this hideous war. Germany and Austria are starving, bedlam in the streets, families separated and the old order in turmoil. The loss of the war has changed Christian, I am afraid."

Desperately Charlotte broke in, "Is he wounded? What has happened? I thought he was at the headquarters with the General Staff, safe . . . in the rear."

Pieter leapt to reassure her: "No, you are correct, he is safe. But he is a different man, an altered man; after all the war has put him through—you needn't know the details. I just returned from a quick Christmas visit with him and his family. Did you know that his father died and now Christian is elevated?" Pieter reached for her white hand. "They, the Austrians who you knew so well, are very bitter about the outcome of this war. They feel that the victory was stolen from them by a conspiracy. The army was never defeated and has been abandoned in the field. So much was riding on a victory, and you know the German people are very proud. He—well, they—don't think the time is right to bring an English woman into the family . . . I'm sorry, dear Charlotte, but we must wait a little while longer."

Charlotte was dumbfounded, and for a moment simply she stared at Pieter in disbelief. "You can't mean that, Pieter. After all I and my son have done for Germany these four years? We have risked our lives every minute of every day for the Kaiser. We are as loyal, more, than those who sat at home waving a flag."

The monsignor tried to calm her down, reaching for her trembling cold hand across the tiny table, which had been cleared for the promise of dessert. "I'm sure, after some time, things will change. After the treaty has been signed, in June. Then maybe attitudes will change, but for now I think we must be patient, put things on hold. You understand, my dear, don't you?"

She did not understand. Pieter left her to her shock and sorrow. And now, as she looked out at the cold river and cold iron bridge, her bitterness boiled in her. Charlotte was abandoned. Her son had left her home and started a new life. He was married into a stratum of English society in which she had little pathway. She had nothing in common with her daughter-in-law or her family. Even her dogs, whom she had never stopped complaining about, had been taken away. And now her one and only Christian, the love of her tortured life, retreated from her affections without regard for her twenty years of unquestioned devotion. Because of him she had denied her family, betrayed her country, and donated her son to his father's cause. She had spied, decried her heritage, all for the reward of his love. The war to end all wars turned against her—destroyed her future when England, in spite of her and her son's efforts, triumphed.

While England moved forward with recovery—even with the vote for women in 1918—Charlotte hardly noticed. Her depression was bringing her down, and she became a recluse in her empty mansion on the river. In the darkness of the empty library, where she and Rolly had written messages hoping to defeat her own country, she stared at the secret cabinet that held copies of their treachery and the Iron Cross that had been earned by their treason.

Christian had betrayed her. Every day she was reminded of that as she sat in the empty library where she and Rolly had composed messages for the Germans. She read the newspaper accounts of the Treaty of Paris, wondering if disclosing the names of spies would be part of the deal. She passed by the secret cabinet that held Rolly's Iron Cross. And she stared out at that bridge—the bridge that represented all of her connection to Christian. It was drop-off and pick-up, site of fear and excitement, the enormous metal antenna that launched her coded offerings through the air to her lover. The spot where she had watched Beryl drop into the Thames so her fairytale future would not be compromised by an East End chit.

Where was her fairytale now?

# Chapter Thirty-Two

# London, 1921

NATHAN FREDERICK STETCHWORTH WAS BORN to an ebullient Rags and Grace in 1921. Lying in the hospital for a week after the birth, per the custom of the day, Grace pondered raising little Freddy in the Sussex Gardens house, Rags' one-time bachelor home and still a quite masculine domain. In particular, she was considering an offer put to her by Charlotte to take the baby directly to the mansion in Fulham, where both mother and son could be looked after in "suitable circumstances." She was assured by Charlotte that the sympathetic household staff, in concert with two nursery maids and a nanny, could free her to enjoy the experience of motherhood.

Grace was a nurse, but not a nursemaid, and was, like most new mothers, unfamiliar with tiny newborns. Although she sometimes found her mother-in-law odd, the offer was tempting. The house near Putney Bridge was spacious and comfortable. The help of servants as well as Charlotte's own keen attention to her new grandson would allow Grace to return to work with the battered veterans at St. Thomas' if she chose to. She felt sure that Rags would have reservations. He was so content outside the closeness of his mother's influence, which he sometimes found smothering. But then again, perhaps the welcome distraction of the adorable Freddy would ease Charlotte's focus on Rags. In the end, Grace accepted.

She let Charlotte know quickly, so that Charlotte had sufficient time to conduct interviews for a nanny. There was no need, though. She had underestimated her mother-in-law, who had transformed the nursery and hired the help as soon as Grace went to the hospital. The grief and bitterness of Christian's betrayal—even the loss of her wartime employment, with its modest prestige and intellectual challenge—had left Charlotte floundering, and living full time with her grandson was just what she needed. She would raise another boy, and this time he would be a proper English gentleman of wealth and circumstance, even if it took the entire family fortune.

As soon as Charlotte received Grace's acquiescence, she traveled to the hospital with a fresh bouquet. "I thought your flowers were looking rather poorly, dear. I don't think the hospital staff has been changing the water as I directed. I think these carnations will weather the storm until we can get you and Freddy out of here and into a suitable place. Your new home is waiting, my dear, complete with all you could want." She gazed up at the ceiling and dropped her voice. "So much better than that dreadful little hovel in Sussex Gardens with the batman and groom to watch over your every move and a decrepit staff who are more of a hindrance than a help." She paused again for effect, taking in a deep breath and casting a knowing eye. "My dear, rest assured that Grandmamma will take care of everything."

Grace was rattled by Charlotte's intensity but shook it off quickly. "I'm so looking forward to leaving here; I hate being a patient. It's the wrong end of the stick for a nurse. I plan to tell Rolly this evening. I hope he takes it well, but no matter, Freddy and I will be home tomorrow, rest assured." There was a welcome finality in Grace's voice.

Charlotte smiled and nodded her head. "Well done, my dear," she offered conspiratorially, "this, after all, is woman's work."

Grace lowered her voice: "I plan to offer him a crumb if it comes to that. When he is on shift, he can stay at Sussex Gardens and play with his soldiers if he wishes. I'll make him a home with us, at Fulham, when he's off and has become a dutiful father. That's fair, Mother, don't you think?"

Charlotte agreed: "I shall do my part and provide him with a valet, you with a lady's maid, and all of us with a chauffeur. It's time he took his place. Between the two of us he will surely surrender. We'll have it our way when Freddy comes home."

That evening a hapless Rags, still in uniform after posting the guard, arrived at the hospital with more flowers. Grace nodded at Charlotte's carnations and went straight to it: "Your mother and I have formed an alliance and have decided to go home to Fulham, where Freddy will have a proper looking-after. She has prepared your old nursery and taken on two nursemaids and a highly qualified nanny. You and I can take over your old rooms, which I am told are redecorated, and an adjoining sitting room. She is employing a lady's maid for me and a valet for you. You can keep your house and staff for duty days. How does that sound, darling?"

It was obviously a fait accompli, but Rags surprised Grace with his enthusiasm. "Grace, I have been pondering over the whole matter, and frankly it suits me as well. Frankly, I've been in a turmoil for weeks over the post-hospital arrangements and no matter which way I turned I couldn't work it out without considerable financial help from Mamma." As it was, his army pay was and had always been highly augmented by the Stetchworth estate. It was rare for a guard's officer to stand the expense of the mess, uniforms, horse and tack on his army pay. When there was something extra, he tapped his mother once again for funds, which she never refused. She could be a bit of a blockage—in his love life many a time, for instance—but that was a small price to pay for her generous support. Charlotte was of the Howard family and conducted herself as a member of a great clan. Rags wondered with a touch of wounded pride if moving into the mansion by the bridge might diminish his standing as head of his little family. But Rags, like Grace, could not resist the obvious advantages of the arrangement.

A few days later the three moved into the mansion. As Grace predicted, the atmosphere in the house was somewhat stifling and Charlotte a bit over-bearing, but the staff stepped in as a buffer and Grace found herself with all the freedom she could want. She knew that, when she was ready, she could continue working with the traumatized soldiers at the rehabilitation center without worrying about Freddy's well-being. She had hated the confinement and the physical restrictions that had plagued those last few months of pregnancy and had no desire to continue being house-bound. Her freedom, which she had enjoyed so much since the war, would have been curtailed by the birth of her son if it hadn't been for Charlotte's generosity.

As much as she told herself that returning to work with the soldiers was her main motivation, Grace found the perks of life under Charlotte's roof to be irresistible. With the nanny at home, she was free to go shopping at Whiteleys department store for Freddy or meet Rolly after work at the Swan. She began to spend the night at Sussex Gardens now and then and enjoyed the time alone with her husband. Charlotte encouraged her to shop for furniture at Harrod's, to decorate and organize, more than happy to have Freddy to herself while Grace played house at Sussex Gardens.

The arrangement made her both a mother and a free woman of means. It was a lifestyle she had never envisioned for herself. Her parents had been well-off but not wealthy, and Grace loved being able to treat her parents. She began to participate in the regimental social life along with her mother and father, spending afternoons with family support for the Guardsmen's families and taking them to dinner at lovely restaurants afterward. On the nights she returned to the mansion in Fulham she took advantage of the chauffeur—no more exhausted shuffling in the Underground during rush hour. London looked so different, lit up like a Christmas tree every night now that the blackout curtains were down. When she came through the doors, someone was always on the great staircase, scurrying up or down, laden with baby's requirements. She'd slip into the library, where Mrs. Alberry would enter with a "Long day, madam—would you like some tea?" Grace would seat herself by the fire, and some good soul would bring Freddy in for her to fuss over and play with.

After all those years of bone-breaking work and heartache in hospitals, she found herself more and more grateful for the life she had now. She had a handsome husband and a beautiful child. She spent Charlotte's money in the best stores in Knightsbridge and treated her mother to shopping trips at Harvey Nichols. She had guaranteed her child's welfare in the postwar world, and the Stetchworth fortune would surely outlast any legacy from the Moss-Jones clan, who had nothing more to offer than social position. Others she knew in society held their chins just above water; in contrast, Charlotte could open any door that mattered, from schools to business, always backed by the Howard family.

Some nights, after the nanny took Freddy back, Grace's mind drifted back to Rory. She remembered him as a childhood playmate on a faraway army post. He was a handsome young man, so warm and funny, and they had loved each other most of her life. But he was gone and nothing could bring him back. She had seen Rory close his eyes for good, seen soldiers scream as their legs were amputated, had lain in an army bed with fever herself, been bone-tired and still gotten up to change bedpans and clean rifle wounds. Despite her blessings, life would be long without him, but her busy days and evening social life kept these thoughts at bay. Perhaps she would take a sabbatical from the hospital until the new year.

AS THE MONTHS WENT BY, Charlotte found herself most content with the new arrangements. Each evening she finished sorting out the staff, the menu, the attire and all the other details for the next day, driving up the tension within the army that now made up the expanded ranks of the Fulham house. Many evenings she would inquire, "Where is Grace?" of Collins, the lady's maid. The new maid looked sheepish. "I don't know, madam; I haven't seen madam since she went shopping. She said that she would be seeing the captain later." Charlotte sniffed, "I suppose she is staying the night at the Gardens then." Then she would dismiss them all to their places and call for her nightly brandy, a new habit that had developed since Freddy took over her life. She took it in bed to warm her bones before going to sleep.

Charlotte felt born again. Giving up Christian had been for her an act of will. It took great discipline to wrench her mind from the habit of decades of mooning over her Austrian aristocrat, but Charlotte was nothing if not determined. Looking at herself in the long mirror she was still thin and good looking for a woman her age. And now there was Freddy. What did treacherous Christian—a spoiled, stupid boy who had turned into a spoiled, stupid man, a failure, from a failed country—mean to her now? With Freddy she would have the chance to raise another boy, and this time he would be a proper gentleman. She prayed for more grandchildren to come. They would form a new dynasty around her, and she would be like an old queen reigning over her court. She didn't need a man to achieve greatness. She would achieve it for herself.

CAPTAIN STETCHWORTH WAS ON ROTATING shifts at Saint James's Palace. One week on duty and one week off suited him down to the ground. He purchased a two-seat roadster to rocket to work across Lambeth Bridge to his house off Bayswater Road. The real reason for the purchase was to keep his brace of terriers with him, who were underfoot at the big house. They were getting on and Valerie, in particular, was having problems negotiating the steps up to Putney Bridge on her beloved walkies. He could see it in her deep black eyes and hear it in her breathing. She enjoyed sitting beside him with the wind in her coat, relegating Teddy to being stuffed behind the driver's seat. She knew who was boss.

Rags found himself quite happy with life in 1921. He was young and full of energy. He had survived the war and, most relieving of all, had survived his spy work undetected. He had a handsome young son and still had time to enjoy his pretty wife, going out on dates to the Swan or spending the night at the townhouse. But occasional nights at Sussex Gardens had consequences. No sooner was Master Freddy wobble-walking and munching on Teddy's carrot-like tail than Grace casually announced one Sunday evening when coffee was served in the library her good news in a very off-hand way. "Rolly, I have chosen Martin for our next son's name, after your grandfather." Rags jiggled his cup in the saucer, and Charlotte nearly dropped hers.

Rags choked as he tried to speak. "A little premature, old girl, I haven't mastered Freddy as yet!"

Charlotte, seated at the head of the table, leapt up and rushed at Grace: "My dear, what a tribute! I never dreamt we Stetchworths had made such a favorable impression. I'm so delighted. To think, he will be named for his great-grandfather."

The Stetchworths had indeed made a favorable impression, and Grace was grateful. She knew how to guarantee the child's future. Raising boys in class-conscious England cost a great deal of money, to be sure, if they were to have a chance in a world that was rushing headlong into an uncertain future. If war were to come again, she wanted her sons to be at Horse Guards, like Rags, not dying on the field like her beloved Rory.

Until that moment Charlotte hadn't thought of her father for years. Looking at Rolly and his burgeoning family, she couldn't help but think of the path that had brought them there. Charlotte did not often allow herself to think back on that night on Putney Bridge, when her Rolly's future was endangered by a most unsuitable match and she took action to stop it. But as she looked at little Freddy and the beaming Grace, she thought, "What a good thing I did then."

*Part III*

# TRANSMISSION (1936–1944)

## Chapter Thirty-Three

# London and Newmarket, 1936

IN 1936 KING GEORGE V died. He had reigned since 1910, and now his playboy son Edward became king.

The ascension of Edward VIII was a worry to Rags. For the past ten years, he had served George V directly, thanks to some maneuvering by his father-in-law. He had been a Welsh Guardsman since 1915, but by the mid-1920s he was bored of the Guardsmen and would soon be the oldest captain on the parade ground. Colonel Moss-Jones had made quiet inquiries to his old friend, the renowned Major J. R. M. Chard, who remembered how the young Captain Stetchworth had offered him a ride to the palace during the war. A few months later, Rags found himself a King's Messenger to George V.

The King's Messengers were formed during the exile of Charles II. Having witnessed the execution of his father by Oliver Cromwell in 1649, Charles was eager to have a select team of messengers whose loyalty and authority were unquestioned. He selected four companions and broke off four silver greyhound handles from his breakfast tray and passed them out as badges to symbolize speed of delivery in the days when they were the fastest and truest beasts in England. The greyhound had ever since been the symbol of the Messengers.

Grace had been proud and Charlotte delighted with Rags' appointment to the court as one of four King's Messengers. The position called for the grade of major, and Rags strolled up Pall Mall, turned left at the Army and Navy Club, crossed St. James's Park, and emerged on Jermyn Street to see the tailor. At a shop in Piccadilly arcade he ordered the appropriate badge, gold aiguillette, and sash of garter blue with gold edges to go with his various uniforms. At the Messengers chambers he was issued a leather case with secret compartments, not unlike the one he had purchased in Italy years before. This pouch was small enough to weight, roll up and stuff through a ship's porthole if he was threatened, according to the clerk who issued all his paraphernalia. A small shiny nickel-coated revolver with concealed holster was issued as well.

When properly attired and extensively briefed, he had been taken, along with the company of the other three messengers, to meet the King in his private rooms. George V was examining a page of stamps in an album and stood up to greet them. "Stetchworth, I have heard your name recently from Hopewell and know of your exploits at Gallipoli and France. We are a small family here, and now you are a member in good standing. I'm pleased to have you with us. I congratulate you and charge you, as a member of the service, to discharge your duties on my behalf and take orders from no other person other than myself. You are *not* to be interfered with on any account."

The King was handed a red leather–covered folder by a smiling equerry. "I have instructions I wish to give you to that effect." Major Stetchworth stepped forward to accept the portfolio with the King's cipher embossed on the surface. The King stood and reached for his right hand. "Rags, is it?" Shocked that the King would use the nickname, "It is, Your Majesty." The King chuckled. "You're one of the family now, Rags. Well then, welcome aboard; I place my full trust in you."

The four messengers backed out of the room together. "That wasn't so bad, was it?" one of his fellow Messengers offered. "By the way, a point of protocol, my boy. We refer to the King when in close quarters as Sir, not His Majesty; he prefers informality from the likes of us."

Rags smiled. "So noted. Less formal, more matey," knowing it was an exaggeration.

IN THE YEARS SINCE THAT first meeting with King George, the role of the King's Messengers had become only more vital. The ease and optimism of the 1920s had ended with the advent of the Depression, and with it the presumption of peace in Europe. Capital, the engine of change, stopped moving, an inescapable death knell. Professors, economists, bankers and experts of all descriptions, across the world, proffered theories, pronounced rational solutions and watched helplessly as wages stagnated, jobs disappeared, and anarchists gained popular support. Lloyd George and other politicians, keenly aware of the danger the anarchists presented, warned the government to listen, talk, and give in to all workers' demands, cooling one crisis after another with social programs that released some of the steam of the pressure-cooker that the decade had become. England financed the relief programs with borrowed money for the present by mortgaging the future. The United States took the paper, knowing that the credit rating of the British Empire was a solid bet. With these mitigating factors in place, it seemed that once again the English Channel represented the stopping point for European chaos.

But that sense of security went only so far. In 1931 Japan invaded Manchuria to gain an agricultural base. In Italy, Mussolini was intent on reestablishing the Roman Empire by snapping up African coastal states on the Mediterranean and in Ethiopia, bolstered by a new, showy navy and air force. By 1936 Francisco Franco's fascists had gained the upper hand against the Republicans in the Spanish Civil War. Across Europe governments floundered and failed as political upheaval ruled the Continent.

Worst of all were developments in Germany. The German people had suffered terribly since the end of the Great War, and their bitterness had blossomed into a frightening nationalism. In 1933 Adolf Hitler, leader of the National Socialist German Workers' Party (NAZI), became chancellor of Germany. He had come to power promising stability and a return to Teutonic glory, vowing to restore the country to its "natural borders" of ethnic Germans; wherever the German language dominated, that land was a part of Germany, according to the Fuhrer.

Hitler solidified his control of the German government with the passage of the Reichstag Fire Decree of 1933, passed after the legislative headquarters of the nation was set aflame by parties unknown. Blaming the communists, Hitler requested and received the passage of the decree, which suspended civil liberties in Germany. A short time later, his dictatorship was ensured by the Enabling Act, which allowed Hitler to rule by decree.

From that point on, Hitler was hell-bent on domination. Opponents were jailed or their assets seized. He rebuilt the German army, in violation of the terms of the Versailles Treaty, and created the Luftwaffe. Pledges of loyalties had to be made to Hitler personally, rather than to Germany itself. He fired generals at will and filled his government and the armed forces with allies and yes-men. He demonized Jews and communists and vowed to cleanse Germany of them. With the whole of Germany under his command, in 1936 he marched his troops, unopposed, across the Rhine River to take back the Rhineland, a prize territory that had been demilitarized by the Treaty of Versailles.

Britain was dismayed by these developments, as was all of Europe. Those who had been embroiled in the war could not fathom that anyone could repeat the sins of the past. Yet each day brought bad news at home and abroad. And no one wanted a new war. No one wanted to ask yet another generation to sacrifice their sons to contain Germany. And surely Hitler was becoming more moderate. He would occasionally hint that his imprecations at the Jews were not heartfelt, but only what the people wanted.

It was understandable that the British public became apathetic toward rearmament as the Depression droned on. In the Great War, the British had lost friends not by ones and twos but by schoolrooms. Of the one quarter of the male population of Great Britain's empire that served in the Great War, more than 800,000 perished. No family was untouched. On their return to the British Isles, society was dealt a heavy blow. The economy collapsed, jobs disappeared, and families were forced to alter circumstances just to survive. Laboring households concentrated on daily living conditions, poor health care, and a search for good jobs. The upper classes put their heads in the sand regardless of warnings from Churchill, who was out of government and regarded as a warmonger. Having seen their young compatriots cut down in the prime of life, their new philosophy was "Life is for the living." Their lives were all sport outings, sports cars, yacht racing at Cowes, shooting in Scotland, garden parties, and first nights at the theater, opera or ballet. Horse racing at Ascot was a moment to display the latest haute couture from Paris. The public was entertained in the new large venue Odeon Cinemas by popular films that turned grand literature into feature motion pictures starring great charismatic actors. It was common to go to the pictures twice or more a week.

However, it was at the movie theaters that newsreels began to make an impact on the people's consciousness. Japan's rape of Manchuria, Mussolini's exploits in the Mediterranean, and the vicious Spanish Civil War impressed on them the impending danger. But rather than arming for defense, the British leadership relied on diplomacy to turn back time and arbitrate squabbles and land disputes to prevent overt war. And the British people encouraged it. Not war again—surely another way could be found.

RAGS HAD BEEN HAPPY WITH his work for George V, but with Edward's ascension in 1936, it was a new world. Edward was a bachelor and a socialite, which on its own could have made Rags' position quite entertaining. But Edward was also an admirer of the Nazi party leadership, and the ascendancy of Germany since Hitler became chancellor in 1933 made Rags extremely nervous.

In all spheres of life, it seemed, the carefree years of the twenties had turned to tension. Grace and Charlotte, who had gotten along well in the early years, were increasingly under strain. Charlotte's drive and ambition had been redirected toward controlling the lives of those in her household. She disapproved of Grace's laxity, as Grace enjoyed romping with the boys and encouraged what her mother-in-law called horseplay. Charlotte deplored such behavior and found it unacceptable to the dignity of her family. Grace insisted that "boys are bound to be boys." She had grown up on army posts, always a member of one gang or another, playing at rough-and-ready ball games of all description, even though her mother discouraged it and hoped she would grow out of such behavior. But army brats never get over the freedom of living in foreign lands where they survived in packs sequestered in compounds.

It came to a head one evening when Freddy brought down the drapes in the library, "swinging like a pirate in the rigging," he told his patient mother. Grace and Charlotte had it out then and there, with the two boys standing by in shock at the women's language. Charlotte demanded, "Get a grip on your sons! They're nothing but vandals, crashing about, destroying my house and furnishings. After all I have given you—you are ungrateful and irresponsible."

Grace exploded for the first time in her life, as the boys looked on dumbfounded. "Enough! I am tired of your constant meddling. They are my sons, and I will raise them as I wish. I hate you and this house; I wish I had never come here!" she sobbed.

"Well," Charlotte said, raising her voice, "that is the thanks I get for saving you from that poky little garden house and a life of toil. Who provided the money for you to shop to your heart's content, given you time to have a career, such as it is—time to pamper yourself with a car and chauffeur, and lady's maid too, and made me take on the responsibility of raising babies to boys while you became a woman of leisure? You ungrateful—"

At that moment Mrs. Alberry entered the library to see what the rumpus was all about. She took the boys away, who were snuffing, heads down, most disturbed. Neither woman apologized. "Grace," Charlotte said, now calm, "I am unable to cope; the boys need discipline."

Grace sat on the sofa with her head in her hands. She felt defeated and rather ashamed of her outburst, which had been pent up for what seemed to be years. She had no more fight in her. "What do you propose?"

The next week the boys were enrolled at the Charterhouse Square School in London. There they would study until they were eleven, when they would transfer full time to Charterhouse in Surrey as their father had done. Grace knew that it was the practice for boys of their age and class to go away to school, where they would be taught to be British gentlemen, but she had dreaded it and tried to avoid it. Her time with her sons was the brightest part of any day. Now, with the boys away in the day and fully engulfed in their studies in the evening, she felt their loss. She had her social schedule and her work at the Royal Hospital near Putney Common, but there was a void that only her sons' presence could fill.

Even worse was the knowledge that in just a few short years her boys would be of military age. Charterhouse's cadet program would ripen them for war, just as it had their father. Grace, who had always been cheery and optimistic, had been battered by the sudden death of her mother the year before and the floundering of her father, who spent far too much time in the officers' mess drinking, trying to cope alone. To lose the company of her sons on top of it was too much, but she knew that the protections offered by Charlotte and the Howard family would be the boys' best promise of safety.

With Rolly traveling frequently as a King's Messenger and the house off Putney Bridge less and less inviting, she joined with a girlfriend in purchasing a little cottage in Newmarket, near Cambridge, where the two enjoyed the horse racing on weekends. Sometimes she would go there alone, visit the shops and have tea on the High Street, where she could linger and watch the strings of racehorses passing out of their paddock at a walking pace and through the village. The magnificent animals, with brushed, bright coats, pranced with heads down, arching their strong necks and eyeing the spectators, who respectfully stopped, fearing they might spook the skittish mounts. Under their brown, polished saddles were striped blankets in the colors of the stable. The jockeys, in work clothes and helmets, steered the horses between cars and lorries as they passed out onto the open green heath for exercise.

As she sipped her black tea, Grace felt she had found a refuge. She would take the train to Cambridge and a bus to Newmarket any time Rolly and his mother—and her father, for that matter—dragged her down. The cottage behind the red brick wall of the Jockey Club would allow her to hide from all that threatened to embitter her: Rolly's travel, her mother-in-law's meddling, her sons' absence, and her worst fear of all—the specter of a new war.

## Chapter Thirty-Four

# Fort Belvedere and Germany, 1936

KING EDWARD VIII DIDN'T MAKE radical changes among his courtiers. The four King's Messengers, on the contrary, became very busy delivering communiqués to the capitals of Europe. Old King George had been concerned with his son's overtures to the German chancellor, Herr Hitler. Edward had always considered his German relatives as close cousins. He had an idea that Britain should ally with Germany in a conquest of Russia. This was borne out in a note from the German ambassador Leopold von Hoesch to Hitler after a dinner with King Edward: "The feelings of the new King towards Germany are so deep and strong that he would resist contrary influences. Would he also want to realize his great-grandfather's [Prince Albert] dream of an Anglo-German alliance?" His report went on: "He wants to attend the Berlin Olympic games and meet with the German veterans association. He will, of course, from the start show restraint regarding tricky questions of foreign policy. But I am convinced that his friendly disposition towards Germany will have some influence on the formation of British foreign policy. There will be a king on the throne who understands Germany and is willing to have good relations between England and Germany."

At the bottom of Edward's feeling was the memory that his father had failed to intervene on behalf of their cousins—the czar and his family—when the Bolsheviks threatened to murder them. Edward harbored dreams of revenge on behalf of the greater royal family. But Edward was not alone in his indulgence of Germany's militarization and radicalization. Driven to prevent war at any cost, the British people and their government searched for reasons to avoid confronting the frightening evolution of Germany under the Nazi Party. When the Saarland voted to return to Germany in 1931, it didn't make the news. Even the seizure of the Rhineland by German soldiers in 1933 hadn't swayed French and British opinion against the Germans. Britain regarded the bold move as merely reclaiming a strip of native land stolen in the turmoil and heat of the 1919 peace talks. In 1936 Hitler had made a great show of the Berlin Olympic Games, which garnered praise from many corners. The Berlin Games were well attended, and Hitler relaxed his anti-Semitic campaign, hinting that he was temperate at heart. These public relations efforts found a receptive ear in many members of Parliament, who were most aware that the Great War had brought near-bankruptcy and that the British Empire had struggled to regain its place among nations ever since.

In addition, Edward—a member of the Windsor family, who had wisely abandoned their original family name of Saxe-Coburg und Gotha in 1917—felt himself to be German at heart. Both Edward and his younger brother, the Duke of Kent, quietly courted German interests, and they were not out of step with many others in England. Hitler was gaining support from surprising sources. The headmaster of Charterhouse School, in an article in the *Times*, praised German unity, which he witnessed on a field trip with his students during school games. They had spent weeks camping out, playing games and hiking with German youths who made them feel at home. Hitler's hard line against communism encouraged the Conservatives in the House of Commons to normalize relations with Germany. England began to blame France for fermenting another war when it signed a pact with the Soviet Union.

EARLY IN 1936 RAGS, BECAUSE of his knowledge of the German language, was assigned to support the private communiques between his sovereign and Chancellor Hitler without the knowledge of the British government. For Rags, this raised the specter of Germany once again, and he reluctantly had to tell Charlotte of the dangers of grubbing up the past they assumed was buried with the war graves. Late one evening, when Grace had retired and the house was quiet, the two sat in the library. He approached the subject carefully, so as not to panic his mother. He was sure it had never crossed her mind: she had thoroughly buried the past with the loss of Christian.

"Mamma, I'm going to be the principal messenger between the King and Hitler." He caught Charlotte looking away from the fire toward the hidden cabinet that held enough material to engage a firing squad for them both. She could feel the blood rising into her neck, causing discomfort in her jaw. But she resisted the thought that it was starting all over again.

"We mustn't be concerned for fear of evoking the sad memories of the past. I don't see the connection between then and now, Rolly. The war has been over for seventeen years. Hitler was a corporal in the trenches in those dreadful days, a mere foot soldier." She reminded him, "Christian isn't even a German; he's out of the picture in Austria with some social-climbing fraulein. The world has changed, turned over; these are all new players, it's a new modern world. Besides, who says Hitler is like the Kaiser? He's interested in putting his poor country back together, not invading England. It's all stuff-and-nonsense. They picked you because of your facility with the language, plain and simple. God knows it's hard to find a German speaker in England since the war."

While she poo-pooed, Rags added an extra ounce or two of cognac to the crystal snifters he was preparing at the sideboard. It was going to be a difficult session, and, true to form, he turned to the climate as a distraction. "Downright frosty evening. This will warm you, Mamma." He handed her the cut-glass goblet. The swirling mist that hung over the river had begun to turn to ice pellets. The string of dull lamps on Putney rail bridge glimmered on and off in the nasty weather. Hunter, a West Highland white terrier, touched his black nose against the cold glass of the French doors, looking for prey scurrying along the low wet embankment wall on the river terrace. Hunter had replaced Valerie and Teddy in the mansion after their passing, and his name bore tribute to his skills at a ratter. Like the others, he valued the walkies across the bridge to Wandsworth Park. Rags knew it would be a nasty tread that evening after the contentious discussion with his mother and hoped the terrier would stick to his business for a quick return.

She continued with her interpretation. "Monsignor Pieter has given up his post at Westminster Cathedral and is back in Regensburg. I had a note from him at Christmas, did I tell you? He believes he is going to be elevated by Pius XII and take on the basilica. You see, even the church has moved on. Rolly, you have taken this personally; leave it be. Think of it as an honor to be in the good graces of His Majesty and don't make a fuss."

Rags interrupted. "You're aware that the pope was the papal delegate to Germany before his elevation. The talk is that even he is pro-German."

She raised her voice and countered. "You men in the palace are always hanging crepe. You see conspiracy around every corner. You mustn't listen to Churchill. He is a bad hat."

Rags judged that enough had been said for the time being. "Perhaps you're right; I guess I am being paranoid. It's just that I had put it all behind me. Now here it is all over again. These years of service to the Crown have changed me. I have learned to love this country and its people, with their indomitable spirit and contagious calm. Working with good-hearted soldiers and an officer corps of fine fellows has worked on me, and now, I suppose, I am one of them."

Rags felt better, composed, as he put the lead on Hunter, who was prepared to take the bridge by storm and trot past the dim amber lights of the Bookers' house at the far end, an unwelcome reminder of times past.

A FEW MONTHS LATER CAME a summons to Fort Belvedere, where King Edward spent the weekends with Mrs. Wallis Simpson and friends. Out of uniform to match the informality of the fort, Rags arrived quietly at a back entrance of the Bombardier's quarter, which was attached to the main house. It was constructed in 1820 as a small artillery park with thirty-one brass cannons arrayed below the tower and main house. It had been extensively renovated and added to over the years into a rather odd folly. Belvedere had been given to Edward by his father in 1919, after his wartime service, and he used it as a retreat from the press where he could entertain close friends with the latest music, trends and fashions. Mrs. Simpson, an intimate friend, had been put in charge of redecorating, which was one of her passions; the other was the King. On the twenty-two-mile drive from London, Rags thought of the goings-on in the eight-bedroom fort in Windsor Great Park that would be filled with couples bent on having a good time. He was apprehensive.

Major Stetchworth stood out from the guests, formally dressed in daytime attire. He was conducted to a small study where the desk was piled high with red boxes from the Foreign Office. The papers strewn on the leather top of the bureau were cables from ambassadors and papers marked "Most Secret." This cavalier treatment of sensitive correspondence concerned Rags. Anyone, including Mrs. Simpson, could browse at will. It was most disturbing, but it was not the place of a mere messenger to mention the danger to the King. He feared a Home Office inquiry. He was aware that the Home Office and Cumming at MI5 were concerned about the lack of security and Mrs. Simpson's close liaisons with Count von Ribbentrop, the rakish German ambassador, and feared she might be a paid German spy. According to a surprise visit from Uncle Hilly to Rags' office, the King was not aware that the phones at the fort were tapped. In confidence, he asked Rags to keep an eye open at the fort and give him a tickle if he saw anything that might be of interest to the security of classified matters. This put Rags in a very precarious position, and he wasn't certain where his loyalties should lie.

Edward entered the study dressed in a sporty tweed jacket and tan slacks, smoking a straight briar pipe. Rags recognized the blend as Dunhill 39. "Ah, Rags, they told me you were here; good. I have something for you to take to the German chancellor—right away." Rags thought it unnecessary to invoke speed; he was not in a habit of lingering over His Majesty's business. "How long will it take you to get to Strasburg if you leave directly? No airplanes, too showy, people know who you are and they can guess where you're going. As always, you must be careful, on the hush-hush, old fellow. If the Foreign Office, that gaggle of old women, knew I was in direct contact with the Fuhrer, they would be on the hop. You understand, I am sure." The King touched the side of nose with his first finger and gave a wink. Edward was always friendly, congenial, and Rags considered him to be a fellow soldier. They were teammates, but he was always careful not to return the congeniality. It was strictly business on Rags' part, professional.

Rags knew the routine. "I'll take a car to Dover, sir, and cross the Channel first thing. Train through Paris, change from Gare du Nord to Gare de l'Est on foot; it's only a few blocks and I can shake off anyone who is interested and take an express to Strasburg. I should be there by before midnight, I should think, sir." Rags had often used that route east.

The King took up the remainder of the itinerary. "Von Ribbentrop has arranged a car to pick you up at the Restaurant Rhinebec on the far side of the bridge in Germany. They have a car to take you to Obersalzberg. Have you been there?"

"No, sir. I have often gone to Berlin but not elsewhere." Rags had seen photos of the Eagle's Nest in magazines and found the prospect of seeing it in person most exciting.

The King placed a dollop of hot wax on the envelope's flap and pressed his seal into it with his royal cipher, which he took from a locked drawer in the desk. Rags placed it into a larger wrapper and sealed it with hot wax, adding his own seal of the running greyhound. Then it went into the leather case, which he tucked under his arm. He saluted the King and backed out of the room. The meeting took only a few minutes, and he was off again like the proverbial greyhound.

Rags left the swirling party that had adjourned to the grounds, where the King directed his guests in his favorite pastime. They begrudgingly began to clear brush and bracken from the grounds around the fort. A bonfire was lit and the happy couples dragged branches to the pyre near the swimming pool. The ones who performed well would receive more attention from the host and hostess.

That Mrs. Simpson was now acting as hostess was undeniable, a fact that caused great consternation to many in the establishment—she was a twice-divorced woman whose husband was still alive, and an American to boot. The Archbishop of Canterbury, Baron Lang of Lambeth, had been a close friend of King George V and shared trepidations when it came to the succession of the throne. He took it upon himself to put a stop to Edward's plan to marry Mrs. Simpson and led a coalition which included the prime minister, Stanley Baldwin, and several press barons "to see Mrs. Simpson off." He saw to it that members of the staff at Fort Belvedere reported the goings-on and circulated slanderous information most shamelessly. Edward counter-proposed a morganatic marriage, which would allow him to marry Wallis Simpson but not include her in the affairs of state or royal succession. It was the most dangerous ploy, and one that could find sympathy among the people if it were handled correctly. The archbishop pounced on it. A newspaper campaign ridiculed it among the pages, but Edward remained unmoved. Recently Rags had heard the King refer to the archbishop as "his nemesis, a specter clad in black gaiters going noiselessly about."

Rags was very careful during this period of leaks to the opposition, ensuring the King would not suspect him as a source. His attitude was "never pass up an opportunity to keep your mouth shut."

AS HIS DRIVER RUSHED HIM toward the port of Dover, Rags marveled that he was taking the same route as the famed pilgrims of the *Canterbury Tales*. He could see the fabled inns along the way, some claiming to be in operation since 1387. With no pilgrims clogging the road today, they made good time to Dover, where they met the newly arrived boat train from London.

Leaving the car, Rags mingled with the rail passengers as they detrained on the dock next to the ship. A ticket was waiting for him and Rags concealed himself for the duration of the crossing in a tiny cabin, away from prying eyes. He knew that tabloid reporters haunted the ships day and night, hoping to catch a film star or politician unaware. More than just peckish, he knew that the food service on board was unremarkable, even worse than railroad cafeterias. A waiter brought him a dish of deep-fried fish and chips, which he covered with malt vinegar to cut the grease. The chips were soggy and so hot from the grease they soaked up that they burned the roof of his mouth. Since the tea was cold, it all leveled out in the end.

For the time of year, the water was surprisingly calm, and they made good time to the waiting Paris train on the dock at Calais. The transfer was quick and painless to a second-class seat next to the window. As the train lurched, a vendor came down the aisle struggling with a cart filled with beer, wine, cigarettes, and sweets. Rags felt he had no other options and bought several bars of Belgian chocolate, which he had learned to live off during the war. He donned a slouch hat and kept his collar turned up, for the train lacked heat and the windows clouded over from the condensation given off in small clouds by the chilly passengers.

It took over two hours to go the short distance to the City of Lights, which, at that time of year, were glowing yellow in the late afternoon. He detrained with the crowd, anxious to find a warm spot before moving on. He chose the Mercure Hotel bar across tangled traffic moving slowly on the wide street in front of Gare du Nord. After a cognac went down with some haste, he plunged into the stream of shivering, wet pedestrians on the pavement and walked a few blocks to a market. The smell of cheese and raw meat mingled with cigarette smoke and wet wool. Rags remained only long enough to ensure that he was not being followed. In the damp air, he crossed Avenue Magenta and took to darkened alleys, arriving at the side entrance of Gare de l'Est and selecting an express train to Strasburg. With any luck, he would be in a hotel on a back street before they stopped serving dinner that evening.

Arriving in Strasburg, he found the dining room closed but managed to convince the staff that he was at death's door. Being France, somehow the kitchen managed to put together a meal of cold seafood delights along with vichyssoise. He was sure that it was part of their leftovers, scraped off plates returned to the kitchen by fussy customers. No matter—the chocolate bars had made him bilious.

A message sent from the Palace alerted the German Foreign Office that the King's Messenger was expected by mid-morning and would identify himself with a code word familiar to Herr Hitler's aide-de-camp. It was a word the two men had agreed upon when they met at the Berlin Games. The word was "blue"—Mrs. Simpson's favorite color. Before leaving the hotel, Rags checked his revolver before seating it in his shoulder holster; then he donned a heavy black Crombie topcoat and tucked the leather case which held the King's communique under his arm. The cases were weighted so that, if a Messenger were accosted, it could be thrown into a nearby river, and the paper inside was designed to disintegrate upon contact with water. Before stepping out, Rags oriented himself to the fast-flowing Rhine, just in case.

At the lobby, he asked the concierge to call for a car to take him to the cathedral. The famous church was bustling with worshippers, mostly tiny old women in dark babushkas, which made him stand out in his smart dress. In the vestibule, he waited a few minutes to see if he had attracted a follower. There was none. He rushed up a side aisle where a few lingered at the stations of the cross and pushed his way clear along with apologies. There were several exits off the choir, and he quick stepped out a side door and into the maze of streets to search for a passing taxi. In the years since he had joined the King's Messengers, his proficiency in French had become nearly fluent and he directed the cabbie to cross the bridge and to stop just short of the far end of the customs station. Alighting, a hand signal alerted two men in civilian dress to emerge from the bridge abutment at the German end to come to his assistance.

Rags greeted them with the word "blue," and they escorted him in silence past the barrier and into a restaurant where breakfast was served. He was told it was a long drive on the high-speed autobahn to Obersalzberg; "stops are not planned." The car was a shiny black Mercedes touring car like the ones seen in the newsreels. Comfortable, alone in the dark leather backseat, he stretched out and attempted to catch up on sleep lost the previous night. He thought that this passage would be pleasurable, unlike the ones he had taken during the height of the war. On the ferry he had been preoccupied with thoughts of his involvement with Germany in the last war. Those thoughts were never far off no matter how hard he tried to squash them. But as they drove through the countryside, he recalled delightful river trips from Baden-Baden down the Rhine to Switzerland in his youth. He recalled the kind face of his father when he told the story of the gallant stag that jumped the rocks at Freiberg. Now that he was here, Germany seemed familiar and safe.

Until he thought about his coming meeting with the Fuhrer. Rags had become accustomed to meeting prominent men and, as a rule, found them quite ordinary. In fact, he felt, in the right circumstance, he would be capable of filling their custom-made shoes. There were exceptions, of course. Churchill was in a league of his own, only because he was a ball of energy and, in a blink, he could change subjects like a magician's sleight of hand trick. Prime Minister Neville Chamberlain, whom he saw often in the halls of the Palace, was rather vague, as though he had just lost something but couldn't remember what it was. But Hitler promised to be something quite different.

Now, comfortable in the great car and fatigued from the tension of the trip, Rags became drowsy. Before dropping off, he noticed similar cars in front and back that had joined the race to their leader's residence. He liked being personally escorted by the mysterious men in black coats and surmised they were a part of Hitler's personal bodyguard, the *Schutzstaffel*. He was surely in the safest hands in all of troubled Germany. Rags was roused when they stopped for fuel and a break in the road trip. They were inside a German army compound with SS markings on the gate. His escorts took him to a well-appointed room where he was given time to refresh himself and have a cup of tea, which he was sure was Earl Grey, no doubt an attempt to coddle him.

The cars began to climb toward Berchtesgaden, Bavaria, according to the road signs, and almost immediately wove through snow-covered hills that soon became mountains. There were checkpoints every few miles manned by the SS, no doubt sent from the barracks they had come from. He knew the reputation of the stormtroopers from the newsreels put out by the Ministry of Propaganda. They were big men, like the Guardsmen who watched over the King in London. Frightening at first, but when they approached the car their faces turned to gallant smiles and they inquired as to his comfort. When he answered in perfect German, a hand salute followed accompanied by "Heil Hitler." He returned a British Army hand salute with the words "Carry on" in English. He was not going to be baited into a "Heil Hitler"; he was the King of England's messenger, by God.

At the final security check, his escort remained behind and the Mercedes roared up the inclined driveway to a large protruding house that seemed to reach out over the road—the famed Eagle's Nest. He was struck by the enormous glass window polished like a diamond that looked out on the mountains across the stunning valley. He was led up a very wide and high set of stone steps to double carved wooden doors. Rags was met at the door by Herr von Ribbentrop, the foreign minister, whom he knew well from days at court. A large, outgoing man, this time he spoke in German and welcomed the major as an old friend with a glad hand and a pat on the back. A young, trim uniformed soldier in a white mess jacket took his coat and asked for his firearm, which Rags surrendered before entering a series of rooms which led to the chamber behind the great glass window.

The German chancellor was standing facing away at a large map table. His hands were clasped behind his back. He wore a plain light brown military coat and black trousers. He must have heard their approach, for he turned and smiled. Surprised, Rags had never seen his image in the press or newsreels in anything but a stern glaring pose. Rags gave a smart salute. The chancellor walked slowly to greet him and reached out his hand. The major dropped his salute and felt a strong, warm hand in his. "Hauptmann Stetchworth, I presume?" He was mimicking the words of the American newspaper man H. M. Stanley when he found the English churchman Doctor Livingstone in Africa. It was a joke but also a subtle message. It meant that Hitler knew everything about Rags' checkered past. Rags' eyes switched from Hitler's face to the black and silver Iron Cross on his left chest pocket. The two men looked at each other for a moment. Rags had an Iron Cross at home in the secret cupboard, and his host knew it.

## Chapter Thirty-Five

# The Eagle's Nest and Sweden, 1936

HITLER ACCEPTED THE SEALED ENVELOPE from the King's Messenger and left the room, followed by a large German Shepherd that had been lying in the sun. Alone, with only a uniformed servant standing by his side, Rags scanned the room, knowing Grace and his mother would demand a detailed description on his return. On entering the building, he had been struck by an enormous painting of Otto von Bismarck, the father of modern Germany. He never thought of Hitler as connected to the past, but there the old man was, looking proud of what he had begun.

The chamber with the map table had a floor of speckled light grey marble which also covered three steps into a very large reception hall. At the far wall was a single pane of glass that reached from floor to ceiling, wall to wall. There were large ceramic stoves on either corner which kept the room comfortably warm in spite of the frigid snow scene of the mountain ridge on the far side of the beautiful valley. Heavy natural wood beams laddered the high ceiling above white walls that reflected the bright sunlight that came through the window in straight shafts. The back wall was paneled with fumed oak around a large stone fireplace. Split logs were on either side on racks of rough iron. A tapestry of Frederick the Great mounted on a white horse dominated a colorful battle scene. A very large map table lay in front of the window with a bright red carpet beneath. Next to a large world globe in dark leather relief was a grand piano. Rags wondered who played—perhaps the lovely Eva Braun, who was not in evidence that day. Off to one side was an arrangement of half a dozen overstuffed chairs with chintz covers. Narrow tables along the walls held pots of cut flowers. A staff member in mess jacket invited him to sit and served him white tea from a rolling wooden cart. There were stacked plates covered with little sandwiches, cakes and sweets, very much like those served in England. Rags marveled at how comfortable and at home he would have felt, were it not for the frightening revelation the Fuhrer had just conveyed to him.

When the chancellor returned a half hour later, he gave Rags a return message and thanked him for his service. As he was escorted out, Rags felt tremendous relief that there had been no further references to "Hauptmann Stetchworth." Rags reversed his journey, which seemed to go much quicker. He asked for the car to take him to Basel, Switzerland. At the frontier, he secured transport to the city and took the cable ferry across the Rhine to Mulhouse, France. He caught a bus to Colmar and stayed the night in a small gasthaus just outside the quaint city. He took a train to Strasburg and hired a car to drive him to Paris. It was an eight-hour drive across the Lorraine south of the Maginot Line, which appeared to still be under construction. Near Verdun his car zoomed down the "Sacred Way," the road that the French army had worked ceaselessly to keep passable to provide supplies to the old fortress in 1916.

Only half of his mission was complete. In a way, he was now the courier for the German chancellor carrying a message to Edward VIII, which he kept safely in the pouch next to his holstered revolver. Once in Paris he took the boat train in reverse to the Channel ferry and was met this time by his driver at Folkstone Pier. He arrived on a weekday and went straight to Buck House. However, the King was out of the city, in Wales on a tour of the mines. It was fortunate that Rags had slept in the car and on the ferry, as it took hours on the country roads to complete his mission. He found the sovereign at Cardiff, where he presented the Fuhrer's compliments and the message. The King asked after his trip, concerned that he was not detected, and was pleased to hear Rags' recitation of the journey. He also inquired after his reception by the Germans along the way and was assured that they were fine hosts. Rags wanted to use the word "comrades" but thought better of it, considering.

Back at Fulham, Rags prepared to violate the Messengers' code as he sat before the fire in the library with his wife and mother to tell them of his adventure. He excused the servants after they had cleared away the evening coffee to ensure that they were out of hearing. "I know, Mamma, Grace, that I'm restricted by my oath not to reveal my mission of late. But it was wizard; I'll bust if I don't tell you what I was sent to do. You must promise not to disclose to anyone what I am about to tell you," he paused, "not any part of what I am about to tell, mind you." His heart pounded in his ears as he questioned his own judgment, but he could not contain an experience only he and the prime minister held in common. "It's a matter of the highest secrecy, but I know I can trust you both. There are many things I have done during my military service that will never pass these lips, as you know, Mamma." Grace looked curiously at her husband and once again remembered the close bond between mother and son. It was a connection that she felt she could never breach. Grace could feel its strength, so let it be.

The two women pledged their loyalty. Charlotte whispered, "You know me, Rolly, I am your devoted confidant and you mine. You needn't ask for my silence." Grace just nodded her head in agreement.

Rags burst forth: "I met Hitler, in his home! It was a moment to remember; who but the most prominent Nazis had seen the inner sanctum of the most feared mischief maker in the world?" He left out the travel arrangements and went straight to the gates of Hitler's compound. The ladies were riveted when he mentioned the Fuhrer's name. He was the mystery man on the lips of every Briton. Only stern cinema images came to mind of a stick-like figure in the center of every shot. No one outside of German speakers had ever heard his voice, which was always dubbed by translators. Rags gave them the prelude as he described the house and the aides that hovered nearby. "I saw him for the first time from the rear leaning over the map table framed by the giant window obscured by shafts of dusty light. When he turned and smiled, I felt my breath contract and couldn't speak for a moment." The women's eyes were wide and they began to ask questions in an uninterrupted flow.

From that moment on Rags was almost never home. Edward was on a crusade of his own. He knew that the prime minister, Chamberlain, and his counterparts twisted in all directions to appease the unappeasable twins, Mussolini and Hitler. The King, a Deutschophile, engaged the French, Dutch and Belgian politicians by appealing through his royal family members spread across Europe to appease Hitler. Edward was related to most ruling families and didn't hesitate to involve them in his vision for the future. It was quite simple, really: Edward viewed communism as the greater evil. He condoned nationalism when it contributed to the stability of Great Britain and its empire. When France balked, he cut them out in order to ally his country with Germany against the Soviet Union. His government didn't agree with his crusade; Edward was out of control.

Rags was sent on a regular basis to Vaduz with messages for Count Toerring, Prince of Lichtenstein. A cousin and prominent Nazi, the Count was leading the charge among the crowned families to back Hitler. Edward wanted to let it be known that he was German at heart and often remarked how good it was to be able to speak his native language when on the Continent. Rags went across London on a regular basis to pass personal messages to Prince Harold von Bismarck, the German ambassador, to assure his government of the King's continued commitment to Hitler's endeavors. Nuremberg became as familiar as London to the Messenger with correspondence for Charles, Duke of Saxe-Coburg und Gotha. Rags spent weeks on trains, so it seemed, as he crisscrossed the land on the east side of the Rhine. Soon there was no need for subterfuge any longer as the views of King Edward became public. The network of family members that Queen Victoria had created by marrying off her children to royal dynasties was tapped by the King to sway nations to build a coalition against communist Russia in favor of the nationalist movement created by Hitler.

IN EARLY OCTOBER, THE PATTERN was broken when Major Stetchworth was given a message for King Gustaf V of Sweden, who was not a member of the modern German royal dynasties. It was a most curious mission; no other Messenger had ever been to Stockholm. Gustaf, who had ascended to the throne in 1907, had kept Sweden out of the Great War. His country held a unique position: Germany needed iron ore to build war machines, which they could only acquire from Sweden. Hitler wanted to sign a pact pledging to respect Sweden's neutrality if another European war were to begin in exchange for an unlimited supply of iron ore. Hitler was courting Gustaf and asked King Edward to intercede.

Rags accepted the mission, happy to rid himself of dusty old palaces where no one spoke English. The trip would be more of an excursion to a new land and he relished the experience. Yet his personal security, as always, was a consideration. On advice, he switched from the revolver to an automatic. He took issue of a 38-caliber Colt automatic with a short barrel, serial number 32831. It looked like a model he had seen in gangster films. It was true that the flat frame was easily concealed and the eight-round capacity, with one in the chamber, was more desirable than the five in his revolver. Additionally, spare clips could be carried attached to the back of his trouser belt.

Once on the Continent, he took a train to Brussels and then another to Copenhagen. It was some distance from the docks, which were spread out over a large inlet several miles long. A taxi let him out at the terminal, where he waited until the evening tide to board. As he lingered on the pier, he remembered his school days and the tales of Vice Admiral Horatio Nelson. In 1801 the Royal Navy caught the Danish navy moored in port along the same docks and proceeded to destroy them at anchor. Nelson had ignored his orders when he raised the telescope to his blind eye and said, "I really don't see the signal." With pride, Rags remembered his teacher saying, "Only an Englishman would do such a thing."

Rags had two choices: a ferry to Stockholm or a shorter ferry ride to Gothenburg and express train to the capital. With security in mind, he opted for the smaller car ferry to the southern tip of Sweden. As they cruised out of the protected harbor, a gale of some force sprang up on the nose of the small steam ship. The waves rose to a dozen feet, plunging the bow under water with each successive roller. The ship rose and yawed, and the screw came out of the water as it bobbed once more. Rags took to the fan tail and clung to the rail, trying to keep his dinner down. A short trip became much longer as the northern waters welcomed him to Sweden. He didn't remember much about the train to Stockholm, sleeping blissfully on the cushioned first-class seats: a reward for surviving the ferry. He was met at the station by the British chargé d'affaires, who questioned him in the car as they crossed the city. The Foreign Office had not notified the British embassy of his visit until a few hours before. Rags fended off the questions, concentrating on the mission.

It was a beautiful city in the chilly morning sun. The car lurched from side to side as it skipped over the shiny tram track that ran down the center of the main street. The azure blue trams crept up to the back bumper and rang bells in an effort to push the diplomatic car out of the way, but they were ignored by the driver. There was a charm to this northern city that surprised Rags. He expected to see drab stone piles, block after block. But there were masonry buildings scrubbed with autumn colors and hung with large long reflecting windows to cheer him up. Waterways were everywhere connecting small lakes with canals to the fourteen islands that made up the city. The islands were roped together with short, thick iron bridges. Miniature ferries, stuffed with anxious riders on their way to work, ringed the rails. The continuous shorelines were fat with autumn-colored leaves, hiding houses of pale green to brown mustard and pale yellow. The sunlit spits of dark wet sand that jutted out into the streams were dyed a light ochre. They passed the city hall, a deep red brick building constructed at the turn of the century that hosted the Nobel Prize ceremony each year in December. The architecture of the central city stood out, with its block buildings of five to seven stories, evoking the feel of Paris. Many had ornamented corroded copper or black iron roofs over Palladian or baroque molded windows. The whole city had a charm that drew the eye to each structure as if painted on a canvas drawn in colorful broad-brush strokes dabbed with earth tones. Thoroughly enchanted, Rags left the city center and climbed up to the diplomatic quarter, which looked down on the archipelago that fed salt water from the sea.

His guide pointed out the German embassy on Skerpog Street and mentioned that there had been a great deal of activity within the last week. It was a stern, dark red brick mansion with green-coppered French gables and a neoclassical arched front that took its look from the Romans. Rags thought he was being baited for a hint to the reason for his mission but ignored the ploy. Turning onto Ostermain, the heart of the Embassy Quarter, they stopped at the British embassy wedged in between those of the United States and China. The German legation was larger than any other, demonstrating its significance to the Swedish nation at this moment.

Rags' private audience with King Gustaf was delayed for a day, which gave him a chance to visit the city sights. He took a tram into the commercial city and across to Riddarholm Church, whose black-spiked spire caught his eye—very striking. Built as a monastery by monks determined to convert the thirteenth-century Swedes, it was splashed with Palladian ornamentation attached to the undercoating of pink and white stone blocks.

With an English brochure in hand, he walked the cool passageways to view the statuary and carved grave images. Soon a fellow tourist with pamphlet in hand approached him. Rags heard the quiet question: "Aren't they just like the ones we saw in Rome so many years ago?"

Rags had been surprised once, but not this time. He turned to see not a man in priest's garb but a figure in a smart suit, neat and well kept.

"Hello, Father," he replied in English.

IT HAD BEEN MORE THAN twenty years since they last met on the ramparts of Castel Sant'Angelo, yet Christian's voice had not changed from when Rags was a boy in Freiburg. Yes, the blond hair was now grey but still thick, combed straight back in a pompadour. Tall as Rags and straight as a Prussian soldier, he smiled and put his hands on his son's shoulders. "Rolly, more and more you resemble your lovely mother. How is she these many years later?"

He didn't apologize. Rags held his temper over this sudden and inappropriate approach. His father had abandoned them after compromising their future, like unneeded servants. "She is alone," he responded. Reflexively, Rags reached his right hand under the flap of his left breast and gripped the square handle of his automatic pistol.

His father put his hand on his son's right elbow. "Now, now, my boy, you'll scare the parishioners. You must understand, the times—they were hard. We were shattered by our government's betrayal. What could I do? I was in the hospital when it all happened, fighting my way back from oblivion. Arranging the retrieval of your mother was simply not possible." Rags didn't believe him; there was never any word of a combat wound. He was convinced that his father was a liar.

"Why are you here, Father?" His voice didn't conceal the anger he held in his heart for the man who had left them at the war's end.

His father stepped back and looked around for prying eyes. "I'm here with a legation from the German General Staff to negotiate an unrestricted supply of iron and timber. We must have it and there is no other place to go. Without it, Germany can't take its rightful place among nations and will become the sick old man of Europe." He paused and then looked Rags directly in the eyes with a firm intensity. "I must appeal to your sense of love for your native country once again. You have been a good and loyal servant to the King, who is a great friend to Germany. You are his messenger, and I hope much more. It was no accident that you were chosen to bring his messages to the Fuhrer. He values your service both now and in the last conflict and would like you to accept his commission once again."

Rags' fists gripped tighter, and Christian saw the fury in his face but was not worried. He smiled indulgently: "I know this is a shock, but we need you at the center of power once again. I'm not going to ask you for your decision here and now. But I wish you to remember, MI6 has not closed the file on spies from the last war. If it were to become known to MI6 that you—and, more importantly, your dear mother—worked for the German government and sent many messages, which, may I say, still exist, you would be shot, the both of you. Mr. Booker will be waiting for your answer on Putney Bridge." With that, he wheeled around, without a goodbye, and strolled down the aisle, reading his pamphlet on the venerable old churches of old Stockholm.

ON THE TENTH OF DECEMBER the nation was stunned by the abdication of Edward VIII. In October Mrs. Simpson had received a divorce from the Ipswich crown court which would become final in spring. She would be free to marry, and Edward intended to do so. By the next morning, December 11, his brother Albert was king, to be known as King George VI.

The feeling in the palace was one of shock and relief. The courtiers and the staff embraced the new king and queen. Those who were close to Edward were no longer in favor, and Major Stetchworth found himself put out in the cold. Feeling too old at age thirty-eight to return to the Changing of the Guard, he went once more to old friends for a billet. Uncle Hilly had lunch with him in the room above the Clarence Pub with Smith-Cumming and Segar, but MI6 needed men who were not as public as Rags, who was well known as one of the former king's retinue. They suggested he apply to the Army General Staff, which was gearing up for another Continental war. Hilly said he would be meeting with Churchill soon and would see if, since the old man knew Rags from a favorable time and was himself a champion for the former king, he might be interested in a staff officer with Rags' background.

And so it was that in early 1937 he joined the General Staff as a minor flunky in the process of putting together a staff cell in a Whitehall basement to do a feasibility study on how to command the armed forces in the light of modern communications. It was going to be a joint effort on behalf of all the forces, which envisioned a single point of information enabling the government to understand the daily situation and be able to react in a timely fashion. Rags felt fortunate to find employment after his close relationship with the disgraced Edward. And he felt grateful to be out of the spotlight, more of an office nobody than an elite King's Messenger. The anonymity would help disguise the fact that he and his mother, for the second time in his short life—though this time with anger and fear—had become German spies.

## Chapter Thirty-Six

# Europe, 1937–1940

ON THE TWELFTH OF MAY 1937, Great Britain and her empire celebrated the coronation of King George VI. His estranged elder brother exiled himself at Baron Rothschild's Schloss Enzesfeld in Austria. In June, Mrs. Simpson, upon her divorce, changed her name back to Wallis Warfield. She married His Royal Highness, the Duke of Windsor, the former king, at a ceremony that took place at Chateau de Candé in France. No member of the extended Windsor family attended. The newlyweds cavorted about Germany to the delight of the international press. In Germany, the couple were met by marching bands and cheering crowds, while the duke reputedly exchanged Nazi salutes with his hosts. In October of 1937, Hitler invited the couple to the Berghof at Berchtesgaden, confirming the impression that the Windsors had strong interests with the Nazi party and its goals. Hitler remarked that Mrs. Simpson "would have made a good Queen," which sealed her fate—the Crown refused to grant the duchess the title "Her Royal Highness," which enraged the Duke of Windsor.

After a short time on the Continent, the Windsors planned to return to England and reside at Fort Belvedere, the house that had been given to the Duke by his father, George V, years before. There the Duke planned to help the new king with his unsolicited counsel. The royal family would have none of it and took back Fort Belvedere and denied his return, granting him a considerable income sufficient to live abroad for the remainder of his life. Soon the Duke of Windsor learned that he had misread the mood of the British people as well, believing that it was only the Archbishop of Canterbury, the government, and the newspapers who were opposed to his marriage. While everyone enjoys a good love story, a king was not entitled to impose his selfish desires over duties to empire. He was not an ordinary citizen but one who had enjoyed the privilege of royalty and therefore was expected to do his duty. He was no longer accepted across the British Empire. His subjects had moved on; the king is dead, long live the king.

Europe had not stood still while Great Britain settled a family squabble. The vicious civil war in Spain between the Nationalists, with military support from Nazi Germany and Italy, and the Republicans, who received reluctant support from the Soviet Union, was raging. A movement of English volunteers with socialist aspirations rose up and went to Spain on their own hook. Some 40,000 served the Republican side in the International Brigade made up of foreign amateur soldiers. The pocket war turned into a testing ground for Germany's latest tank and aircraft models accompanied by a considerable number of regular Nazi soldiers. The war raged before a stalemate set in by mid-1938 with the Republicans holding onto the north by their fingernails and the Nationalists consolidating the middle and south of Spain under Francisco Franco.

While many in the English socialist movement were intent on making a stand in Spain, there were others just as militant who judged that fascism was the path to the future for the working man in England. In East London, in particular, fascism found a home in an element of the working and lower middle classes. The British Union of Fascists (BUF) was founded and led by a charismatic demagogue, Sir Oswald Mosley, the 6th Baronet of Ancoats. As a Member of Parliament and vocal veteran of the Great War, Mosley surrounded himself with black-shirted followers and stirred up British politics. The affiliation with Hitler's stormtroopers was obvious, as was his rhetoric, which blamed Europe's ills on the plotting of international Jewry. The movement gained prominence in October 1936 when socialists pushed back a BUF march at Cable Street in East London. The newspaper reported the shouts of "they shall not pass," which became a socialist rallying cry. The contests continued in the streets until the Public Order Act of 1937 banned political uniforms and quasi-military-style organizations. The BUF changed tactics and offered candidates for Parliament from then on, and they gained a number of seats from the London area. Mosley renewed his earlier campaign and enjoyed success in many quarters, pressing the theme that the Jews were at the bottom of all troubles in international relations.

In Berlin, members of the intellectual community remained neutral, since opposing Hitler led to a sticky end. In 1938 the mayor of Leipzig resigned when the statue of Mendelssohn, a Jewish composer, was removed by fascists. England was flooded with high-ranking professionals, as well as wealthy and educated Jewish families. A passageway was set up for Jewish children to flee to England, though their parents remained in Germany. Sixty thousand volumes of the famous Warburg Library were moved from Hamburg to England for fear of them being burned by the Nazis. English universities looted the faculties of German colleges, offering sanctuary to mathematicians and scientists. Of the 75,000 Jewish refugees from Germany, 55,000 chose England. When Germany annexed Austria in the spring of 1938, it became clear to the British that not only were the Germans badly led but they were inherently bad people. As a result, the vast majority of the nation believed that Germany was beyond redemption, leaving no chance to reconcile.

The Chamberlain government had not reached that conclusion. It continued to search for a peaceful solution and, in that spirit, signed the Munich Agreement, along with Italy, France, and the United States—most of the European powers, in fact, with the exception of the Soviet Union—in September of 1938. The agreement allowed Germany to annex a portion of Czechoslovakia, which it then designated Sudentenland. With the peaceful *Anschluss* of Austria earlier in the year, Germany had now annexed two important territories with the blessing of Britain. The Nazis were becoming confident in their designs. But Chamberlain pronounced that the agreement would bring "peace in our time."

RAGS WATCHED WITH DESPAIR THE success of Hitler's experimental blitzkrieg in Spain. The only beneficiary of the civil war was the successful battlefield test of Hitler's new war machines as they outstripped the pitiful Republicans, who fought like soldiers from a bygone era with obsolete tactics. If Germany brought those weapons and blitzkrieg to the rest of Europe, the result would be the same; Great Britain and the other nations were unprepared. In view of the fast-moving action on the Continent, Rags applauded his decision to get away from the British Army, which was beginning to prepare and expand at an electrifying rate.

Due to his inexperience, his new duties in public works were light but interesting. The government debated using the vast complex of the Underground network as bomb shelters but were hesitant to interfere with London transport, which brought thousands of workers to their jobs every day. The government insisted that above-ground facilities would do. First they dug trenches in the London parks, but within days the trenches filled with water. The solution was to build hundreds of above-ground brick shelters. These oblong windowless one-story buildings less than 100 feet long were meant to accommodate a few hundred people in very close quarters. There was no plan for electricity, water, or plumbing in the bomb shelters. The government, still fighting the last war in their heads, expected that the attacks would be of short duration since German aircraft would be near fuel exhaustion by the time they reached London and unable to linger. The shelters were erected on waste ground and park land. The government departments would be expected to remain in operation day and night no matter the conditions, and so were dug in deep under existing structures on either side of Whitehall.

While Rags changed roles from soldier to civil works, Grace was nursing at the Royal Hospital and reviewing reports from Spain. Grace, at her post in the psychiatric ward of the Putney hospital, carefully read the accounts from the International Brigade volunteer medical team about trauma in modern warfare. She recognized the threat that air attacks would bring to the civilian population of London. As before, there would be no mercy for civilians, once again considered legitimate targets by the Germans. She recalled the frightening experience of the night she and Rags met in the middle of a zeppelin raid in 1915. But the accounts from Spain were much more harrowing because of massive formations of German war planes. While the zeppelins dropped sixty high-explosive bombs and twice that number of incendiary devices, accounts from Spain were exponentially larger and more destructive. These were high-speed attacks which bombed as well as strafed with machine gun bullets from low-flying, fast aircraft. The German dive bombers were equipped with sirens that howled during their low-level attacks, frightening those nearby. Grace could see that Spain was merely a rehearsal for what the Germans had in store for England. It wouldn't be just soldiers who were traumatized but women and children who would fill the neurological wards where she toiled. In the evening after dinner she questioned Rags about the newspaper reports, but he could offer little comfort regarding her well-founded projections.

On a chilled spring evening, when Grace retired early, Rags remained up to have a nightcap with his mother. The two were tense as they gazed into the leaping orange flames of the fireplace coals. Twenty years had passed since they had enthusiastically offered to spy for Germany, but this time was entirely different. They were edgy, dismayed at the compulsion that had led them to this most unwelcome renewal of relations with Christian. The Bookers were no longer the sad little shopkeepers that Charlotte had sniffed at but their watchers, enemies who spied on the spies. Likewise, she and her son were no longer co-conspirators but something more like fellow inmates, trapped and played like puppets. And all for the gauche, clownish Hitler, a failed Austrian art student—so unlike the aristocratic Kaiser, Queen Victoria's grandson. The two sat in strained silence, and Charlotte held her glass tumbler so tightly it might break.

"Do you have anything to transmit tonight, Rolly?" Charlotte asked with her usual weariness. "The Bookers will be looking for something."

His new position at the General Staff provided him with some protection from excessive demands, but Rags knew that he had to produce some intelligence to keep his father from betraying them. Painfully aware that he was expected to contribute to his body of purloined sensitive statistics, Rags began to send Christian the figures of the American army build-up. Their cantonments in Scotland and the Northern Midlands were set up at the very edge of German bomber range stationed in Norway. He also confirmed rumors from German spies in the Republic of Ireland that American flying fortresses were in rehab in northern Ulster after the long trip across the Atlantic.

It was a sleepless night for them both. In the morning, they looked knowingly across the breakfast table while Grace twittered on about the boys' school play and her friends at the hospital. Charlotte, not wanting to seem strange, reviewed the instructions for the staff and who would be home for dinner. She suggested something light since the boys were at school on weekdays. When Rolly and Grace had gone to work, she secreted herself in the library, telling the staff that she was not to be disturbed, as she had letters to write to the family. She could see that rationing was in the offing if war broke out and wanted the relatives up north to send preserved vegetables and hampers of other goods to London to support their comings and goings in that event. Was it going to be as bad as the last war, or worse, she wondered.

She also wanted the privacy to clean out the cabinet stuffed with years of messages and other objects that implicated them in treason. For some time she had been planning this day. She reached behind her neck with some difficulty and undid the tight chain clasp that held the ornate cross of silver and black enamel from around her neck. The metal was warm from lying under her blouse on her breast. She turned the cross in her firm grasp so the cross bar was in her palm and the bottom free to slide into a crack that was hardly discernable. The lock resisted; then the hidden spring released its tensions. It had held its secrets for twenty years and was reluctant to move, still protecting the family secret. There was a click, and the panel sprang open. There was a series of shelves a foot deep, most of which were stuffed with loose paper. Charlotte retrieved an empty wastebin and then dragged a set of library steps in place. She climbed up to start from the top. There was a great deal more then she had imagined. A clearout was not as simple as she thought. She could easily fill that container and several more. It occurred to her, there up on the third step, that she could not empty it out without the help of the staff. Burning it in the fireplace would cause far too much ash. The draw of the stack would take some of the unburned fragments up and out in the air currents. It would spread them all over London. They would have to be cut up with scissors into unreadable fragments. Even so, many would remain in the fireplace unburned and the servants would see them when they cleaned the grate. No, no, she thought. This would not do, yet it had to be emptied out for no other reason than there would be a need for more space in the campaign to come. What was she to do?

Climbing down, she locked the cabinet and returned the room to its original condition. She stood there defeated and said in a whisper, "My God, what are we to do?"

ON SEPTEMBER 3, 1939, THE RESIDENTS of the mansion north of Putney Bridge tuned in to the wireless, as all the rest of Britain—and indeed nearly all the world—did. Soon they heard Neville Chamberlain's voice, weary and disappointed, announcing that Britain had declared war on Germany. Hitler's invasion of Poland two days before, he said, "shows convincingly that there is no chance of expecting that this man will ever give up his practice of using force to gain his will. He can only be stopped by force, and we and France are today, in fulfillment of our obligations, going to the aid of Poland, who is so bravely resisting this wicked and unprovoked attack upon her people. We have a clear conscience. We have done all that any country could do to establish peace. The situation in which no word given by Germany's ruler could be trusted and no people or country could feel itself safe has become intolerable."

The Soviet Union's pact with Germany in August had been observed with anguish by France and Britain. The Soviets pledged to support Germany's invasion of Poland from the west in exchange for rights to invade from the east. Within a month of the invasion, Poland was no more, Germany was relieved of the prospect of a two-front war, and Britain began sending troops to France for support.

In the British civilian sector, the population watched over their shoulders at Hitler's machinations and looked to the government to protect them. Bomb shelters and plenty of them were demanded, and Rags found himself in the thick of it as he performed field site surveys. Many of London's eight million citizens sought protection below ground, but the government continued its plans for above-ground shelters, reminding them that only 670 Londoners had been killed in the zeppelin attacks of the Great War. Rags, however, knew better. He had attended secret briefings that wove a much darker picture. The modern aircraft of the Luftwaffe had ten times the firepower of an airship. It became obvious from the start that municipal accommodation for the masses could not be built and the majority would have to shelter at their residence.

Chamberlain had urged the British people, "Now that we have resolved to finish it, I know that you will all play your part with calmness and courage." It started with the distribution of the Anderson backyard shelters—developed by John Anderson, who had been placed in charge of air raid preparations. They were issued in sections of semi-circular corrugated metal hoops to be dug into the soil at a depth of four feet while the soil was to be packed on top for overhead stand-off. Large enough to protect a family of six, they were damp, smelly and cold sanctuaries for families, pets and all kinds of creepy-crawlies. Starting in February 1939, they were given for free to families that earned less than 250 pounds a month and for a small charge to others, and by the time of Chamberlain's declaration, more than a million of the shelters had been erected in British backyards. The citizens dusted off their old blackout curtains, filled buckets with sand, and stocked up on everything from preserved food to silk stockings. They had been told once before that if there was to be war, it could not last because none of the European economies could afford the cost. While the British had been served a "load of cobblers" in 1914, they weren't about to buy it again.

For months after the September 3 declaration, the two sides were cautious. It seemed that Hitler was not ready for war in the west after the Polish campaign and stood down that winter and spring of 1940. Strangely, France simply watched the German formations from the safety of the Maginot Line. When a reporter asked a French soldier in Strasburg why he didn't shoot, he replied, "He's not bothering me, why should I bother him?" The British Expeditionary Force, cozy and idle on the Belgian border, "carefully observed" the nearby German activity. It was only in late spring, when it was observed that the Germans were carefully preparing an airdrome as a decoy in Holland, that things came to life. The airfield was constructed with painstaking care of nothing but wood. There were hangers, fuel tanks, gun pits with wooden anti-aircraft cannons, lorries, barracks, mess halls and fake Junker aircraft. The RAF recon flights watched patiently until the airfield was completed. The next morning a lone British bomber crossed the Channel as the sun rose, buzzed the fake field at low level, and dropped a single, large wooden bomb.

Shortly after, the bombs went from wooden to real. In May 1940, the Germans attacked France, Belgium, and the Netherlands, just as they had done in 1914. Initially the plan appeared to be a true copy. They engaged the combined British and French forces, who were aligned as before. But instead of concentrating the main attack in Belgium, a primary portion of Hitler's combined force struck through the Ardennes forest, routing first the French and then the British. Within six weeks his panzers were crushing the BEF against the Channel at Dunkirk. The troops abandoned their equipment on the beaches. A herculean effort was initiated by the Royal Navy, augmented by small civilian watercraft, to evacuate the troops across the Channel to Dover while the Royal Air Force flew cover. The trains brought 225,000 survivors to London and dispersed them to their regimental depots for recovery and refit. Only one unequipped British Army division was left intact to defend the island nation, and it borrowed the tanks and guns from a newly arrived New Zealand division. England stood alone on the west side of the English Channel. The Royal Navy and Air Force took up the action.

By July things were heating up in London while the southern coast was taking a pasting from the first wave of German bombers. Rags became involved in several underground projects meant to secure the new Prime Minister Churchill's War Cabinet. Three underground stations were scouted, and Downs Street, near Green Park, was selected along with a very ambitious project to dig in a three-story office-style building outside central Westminster to be called the Paddock. Rags became the project officer for the office of public works. The Paddock cost a fortune but was too far from Whitehall to be used. Churchill attempted to operate from it but abandoned the idea after just two meetings. Brigadier Leslie Chasemore Hollis altered shelter plans and began a reconstruction of the basements between the Treasury and Foreign Offices just yards from the prime minister's number 10 Downing Street residence. It needed to contain not only office space for the Cabinet but sleeping quarters and mess for the staff, which was growing at an alarming rate. The danger of high-explosive, incendiary and poison gas attacks complicated construction design.

Churchill was aware that the first and most critical element of the German Luftwaffe attack on England would be to knock out the RAF, allowing for a naval crossing of the English Channel while bombing the civilian population into capitulation. Churchill couldn't risk the elimination of the British government in such an onslaught. In the summer of 1940, Rags watched as the yard between the two-government buildings was overburdened with concrete and steel reinforcement to protect a two-story complex of rooms below. They would be the Cabinet War Rooms, or CWR. Rags had a hand in the design of the spaces to accommodate the military and civilian working staff, which were expected to operate twenty-four hours a day, including a considerable number of resident officers and secretaries.

He knew that it was essential that the War Rooms have access to two-way communications to the rest of the world. A tunnel was constructed up Whitehall to Trafalgar Square, where it intersected with commercial cables. From there it crossed the river to Waterloo Station and then east to the Faraday Building and the 40,000-line undersea cable head buried a hundred feet down. Rags became the briefing officer on all things concerned with the project, drawing him back into the military establishment. Slowly he became recognized as the liaison between the potential customers and the public works establishment, able to speak both languages. He was increasingly uncomfortable with the work, fearing that he was going to be drawn back into vital military circles—just what his father was hoping.

In August, he was called to the office of Brigadier Hollis, his superior at the General Staff. The stocky Royal Marine congratulated himself: "My judgment was correct—remember that first day we met in your father-in-law's office at the old palace?" The brigadier was in a jovial mood and had his happy face on. Rags had not seen that face in months and wondered what he had up his sleeve. It usually heralded the unveiling of a steaming hot potato. Like the day when he told his errand-boy to alter the plans for the Paddock because they forgot to install toilets.

"I knew you were a *good'n* the moment I laid eyes on you. Were you aware that I had a visit the following day from old Captain Smith-Cumming, who said what a good job you'd done for Hilly? He thought I should take you on. Well, even if I had second thoughts, which I didn't, that turned it. That kind of endorsement rarely comes my way, Rags." He paused, taking his time to light a cigar, failing to offer one to his protege.

"But I'm sorry to say that I'm losing you now. You have been seconded by Churchill himself, according to your uncle. He liked those briefings you gave, can't imagine why." Laugh lines wrinkled the corners of his blue eyes. "They need you back in the army—been told to let you go. I suppose they require a loony with your background to run the place on a daily basis. I made the bastards pay, though. I told them it was no job for a mere major, and they agreed."

Hollis handed Rags a commission as a lieutenant colonel accompanied by a set of orders assigning him as the Cabinet War Rooms adjutant. Rags stared, shocked and speechless, and stepped forward to take the parchment. It was the last thing he had expected. Churchill, promotion . . . what had just happened? He was mute.

Hollis could see Rags' surprise and was pleased with himself for pulling it off so well. It was a good story to tell at the mess that night. "Well, Colonel, what do you have to say for yourself?"

Rags had never thought of himself as a colonel. Colonels were old men, self-assured, crotchety, blockheads, always in the way with unsolicited advice. Now he was one. My God. He wanted to salute the man he admired so much, but Hollis grabbed his right hand and shook it very hard. "A word of advice, Colonel. Play up, play up and don't let the side down."

Rags wasn't concerned about becoming the CWR adjutant; he could handle that. But this new position would raise the expectations of his father in Germany, and the newly minted colonel was alarmed that he was to be propelled into the very center of the war operation, where he could do irrefutable harm.

Rags bowed his head, a little ashamed that, unlike his fellow guardsmen, he had skirted combat in the Great War and was going to accept a position that must be the safest billet in the new war. "I must say, sir—" He paused as the words stuck in his throat. "I'm grateful for the trust you have placed in me. It's been an honor to serve under you these past months. We've been doing God's work to protect the innocent subjects of the King; there is no higher calling in my mind. I hope I deserve your faithful support." Inside he wanted to confess that he indeed did not deserve the faith Hollis placed in him. If only he could yell out loud, "I've been a poxy spy, leave me where I am, where I can do no more harm." But instead he gave a smart salute and exited. He had to pretend it was a blessing when it was actually a burden that he had planned so carefully to avoid. He asked himself, "Why can't I make this nightmare end?"

He didn't run to his tailors, as he had after every other promotion; that could wait until morning. He cleared out the remnants of his desk to be transferred to his new office in the Cabinet War Rooms, which had just become operational that month. On the way home that evening he examined the Tube station structure at Westminster situated safely under a block of office buildings. It was a habit he had developed over the past two years. On the train to Putney Bridge he couldn't help recalling that terrifying evening when he met Grace on the same line and the horror of those hours above ground dodging bombs. He reminded himself as he de-trained, exited the ticket hall, and passed through the arch that times had moved on but not changed. The war would be brutal. The sun was still bright in the summer sky even though it was well past happy hour, but the humidity oozed up over the riverbank. He paused at the gate and braced himself for the ordeal to come. To the unwitting Grace, the promotion would seem a blessing, and he would have to play the part, all the while exchanging glances of the greatest dismay with his mother.

The only one not concerned with family matters was Hunter the terrier, who greeted him inside the entryway with his usual demand for a good scratch and a well-placed kiss on the top of his fury noggin. When Rags had lost Valerie and Teddy to age and cancer, he had found the loss of their warmth and enthusiasm unbearable, and the family was startled when he came home with Hunter a mere two weeks later. Now when he entered the library his wife and mother were listening to Lord Haw-Haw speaking on the wireless in his posh trader's voice. "You know, you're all done for. Your army is disarmed by our unstoppable panzers, and your navy is floundering, unable to slow the glorious submarine fleet from cutting your throats in the wide Atlantic. Your Royal Air Force has been nobbled. Soon you will be turning to eating your pets. Now let us make a little sense of your predicament. Give it up. Tell those ninnies in Whitehall to sign a peace treaty. What do you care of Eastern Europe, they don't even speak English out there."

Rags took wide strides across the room and snapped it off. "I have news, my dears." He put on a pleasant smile for their benefit. "Today I got a double surprise. You are looking at Lieutenant Colonel Stetchworth, adjutant of the Cabinet War Rooms at the request of the prime minister."

Grace jumped out of her chair and rushed him. She squealed with delight, happy to see him back in the army where he belonged. "Does that mean that you won't be deploying with the regiment?" she said with hope in her voice.

Rags assured them both, "Yes, my dears, I'll be a slacker once again; that is indeed the case. I'm out of the war, just a mole in the ground, blind, deaf and dumb, my favorite state."

Grace danced to the drinks tray and poured out a sherry to toast the new colonel. "Oh, Rags, of course you're not a slacker. Serving in the War Rooms is a high honor. You'll be protecting your country at the highest levels. I'm very proud of you, my dear." The new colonel was surprised to realize it was the first time she had called him anything but Rolly in many years.

# Chapter Thirty-Seven

# London, 1940–1941

AT THE BEGINNING OF SEPTEMBER, Reichsmarshal Herman Goring, who had promised the Fuhrer a quick victory, had changed tactics. His new approach: bombing the daylights out of the city and docks of London. As in the Great War, the Germans combined high explosives with incendiaries. While the British had prepared for poison gas, it didn't come. It seemed that all sides of the Great War had learned at least one thing: gas could be disruptive to both friend and foe.

The earliest reports to the CWR were hysterical. Rags posted them on a bulletin board in the hallway of the dormitory on the lower floor: "German paratroopers have been reported in Cricklewood dressed as nuns." As the adjutant, Lieutenant Colonel Stetchworth was the next best thing to a commander of the sprawling staff, which consisted of over-the-hill field grade officers and young female stenographers and typists. The combination was awkward and a challenge to schedule. Fortunately, the workload was frenetic, leaving little time or opportunity for disreputable behavior. He set up teams on eight-hour shifts that rotated every four days. Theoretically, between shift changes a day off was included. In wartime, it would become a generous and necessary break. However, as the bombing of the city commenced on September 7, it was difficult to honor the schedule. The prime minister in particular had his favorites who were always on call for the great man, who rarely got a night's uninterrupted sleep himself. Rags found a bed in a corner of a utility room where he kipped, only going home for a few hours at a time to bathe and change uniforms.

The Cabinet War Rooms would likely never be seen by anyone outside a small elite group of civil servants and select military members of the services. A small, grey metal door, tucked into the side of the broad granite steps leading to the space between the two massive state buildings, was the only outside entrance into the CWR. Neatly stacked tan sandbags, like giant bricks, protected the outer entryway. The guard was inside, out of view of the public. A royal military police officer inspected passes as well as incoming and outgoing packages, crates, and cases. A long concrete staircase descended down twenty feet to a short damp corridor which led to the War Cabinet Room, where the members met. Further on, around two ninety-degree corners along a rather narrow fifty-yard passageway, was a jumble of chambers on either side.

There, on the immediate right, were three twenty-foot square interconnected rooms. They were the heart of the operations. The walls were covered floor-to-ten-foot-ceiling with sepia-colored paper maps illustrating every area, land and sea, concerned with the war. In the center of each room were wide rectangular tables with twelve-inch wooden shelves down the center that held a bank of colored Bakelite telephones. Most were direct lines and were marked as such with notes tacked underneath. The pale green phone conversations were protected by a Sigsaly Scrambler, an encoded telephone system whose base was installed in the basement of Selfridge's department store. Eight-inch-thick, pale yellow painted upright timbers were ten feet apart, fashioned at the top to overhead wooden beams. On each, a curious device was tacked on at five feet from the floor: a four-inch white ceramic square with four open wires coming from the corners that were coiled like small springs. The pattern left an open space the size of a penny in the center. It was an open electrical circuit that produced a considerable shock if touched. But if a smoker, with a cigarette protruding from his mouth, leaned forward to touch it, the end became lit. No open flames were permitted in the CWR.

Several small desks were dotted about and a cot was up against an inner wall. Paper, in all sizes and colors, abounded in folders, desks, shelves and on the floors in stacks. Twisted light and telephone cords hung on black strings above comfortable armchairs, the only amenity in the rooms. Bookcases were crammed with volumes of regulations, histories, and records. Small paper boxes containing colored map pins and rolls of string were on the floor near the maps. Wooden stools were scattered about for officers to stand on when posting maps.

Next door to the map room was Churchill's spartan bedroom, which was small and contained a single bed, nightstand, lamp, and small dresser. The back wall was completely covered with a world map. A small table held the BBC broadcast microphones. The floor was carpeted and the room equipped with emergency lighting. Churchill was not fond of remaining underground but did so when air raids were imminent, which in the fall of 1940 seemed continuous. Across the hall was the transatlantic telephone closet where Churchill conversed with Franklin Delano Roosevelt. The remainder of a dozen small chambers down the hallway were known as the courtyard rooms and used by senior officials for sleeping and meeting areas. Toilet facilities throughout were chemical and gave off an acrid scent, which, when combined with clouds of cigarette and cigar smoke, was the cause of numerous respiratory complaints. The aroma of Churchill's minuscule kitchen, ruled over by Mrs. Landemare and her granddaughter—sequestered for the duration—could be noxious. They were limited to two small electric stoves for cooking the exotic dishes the prime minister preferred. The constant droning hum of the air-handling system assaulted the eardrums day and night. The staff, supervised by Rags, were relegated to a lower level when resting. Its only access was a single narrow metal ship staircase—more of a ladder, really—guarded by a Royal Marine. Below in the damp, row upon row of metal bunkbeds stood cheek by jowl. The toilets and washing facilities were on the floor above, which required the women to walk in their night attire past the guard when necessity called.

While every effort had been made to blow fresh air through both floors, the crush of narrow hallways confined a great deal of body heat during the day shift and a cool damp atmosphere thereafter. The working end of the complex was close to the outer door, where the environment was pleasant. The conference chamber was dominated by a large U-shaped table with just enough space to accommodate wooden armchairs. The walls were covered with beige paper maps, floor to ceiling, that represented that portion of the earth's surface inflamed by the war on land and sea. At the head of the table was a sturdy wooden captain's chair for Churchill. There was just enough space in the corner for a briefer to illuminate the markings on the maps, which were in constant flux. A glass-panel side door allowed briefers to switch with little interruption. Stenographers were seated on wooden folding chairs that creaked and squawked as they sat through interminable discussions of the utmost critical topics. There were few discussions that weren't most secret. Rags stood by just outside in the hallway, where he could hear current discussion yet be aware of the next item on the agenda. It was unfortunately the perfect place for an enemy spy.

BY THE 15th OF SEPTEMBER, the Luftwaffe threw everything they had at the city, expecting Londoners to crumble and sue for peace. Hitler believed he could break the citizens, who would surely demand an end to the war.

Churchill would have none of it. Churchill's words of June 4, after the unexpected triumph at Dunkirk, echoed across the nation: "We shall go on to the end. We shall fight in France, we shall fight on the seas and oceans, we shall fight with growing confidence and growing strength in the air, we shall defend our Island, whatever the cost may be. We shall fight on the beaches, we shall fight on the landing grounds, we shall fight in the fields and in the streets, we shall fight in the hills; we shall never surrender!" The mood of defiance was everywhere. One night an audience was trapped in the Troxy cinema when bombs began to fall. The manager led the patrons in a sing-along of "There'll Always Be an England"—despite one heckler yelling "I'm not so sure of that!"—and the audience sang and laughed and made merry until midnight.

Churchill himself, never content to stay put for long, would abandon the CWR regularly in the evenings to climb up to the roof of the Treasury Build-ing to witness the bombing raids. Exposed to enemy fire, he was not alone. Londoners adapted to the new reality. When the bombs fell, some sheltered in terrace house entryways, full of hot, sulfurous air. Some took cover in their backyard Anderson shelters of corrugated steel. Others had the newer Mor-rison shelter, a type of low cage with a reinforced top meant to be installed in living rooms. Larger air raid shelters were available to some communities, but the Underground was available to nearly all, which made it a popular refuge. The government strenuously opposed the use of the Underground as a shelter, but it was no match for the Londoners who pushed their way in.

Rags found himself to be one of those pushy Londoners several weeks after the bombings began. Walking home to his townhouse at Sussex Gardens in the blacked-out city, he heard the drone of German bombers just before the warning warble to take cover. At Hyde Park corner he looked up at the black sky striped with the bright white shafts from searchlights, knowing that the anti-aircraft guns were about to rattle. In the park, London's big guns lit off a cacophonous crash while German bombs screamed home. Out on the unpro-tected streets, thunderclaps brought down whirling molten fragments that peppered the walls and shattered storefront glass windows. With his fellow pedestrians, Rags ran past a small neighborhood church that exploded just short of the Lancaster Gate Tube station. Brushing off the guards who tried to keep order, he joined the scramble down the circular staircase that surrounded the elevator shaft for the safety of the underground platform.

Rags bundled his coat beneath him and leaned against one of the tiled walls, ready to wait it out. He could see that it was going to be an all-nighter, and the station soon filled to capacity. The two large elevator cars were stopped and stuffed with assorted bodies lying uncomfortably on bedding brought from home. They appeared like the "crooked little people" of the nursery rhyme. Newcomers searched past pallid faces for a vacant bit of floor, putting hand-kerchief to nose to fend off the smell of warm bodies, sick children, and open buckets serving duty as toilets. An older man with a yellow smile teased, "No one ever died of a bad smell, guv'nor. It's all right—the last train gone by; you're safe 'til six in the morning." Rags was grateful to find it to be so.

The next night he related his tale to Charlotte and Grace at the Fulham house. "God help and preserve us," whispered Grace. Rags squeezed her hand. "No need for you to concern yourself with me, my dear, down there in the mole hole; but what of you sequestered in the wards filled with war neuroses victims? Putney Bridge may be a target, and I am sure the Germans will not give the hospital a miss." He turned to his mother, who was pouting. "And you, Mamma, must have the servants prepare a safe spot in the cellar with all the comforts you need. Hunter will provide the entertainment, I am sure." Charlotte refused to have one of the common Anderson shelters outside the house, much less the cage-like Morrison shelter that required users to crawl on the floor to take cover inside.

Rags was concerned for the Bookers as well. Their home was only yards from the rail bridge, which was surely marked on the enemy target map. That evening Rags penned a cautionary note to be transmitted to his father to the effect that special care should be taken to ensure that Putney Bridge be exempt. It wouldn't take much to disrupt the delicate antenna they depended upon if the bridge structure was compromised. To repair it in wartime conditions was not possible since a machine gun bunker had been constructed on the station end of the span and Rags had to wear his uniform to take his evening walk with Hunter. The slight curve at the Putney end of the bridge would block the guards from observing the message drop. Booker had become known to them since he passed that way every night after 9:00 p.m. on his obligatory march to the Eight Bells Pub for a few pints with his mates. He never failed to make a courtesy stop and leave a couple of bottles at the top of the steps to warm the guards.

In the morning, Rags took his coffee on the terrace overlooking the Thames and witnessed a most peculiar event. Across the river, on Deodar Road, a pair of barrage balloons were fighting their way into the air. He could see between the houses a number of lorries and a scattering of men attempting to launch the obstinate craft. Sixty feet long and twenty-five feet in diameter, they were expected to drag their tethering cable to an altitude of 5,000 feet, forcing German aircraft to higher altitude in hopes of ruining their aim. It was a struggle and he could hear the shouting and cursing clear across the tidal river. It was no different when he left the Tube station at Westminster, where he encountered another crew struggling with a pugnacious balloon meant for Parliament Square. The light grey sausage skimmed its way toward Westminster Bridge with a good portion of the crew still clinging to the restraining lines. Rags veered back inside the station along with dozens of passengers as the soldiers managed to snag a couple of ropes on the iron fence across the road, ending the drama. It seemed the very air of London had become a battlefield, and Rags, like his fellow countrymen, was happy to escape below ground.

RAGS FOUND SUPERVISION OF SENIOR officers and women at the CWR a daunting task, quite unlike overseeing the disciplined soldiers of the Welsh Guards he loved. While the stenographers tended to work with almost martial efficiency, the officers could be obstinate and argumentative. One in particular, a spit-and-polish major of the Royal Signal Regiment, had become a thorn in Rags' side. Major William Ornbee Wittles—as Rags always referred to him in his head—had become obsessed with security and demanded that protocol for classified material be more stringently supervised. Rags' experience with the document library during the Great War did not seem to cut the mustard with Major Wittles, and his constant interference began to worry Rags. He needed clear access to materials he could send to his father, and it was already a very delicate act to cull out useful information that could not be tracked back to him. He didn't need Wittles' prying eyes as well.

Just as Rags had begun to worry seriously about the snooping major, a set of orders for one of his crew crossed his desk. The order specified one soldier in particular, but Horse Guards sent out hundreds of assignments a day and would not notice or care if a staff manager made a comparable substitution. He enlisted a young typist to alter the copy and change the name at the top to Major William Ornbee Wittles, and the next morning he presented Wittles with the good news: He was being assigned to a liaison officer's billet with the American Army Theater Command headquarters, Schofield Barracks, in the tropical paradise of Hawaii. He was to leave immediately. "Well, Wittles, I'm truly sorry to lose such a valuable colleague, but you have landed a plum assignment; we're all envious of your good luck. You must know someone at Horse Guards—good on you, Major." Rags gave him his order with his left hand and returned his salute with the other. Wittles' eyes had gotten as large as charger platters. "You're expected to board at Liverpool within the week, so I'll have to scratch around for a replacement while you are off putting your kit together. God speed, Wittles."

Pleased with the efficient solution to the Wittles problem, Rags walked along the embankment on his way to lunch at the Charing Cross Lyons' Tea Room. A special arrangement had been made for those from CWR to eat no matter the hour. He became entangled with a crew of running soldiers hanging on to restraining ropes of a rogue barrage balloon. It had broken free once again, and a dozen men, who were hanging on for dear life, were being dragged toward the Thames. Passersby jumped into the fray, snatching at snapping lines—a foolish decision. His Majesty had plenty of balloons. Amused, Rags refrained from engaging in the show. The sight of one of His Majesty's colonels being deposited in the river was not going to appear on the front page of the *Evening Standard* if Rags had any say. For this or any other reason.

The loss of busybody Wittles allowed Rags to attempt to satisfy his father with items carefully picked out from filed staff briefings which were under his direct control. At that early stage of the war the Germans were primarily concerned with the positions of Atlantic naval convoys. Rags assured Christian that that information was held at the Admiralty and not briefed in Churchill's war room. One of Christian's other spies in London should be assigned to that field. Rags supplied troop movement schedules as the North African campaign heated up all, assuring his father that that was all he could provide there among the "worms," as the underground staffers called themselves. Churchill, naturally, referred to himself as the "head glowworm."

For fifty-seven continuous days and night the Luftwaffe plastered the defiant Londoners. The noise alone should have sent them to Grace's mental ward with war neuroses, but the prediction of mass mental casualties proved to be wrong. Her prepared psychiatric wards remained vacant. The bombing raids gradually lessened as spring approached, and summer provided some relief to Rag's confined people when Churchill shared his time at the Number 10 annex, the above-ground chambers in the State building.

Throughout 1940 and into 1941, Britain had stood alone, unable to see her way out of the deep dark hole of German aggression. The naval replenishment convoys from America and Canada containing war material and food suffered badly from German submarine wolfpack tactics. Churchill had repeatedly tried to convince Roosevelt to bring America into the war, but for nearly two years Roosevelt had resisted.

It all changed on the morning of December 8, when the hotline from Washington, DC, flashed in the CWR. The Japanese had attacked Pearl Harbor at Hawaii. The British Army liaison contingent in Honolulu confirmed the strike, and soon it was official: America declared war on Japan, Germany, and Italy. America was now one of the Allies.

Rags' jubilation was tempered when, soon after, a casualty report clattered in on the teletype. Among the dead in Hawaii was one Major W. O. Wittles.

# Chapter Thirty-Eight

# London, 1942–1943

THE NEW YEAR SAW THE first glimmer of hope for the British. They were no longer alone. As in the Great War, the Americans' hand had been forced by outside events, but once in, they were all in, bringing the might of the arsenal of democracy with them. Since 1939 the conflict had begun to be referred to as a World War, and the Great War was dubbed World War I to distinguish it. Now American staff officers flooded into London, camped out in hotels to swell the planning staffs to capacity. Norfolk House, St. James Square, a block off Piccadilly in center of the West End, became the focal point for joint efforts.

IN APRIL RAGS WAS AT home in Fulham, ready to catch up on sleep in a quiet house. His sons had graduated and joined the Welsh Guards but were thankfully still in London. Grace was home, spending a few hours that week at the hospital, where she was now only an occasional volunteer. That evening the air raid sirens began just after dark. The Germans had shifted to nighttime raids to cut their losses. Recently the targets swung south of the Thames, obliterating Lambeth and creeping toward Putney. There were few military targets there, and it was plain that they were after the workers and their families, so vital to the manufacture of war material. Rags had warned his father to keep the Putney rail bridge off the target list.

Everyone in London was desperate for uninterrupted sleep as a result of the aerial onslaught. Prepared for an early night, Rags was winding the clock as Grace put her hair up in braids. "Ready, I've got the lights." He moved to the windows that looked over the river and parted the heavy blackout drapes. As he did, the air raid siren wailed. "Oh no," Grace moaned, "not again. I can't go to that cellar once more. Can't we take a chance and give this one a miss, Rolly?" With that a flash of light blasted through the rattling windows.

Rags saw a string of explosions three hundred yards away across the Thames along Deodar Road. Like daisies on a string, they rippled toward Putney High Street. He dropped to the floor, expecting the windows to shatter, but they held their place. The bombs had ripped through the houses, and he could see their silhouetted chimneys against the darken sky. Flames shot up within the red and orange glow that became a boiling mass. On his knees, he peeked over the sill. The rail bridge was not hit. He could see beyond to Saint Mary's crenelated church steeple, clearly visible through the cross-hatched iron work of the bridge.

Not waiting for a second string of bombs on his side of the river, he grabbed at Grace, who was on the floor searching for her slippers. "They've got our range—let's go!" he yelled over the din. They met the other members of the household staff as they descended from the floor above. He entrusted Grace to their care as he ran down the darkened wing to his mother's suite.

She was already at her door. "What's happening? Is anyone hurt?" She was tearing at her robe trying to button it in the dark. Rags grabbed at her hand and pulled her behind him as a second string of bombs shook the house and loosened plaster began to fall. The compression from the bomb blast, pushing and pulling, made them feel that their eyeballs were being sucked out. "My God, that was close," she said. As they reached the top of the cellar stairs, Rags snapped on the stairway light. It was internal to the structure, which didn't show outside. The others had made it down safely in the dark, forgetting in that moment that they could have used the light and seen where they were going. The German bombers passed on up the river, yet no one left the safety of the basement until dawn.

The next morning, Grace and Rags dressed while the kitchen staff, grateful for surviving the night and finding the house shaken but intact, rustled up breakfast. "I was thinking, Rolly . . . I may go down to the Newmarket house today." He nodded distractedly, as this was a more and more common announcement in recent months. Grace flattened her mouth at her husband's inattentiveness and left to pack, while Charlotte read the newspaper and sipped her tea.

Concerned about the Bookers, whose house was adjacent to the far end of the rail bridge, Rags put on his uniform and walked to the metal steps a hundred yards from the Fulham mansion. He gave a wave to the Home Guard sergeant peeking out through the machine-gun slit in the concrete bunker at the south end of the platform. "I see you made it through the night, guv'nor. So'd the bridge, I'm thinken—though the trains are stopped. Trouble down the line, they say. Old Herman's not such a good shot, is the bastard?" He stuck his fat thumb out through the slit and turned it upwards. "Keep your pecker up, Sergeant," the colonel yelled.

Rags kicked bits of debris off into swirls of wreckage floating by in the swift morning tide as he crossed over to the Putney side. On the other end he found the Bookers' house, which abutted the underside of the bridge, intact and assumed his radio operator must have gone to his shop in the High Street to assess the damage. At the bottom of the steps, he was stunned by the smoldering wreckage strewn on the pavement closing off the street. The home of his housekeeper, which had been destroyed in the World War I, was once again flattened, along with her neighbors' all along the south side of the street. Passing under the railway arch, he managed to get a look at the underside of the rail bridge, which was fortunately untouched. The radio link to Germany survived.

A block closer to the High Street he was diverted around Brewers Lane into the back garden of Saint Mary's churchyard. The lane was still on fire and the building had collapsed into piles of stones and timbers. The vicar was tending to an older lady on a bench who was covered in dust and her small hands were bloody. "My daughter was in the Castle Pub last evening for a birthday party with all her friends. They had stayed open late to keep the party go'en. I left for my bed, you know. She's lost in there somewhere, I was trying to clear the rubble but just couldn't do any more," she sobbed. Rags never got to the stamp shop, but stayed at the church moving debris and hoping against hope for signs of life.

THROUGHOUT THE SPRING AND SUMMER a wildly adventuresome plan was being devised by the Combined Operations headquarters, led by Lord Louis Mountbatten. The target was the French Channel port of Dieppe. According to plan, the operation would involve transport and gunfire support by the Royal Navy and a landing force of some 6,000 troops made up primarily of Canadian soldiers. Its primary purpose was not so much to gain ground but to build morale and prove that the German defenses could be breeched. Additionally, Stalin, who had joined France and England after the German invasion of the Soviet Union, required a second front in the west to lessen the intensity of the fighting facing him on the eastern front. Churchill was convinced by Mountbatten that the raid would be a decisive show of force.

Rags was added to the liaison list at Norfolk House's planning group. He was not pleased. Rags had shied away from key assignments, not wanting to be added to the need-to-know list. He was determined to be a bad and ineffectual spy this time around, yet he kept being thrown into the fray in spite of his careful planning to remain on the sidelines. As in the First World War, spies and secrecy were on everyone's mind. Graphic posters abounded on every blank wall reminding folks that "loose lips sink ships." Rags' only solution was to transmit classified information that was of little consequence or those bits that would be overtaken by events before the Germans could react. That way he could build his credibility with his father in Germany with little consequence for Britain.

In a way, his concern was unwarranted. Lord Louis, as Mountbatten was known, had briefed the brass hats and crowned heads—those European heads of state who had sought refuge in London—at the theater on the top floor of Norfolk House. But so many hands had been involved in the planning that it had been leaked in the bars, nightclubs, officers' clubs and to key members of the London newspapers, who promised to keep it secret until the raid was underway. Rags' own driver from the CWR had asked about it, and Rags thought at the time that he dare not have a shoeshine in the Underground station for fear of hearing it from the shoeshine boy.

Weeks later, on a clear and bright morning, 0500 hours on August 19, 1942, Operation Jubilee kicked off. The troops hit the beach at Dieppe and naval gunfire covered them on their scramble ashore. By 1100 hours that same morning, nearly 3,700 troops—60 percent of the invading force—had been killed, wounded, or captured. The Allies had no choice but to evacuate the remaining troops and return home.

It was a total failure publicly enjoyed by Hitler. Air support had been woefully insufficient, and the RAF lost 106 aircraft. None of the operation's objectives—engaging the Luftwaffe, holding the port even briefly, and knocking out German defenses along the coast—had been achieved. Worst of all, it broadcast to the world that the Allies were unprepared to invade central Europe from the Channel. The newspapers commented, "It was as if the enemy knew we were coming." During the review, watched carefully by Rags, the question of spy activity was examined in detail. It was agreed that the lack of an effective security program and procedure within the war plans headquarter at Norfolk House had alerted the Germans to the attack. Rags, who had communicated the night before with his father tipping him off to the raid, agreed with the assessment.

At a meeting of the planning group in Norfolk House the following week Mountbatten and his staff were absent. However, forgetting the losses as best they could, something of great importance resulted. Not only was there a need to strictly compartmentalize operational plans, a requirement for a credible strategic diversion was integrated into all future operations. It was acknowledged that spies could be anywhere. War plans became protected with code words and restricted access. Only a few could be trusted. In the mill was a plan for an amphibious invasion of North Africa by the Americans to land in Morocco and attack east along the southern Mediterranean coast in support of British formations in contact with Rommel's Africa Corps. It mustn't go the way of Dieppe.

THE GERMAN BOMING RAIDS EBBED but continued on a smaller scale in the months to come through Christmas and on into the new year of 1943. Now they were retaliatory for the Allied bombing over Germany, specifically Berlin. Christian demanded a list of precise targets from his well-placed son, and Rags was scrambling to respond. One morning his mother pointed to the water pitcher that stood on the sideboard and marveled at its contents. "You know, Rolly, it is a miracle that they have not bombed our water supply. Not only do we drink it, we must be using a terrible lot on putting out all these fires, night after night. It was a great day when Mr. Bazalgette modernized the drains and the water companies built the pumping stations. My mother told me that when she was a small child the drains overflowed and the Thames was an open sewer. There used to be water carriers, men with tankards that held gallons of water fresh from streams north of the city. She said they had a dedicated water-bearer they could count on to deliver clean water twice a day. What a sight that must have been. Shabby men burdened, like pack animals, down every alley with great hogs of water on their backs. Behind every house was a concrete cistern for the servants to dip out the water. Can you imagine, all across the city?"

Back in his cubbyhole of an office in the CWR, he had been searching for a major target for the German bombers to maintain his credibility. He went to his old public works cronies and investigated how potable water was brought to the city. He found that there were deep wells in three segments north of the Thames. He took the time to examine how they supplied the city by visiting the one at Kew Bridge and another north of Paddington Station. They were identical operations. A compound of yellow brick structures was husbanded behind high walls on a plot a hundred yards square. His uniform and credentials provided an introduction to the site manager. Rags mentioned the names of a few friends in the public works headquarters and reminisced over his past service in the department during the shelter crisis. He was welcome if for no other reason than no one of any stature had ever visited the site before.

He was given a walking tour that explained how the giant central pump—designed by Mr. Watt to clear the tin mines of Cornwall of contaminated groundwater—brought clean water out of deep, deep wells and deposited its contents into a sluice for the reservoir. "You know, Colonel, if Herman could knock us out of action, we'd be in a sorry state in London and have to bring in water by the train load."

Just so—Rags had his target. After detailed consultation with the public works office, he picked the Paddington pumping works that supplied the West End. A few weeks in, a formation of three Heinkel bombers came roaring in as dawn broke and plastered the Paddington pumping station compound, felling the ten-story tower and smashing the great beam engine. The pump was destroyed, and Rags' credibility rebuilt.

# Chapter Thirty-Nine

# London, 1944

BRITAIN WAS BUOYED BY THE naming of American General Dwight D. Eisenhower as Supreme Commander of the Allied forces in January of 1944. With the success of the North African campaign in 1943 and the invasion of Sicily which followed, everyone—Allies and Axis alike—had their eyes on France. Eisenhower's headquarters at Norfolk House and Camp Griffiss were humming by the earliest days of the winter of 1944.

Mussolini was gone, Italy signed an armistice in July of 1943, and the Germans were struggling on the Eastern Front. But the optimism spreading throughout London did not penetrate the walls of the mansion in Fulham. The war-weary Stetchworths had spent their adult lives tied to the military in war and peace. Their sons were being deployed to the battlefield, as the forces demanded younger and younger candidates to fill the regiments depleted by combat in the Mediterranean. Rags was nearly always at the War Rooms, and Grace was nearly always absented to the house in Newmarket.

With their sons now in danger, harrowing memories of loss haunted them. In Grace's tortured reminiscences she pictured the storied Chateau Chenonceau with its four graceful arches over the Loire—and her lithe, beautiful Rory turned to cannon fodder. Rags worked, and when he wasn't working he slept, troubled by dreams of a vivacious young girl who vanished like a vapor in the wind, with a malevolent threat left in its wake. War had ground up the promise of their idyllic childhoods and their youthful hopes, leaving an ash heap of regrets, compromises, and staleness—and, for Rags, fear.

Christian had become frantic for news of an invasion. Hundreds of thousands of fighting men were gathering on both shores of the English Channel. According to the newspapers, "England was crammed full of foreign fighters who would surely sink the island if they didn't get off soon." Germany kept pouring concrete along the Atlantic wall, making it higher, stronger, tougher.

Hitler built 2,000 miles of defenses and stocked them with all the men he could spare from the Eastern Front. Yet it was still vulnerable. Christian knew that Rags was the Axis's best hope, for in the course of two world wars he had never sent a communiqué that proved false.

Rags was frantic himself. Air reconnaissance had discovered odd-shaped buildings along the beaches north of Hamburg. Peculiar rail ramps were seen, but they were unexplained in spite of efforts to decipher the photos. There was fear that Hitler was developing a new powerful weapon that would drive Britain to the treaty table, perhaps an unpiloted flying bomb launched by rail to be deployed along the French coast, well within range of London. Rags could not believe how quickly things were moving. Days passed by in a flash as the pages of the calendar were torn from the wall in the deep confines of the bunker and discarded in the trash. May was a frenetic blur, as his father's threats grew clearer and the window for intelligence more immediate. As the last days of May arrived, Rags learned that the command group was no longer in London but at Portsmouth. The supreme commander had been given the options for the attack date and the CWR was in direct contact with Eisenhower's forward command post. Rags arrived home every night shaken and almost in despair, but his mother had retreated into her bedroom with a steady supply of brandy, walling herself in from the frightening threats that her son and his father represented. His sons were at locations unknown, and his wife was sequestered in what seemed to be her true home now, the cottage in Newmarket.

THAT IS WHY IT WAS unexpected that Grace found herself in the library at Fulham in early June relaxing in a high-backed shelter-chair drawn up to the low glowing coal fire. Her nurse friends had left the cottage to be back in London, and the feeling that invasion was imminent drove her back to the house, where she might get word of her sons when the inevitable happened. She had slipped in earlier that day, wanting to avoid the pestering solicitude of the servants and the unwelcome company of Charlotte. But as she sat with her back to the double doors that led in from the hall, curled up for warmth and invisible to other eyes, Charlotte and Rags entered, heavily engaged in conversation. They stopped along the inside wall by the built-in bookcase that ran the length of the room. Intense, Rags began to speak to his mother.

"It has come to this, Mamma. We knew from the start the risks. We must send Father the place and date of the invasion. Otherwise we are caught for sure. Our lives will be forfeited, and our name and that of our children, if they survive the war, will be cursed forever. We have no choice. And if the Allies are thrown back into the sea, perhaps England will give up this monstrous war and sue for peace. The Germans will stop the Russian hordes from overrunning the Continent and we will all settle down into a new era of peace and prosperity. We can contribute to that tonight with just a very few words."

Charlotte was wavering. "To give up the invasion site could change history. It's too much to ask of two little people."

"Mamma, it will be over in a few hours; trust me, I know the plans in detail. We have no choice. We must send him the information tonight. And to guarantee reception, it must be short and transmitted over and over again. The key, Mamma."

From the edge of the high-backed chair, Grace dared to lift her eyes up enough to see the bookcase. She watched as the old lady took the heavy black and silver cross that hung from chain around her neck, the one she always wore no matter the dress or occasion, and plunged the long end into a small crack between the oak panels that framed the open shelves. She heard a click, something dropped and the tall panel snapped open. Charlotte swung the panel away to reveal half a dozen wooden shelves and drawers, and she slid out a drawer. "Your Iron Cross, Rolly. After tonight, Germany will change this 2nd class Iron Cross to one of 1st class, I shouldn't wonder."

Rags smiled grimly. "Now the note pad, just three words. The place and the date is all they want." He put down the pen and folded the paper to put in his tunic pocket. "I'll drop it on the way to the Spotted Horse now that it's getting dark." Charlotte made a notation in her record book, locked the secret panel with the base of her cross, and they both left the room for the front hall.

For a full minute Grace's vision went black, and she gripped the arms of the chair to keep herself upright. Her heart pounded and her stomach churned. She didn't dare to move for fear she'd be violently ill. After that minute of dread, her whole body was convulsed with anger. Her sons. Her father. Her city. Her love. And this vile, hateful imposter and his vile, evil mother.

She dashed from her chair out through the French doors to the garden that lined the river wall. She wore only a sweater to protect her from the damp fog that shrouded the shoreline. At the garden shed she took a torch to light her footsteps. It was so dense that she could barely follow Rags as he left by the front door for the bridge. Blackout rules had been eased that spring of 1944, but the dim light made the wet cobblestone pavement hazardous. It was twilight in the June sky even though it was getting late. The thick river fog hung on to every surface, dampening everything. The bridge lights had been shrouded, casting a glow straight down on the narrow metal walkway that hung precariously on the west end of the iron bridge.

Trains clattered by as she followed Rags, masking her steps. She could see him, dimly, just ahead. Intent on getting up the three sets of wet steps, he never looked back. It was just after 9:00 p.m., the time set to make the drop. Once Grace gained the metal rungs, her footsteps, rapid now, caught

Rags' attention. He stopped in the center of the bridge to see who was briskly approaching at this time of night. Had he been followed by the army or the police? He thought of casting the unencrypted message into the water. Cursing himself, he had forgotten, in his haste, to put it in a weighted envelope. "What an amateur mistake," he thought. He mashed it up in his fist and was about to drop it over the rail when he saw her.

Grace came at him like a bat out of hell. "You bastard! You ugly, hateful, German bastard!"

"Grace!" Rags was beside himself with confusion and alarm. How did she know? Why was she here?

"I was in the library by the fire, just now. You miserable traitor. You've killed me, do you realize that? And you've killed my sons.

"Grace, you don't understand," he beseeched her. "Go back home. I swear I can explain."

"No!" she screamed. "There's no explanation you can give!" His refusal to throw out his message and his calm, sure persistence was undoing her. "What is the matter with you? What is the matter with you??" With fury in her eyes, she raised her hands and pushed Rags with all her might, sending him flying backward.

The last that she ever saw of Roland Augustus Grayling Stetchworth were his eyes growing wide as he fell between the cross pieces and onto the track. Seconds later a speeding train thundered at him. He was swept up like a piece of debris and cast between the rails and the carriage. In a second the train was gone, and Grace stared in horror, first at the remnants of her husband's utterly destroyed body, and then at the small packet of paper at her feet. Heaving, sick, she kicked it into the dark water and ran as fast as she could back to the house.

*Part IV*

# KEY (1945)

## Chapter Forty

# London, Just After Christmas, 1945

FREDDY WOKE UP TO A feeling of determination. Christmas had come and gone, and he was off today to meet with his distant Uncle Hilliard Hopewell, hoping to crack the code of his father's life. Last June he had received the news of his father's death on the rails of Putney Bridge. An accidental death—no one knew what he had been doing on the bridge at that hour alone, although Freddy was beginning to understand. It had made a difficult year even more difficult, especially since his mother had retreated to her cottage, bitter and closed off in a way that worried Freddy. From the state of their marriage for the last ten years, Freddy was frankly surprised that she had taken his father's death so hard. He was even more surprised at how closed she remained to him and his brother Martin.

Talking with Uncle Hilly had become urgent for Freddy because whatever additional secrets his grandmother had held were now lost forever. The day after her confession to Freddy, Christmas Day, Charlotte didn't appear at the breakfast table. This was worrisome, as she usually reveled in ruling the table when family was in town and also because Freddy has seen the toll that telling her story had taken on her. When they had parted for bed the night before, Charlotte looked as frail and worn down as he had ever seen her. He sent a servant to find if she was going to have her breakfast in bed, and a few minutes later there was a scurry on the stairs and noise in the hall. Mrs. Brooks was heard to go up the main staircase . . . unusual, he thought. She descended in like manner moments later, going to the telephone and calling for the doctor. Freddy was soon at her side as she hung up and told him, "I can't rouse Madam." He rushed the staircase, Hunter the terrier in the lead, but it was clearly too late. Her hand was cold and her face rigid.

His grandmother's last words to him the night before she died had echoed in his head ever since: "I will never know how Rolly got it wrong." With this memory in mind this morning, as on every morning since her death, he couldn't shake the doubt and confusion that dogged him. So it was with resoluteness that he set off for Green Park Tube station and then to Cambridge House, site of the Naval and Military Club, where he was scheduled to meet Uncle Hilly for tea. He had asked Hilly to meet him to discuss his father's career, and now they sat comfortably at a large front window that looked out on the small parking lot just inside the outer wall that opened onto Piccadilly and directly across from Green Park. Hilly inquired about his wounded leg, and Freddy said he intended to remain active in the regiment. Hilly winked. "That's my boy." Nothing could recommend Freddy to him more highly than a determination to continue his service.

Lord Palmerston's old parlor was a perfect setting for a quiet, discreet discussion. The room was very large, with two fireplaces blazing away trying to keep the cold and damp in the courtyard. The brushed carpet held any number of small tables in clusters with an arrangement of comfortable brown leather chairs for each in a tight circle. There were other lounging chairs against the wall meant for dozing, filled by the usual subjects. Newspapers rustled and light grey smoke swirled just above conversing heads. Groups of seating were spaced apart generously for the sake of discretion.

Tea was served, and Hilly offered an opening volley. "So you are interested in your father's career? May I ask what prompted this inquiry, Lieutenant?"

Freddy hesitated, but then he noticed how comfortable Hilly seemed, with almost a knowing air, and this freed his tongue. Ten minutes later, his tale was done and he looked at Hilly expectantly. Hilly puffed on his cigar calmly while Freddy held his anxiety in check. When he responded, his words were unexpected.

"My grandniece could be a difficult woman. I never took to her, you know. I must have known her or known of her much of my adult life. Her behavior in Austria. That quick marriage and even quicker childbirth. Her belated husband, Stetchworth . . . he seemed an odd choice for Charlotte. And then suddenly he was gone. Chemical poisoning, they say." He eyed Freddy meaningfully.

"But still, when she approached me about a commission for your father, I was happy to help. He seemed a good boy, though a bit full of himself, as young men often are." Hilly waved his hand at the waiter stationed by the white columns that marched across the chamber and asked for two dry sherries.

"I hired Rags to be my military aide and found he was quite quick to the ladder. Very bright, you know. Well, of course you do. Within a few months he came to me one morning at the office and asked to close the door. Most puzzling. I thought he was having second thoughts about being what amounted to a servant to an old man and wanted some adventure, you know, like his pals. It seemed he had met a girl the night before in the middle of a zeppelin raid and they had nearly bought it."

"That was my mother?" Freddy asked. He had heard the story many times.

"Oh yes, that was your mother. He was smitten with her, but that was not what he came to discuss. He had a rather more fascinating tale. Of an aristocratic Austrian father and a mother so devoted to him that she was prepared to spy for the Kaiser to earn his love. And a young son too brainwashed about glorious Austria and evil England to know better. He had been sending messages to Christian in Germany, a member of the enemy intelligence community, but he couldn't go on. When he witnessed war firsthand that terrible night, he knew he couldn't play on both sides."

"You knew, sir? As early as that?" Freddy asked.

"I knew. I must admit I was flummoxed, didn't know where to turn. It isn't every day a German spy comes to your office to confess, much less a German spy who happens to be a member of your family and who you had placed smack dab in the middle of army command!" Hilly was nearly chortling at this point, and Freddy could not have been more amazed.

"What in the world did you do?"

"I did something quite smart, if I say so myself. I called for Smith-Cumming, an old acquaintance from the Home Office, to meet me at the Clarence Pub in an upper room that very day. In those days, he was a one-man snout defending our borders from such matters. He headed a very small national effort dealing with foreign espionage. A man to be reckoned with, I can tell you—he turned out to be a godsend. The army didn't have an intelligence corps as such; it manufactured one of sorts each time we were in a conflict. When a campaign was concluded, the office was dissolved. We were rank amateurs, not equipped to deal with the threat posed by Rags' revelation. Over supper that night, we went over the traffic he and his 'dear' mother had sent and concluded that, while disturbing, it hadn't caused any real harm. Cumming was particularly distressed that there was an enemy radio station in Putney.

"But Cumming was a crafty old bird who thought before he acted. I had some fear he might want to jail Rags, but he rewarded my confidence in him. We agreed that this was a blessing in disguise: Rags would become a double agent. He would keep his mother in the dark, and Cumming and I would feed him correct information of two types: intelligence that was time sensitive and couldn't be acted on by a tactical army, or political information about conflicts inside the War Cabinet which would soon be aired in public. These streams of verifiable intelligence would give him credibility and would give us a priceless return. We monitored the radio station so we could get a look at the codes the Germans were using. Most helpful since we knew how the messages read before they were encrypted by the operator, a Mr. Booker. It was invaluable in understanding how they constructed their one-time pad system."

"Sir, this is simply incredible."

Hilly smiled, relishing the story of his genius operation. "Your father's mentor became Henry Segar, a close confidant and a member of a cell at MI6. Henry has a most devious mind, you know, a real intriguer. Their first joint message was to reveal that the Royal Society for Improving National Knowledge had allied with the War Cabinet to engage the nation's brightest in the conduct of war. We thought that would put the cat among the pigeons for Herr Christian. We wanted the Bosch to know that we were engaged at the national level in an all-out war, just as they claimed to be. It also showed that Rags was at the heart of the war effort. It gave him real credibility without injuring our efforts. Later, we were sorely impressed by the guile of his father with his surprise appearance in Rome. We hadn't understood the relationship between the Monsignor Merchanti, the papal legate at Westminster Cathedral, and the plot as a whole. That was a helpful bit of intelligence, I can tell you. His father's boldness and cunning alerted us to the danger, and we redoubled out efforts to keep Rags' true role secret. We followed the first rule of warfare: 'don't underestimate the ability of the enemy.' Rags' purchase of a special diplomatic case in Rome showed that he could think for himself, most refreshing but at the same time worrying. We hoped we were backing the right horse. I soon learned that spying is a tricky game."

Freddy agreed. "My grandmother was quite impressed with that leather case. She thought it gave him an air of sophistication. She was proud of their work. I don't think she suspected that her son was anything but sincere in his pursuit of increasing the chances of a German victory. I can tell you, sir, you never tipped your hand to her. She had no idea."

Freddy was euphoric. He had been crushed by his grandmother's story but had gradually noticed cracks in the framework here and there—nothing definitive but enough to make him wonder. From that first night when he had lain awake distraught that he was the son of a Nazi spy, he had moved to confusion, then hope, and now utter exoneration. His relief made him forget all formalities: "Uncle Hilly, I am so relieved!"

The old general smiled at his success, happy to tell an outsider for the first time a truly remarkable tale worthy of a good book. "Well, that is some consolation. It's a story that will play out over the next thirty years. That's a long time to keep the narrative going, don't you know? But I must credit Segar with keeping the thread from breaking. At the end of the trip to Gallipoli and Rome, Henry suggested that we tell the Germans about Kitchener's plans to relieve the commander in Gallipoli and that he planned a visit. It was the old man himself that let us tell about his pending trip, which was highly classified because of the danger it posed to himself. He was onboard with Henry's plan. They had been together since Egypt and he trusted Segar's instincts."

Comforted to see how well the situation was managed, Freddy asked, "When Christian presented Rags with a Hauptmann's commission in the Imperial Army and the award of the Iron Cross second class, you must have been gratified that your concealment of his true mission wasn't compromised."

Freddy then saw what very few people had ever witnessed: Hilly's jaw drop in momentary shock. "What commission? The Iron Cross? Are you sure? We knew nothing of that!" the old general barked.

"Well, sir, I saw them. They are in the cupboard in the library at home where Grandmamma kept everything from those times. I held them in my hands. Didn't you know, didn't Father tell you?"

The old man stopped and raised his eyebrows, turned his eyes to the ornate plastered celling, and then grinned and laughed loud enough to make his fellow sherry drinkers look disapprovingly in his direction. "Well, well, well . . . Rags, you scamp. I suppose a good spy never tells you everything. That's one on old Segar, I must tell him, I really must." He laughed again at the prospect of springing the existence of an Iron Cross on Henry. "You must tell me more about the record of their espionage kept in the panels of the library. Of course, that must be preserved and given to Cumming; I'll have to see to that. I had no idea that she would do something like that; shows you that spying is no game for amateurs."

Freddy, a little relaxed now, grinned. "They pulled it off pretty well, those amateurs, didn't they?"

Hilly smiled and took a deep breath. "Yes, but there is a long way to go. Cumming announced to all that there was a German spy embedded in the army and navy HQ. Of course, he was aware of Rags, but he had reason to believe that he was not alone. There were more than just Rags working for another segment of the Imperial German General Staff that had to be found. To prevent someone stumbling over Rags in pursuit of the threat, he had to put Rags in charge of the effort to improve internal security and had everyone in the search report any suspicions to him. In the end, some other effort found the spy in the office of the Royal Navy. We were relieved, I can tell you."

Freddy had an unresolved crisis concerning the aftermath of that intervention. "You are aware, sir, that my father became involved with MI6 to find a quiet place for his mother to do war work, to keep her busy and out of the way."

"Yes, yes, Segar arranged for a discreet spot in censoring the mail from Europe and put her near Rags across the parade ground at Horse Guards. That did the trick."

Freddy thought for a moment. "So how is it that it worked? When she got promoted and moved up to the top deck, she was able to warn Christian of suspicion cast on the possible German agents. She warned Christian to pull the agent before he was compromised. She did it to make herself more valuable to Christian. She wanted to become a spy in her own right, so to speak. Essentially, she opened a separate channel through Monsignor Merchanti to Christian."

Hilly shook his head. "No, no, she couldn't have done that. We were watching the monsignor closely; they never met."

Freddy smiled. "They never met, but she left messages under the seat in the confessional at the cathedral. You knew she converted to Catholicism, didn't you?"

"No, I didn't, but Segar must have known, I'll check with him. He didn't tell me every little item; I was very busy with my own mission. He would know, I'll check with him." For the first time Hilly sounded unsure, and Freddy wondered if there were other things his great uncle didn't know.

"You know, sir, about the girl my father was dating . . . Beryl, his secretary at the Classified Library? She was killed while my father was in France."

Hilly was immediately on guard. "Yes, I remember. Lovely girl, quite smart . . . killed in a zeppelin attack, if I remember correctly."

"Sir, my grandmother said that she was stabbed on Putney Bridge by Mr. Booker and thrown into the river." Freddy's delight in the tale was suddenly dashed. His feelings of dread and anger at his grandmother returned. "She was afraid that Beryl would ruin her son's life and he wouldn't return to Austria with her after the war. So she asked Booker to kill her," he said quietly.

Hilly looked stunned and was quiet for a moment. "I hope that isn't true, Freddy. I sincerely hope that isn't true."

Freddy suddenly felt quite ashamed. He looked down and scrambled to find a new topic, anything to take away the look of reproach in his uncle's eyes.

"And what about this war, sir? How did you carry on?"

"Rags was relieved by the ending of the 'war to end all wars,' as we all were. The secret was kept and solidified in place when Charlotte's plans to emigrate to Austria were shelved by Christian. You and your brother marked the beginning of a new era. Your father and I kept in touch, but of course we never thought to engage in spycraft together again. And then Hitler came. Damn Hitler. The King looked to Cumming for a replacement for one of his trusted messengers. Segar—such a wise man, he truly has a crystal ball. He saw an opportunity to put Rags back in the picture. With the uncertainty of a declining king and a suspicious successor, Henry found it prudent to have someone on the inside who would be carrying highly classified and privileged communications of interest to the empire in the Secret Service. It turned out better than we could have expected. Edward VIII was at cross purposes with the government, and we were able not only to read his correspondence but have an A-1 witness to the royals in Europe and in fact to Hitler himself. It was a tremendous advantage, and for that alone your father has the thanks of all of us. It is too bad that it cannot be made public."

"I think my father must have fainted when Hitler called him Hauptmann Stetchworth when they met at the Eagle's Nest."

"Did he, then? I hadn't heard that. I must consult Segar, he'll know." The old general thought a moment and then resumed. "Then we had another surprise. Christian popped up in Sweden, insisting that Rags and Charlotte continue in German service under threat of exposure. Christian was keeping a step ahead, and Rags was truly worried now. His mother had reluctantly moved on and put all her energy into you and your brother. Rags dreaded the prospect of becoming enmeshed in spying again, and especially of exposing his mother to the fears and threats of exposure. But Segar was insistent. Rags was too valuable an asset, and as for the stress on Charlotte . . . well, she made her bed and now must lie in it. Your father disagreed and threatened to quit, and we diverted him to Public Works while we sorted it out, to keep his father from making demands.

"But Segar stepped in once again and said we must have a German spy with unquestioned credentials at the heart of our deception plan. The Dieppe Raid was our golden opportunity, and we moved Rags into the planning process by putting him in the CWR. Dieppe was a tricky one. Churchill had a dilemma. Stalin wanted added pressure on the Western Front since he was bearing the war on his own shoulders. Roosevelt wanted an attack on the French Channel coast, the shortest route to Berlin. That peacock Mountbatten wanted to lead a spearhead raid on the French coast to bloody Hitler's nose, as he put it. Churchill, instead, wanted the efforts to strike at the soft underbelly of Europe. If the Germans were tipped off by a credible source, they would stop Mountbatten and there would be no more talk of a Channel crossing and Churchill could get on with his plans in the Mediterranean. So it was left to Rags to tip them off. Good plan, really. I was opposed. I couldn't see us sacrificing those Canadian soldiers for high diplomacy. But that is why I am just a retired general."

The pair were alerted that their table was prepared in the dining room for afternoon tea. They strolled together out of the smoking room and Hilly greeted old friends as they walked down the long passage lined with musty old big-game trophy heads and a bank of regimental crests emblazoned on wooden plaques. In a small side garden a bronze statue of a nude young woman stood coolly in the midst of some potted palms. They passed the broad steps to the upper rooms where the billiard and snooker tables were sequestered next to the Goat Club. They were both hungry, and the china plates and trays offered dainty crustless beef and cucumber sandwiches, scones and chocolate desserts. They were offered China tea poured from a Wedgewood pot heated to just the correct temperature.

As they put their serviettes on their knees, Uncle Hilly smiled and said, "You know, there were lighter moments. Booker was getting on, and an inspection of his twenty-year-old antenna was corroding away under the superstructure of the rail bridge. We suspected he would kill himself if he tried to climb underneath as he had done as a young man and check it out. So we watched his shop, and when a notice appeared that he was closing up for a week, we made inquiries. We found that his grown son, Horatio, was in Dublin, out of the reach of conscription, and Booker and Flopbottom, as your grandmother called Mrs. Booker, would be gone." Hilly burst out laughing and slapped his knee: "So we repaired the damn thing! And since his messages got through, Booker never concerned himself with the matter. That was my idea; Segar was impressed."

Freddy was relieved to have their discussion return to more light-hearted topics. "There is one matter I am concerned about, though. You said that my father's messages had little consequence, but he arranged for an entire pumping station to be destroyed, leaving much of the West End without drinking water."

"Things aren't always as they seem, Freddy. The pumping station near Paddington was under renovation at another nearby location. We were replacing the old steam engines with electric pumps that were deep underground. The bombing of a deserted plant was more reclamation than destruction. After the raid, we covered it with false news stories claiming a shortage of drinking water when none existed. That was your father's idea—a smart one. It helped confirm his credibility as we built up to the big one: the date and place of the D-Day invasion."

"Grandmamma told me that she helped compose that short message the night my father died trying to deliver it to Booker. Her last words to me were, 'I will never know how Rolly got it wrong.'"

"She never will," Hilly replied. "But now you do."

## Chapter Forty-One

# Putney Bridge

AT THE TIME OF HIS father's accident in June of 1944, Freddy had been on a troop ship bobbing around expectantly off the coast of Normandy. He remembered his own peril that night, caught in a Channel rain squall, wishing he could get off that ship from hell and onto the beach ahead. It was weeks before a letter from his mother telling of his father's accident reached him. He never quizzed his mother about that night. There was very little she knew or could tell.

Now, as he came home from his meeting with Hilly, he was excited to tell her something wonderful—that his father hadn't been just another casualty of war but one of England's great unsung heroes. His mother had met them at the mansion in Fulham after Christmas, although his brother Martin had been unable to join them. His mother had suffered as he had at the untimely death of his father, becoming almost a recluse, someone he hardly knew any-more. For some time she had refused to visit the mansion at Fulham, but now that Charlotte was dead she relented. Now, at least he could tell her that her husband was a great hero of the empire, though destined to remain unsung.

It was dark when he opened the front door and was greeted by Hunter, who was expecting his walkies. "Not yet, bucko, in a little while, I promise." The dancing terrier dogged him to the library door, nipping his pant leg. He was intercepted by Mrs. Brooks. "Your mother asked that no one be allowed to disturb her, sir. Could I get you something for the damp and cold, perhaps with Mrs. Jayson in the kitchen?

Freddy waved her off. "I must see her, it is most important," softening his voice, "it's all right."

He entered to find Grace at the fireplace. The door to the hidden cupboard was wide open and she was burning papers. Intent, she didn't hear him approach. He suddenly realized that she was destroying the documentation of his father's espionage, which had historic value. "Mamma, stop, don't put that in the fire!"

She wheeled around, startled. "Freddy, you're here." She stared at him, almost in a trance, it seemed. "I said I was not to be disturbed."

"Mamma, I see what you have. Please don't worry—I know what it is."

"You know?"

"Yes, I know. But Mamma, do you know what it really is?"

"I know what it is!" she spat out. "I know what he was! Him and his filthy mother. Freddy, we have to destroy it. It must never see the light of day."

He stayed her hand, alarmed at her state. "No, no, Mamma, let me explain—"

"No! There's no explanation you can give!" she screamed in an eerie echo of that night long ago. It brought her up short. This was Freddy. He was not his father.

"Freddy, I'm sorry, but I can't talk now." There was real emotion in her voice as she took one ledger with a red leather cover and tore out pages, ready to drop them into the fire.

Freddy stepped in between Grace and the blazing fire. "Mamma, please sit down; we have to talk." He guided her to the chairs where so recently Charlotte had given him the message of his father's treason, mistranslated and misapprehended.

"Mamma, I know how this looks. You must think Father was a spy for the Germans. It's not true. I just spent the afternoon with Uncle Hilly. He wasn't a spy for the Germans, Mamma. He was a double agent working for the British special intelligence office."

He took the portfolio that she was still clutching in her hand, but she recoiled. "What are you saying?"

Freddy pulled away from the fire and crossed the room to place the record back into the cupboard. "There are thirty years of spy records here that Uncle Hilly says must be preserved. It's true that Grandmamma initiated a plot to spy for Germany, but when he met you, that night of the zeppelin attack that you both recounted to me over the dining table time and time again, he lost heart. He went to Uncle Hilly and confessed. Captain Smith-Cumming and Henry Segar then turned the enterprise against the Germans for the next thirty years.

"Don't you understand? You altered the plot that night on the bridge when London burned. He couldn't tell you, he couldn't tell Grandmamma, he lived with it every day for the remainder of his life. He's a hero, Mamma, and so are you."

Grace's head swooned. "It can't be."

"Here, look." Freddy fumbled through the shelves and plucked out one of the record books. He scratched through the pages to the last entry. "Here is the diary from 1944, the last page." He read it before showing it to her: "There . . . look." He leaned over Grace and pointed to the last message sent to Germany. It read: *Calais 7 June.* "You see, Father sent the wrong place and date to the Germans, a part of the Normandy deception plan, worked out months before. The Germans, Hitler, would believe him; he never sent wrong information in thirty years. I wonder if he got it off before the train accident."

Grace throbbed with anguish. The writing was right in front of her: Calais 7 June. Rags had tried to explain, tried to interpret the confusing message of his treachery for her, and she had refused to hear. She had got it all wrong, and now he was dead. She dropped the portfolio, stood up, grasped Freddy's hands and buried her head in her son's chest. "Why didn't he trust me?" she wailed. "Why didn't he tell me? I could have kept his secret, I could have helped!" Her mind was racing now. She thought of the years focusing on the boys, fighting with Charlotte, being disappointed that Rags was not the hero that Rory had been. He must have been disheartened in their marriage, in her—that she believed him to be no more than just a bit of a slacker who had found a safe place to plant himself. He kept it all bottled up, like a good Englishman. And she had let him go on alone, sniping at him and resenting him, ultimately going off to live her own separate life.

Freddy was alarmed at his mother's reaction. Rather than being relieved or proud, she seemed devastated. He understood her shock at the discovery of the spy papers, but now that he had told her the good news of his true service to England, she seemed even more distraught.

"Mamma, please tell me what you're thinking, why you're so upset."

"Oh, Freddy . . . There was no accident on the bridge that night. I discovered that he and your grandmamma were spies, that they were going to send Hitler the date and place of the invasion. I followed him up on to the bridge and confronted him, begging him not give up the secret of the invasion, and he just wouldn't."

Freddy, confused and scared, asked, "What do you mean there was no accident?"

"He just wouldn't stop, Freddy. He held on to that paper and kept saying he could explain. I was out of my mind with anger, Freddy. I drove myself into him with all my might. I pushed him—onto the train tracks." She fell to her knees sobbing.

Freddy's heart gave a twist, and all his joy turned to ash. The pride, the relief, dissolved in a swell of grief. "Why, Mamma?" he whispered. "Why couldn't you have trusted him? Just given him a chance? He was a good man—you knew that." Here, finally, was something that truly couldn't be explained. Freddy turned and walked away.

IN THE MORNING, AFTER A fitful night, Freddy arose and sat on the side of his bed. He was completely drained by the events of the last few years: the war, his injury, his father's unexpected death, his grandmother's confession, her own death Christmas morning, the joyous revelation of his father's heroism, and then the devastating admission that his mother had misread his father's actions and killed him.

He was drained but, he realized, strangely peaceful. The losses were too much—he couldn't afford any more of them. His mother had been deceived and acted only with grief and righteous anger—not her fault. He was determined to make peace, to move forward with forgiveness and love, to treasure the family that he had left, those who had survived the heartbreak of two world wars.

He walked down to his mother's bedroom, ready to wake her and let her know he had forgiven her. He tapped on her door to take her down to breakfast and make peace—to share their grief together and make sure that the two of them would never become strangers to each other, as Grace and Rags had. But there was no answer. He creeped in and found that she had gone.

He called for the maid. She was in the hallway gathering linen. "Madam has been up since early this morning; I heard her go out."

Freddy dressed to take Hunter with him to look for her. On Putney Bridge walkway, halfway across, he found her shoes.